T0156566

DEATH IN CHICAGO
• A SANCTUARY CITY •

DEATH IN CHICAGO
• A SANCTUARY CITY •

THE SAD SAGA OF THE UNTIMELY DEATH OF DENNY MCGURN IN 2011

BRIAN MCCANN

DEATH IN CHICAGO A SANCTUARY CITY
The Sad Saga of the Untimely Death of Denny McGurn in 2011

iUniverse books may be ordered through booksellers or by contacting:

iUniverse
1663 Liberty Drive
Bloomington, IN 47403
www.iuniverse.com
1-800-Authors (1-800-288-4677)

ISBN: 978-1-4917-8484-6 (sc)
ISBN: 978-1-4917-8483-9 (e)

Library of Congress Control Number: 2015921477

Print information available on the last page.

iUniverse rev. date: 02/17/2016

PRELUDE

Around 10:00 a.m., in a dark corner of a dark basement, Raul Orizaga was as free as a bird. It was two days after his release and he owed his freedom to careful planning and a payment of 5K to his lawyer. Now, all he had to do was lie low and hide in this "safe house" for a few weeks, before deciding where to go next. The night before he'd had a grand time. He had hung out with a few of his homeys, drinking shots as a "Fuck you!" to the gringos, at the place his brother, Roberto, knew about.

Raul's throwaway cell rang.

"Rauly, Robby here, man."

"Why you not call yesterday, bro?"

"Look, you idiot. The Man all over this place yesterday; I give him some bullshit. I told them you live in a cellar, and I never see you—I think they bought it."

"What you think?"

"Lay low, man. They going think you split to Mexico, and they forget about you."

"So what's up now?"

"Listen. Shit happens, as they say. Just forget about it, but don't forget you gotta pay back the club."

"*Si, si.* I know. That means back on the street, but I gotta be careful, man. The lawyer—Simpkus—says they gonna get a warrant or something."

"You got that right, and the motherfuckin' federales gonna be lookin', too. But the gringo Feds got so much shit to do, they probably don't give a shit about you. Still, you gotta lay low, dude. In a few week, the club gonna give you an assignment, cause you owe some big *dineros*—like 30K."

1

"Sure, bro. I know the deal—and I gotta stay in Chicago."

"Yeah. That's the deal. And remember, the lawyer knows nothing."

"Say, can I at least take a walk—get a *cerveza* or cigarettes, man?"

"Look, bro, we got you hidden in Sout' Chicago. The Man all over the fuckin' place, lookin' for shit. Bro, the old man—he cool, okay? You got it? Like, you be invisible, 'cause he no want trouble. You cool with that?"

"Yeah, man. He leaves food in the morning—not bad, bro. Hey, I never seen him."

"That's the deal, Rauly. I give him $500 every two weeks. The old dude needs the cash 'cause his lady sick."

"Okay, bro. I'm a ghost down here."

"Cool, Rauly. Maybe you get out in a week or two—and don't you use that cell to call. If I call, it will always be 8:00 p.m."

"And I gotta kill some motherfucker, right?"

"That's the deal, bro—could be more!"

DAY ONE, SUNDAY, AUGUST 28, 2011

Pat McGurn was at home reading a book when his cell phone rang, shortly after 2:00 p.m. The caller ID read, "Cook County Sheriff," but there was only a recorded message: "*This call is to inform you that Raul Orizaga was released on bond this morning, at 10:00 a.m.*"

The book fell to the floor. Pat listened, dumbfounded, barely able to contain his rage. Orizaga had killed his brother, Denny, almost three months before, and now the son of a bitch—an illegal—was going to flee to Mexico.

"Okay," he said grimly. "The first step's to confirm this and, the second, to notify Denny's daughters."

Plan of action in place, Pat called his niece, Judy, a Cook County deputy.

"Uncle Pat, what's going on?"

"Judy, sounds like you're watching the Sox game," said Pat, his voice straining from the effort of trying to sound normal.

"Yeah, out with a few friends up at *Kerry's* on Western. So, everything's okay?"

"Well, I'm fine, I guess, but I just got a call from the jail—they let Orizaga out!"

"You're kidding! Wait a second—they had a hold on him, right?"

"That's what Murphy, the Assistant State's Attorney, said. Look, I need confirmation—can you make a call to verify?"

"For sure—I'll call you right back."

Pat knew Judy had friends on weekend duty at the County jail. If they

3

confirmed the release, he'd have to call Denny's daughter, Christy and Nataly first and, later, his siblings—Catherine, Eddy, Marie and Therese. Slowly, he pulled himself out of his armchair, suddenly remembering the detective who had notified Christy the night of Denny's death. Pat went down into the basement to look at the file he had kept on the case. Barely glancing at his model train workshop or at the trains ready to roll at the push of a button, he headed towards a vertical file cabinet. Sure enough, there was a record of his phone call to Detective Skolickwitcz, the day after the murder, for specifics on the arrest. He skimmed through the police report as well as through an article in *The Daily Globe*. The article re-awakened all the sadness that had descended on the entire family.

It was unbelievable that his brother had been run over and dragged by an illegal alien! Denny, a commercial insurance broker, was crossing Kedzie Avenue in Logan Square when it happened, heading for *Hacienda Leon* restaurant to enjoy a *Mojito* with the owner who happened to be one of his clients. The phone rang again, interrupting his musings.

"Uncle Pat? Yep, he's out. Looks like the brother made the bond in cash."

"Thanks, Judy. *Anything else?* Like who handled it and receipted the money?"

"My source—a guy named Steve—works in E wing down there, and I got him on his cell, you know. He just said, 'Raul Orizaga released a few hours ago.' Look, I know one of the supervisors. I'll call him tomorrow and see if he'll talk. You know these people are—well, you know—pretty guarded."

"Judy, that would help big-time! I'll wait till tomorrow and call Eileen Murphy, the Assistant State's Attorney who prosecuted Orizaga—we met her during the discovery process."

"Any time, Uncle Pat. And, hey, this really is bad news. I'm thinking somebody screwed up."

"That's right, because there was a hold or detainer on the creep, and we were promised he couldn't make bond. Okay, be seeing you."

Now that the worst had been confirmed, Pat tried phoning Detective Skolickwitcz, but he was off and wouldn't be in until the next day. Next, he called all the family members, including his son, Michael, and daughter, Molly. Needless to say, they were shocked at the news. Meanwhile, Pat's wife, Clare, had returned from a luncheon at the *Oak Forest Country Club*. A former youth officer and legal investigator, Clare knew a thing or two about the courts. She had all sorts of contacts in her present role as Senior Investigator at the *Illinois Grievance Commission* where her main responsibility was investigating attorney misconduct.

"Pat, let me get this straight. *You got a recorded message?*"

"That's it, and it simply said he posted at, I don't know, I think at 10:00 a.m.

Like I said, Judy confirmed, so he's out."

"On his way to Mexico, I bet," said Clare, her mouth twisted in disgust.

Pat put his arms around her.

"Here, Honey. Give me a hug. This is crazy. You know I'm going to fight this."

"You mean, *we're* going to fight this," said Clare, holding him tightly. "When have you ever had to face anything alone since I met you? Let's go down to *Zorba's* for dinner tonight—I think we need some downtime."

Zorba's had been Denny's favorite restaurant in Greek Town, so Pat was pleased with the suggestion. Because of the continuing late August heat wave, he made reservations for 6:30 p.m. on the restaurant rooftop which would be much cooler than having a table inside. Once they were seated, they ordered drinks. Pat's mood improved considerably, especially as Clare, elegant in her sundress, looked radiant; in fact, her laughing Irish eyes made her seem twenty years younger. From the vantage point of the rooftop, they enjoyed the view overlooking the downtown Chicago, with the spires of *Old St. Patrick's Church* just a few blocks away.

"It's a great town, Clare, don't you think?"

Clare smiled and took Pat's hand re-assuringly. Yes, Chicago was a great town and it would be again, once justice had been returned to the McGurn family.

DAY TWO, MONDAY, AUGUST 29, 2011

The next morning, Pat drove Clare to the train station at 91st Street. It was only a short distance from their home, but Pat, a retired teacher, always insisted on giving Clare a ride. Usually, she would wait with him in the car until they saw the lights flashing at the 95th Street station; that was Clare's cue to kiss him goodbye and make for the train, leather brief case in hand. She enjoyed her work, but had many responsibilities which often left her drained at the end of the day. By the time she had finished interviewing witnesses, writing memos and pouring over the fine print of legal documents, she was exhausted. Pat was only too happy to lighten her load in whatever way he could.

Once back home, he called Eileen Murphy. He and Clare had met her several times now, and they found her both approachable and sensitive to their concerns. She picked up right away.

"Oh, Pat. Let's see, the court date is Thursday. Is that why you're calling?"

"No, Eileen—my guess is the court date may be a waste of time."

Voice shaking, Pat went over the events of the previous day.

"Oh, my God—this is unbelievable!" exclaimed Eileen. There was no mistaking the shock in her reaction. She told the McGurn family two months earlier that *Immigration Custom Enforcement* or ICE would pick Orizaga up and place him in a federal detention facility if a $25,000.00 bond was produced.

"I'll head to court right away and get my judge to start warrant proceedings to get Orizaga back. I'll also change the bond and send out deputies to look for him."

"Hey, Eileen, what happened here?" Pat blurted. "This looks like—well, you know—a screw-up."

"For sure Pat. I had no idea, but let me get back to you, and—who knows?—maybe we can find him."

Slowly, Pat began cleaning up the breakfast dishes. There was not much to do since it was just him and Clare—they had been "empty nesters" for some time. As he stacked the stainless steel dishwasher, he brooded over "next steps." He was facing new territory and needed to figure out who he could trust to be of assistance. Clare, of course, was his main confidante and advisor—always had been. Michael, his lawyer son, would also help. So would his daughter, Molly, and her husband, Frank, both journalists. Eileen Murphy—probably, but she was part of the bureaucracy and had to play the game. Perhaps Clare could get a lead on the lawyer, since she worked for the *Illinois Grievance Commission*.

As ideas surfaced, Pat jotted down a few notes on some scrap paper. He remembered that Eileen had told the family of Orizaga's prior felony conviction in 2009. "Why didn't they deport this creep the first time? How could they let him out?" he muttered to himself. In all likelihood, some part-timer had failed to look at the sheet. Who was on duty? Wasn't there a detainer flag? *Better call Judy and see who signed the release*, he wrote. Then he added, *Get out my notes on the Secure Communities Task Force testimony*. Pat had given that report three weeks earlier. Who knows? Maybe there was a lead there.

He recalled the emotion from that day when he had recounted, with graphic detail, the tragic event of two months prior. *The Department of Homeland Security* had commissioned the *Task Force* that was on a five-city tour to elicit input from various communities. Chicago was the third stop, scheduled after L.A. and Dallas. This *Task Force* was charged with preparing a report on how best to deal with the growing problem of undocumented immigrants. From press reports in mid-July, Pat had learned of the meeting scheduled in Chicago and had signed up to testify. He figured that the *Task Force* should hear his testimony. Arriving early, he was scheduled as the second speaker; he would be permitted to give a four-minute speech.

The meeting was held at *Haymarket Hall*, on Washington Street.

When Pat arrived, the place was filled with hundreds of demonstrators, mainly Mexicans. There were also a number of people who appeared to be old 60's radicals there, along with ten or more Catholic priests. The crowd was extremely noisy and aggressive, carrying signs that read, "STOP DEPORTATIONS AND FUCK ICE." The scene at *Haymarket Hall*, complete with heated interruptions and fist pounding, was unsettling, to say the least, but the whole demonstration seemed well-organized. Pat figured that if the demonstrators knew the truth about what happened to his brother, maybe wisdom would prevail.

It took almost twenty minutes for the raucous crowd to settle down. The first speaker was a middle-aged Mexican woman who testified that her husband had been deported some months back, in what she described as a set-up. Hearing her emotional testimony, the crowd again grew angry, even insisting that all cops leave the building. Unprepared for this turn of events, the *Task Force* seemed to be somewhat intimidated. There were more delays, but, finally, the chair called his name. The noise was deafening, but, determined to have his say, Pat yelled into the microphone, "*SILENZIO!*" Surprisingly, some four hundred people settled down, and he proceeded, in his best teacher manner, to go over the events of that fateful June 8, 2011. Near the end of his presentation, no one could hear a pin drop.

Pat walked out quietly, followed by two news reporters and a representative of Public Radio, which would broadcast his remarks off and on for the next forty-eight hours. After about ten minutes of interviews, Pat excused himself and said he had to meet someone. He was emotionally drained.

Setting that memory aside, Pat poured himself a cup of coffee. The large red mug—his favorite—gave a touch of ordinariness to the day, something he desperately needed! The whole saga was a real mystery, with all sorts of fuck-ups—maybe going back three years, because of Orizaga's prior felony. To make this a larger story, he would not only need a journalist, but, more urgently, advice from someone who knew about criminality and alien criminal immigrants. There was a chance, of course, that human error was behind Orizaga's release, but the signs were pointing to something more sinister.

As he continued compiling an inventory of helpful resources, his phone rang yet again.

"Pat, Eileen Murphy here—here's the deal. There's this new ordinance that effectively lets guys like Orizaga post and get out."

"Ordinance, you say? What—from the Cook County Board?"

"Yeah, passed a few weeks ago on August 11—I'm trying to get a copy, but you can download it from the County Board website."

"Okay, I'll do that, but what about this detainer you told us about?"

"Well, that's the point. This ordinance effectively allows the Sheriff to ignore detainers, or I should say, it *mandates* that he release them if they post bond."

"Wait, wait. Isn't this federal law we're talking here?" objected Pat, unable to believe what he was hearing.

"Well, yes, one might say that, but it appears that the Cook County commissioners felt they could ignore it."

"That's crazy. Was it in the papers?"

"I don't know. I suppose you could try *The Globe* or *The Chicago Times*— or try Googling 'Cook County and detainers.'"

"I'll try that, Eileen. Can I call back later?"

"Sure. I want to update you on the new bond and warrant I worked on this morning."

Abandoning his coffee, which was now cold, Pat got out his Mac Air. Still numb from his exchange with Ellen, he began surfing the net. Eventually, his search produced a news report in *The Globe*, dated August 12, 2011; it recounted the passing of the ordinance. It was written by Ron Ralston, so Pat sent him an e-mail explaining who he was, leaving his phone number. Ten minutes later, the phone rang.

"Pat McGurn, please."

"Speaking."

"You just e-mailed me. Can I ask a few questions? I'm Ralston, from *The Globe*."

"Hi Ron—I was expecting your call."

"So how do you feel about Mr. Orizaga's flight?"

Ignoring the question, Pat said, "So you know about Orizaga's release?"

"Yeah, it's all over the newsroom. Somebody, probably at Cook County Sheriff Dypsky's office, left an anonymous message."

"Well, that's good. Let the public get up in arms, don't you think, Ron? Let me ask a question—"

"Mr. McGurn, *I'm* supposed to ask the questions."

"Sure, but I need to know what you know, so c'mon. Let's start with what you're going to write."

"Okay, fair enough. It will go something like this," said Ralston.

"Ten Cook County commissioners including chief sponsor Vic Varbanov and President Korshak have taken the position that they have no responsibility to enforce federal law. Immigration and Customs Enforcement, or ICE, will argue that federal law preempts local law with respect to immigration. ICE will also argue that Sheriff Dypsky should have ignored the ordinance and notified ICE of Orizaga's release within forty-eight hours, as the law requires."

"Okay," said Pat. "So now the picture is getting a bit clearer, but what I still don't get is that, apparently, the Assistant State's Attorney, Eileen Murphy, had no idea the law had been passed."

"That's right, Pat, and I'm guessing none of the other staff attorneys did, either. I also learned that ICE headquarters in Washington is furious about this. I'm trying to obtain a letter that went out to Cook County President Korshak a few hours ago."

"So may be State's Attorney g is complicit in all of this?"

"Good bet, but she will have cover—you can bank on it. She got some bald headed guy keeping her out of trouble as her deputy. I think his name is Sheehan. Let me tell you, the whole lot of them—I mean, from Korshak on down—will figure out a cover."

"Leaving my family and me with nothing but a bunch of hollow condolences," exclaimed Pat bitterly.

"Well, Pat, at least I can expose some of these shenanigans for you and the general public. But it's going to take a while, because these people won't cooperate."

"Alright, Ron, before you go, tell me what happened last month, when the ordinance was passed; your article gave a good summary, but I want to know the vote and if there was a debate."

"Well, I really wasn't there—the story was from a press release. But I did a lot of research—or, I should say, my legman did. We heard that it was rushed through, and that just yesterday they released the vote."

"Wait a second. Just yesterday, you say?"

"Yeah, they're supposed to post the minutes within a few days, and it took them a month."

"Jeez," Pat said, "I should have followed this. And others wrote it up, too, you say?"

"Oh, yeah. Some new kid at *The Sun* and another story in *The Daily Report*, but I'm the one that hounded them on the minutes."

"What else, Ron?"

"Commissioner Tom Wagner was on *Wolf News* and said he thought a law suit is inevitable."

"Think I should call him?"

"Worth a try, I guess."

"What was the vote?"

"Googan, Giglio Guest and, of course, Wagner voted against it. Riley—a former governor's nephew—also voted against it. Oh, and one commissioner was absent, and the indicted one—you know, James, the ladies' man and gambler—voted 'present.'"

"So, let's see, ten voted for it and looks like these spineless bastards didn't want it to go public. Un-fuckin' believable, as we used to say back in the day. I'll tell you what, Ron. I'll give you everything you ask, if you go over some of your notes with me."

"Really, I shouldn't be doing this, but here's what I got. Orizaga spent seventeen months going in and out of the court of this idiot judge named O'Fallon, up in Skokie, between his October 2008 arrest and his release from probation, February 2011. Court personnel never contacted ICE."

"Hold on—did they have to?"

"Well, yes and no," Ron said. "O'Fallon and the attorneys knew he was illegal and they also knew immigration enforcement was a federal responsibility. But get this—my legman found a Cook County resolution that somehow gives court personnel permission to ignore federal law."

And there was more. Ralston had called the press spokesperson at the Chicago ICE office who claimed they had no knowledge of Orizaga until June 8, 2011. That was when a new reporting procedure linked state and FBI criminal history databases with those of the Department of Homeland Security.

"And as you know, ICE is part of that federal agency," said Ron, his voice heavy with meaning.

"So when Orizaga got booked the night of your brother's death, the Feds issued a detainer, probably the next day."

"Okay," said Pat, trying to absorb the information overload.

"So now I see why the Feds were not contacted the first time. Let's be clear. Denny would be *alive* today because Orizaga would have been deported. We now can point the finger at no less than twenty Cook County assholes! Pardon the French, Ron."

"We contacted Hunter-Goss at the State's Attorney, and her press gal, Suzy Sorich, said it was not their responsibility, period, and she hung up. I also left a message for your prosecutor, Murphy, but she won't talk to me, I'm sure. A detainer was definitely issued on June 9, 2011, and Sheriff Dan Dypsky knew about it. It would have been in Orizaga's file when he was released."

"Did you call Dypsky?"

"Never returned my calls. Word is out that he fired his press guy, most likely over this."

"Did he hire a new guy?"

"Yeah, we think it's some 19th Ward family friend named Guy Grodecki. I plan to call him in a day or two, but doubt he'll be helpful."

"Look, Ron, I owe you for this, but let me get back to you. I'm going to call Murphy—I got to tell you, I don't think she knows about the judge up at Skokie Branch, or this other stuff."

"Good point, but I'd bet a grand Hunter-Goss's people will get to her and read her the facts of life."

"Yeah, good bet, but when she told me about the ordinance it seemed like she was blindsided on this."

"Look, Pat, the question is why *didn't* she know about the ordinance? I mean, she shouldn't have to follow County Board proceedings, but Hunter-Goss surely should have known, as well as her deputy, Sheehan, who was there for the vote! They should have issued a memo to her. Four hundred or more assistant states attorney and Murphy could have gone back to court and increased the bond to, say, a million!"

"So your article comes out tomorrow, Ron?"

"Yeah, I'll focus on your concerns, the vote, and the refusal to comment on the part of those responsible. Maybe later, say in a few days, I'll get into to some of the other stuff like the prior conviction, so I'll be in touch. And, Pat—I'm real sorry about your brother."

After the call ended, Pat went over the chronology of events, making sure that he had not omitted anything of importance. Then, when he had a clear idea as to what he wanted to say, he phoned Eileen Murphy.

"Eileen, Pat here. You won't believe what I just learned," said Pat as he launched into his summary of the conversation with Ralston.

"My goodness, Pat. Well, politics are out of my jurisdiction," protested Eileen, a faint touch of humor in her voice.

"What about your boss, Hunter-Goss?"

"Well, aahh, you know I have to be careful, because things can get—you know."

"Okay, okay, I get it," said Pat, frustration rising. Ralston had been right. Someone had already gotten to Eileen.

"Sounds like you were called to the principal's office," he observed.

"She's real political, Pat, so you have to be careful."

"No—*you* have to be careful. I understand. I bet she's part of this cover-up."

There was an awkward silence.

"Pat, you know I can't …"

"Yeah, I know. Well, what *can* you tell me?" said Pat, barely conscious of the aggressive edge to his voice.

"Well, I increased the bond to 500K, and there is now a warrant out for his arrest. They sent Cook County Sheriff's deputies and Chicago cops to look for him. I haven't heard anything yet."

"Fat chance! C'mon. You and I know he's long gone, for God's sake."

"Yeah, probably, but that's all I could do," Murphy continued, almost apologetically.

"You know there's a court date Thursday, right?" she continued.

"Sure, but why bother? We both know Orizaga skipped."

"Well, the court will convene, with or without him."

"Maybe some of my family should be there, but if Orizaga doesn't show, that will further add insult to injury."

"I'm so sorry, Pat."

Pat, barely hearing her, looked at his notes.

"Okay, let me ask about the ordinance."

"Pat, we already went over that."

"I know, but did you ask other prosecutors, judges, supervisors—you know, talk around the courthouse—if any others knew about this ordinance?"

There was dead silence.

"C'mon, Eileen. Help me out."

"Well, Pat, I got to tell you—no one knew, not even Judge Martin, the guy assigned to your case."

"So no memo—what about that bald assistant to Hunter-Goss? Sheehan, I think his name. I'm told he's always at these Cook County Board meetings."

"I didn't see anything from him, Pat."

"Jeez, this looks worse than the Chicago Public School boondoggles I put up with at the *Board of Education* for thirty years. I'm going to pursue this and, for starters, find out about this idiotic ordinance."

"Pat, I'm with you, but you know it's difficult."

"Hey, Hunter-Goss really screwed this up, along with ten commissioners—Dypsky, Korshak, and God knows who else. I mean, there must be other illegal felons in the system, right?"

"I just had the one, Pat, but you're probably right. The talk around here is that a whole bunch more got out."

"Think Hunter-Goss will talk to me?"

"She *won't* talk to you. Trust me."

"Oh, and do you think Judge Martin or the bond judge, Santiago, knew Orizaga had a prior felony conviction?"

"Well, for sure Martin did, because it came up, back in July—I think you were there. And the Rice girl—I doubt she told the bond judge of Orizaga's prior felony."

"Rice? Who's that"?

"Oh, she's new here and was assigned to the bond hearing. I got the file after that."

"So a wet-behind-the-ears new kid agrees to a low bond for an illegal prior-convicted felon who then kills my brother."

"Well, that's one way to put it, I guess, but we all thought the detainer was sufficient."

"Maybe this guy, Judge Santiago, knew something you didn't—that the ordinance was coming down the pike."

Again, that deafening silence.

"Okay. Thanks, Eileen—please call if you have anything."

"You bet," she said but her words sounded flat.

"What a bunch of bullshit!" muttered Pat as he clicked the "End Call" button on his phone. Here it was, the end of August, and his brother had been dead almost three months. These clowns had let Orizaga walk, and only God knew how many other illegals were out there hurting people. Noting that his cell battery was low, he connected the charger and turned again to his Mac Air. He was curious about Cook County State's Attorney Hunter-Goss' background. If his memory served him well, this was her first County office. A quick search revealed she had been elected in 2008. Prior to that, she had run the *Gang Crimes Unit*. Pat also recalled she served on the *City Council* from the Austin community on the West Side.

"Wonder if she ever prosecuted anyone?" he said out loud. He needed to know the players and everything about them. Though Eileen may have overlooked a few things, his gut told him not to hold her responsible because there were bigger fools out there that owed his family explanations. Even if it was the last thing he did on this earth, he planned to go after every one of those sons o'bitches …

Pat's thoughts turned to his long time friend and mentor, Professor Joe Vanderbiezen. Well into his 70's, he was still as sharp as a tack and was a long-time vocal critic of the Chicago and Cook County machines. Joe would have read Ralston's article by noon the next day—that would be the best time to call him and get his take on the foolish ordinance. He was certain it involved corrupt political machine shenanigans of some sort, and Joe would be the one to understand them.

DAY THREE, TUESDAY, AUGUST 30, 2011

W hen Eileen called the next day, she had nothing new to report. Pat could have given her a hard time, but then reasoned that she most likely had a heavy caseload. Moreover, although there was something shady about the goings on at the *Cook County Board*, it was unlikely she was involved. Instead of venting his frustration, he calmly informed her that he had decided to contact Detective Skolickwitcz. He had been the first person to notify his niece, Christy, of her father's death; it would stand to reason that he could be a part of the task force that had gone after Orizaga.

"Say, did you read Ralston, this morning, Eileen?"

"Didn't have to. It's all over our place. My boss is really angry."

"I'm glad to hear it—I'm going to call this copper."

"Pat, as I recall from last June, he works the afternoon watch. They went out late yesterday, and if they got Orizaga, I would've heard about it."

Just as he was about to hang up, Pat remembered something.

"Okay, Eileen, let's stay in touch. Oh, and by the way, what about a federal warrant so the FBI can look for this guy?"

"Well, I was going to get into that later, because going that route could take time."

"Wait a second, Eileen. Are you telling me that you have been in touch with the FBI?"

Pat, who until then had been sitting on his deck, enjoying the tranquility of his garden, stood up abruptly, almost turning over his chair.

"Well, yes and—"

"Hold on, Eileen. Look, please don't hold back anything!"

"Pat, there's some things the Bureau wants to keep 'need-to-know.'"

"That's nonsense and you know it. Now, what's going on?"

"Okay, getting a federal warrant can only follow a local warrant, which we have. An agent has to prepare an affidavit. I will be the chief source. After that, a federal court date is set, and a federal judge issues the warrant. Then agents can look for Orizaga in all fifty states while working with Mexican authorities."

"Timeline?"

"Could take a few weeks, Pat."

"Okay, this whole process is a joke. Look, sorry for the outburst, but I need all the information you have. Can you promise that?"

"Will try, Pat."

His conversation with Eileen had left him drained. Had he not badgered her, he would have been completely unaware of the latest developments and of the time frame involved in securing a federal warrant. Everything took too long; no one seemed to have a sense of urgency, even Eileen whom he believed to be on his side. Bracing himself for further frustration, Pat picked up the phone and called *Area Three Detective Division, Chicago Police Department.*

"Skolickwitcz here."

"Detective, this is Pat McGurn. You were the guy assigned to my brother's killer. You took five or six weeks to complete the report, and I was a day away from blabbing to your supervisor and going to the press. Now are we clear?"

Pat made no effort to hide the irritation in his voice.

"Yeah," came the indifferent reply. "So you're the brother that's been calling the State's Attorney—"

"Look, how d'you say your name, Detective?"

"Just call me Alphy."

"Alphy?"

"Well, nobody can say my name, see? So they call me Alphabet—now it's Alphy."

"Okay, whatever, Alphy. Now you went looking for Orizaga, right?"

"Yeah, with Sergeant Skeeter and a guy guy from the Sheriff."

"Well, you have any luck?"

"We talked to his brother who said Raul lived in the basement. He showed us a hot plate and a bed—said the brother comes and goes."

"Comes and goes," Pat repeated, unable to believe what he was hearing.

"Look, we're going to go back and check this out, but I only work afternoons. Maybe some of the other shifts will stop by, but we've a manpower shortage—you know, courtesy of the new mayor."

"You knew he was illegal when they caught him the night Denny was killed right?"

"Well, we figured and the Feds knew to and they issued the detainer."

"And you didn't think to call *Immigration and Customs Enforcement?*"

"Didn't have to."

"What d'you mean?"

"Well, like I said the Feds issued a detainer. When a guy is booked— like this Orizaga—the Illinois State Police get notified, and somehow the Feds can check. And if a guy is illegal, they issue a detainer."

"So this policy is new?"

"Yeah. Before, we were told not to call the Feds if we figured a bad guy was illegal."

"*Really?*"

"Yeah. I guess the word went out to treat these Mexicans like they were citizens. Nobody I know ever called the Feds."

"I gotta look into this, Alphy."

"Hey man, don't let on where you heard it!"

"Lips are sealed," said Pat, shaking his head in disgust. Fucking goof ball and one of Chicago's finest, to boot.

"Look, I have to go. If you learn something, give me a call, okay? Here's my cell."

"You got it, Mr. McCraw."

"McGurn, Alph. McGurn"

"Got it."

By now, Pat needed a beer and a change of scene. The flowers on his deck had begun to overpower him with their fragrance, and he had the start of a migraine. It was still early in the afternoon, but he headed for *Ruth's* on Western, hoping that the walk—or the beer—would clear his head. A 'Nam vet named Dooley was playing *The Band* songs on the jukebox. On came "*The Weight*" and the familiar lyrics to, "*Take a Load off Fannie.*" The song somehow relaxed Pat.

"Hey, Slim, gimme a pint of Molanger, please, and get Dooley a backup."

"Sure. How you doing, Pat?" asked the bartender who was anything but slim. His 300 lb. frame loomed over his customers like some hulk from a comic book. He served up two rounds of Molanger, the thick foamy head mounding over the top of the beer mugs the way his customers liked it.

"Not so good. You won't believe what happened Sunday."

Pat went over the last couple of days, while Slim listened intently. He was the neighborhood "confessor," serving up therapy with a dose of booze—or the other way round!

"You gotta be fuckin' kidding! What you gonna do?"

"Tonight, I'm going to research this ordinance, and call Riley, our former sainted governor's nephew or maybe this guy, Wagner."

"Wagner—who's he?"

"Commissioner Wagner—he was the outspoken one—got a lot of ink because he thought the ordinance was bad news, Slim."

"Why not call Commissioner Riley? He's got all the clout, you know, on account of his name," chimed in Dooley, the only other patron. He was sitting on the stool next to Pat's hunched over his beer mug. The pale golden lager had little flavor—not much better than Drews Light, but twice the price. Not the type of product one would expect from the famous German brewery, but then, it was probably packaged in the good ol' USA.

"I got to tell ya, Dools," slurred Pat, now into his second beer. He had skipped lunch and the alcohol had gone straight to his head.

"I always hated this clout stuff, but I'll call Riley. Read today's paper, Slim?"

"You tellin' me all this is in the news, Pat?"

"Page two—Ralston in *The Globe*."

Dooley put more money into the jukebox, and in a few seconds, Levon was blaring, "*The Night They Drove Old Dixie Down.*" Pat drained his beer mug, placing it heavily on the counter.

"You driving, Pat?" asked Slim, studying his customer over the rims of his round bi-focals. The glass was as thick as the bottom of a coke bottle.

"Nope, but I'm out of here. Not quite the Molanger I remember—just an inoffensive beer, don't you think? Thanks for listening, guys."

And with that, he began the trek home.

Clare was waiting for him in the living room, sitting in the Mission-style armchair closest to the fireplace. From her vantage point, she had a clear view of the front door which she had evidently been watching for some time. Their initial exchange was testy. No, Pat had not heard her call—he'd put the phone on mute after dealing with that fucking goof, Alphy. And, no, he hadn't received Clare's text. And as for drinking too much, absolutely not—just two Molanger which tasted like dishwater and left him with a buzz. Clare, still in her work slacks and blazer, had taken off work early because she was worried about the way Pat had reacted to the news of Orizaga's release. Until then, he had been doing quite well, or as well as could be expected.

"Looks like you could do with a meal!' said Clare sympathetically. She had been more anxious than annoyed by Pat's failure to keep in touch with her. Since his brother's death, he had been preoccupied with seeking justice, and Orizaga's release was definitely an emotional setback, not only for him but for the whole family.

Dinner was lasagna and a salad Clare had made. They sat out on the deck, side by side, overlooking the long back yard which was ablaze with orange day lilies. Though the sun was beginning to set, neither of them made any effort to close the umbrella over the picnic table. It was good just to relax and go over the events of the day.

"You still got the police report?"

"Sure I do, Clare, but what good is it now that he's skipped?"

"This could be a long and painful ordeal," said Clare, looking at him steadily. She reached out for the hand closest to her.

"You know, Pat, some will say, 'Why bother? Orizaga skipped. Forget about it.' But I I know you want to fight these people—there's something terribly wrong here. Given Denny's view of politicians, he would have agreed with what you're doing. Of course, I'll help. I can check on the judge and check out Orizaga's lawyer as well."

"Thanks, Clare—I knew I could count on you! The real issue for now is this ordinance. After dinner, I'll do a Google search and see what I can find.

With little effort at all, Pat found the ordinance at the Cook County website. He couldn't believe the absurdity of the document or that ten commissioners had voted for it. They must have known the shit would hit the fan once one of these felons killed someone.

At about 8:00 p.m. the phone rang. It was Ron Ralston, on a deadline with a follow-up story.

"I'm going to recap the ordinance, Pat. I got a quote from Wagner, claiming there's going to be lawsuits up the you-know-what and another from the Cook County President's office, claiming it's the bond court's fault."

"Bond court, Ron? What's Korshak talking about?"

Pat's raised voice echoed into the kitchen where Clare was in the process of loading their supper plates into the dishwasher. Wiping her hands in her apron, she hurried into the dining room. Pat, clearly agitated, was sitting at the table in front of his lap top, cell phone in hand. He pressed the speaker button so that his wife could hear the conversation. Quietly, Clare pulled out a chair and sat by his side.

"Well, she argues that maybe the bond was set too low."

"Hey, Ron, that's bullshit!" exploded Pat, shaking with anger.

"The fucking issue is that she and the other fools ignored the Feds—you know that, Ron! Did you talk to Commissioner Varbanov?"

"Oh, yeah, and he claims it's all about civil rights and innocents getting deported."

"Did you remind him about Denny?"

"Yeah," said Ron with a bitter laugh. "All he did was stammer and say that he was sorry."

"'Sorry!'—that's not going to bring back Denny! Who did you speak to in Korshak's office?"

"Legal Council woman named Inger Nordquist."

"Did she mention Denny?"

By now, the veins were standing out across Pat's forehead. Clare looked at him anxiously, wondering how much more stress he could take. This whole ordeal was taking its toll on him, physically as well as emotionally. The chandelier shone directly on his head, illuminating his thinning hair that now seemed more white than salt and pepper.

"No comment when I asked her."

"How 'bout States Attorney Hunter-Goss?"

"I told her press gal I wanted a quote, but got no comment."

"Did you talk to Eileen Murphy?"

"Yeah. Looks like her boss gagged her as well."

"Look, Ron, print this statement—print everything. Are you ready?"

"Okay. Fire ahead!"

"Pat McGurn will do everything in his power to get to the bottom of Raul Orizaga's release. If this means reviewing old County agendas, writing letters, or whatever it takes, his family will not rest until those that allowed the convicted felon who killed his brother to flee are held accountable."

"I'll print all of that Pat."

"Say Ron, tell me what's with Commissioner Varbanov pushing this ordinance? Name sounds Slavic."

"My editor told me his mother's from Argentina."

Pat knew the phone would be ringing after this statement became public, but he didn't care. Once the conversation ended, he slumped back in his chair, too tired to move. Clare disappeared into the kitchen, returning with a chamomile tea served in a green and beige pottery mug with "Grandfather" inscribed on it—a gift from the kids. Clare put on a Lorena McKenna album from Ireland.

•

Pat did not sleep well that night. He tossed and turned, awakening Clare several times. It seemed to her that he was mumbling something, but she couldn't make out the words. Whatever he was dreaming could not have been pleasant. No doubt he was being haunted by the whole cast of unsavory characters responsible for Orizaga's release: Shirley Korshak, perhaps, discussing Ralston's first column with State's Attorney, Lisa Hunter-Goss; or Hunter-Goss recapping all she knew about the McGurn affair with Korshak. Or perhaps the Cook County President and States Attorney discussing the new column that would appear the next day …

Her thoughts now racing, Clare imagined how such a conversation would flow.

"Shirley, Lisa here. You got a minute?"

"Sure. Lisa you're calling about Ralston's piece today, right?"

"You got it. I'm sure you're busy, and you can bet we are working a strategy, too. So here's what I got, Shirley. Well, McGurn has not only called Murphy,

but also the detective and he's talked to Ralston, of course. Oh, yeah, Ralston has most of it and looks like he's got another column out tomorrow."

At this news, Korshak utters an expletive unbefitting the Cook County President.

"Hmmm, let me think, Lisa. First, both of us need stock answers when other reporters call—I'll get Ms. Nordquist on it and you do the same. You know, something like, 'In the wisdom of the Cook County commissioners, who believe in due process for all people in Cook County, and that includes posting bond … '"

"You bet, Shirley. We can say it was commissioners, because they passed the ordinance. And we followed, right?"

"Well, I don't know about that because it's on record that I supported the ordinance, so this will get hot, and who knows what this McGurn's up to. Okay, Lisa. So Murphy upped the bond, and cops went looking for him. So any luck?"

"Not a chance, Shirley. Everybody knew he'd run. And, oh yeah, Murphy told me he had a prior felony conviction, but no federal detainer was issued as far as she could tell. She also said that since it was federal, it might not be in the file."

"Really, Lisa, tell me more."

"Well, it's like this. The Cook County Board passed this resolution in 2007 that strongly urged the State's Attorney, Sheriff and, frankly, everybody in the criminal justice system not to cooperate with Immigration Custom Enforcement or ICE."

"So what was this Orizaga charged with in 2008?"

"He was convicted of aggravated DUI in February 2009 and put on probation. Two years later, he was taken off probation and, unfortunately, killed Denny McGurn five months after that."

"Talk about a perfect storm."

"Perfect storm, Lisa. You and I know just the right people to bring calm to all concerned. McGurn can make all the noise he want—it won't mean anything."

"Won't mean anything …," murmured Clare, now in a deep sleep. "Won't mean anything …

DAY FOUR, WEDNESDAY, AUGUST 31, 2011

Pat got up Wednesday morning and began taking care of the usual chores. It was his responsibility to water the flowers on the deck and to turn the sprinkler on in the yard. Clare usually watered the indoor plants but she had left on the 8:20 a.m. train for downtown—in fact, he had driven her to the station at 91st Street. Neither of them had slept well, and he thought she looked quite tired, even though they had both gone to bed early. He checked the few low-light plants in the living room and dining room, before moving on to other tasks—carrying out the recyclables (it was pick up day), filling the bird feeder and taking meat out of the freezer to de-frost for the evening meal. He saw there had been seven or eight calls, most likely because of the article in the paper. He was not in a hurry to return any of the calls. It was good that people were reading Ralston, but he hoped they would get the facts straight. Ralston did a good job, but people tended to scan rather than read, often misinterpreting all the facts; for now, Pat didn't want to deal with explanations.

Eventually, he listened to his recorded messages. One of the calls was from a pro-immigrant activist who accused Pat of being a lying racist; the rest were from friends and family offering support. He pressed the delete button, keeping only a couple of the family messages to share with Clare.

Mid morning, he got into his Ford Explorer and stopped at the *Moonscape Coffee Shop* at 107th and Dotson. There he picked up a copy of *The Globe* and a mug of Mocha Java, then sat down at an empty table to collect his thoughts and jot down a strategy of sorts. He had already seen Ralston's article online, but there was something satisfying about having a print copy in hand, a tangible reminder that things were moving forward at last. Pat waved to old crazy Swiney who was reading a tattered copy of *Mad Magazine*; Swiney growled a "Good morning," and continued re-reading the same page he was reading the last time Pat had seen him. No doubt his favorite page, Pat thought, observing the way Swiney used his gnarled yellow fingers to keep track of each line of print. Pat turned to look at some notes and began studying the original police report from June, together with some of the press clippings. He then took out his Mac Book Air and started typing when Daddy Wags walked in, another neighborhood character who lived at the end of Dotson Avenue in a rundown frame house surrounded by rambling weeds. From his table, Pat could smell the whiskey on his breath as he came through the door.

"Hey, my man, Pat—I seen the paper. You know that's real fucked up—say, let me buy you a coffee or something."

Not wanting company, Pat looked up at Wags, trying to hide his irritation.

"Thanks Wags. I'm busy now—maybe later. Swiney's been smiling big-time over there—why not treat him?"

"You got it, bro," said Wags, ambling towards Swiney who was still engrossed with the same page of *Mad Magazine*. Pat took out a notebook and began writing:

6/8/2011. Accident. Denny killed; Orizaga arrested.

6/9/2011. Bond set at $250,000.00 by Judge Santiago presiding.

6/12/2011. Arraignment. Family met with Eileen Murphy and assured of federal detainer. "He will never be able to post bond."

7/27/2011-8/12/2011. Discovery proceedings; family assured all was okay.

8/11/2011. Ordinance passed, effective 8-14-2011.

9/7/2011. Orizaga bonds out by brother, Roberto. Presumed to have fled to Mexico.

9/8/2011. State's Attorney Murphy sends deputies to look for Orizaga.

Having established the timeline, Pat then took out a copy of the ordinance. As he read through it, he could feel his blood pressure rise. Hands shaking, he forced himself to take a deep breath before writing a single-sentence synopsis:

This ordinance, passed by ten members of the Cook County Board, mandates that the County Sheriff ignore immigration and customs detainers that are issued by the federal government; now the scores of illegal alien felons can post bond and commit more crimes. The McGurn family's beloved brother was killed by an illegal alien and the *Cook County Commissioners' Board* is responsible.

"Let's see," he said to himself, mentally going over the list of culprits. Korshak was the chief non-voting sponsor; Varbanov, Houma, Fanning, McAbee, Petrutis, Mayfield, Chico, Rucker, Alport and Murray all voted for the ordinance. Chief sponsor Varbanov was a former state representative and active with a radical organization called the *HCC* or the *Hispanic Community Council*—perhaps a friend of that other alderman whose father ran a phony identification ring for illegals down in Pilsen? Next was Chico who was appointed because of former Cook County Commissioner Escobar's chronic illness. McAbee had inherited the job from his brother after he died—he seemed pretty useless. Mayfield was a former gym teacher and Boller—who could tell?

"Let's see." There was Petrutis, sort of lazy and a double dipper. Davida Alport was the brains of the bunch, former civil rights activist in the 60's. As for Lori Fanning, she was related to an old high school chum, probably through marriage and was new on the job. Murray? Well, she hung onto her position in the suburbs by promising constituents everything; she was notorious for all the patronage jobs and contracts she had milked out of Korshak's corrupt predecessor. There were a few other supporters; most likely they just went along with the other nine. Oh, and then there was James, a libertine gambler who was being investigated by Fitzgibbons, the U.S. Attorney for Northern Illinois. James had not been to a meeting in months."

Not a stellar bunch to say the least, Pat thought. He hoped that Joe, his old Political Science professor could fill in the blanks about the so called county commissioners. Joe had undoubtedly read Ralston that morning and would be sure to have some perspective as to why the ordinance had been passed. Riley, who voted against the ordinance, might also be helpful, but Pat knew he was supportive of President Korshak. Wagner, however, was the most outspoken commissioner; it would be worth scheduling an appointment with him in a day or two. He knew little about the others, all Republicans, with the exception of Julie Googan, a South Side gal who had attended Lynwood Academy. Pat recalled having read something about her having been involved in bankruptcy and some failed business—not a pristine record!

The coffee shop was becoming quite crowded and Pat could see that several customers who were paying for their purchases were eyeing the empty chairs at his table. Quickly, he gathered up his papers, said a perfunctory "Have a great day!" to Swiney and Wags, and headed for his car. Once in the driver's seat, he checked his phone messages. Two commissioners had called—one who voted for the ordinance and one against. The rest were from family and from four or five people who just wanted to garner gossip. "Miserable assholes," said Pat out loud, not caring if anyone heard him. Last, there was a cryptic message from a George Hallet who left the following voice mail: *"Mr. McGurn, so sorry for your loss. We have not met, but I can explain a thing or two—perhaps over coffee—so please call."* Pat jotted down his name and number, then turned the key in the ignition.

Now that some of the facts were clearer, Pat felt he could represent himself from a more informed vantage point. He and Joe had spent some time together at the Midwest Political Science meetings the previous May at *The Palmer House* and so it had not been that long since their last communication. Joe, having retired from academia years before, was now running a bed and breakfast in Champaign, Illinois, with his wife, Judy— *Serendipity Place.*

"Joe, Pat McGurn here."

"Hey, Pat" exclaimed the familiar voice. "I was thinking of calling you after reading Ralston this morning."

"Yeah, I figured you'd be on it. So any thoughts, Professor?"

In spite of the years that had passed since Pat last took one of Joe's courses, the younger man sometimes still had a hard time calling his former teacher by his first name.

"Well, I read the ordinance—it's a farce and no question about it. You know the Cook County Board tried to pass a similar law back in 2007 and the vote was deadlocked, seven to seven. Korshak's predecessor refused to vote the tiebreaker."

"You mean Rod Streger did something right, Prof?

"Yep. Junior wanted no part of it."

"I'll be damned," said Pat, not expecting this news. "Jeez, he was so maligned in the press." "Look, there's more, Pat. Somehow the Cook County Board got a resolution through later that year that effectively turned Cook County into a sanctuary region."

"Yeah, Ralston mentioned that but it wasn't in his article this morning—space limitations, I guess, but it's unbelievable. Okay, Joe—please continue."

"Well, it looks like the Chicago and Cook County cops, along with State's Attorneys and judges have all more or less complied. However, *Immigration and Custom Enforcement* (ICE) was applying pressure with their *Secure Community Initiative*, so that's why they got this ordinance passed."

"I got to tell you—I'm finding all of this quite overwhelming," said Pat.

"There's more Pat—I'm learning a lot from a visiting professor down here by the name of Joan Farnsworth who works full time for a DC group called *Center for Immigration Analysis*. She's following several so called sanctuary cities across the country, and will be staying with us through the end of October. You'd be welcome to meet her."

"Great!" said Pat, jumping at the opportunity. "Tomorrow too soon, Joe?"

"Fine with me—I don't think Farnsworth going away so let's set a time. Your call, Pat."

"11:30 a.m.?"

"Okay, but before you come down, maybe a little perspective. Remember Schwab and political cultures?"

"How could I forget, Prof? Your seminars back in the day were all about them!"

"Still relevant, Pat. Why don't you Google my name, political cultures & Schwab and just refresh your mind a bit. This might help you understand what's going on up there in Crook County."

Pat chuckled for the first time that day.

DAY FIVE, THURSDAY, SEPTEMBER 1, 2011

P at was on the road early the next day. It was a straight run south on I -57, but, nevertheless, there was no quick way of travelling 135 miles. With his early start, he figured he'd get to Joe's bed and breakfast about 11:00 a.m., as planned. In his college days in the early 1970's, as a student at the *University of Illinois at Urbana—Champaign*, he had always enjoyed this drive. He loved the stretches of empty highway and the small sleepy towns scattered along the way, each with its own version of "Main Street" and a few "Mom & Pop" stores where one could stop for supplies. It was also a thrill to be approaching university territory. To Pat, UIUC was a special place indeed and he often argued that the school was the most important secular institution in the state. Known primarily for its research, it was a founding member of *The Big Ten Conference* and home to *The Fighting Illini*. Its stately architecture alone was significant and T.A. Gaines had designated the university as a "work of art" in his book, *The Campus as a Work of Art*. It was also one of the few universities, nationwide, to own its own airport and aviation center.

After about two hours on the road, Pat caught sight of *Memorial Stadium*, built in 1923 in memory of the men and women of Illinois who had lost their lives during World War I. It always made him feel proud to know that the famous landmark was dedicated to those who had fallen in battle. In fact, there had been countless times when he had studied the names displayed on the 200 columns supporting the east and west sides of the stadium.

Within a few minutes, he was parked in front of *Serendipity Place*. It was an old building, pre-Civil War, by all accounts, with a classic box form and a steeply pitched roof. Two stories high, it had a magnificent porch with a flat roof that was supported by two classical columns. *Doric* most likely, Pat thought. The building was covered in shingles and was painted white; window boxes filled with cascading purple and white petunias added to the charm, as did the beautifully landscaped front yard. The building was truly a gem.

When he rang the bell, an elderly woman came to the door. She greeted Pat with a smile and invited him in.

"Pat, so good to see you. I'm so sorry about your brother, Denny, and now this situation!"

"Thanks, Judy—your support means a lot to me! Hope you can spare Joe for a few hours while I pick his brain."

"The least we can do, Pat," she said as Joe walked in from the library. Standing in the hallway, he looked every bit of the proverbial college professor—bearded, wearing dark jeans, open necked white shirt and the trademark tweed jacket with leather patched elbows that he wore year round.

"Pat, my good man—so no problem with the drive down?"

"I always enjoyed this drive, Prof, and today the weather is only 75F. So the place's doing okay?"

Joe and Judy exchanged smiles, obviously content with this phase of married life.

"We just love this place," said Joe. "Conversations with visiting professors or parents most weekend mornings are a real joy—we talk over Judy's country breakfasts for sometimes two hours. Say, let's leave Judy to her cooking. We'll take your car and drive around campus where we can discuss a thing or two about our shared academic interests. I'll make my own way back as I have some business to attend to. I think you will find Joan Farnsworth's input more useful in the short term."

"Sounds good, Joe. I'm sure looking forward to meeting Dr. Farnsworth. Judy, I promise Clare and I will be down before the holidays for a stay."

"*The Lincoln Suite* is reserved anytime you wish, Pat—please give Clare our best."

Once on campus, Joe pointed out renovations and a new construction site near *Memorial Stadium*. Pat pulled over so as to take in all the changes. He found it difficult to drive, listen and observe all at the same time.

"So, Pat, I hope you got a chance to read Schwab."

"You bet, and I now know why you suggested that."

"Good, good, but I don't think Schwab was thinking of Hispanics that much forty years ago. Schwab was referring to the prevalent 'ME and MINE' political culture that runs from New England in an almost direct line through most large urban areas all the way to Kansas City. Or you might say that it starts with fictional Boston Mayor Skeffington in *The Last Hurrah* on one end and ends with the non-fictional Prendergast machine on the other end in Kansas City. Both the Boston novel and the KC political machine were in play 60 years ago and continue to this day. Look, I know all this academic gibberish won't get your man or change the ordinance, but I hope it will explain things—"

"Joe, I get it and you're absolutely right—without perspective, my efforts could go haywire long term."

Joe gave Pat the old familiar smile.

"Indeed, I recall reading Truman having said something to the effect that it is understanding that gives us the ability to have peace."

"Thanks for that, Joe. I don't know about peace, but maybe it will help me to be more resolute in the weeks to come."

Joe nodded.

"Well said! So as I was saying, perhaps the more egregious examples of corruption on the Schwab model would be Newark, Detroit, Cleveland and Chicago—with Chicago taking the prize. In short, the vast majority of the residents view political institutions as an open market to access when you want something. They believe politics exist for individual wealth, not for the commonwealth, as the founders envisioned. In highly charged 'ME and MINE' cities like Chicago, politics simply mean, 'I want something for me and my family and close friends from the public treasury."

Pat pushed back his car seat and stretched out his legs. Through the open car windows, he could breathe in the fragrance of late summer flowers and hear the songbirds warbling in the trees and shrubbery flanking the stately buildings. In the distance, he could see a massive six-sided building topped by a dome-like structure. The new library? If he remembered rightly, this was the *Aces Library, Information and Alumni Center* that had been built about a decade before. He had seen plans of the building when he had donated to the alumni fund raising effort—that was way back in the spring of 2000 or thereabouts. A twenty-one million dollar facility of over 52,000 square feet …

"Okay Joe, I remember your lectures well. I'll bet you're about to tell me that, according to Schwab, a few hundred miles north in the upper Midwest the 'ME and MINE' notion does not exist.'"

"Right on, Pat!" chuckled Joe. "But there are exceptions. Schwab simply argued that cultural norms make a difference. For example, the predominant thinking in Chicago is that politics are a market to get power and money while in small cities like St. Cloud or Bismark, the general rule is politics represent service for the entire citizenry. Come to think of it, the term "clout" originated in Chicago."

"Yeah, I remember—Len O'Connor published a book with that name forty plus years ago. Also wrote *Requiem*, if I'm not mistaken."

"You always were a good student—glad something stuck in that graying head of yours! I will argue that Schwab's theory applies to your situation. Every ethnic group that gravitated to large northern industrial cities looked for power politically and had its own agenda—like your very own Irish ancestors, Pat. These days the Hispanics have at the top of their list an open border, lax internal enforcement, free education and other entitlements, short of citizenship. You see, legal citizenship takes a long time, but things like licensing, access to higher education and entitlements can be acquired from chief executives."

"Like President Haesi, Cook County President Korshak and the governor, Joe?"

Pat was listening intently now, focusing on every word. He pushed the driver's seat to upright position again and turned to face Joe, the lines across his forehead tightening.

"Yep, and they have submissive legislative branches or, at least, Haesi does in the Senate.

Just recently, President Haesi used an Executive Order to grant status for up to two million illegals for the so-called Dreamers—those from about 16-30 years of age—while the governor trashed *Secure Communities in Illinois*."

"So ordinances like in Cook County and Haesi's Executive Order are a clear manifestation of this?"

"You bet," said Joe, his voice becoming more animated as he and Pat shifted back into the old roles of professor-student. He loved nothing more than to share his knowledge, especially to a receptive audience.

"Joan's research shows there are over fifty of these sanctuary jurisdictions in the US. That's it, in short. I'll send along more for you to read because I'm in the midst of writing a massive tome with five other scholars and my chapter delves into this very topic. Oh yeah, one of our contributors—a guy named McLaughlin from *Southern Illinois University*—has documented every political conviction in Cook County/Chicago for the past 60 years. Just last week he told me that one of his graduate students has proof that there is considerable nepotism with state legislators getting jobs for family members. We also have a historian from Carlyle in Atlanta who will do a biography on Roy Dunne, the first Irish Mayor of Chicago—a brilliant lawyer, clean as whistle. He contrasts Dunne with some of the other Irishmen who, shall we say, were less than honorable clout hounds. So you see, Pat, the book is pretty comprehensive, with different takes by different scholars as to what's wrong with Chicago, Cook County and Illinois."

"You guys may pivot the structure of Illinois politics with this book!" exclaimed Pat. He had always admired Professor Vanderbiezen, but in recent years had associated him more with *Serendipity Place* than with academia. It was clear to him now that Joe was as sharp as he had been during Pat's undergrad days; if anything, his knowledge base had deepened.

"Hardly, Pat. The politicians only look at our work when it suits them, but maybe we might get a better governor and get rid of this incumbent governor. Look, we got a few minutes before we meet Joan, so I'll give you a two minute synopsis of the rest."

Joe explained that Chicago and Cook County were in the midst of an impending financial disaster. It was likely the state would have to declare bankruptcy in the near future, due largely to unfunded pension liabilities, Medicaid bills, school funding and other drains on the Illinois budget. A report released just the day before revealed that the state had over one hundred billion in unfunded pension liabilities and would potentially run out of money as early as 2020. Bond ratings were "heading south" and many analysts were beginning to compare Illinois with Greece.

"Well, Pat, as I was saying there's corruption everywhere, and I'm afraid it's led by Democrats who have enriched themselves to the tune of millions of dollars with sweetheart legal and illegal construction contracts, hundreds of double dippers, do nothing jobs and tax breaks offered by the party leadership. The trend continues, in spite of the fact that U.S. Attorney Fitzgibbons and his predecessors have successfully prosecuted many of these crooks."

Joe went on to explain that a major thesis of his book was that this corruption—be it voter fraud, malfeasance, pension scams, tax dodges and politically motivated criminality—would lead to an eventual breakdown to the rule of law at all levels. The State of Illinois, led by Cook County, would become a veritable war zone on a par with Detroit. The long and short of the book, then, was to convince the electorate that corruption yields violence. The authors hoped that, over the next ten years or so, the rule of law would become the general will of the people, and the public, finally understanding the notion of the commonwealth, would start electing ethical men and women. As things stood, far left academic cabals had plagued the American landscape for over fifty years; they used the current President and he, in turn, used them. Several of the authors—Joe, included—intended to argue that Haesi's successful run for U.S. Senator in 2006 and for President in 2008 was due, in large part, to the diseased political culture in Cook County and Illinois.

"Whew, Joe—no one else has gone there! I mean, *diseased!*"

"Well, they have, Pat, but they refer to the so-called 'Chicago Way' as if Haesi was a product of the 11th Ward Democratic machine—as you know, that's not the case at all. So what we're going to argue is that Chicago politicians accepted Haesi not because they were enamored with him, but because they knew his empowerment would guarantee their continued claim on the spoils."

"So Haesi more or less promised them they could maintain the status quo?"

"You bet—and his stimulus packages wound up in all sorts of silly government programs. In other words, the unwritten rule is that the old machine stays as long as you don't tread on what's mine. Oh, and don't forget the powerful political families that need to be protected—like in your Ward you have the Heaney, Shannon and Conlon families."

"For sure, Joe—let's see, in the 19th we have the new alderman who married into the Shannon family. Oh, and I can't forget Sheriff Dypsky's old man was a ward political operative."

"Okay, you get the picture," said Joe. "We could name any number of corrupt enclaves like the 19th Ward, but your community is at the top. The old political machine regime led by old man Daley would never have favored the lax immigration enforcement ensconced in sanctuary city/counties like Chicago."

"I get it alright," muttered Pat, shaking his head. "And now their sons and daughters and scores of surrogates do so willingly because they keep the spoils."

"You always caught on fast, Pat. In the old days, I'd beat up the machine because of the spoils—now the key to understanding this new reality is increased lawlessness and violence."

"Yeah, and my brother Denny a victim," said Pat bitterly, drumming on the steering wheel with his right hand. For a few minutes, the men sat in silence.

"Okay, I know this is upsetting, Pat, but you wanted the full picture. Earlier, I mentioned George McLaughlin. Well, he and his team of graduate students have connected all the dots that chronicle the politicians from the mid 50's who ended up in jail. They spent five to seven years on the project, and, in fact, I think one of his students is writing a doctoral dissertation. Oh, and before I forget, it was family sponsorship that gave us Simon Lilly, arguably the most corrupt Governor in Illinois History."

"Yeah, good ole Rick Lyons the former Cook County Assessor is his father in law," observed Pat. "Remember how daddy in law and jailbird have been estranged for some time due to certain indiscretions?"

"I forgot about that," chuckled Joe. "Look, we better meet Joan who will be a big help, but when the dust settles on this issue, maybe we can get you down here and you can work with me on the book."

"Really Joe, I'm flattered ..."

They drove towards *The Illini Union*, conveniently finding metered parking on Mathews Street, just two blocks away. Entering the building, they made their way to the *Courtyard Café* on the main level where Joan had agreed to meet them at *Espresso Royale*. An attractive brunette in her early forties, she was sitting at a table, working on her iPhone. After introductions, they ordered Iced Vanilla Lattes and chicken salad sandwiches.

"Joan, while we're waiting, let's start with you, so Pat has some idea of your work. I already gave him some background about our forthcoming book."

"Okay," said Joan, putting aside the iPhone. "Pat, first of all I'm really sorry about all that's happened these past few months. Part of my work involves interviewing family members of victims, so, in some ways, I've heard your story before—countless times, in fact! Before I go on, though, let me tell you Ralston will be a big help, because these issues have really been under reported nationally. He's a good guy."

"Yeah," agreed Pat. "I'm hoping he'll give us at least one more article. So, tell me, Joan, how big a problem is this illegal immigration?"

"Well, we're still working the numbers at the *Center for Immigration Analysis* for forthcoming congressional testimonies, but I can tell you it's a serious issue. You see, when I testify I use hard data and generally conclude with victim references. In fact, near my home in Providence a young college student was run over by an illegal just last month. Perhaps one of the most newsworthy stories involved a popular History teacher from Ashville, North Carolina, who was killed a year ago; his wife is still in the hospital on life support. I'm going to interview the family over the Thanksgiving weekend. I could go on and on, Pat, and when my next congressional document is completed I'll send it to you. In fact, I'll send you a batch of PDF documents over the weekend."

"Thanks—that would be really helpful! So do you have a ballpark figure about how many other citizen victims there have been in the U.S.?"

"I'd say that in the last ten years or so perhaps there have been as many as a thousand victims—the numbers increase yearly. And we're only looking at aggravated felonies such as rape, murder, kidnapping, drug distribution—you name it."

Pat looked aghast. Catching his eye, Joe pulled a face as if to say, "I told you so!"

"This is incredible! So you will present these figures to Congress, Joan?"

"Yes, before the *Judiciary Committee*—my guess in two weeks. So there's a lot to read, Pat."

"Trust me, Pat here will read every single word—and don't be surprised if you get e-mailed questions," cut in Joe, grinning at his former student. Pat smiled appreciatively.

"I'll answer anything you send me—don't hesitate," said Joan. She waited for the waiter to place the Iced Vanilla Lattes and chicken salad sandwiches on the table before continuing. Joe reached for the sandwiches and passed one to Pat. Ignoring the plate in front of her, Joan sat up straight, as if about to give a deposition.

"First, let me explain my affiliation with the *Center for Immigration Analysis*," she said, clearing her throat.

"The center has been operational for about fifteen years and was set up originally by a few anonymous donors and subsequently by many more. We focus on immigration enforcement issues across the several states, appearing before congressional committees, writing position papers, giving speeches and interviews in the interest of supporting what we think are reasonable enforcement procedures under the law. The problem of late is that so called 'sanctuary cities' have emerged in counties and municipalities with large Hispanic populations. These have adopted policies and, in some cases like Cook County, have passed laws and ordinances that allow local authorities to ignore federal law. So, I and a few other colleagues spend as much time as we can with congressional staffers in preparation for testimony."

"Joan, give us some other examples of sanctuary cities," said Joe, before taking a bite out of his sandwich.

"Oh God, where do I start? Every major city on the East Coast, LA, Frisco, major cities in the Pacific Northwest, Houston and, let's see, in the interior Minneapolis, Denver and, of course, Chicago. The list keeps on growing, so I'll send you both a comprehensive list. At present we are looking at Camden because of the murders of four black college students by illegal aliens with priors."

"Yeah, Joan—that was a few years ago. Sure I remember," Pat interjected.

"Get this, continued Joan, less formally now. "The police chief, Chang, said he thought it was 'irrelevant" when asked about their illegal status."

"Are you telling me that our guy in Chicago is the same Chang hired by Mayor Gill?"

Joe nodded, calmly taking a sip from his latte.

"That stupid insensitive, ignorant crack was reported in several papers—and no apologies!"

Pat dabbed his forehead with a paper napkin. Beads of sweat were beginning to form and his face was by now quite flushed.

"So you see the problem?" said Joan, gently. She began to reach across the table, as if to take his hand, then hesitated and pulled back. Instead, she stirred her latte which by now consisted mostly of dirty-looking water, the ice having melted. Pat glanced at her and then at Joe.

"What do you suggest?"

"Well, Pat, maybe I can offer something here. We talked about it earlier and perhaps, down the line, Joan can help as well."

"For sure, but first I need to talk with Wagner, Riley and maybe the other non-supporters of the ordinance as well."

"My guess is that the pro-ordinance people will stonewall any initiative and throw all sorts of curveballs to confuse the issue, but maybe somebody like Wagner might want to offer an amendment. What d'you think, Joan?"

"Maybe, and a call might help from you, Joe—don't leave yourself out of the equation."

"Well, I've already met Riley, but first, Pat, why don't you talk to Wagner and give me a day or two to call them myself."

"Joe, if you're willing to talk to Wagner or Riley, I'm all for it. With the holiday and all, however, I might not get through until next week, so I guess it would be best to wait until you contact them."

"Fair enough, but I'll have to say the initiative started here with our conversation. I've already looked at the ordinance, and it can be amended. I've actually had some experience with writing statues at the state level. I would suggest that an amendment should read that, '*The Sheriff of Cook County should have the responsibility to contact Immigration and Customs Enforcement when a detained illegal alien either posts bond or is released from custody.*' Language of that sort would have prevented Orizaga from being released, provided the Feds had picked him up within the forty-eight hours prescribed by ICE. I'll start with Wagner and get a call in after I do some more research. Okay, Pat—we have a plan here! For now, why don't you go over what you have done thus far?"

Pat reviewed his conversations with Eileen Murphy, explaining how the family had attended two discovery hearings at 26th and California; both times she had assured them that the detainer or hold would prevent his release. Clearly, Hunter-Goss's staff had failed to issue an inner office memo about the ordinance, which is why Murphy knew little more than the McGurns. Then he went over details of the warrant.

"Nothing surprising here—and I'm afraid the probability of catching him is pretty slim," remarked Joan.

"By the way, before you go, Pat, we've been looking at a character up there in Cook County by the name of George Hallet. One of Joe's co-authors has been looking at the many pro immigration groups around the country and this Hallet's name has surfaced from time to time."

Pat winced, as if jolted by an unpleasant memory.

"You won't believe this—I had eight or nine messages on my phone before I left this morning, and I think one was from a guy named Hallet. In fact that was the second time he left a message. So you know something about this Hallet"

Joe raised his eyebrows and whistled; he looked at Joan, who nodded at him.

"Hmmm, not surprised. Look, Pat, here's what is emerging. We still have to explore this further, but we're pretty convinced Hallet is behind this ordinance and other efforts across the country."

"Now, this is getting interesting—so what's his affiliation? Who *is* this guy?"

"Well, he's an 'under the radar' sort of character who belongs to the *Illinois Immigration Cooperative*. It's one of the largest organizations of its kind in the United States and is affiliated with *La Fuerza*, the national Hispanic group and he also works with the Hispanic caucus in the U.S. House of Representatives."

"I heard of *La Fuerza*, Joe—big-time national, I think."

"Oh yeah—been around a long time, heavily funded by huge foundations. We recently learned that Hallet orchestrated a six million dollar stipend for *The Cooperative* under the stimulus package sponsored by his old buddy, President Haesi."

At this point, Joan jumped in, looking decidedly more animated than when she had been giving Pat her "canned" speech.

"Just recently we learned that Hallet has visited the White House three times this year."

"What? How d'you know that?" asked Pat, his face now drained of color.

"*Freedom of Information* request."

"So the Federal Government as well as Cook County is responsible for the jerk running away because this Hallet helped write the ordinance. And you're telling me he's buddy buddy with the President?"

"They go back some years," explained Joe. "We think this Hallet and President Haesi worked together on the South Side in the Roseland and Burnside communities back in the 80's. But I don't want to get sidetracked on the Haesi story, so back to this ordinance. When you talk to Wagner and Riley, I would simply tell them you want the ordinance amended so that felons get deported, and, believe me, that's doable. After that, mention Hallet's role to see their reaction!"

"Couldn't that turn Riley off? From what I've learned over the years, he will always be loyal to the party."

Joe shrugged his shoulders and gestured to Pat, as if to say, "It's your call!" Pat grimaced.

"Okay, I got the weekend to mull stuff over. I'll just try to be assertive and dismiss any excuses, even if they come from the five who voted against it, like Riley. One more thing, a priest left a message as well. Father Ryan, I think is his name."

"My guess he's part of that Catholic social justice group up there and likely pals with Hallet," said Joe.

"He's probably affiliated with that *Immigrant Cooperative* group we talked about. If my memory serves me well, they also have a relationship with an organization called *Illinois Celts for Immigration Reform* or something like that."

Pat closed his eyes for a moment, trying to digest this new information. As a staunch Catholic, he had a hard time visualizing religion and politics working together; or, more precisely, he found it hard to conceive of clergy hobnobbing with politicians. He was of the "old school," and, though liberal in his theology, preferred to see men and women religious focusing on ministry rather than political activism. On the other hand, there were those who would claim that activism was a form of ministry ...

"So you think this Hallet you mentioned works with priests?"

Joan nodded. She went on to explain that, in their quest to control the far left of the Democratic Party, pro-immigration reform groups all over the country sought out alliances with all types of groups ranging from Catholic religious orders to LGBTQ marriage equality advocates. She also mentioned that a colleague of hers had looked at some of the documents issued by the *National Conference of Catholic Bishops* and it was pretty clear they were pro-immigrant.

"You know, why not just talk to this Father Ryan, Pat, and see what he has to say?" suggested Joe. "There are probably 50,000 or more Irish visa over-stayers in the U.S. and it's my guess there are 5,000 or more here in Illinois, so you can see their reason for working in *The Cooperative*. But I can tell you there are very few criminals in that group—it's statistically verifiable that the vast majority of criminal felon illegal aliens are Hispanic."

"What if this priest pastors Mexican immigrants? Just because he has an Irish name doesn't mean to say he's working within the Irish community," countered Pat. Joan caught the defensiveness in his tone.

"Well, just hear him out—after all you're Catholic and you should listen to what he has to say, " advised Joe, sounding his most professorial.

"So who else called?" asked Joan lightly.

"Let's see. Apart from a couple of friends, there was somebody from Korshak's office—I think her chief counsel, a woman named Nordquist."

"For sure make *that* call," said Joe. "And don't forget to make your amendment pitch."

"Well, now that I have talked to you two, I'm all for delving into this— not to get revenge, but to get an amendment and maybe to expose the sordid politics that led to Denny's death."

"Well, based on our work at the university and now with your tragic issue, I would say there is a unique opportunity to direct public debate toward a more reasonable immigration policy with respect to criminals. What do you think, Joan?"

"Absolutely! I couldn't agree more! What's been going on nationally on this immigration issue is a push largely by the Democratic Party to foster a massive open border policy that will move all Hispanics into the party's ranks, thereby destroying the Republican Party for generations. You see the far left has taken over."

"But Joan, criminals are the issue—surely law abiding people are not pro criminal?" objected Pat, slowly shaking his head.

Joe cleared his throat, as if preparing for one of his lectures.

"Trust me, the far left views our current criminal justice system as racist toward all people of color, including Hispanics who are here illegally. Just a few years ago, two of your commissioners, both female, were down here at a conference and shocked everyone by saying that Ronald Reagan should have a special place in hell for his get-tough policies on crime. Executive orders will likely be issued to release thousands of drug traffickers from federal prisons in the next few years. Moreover, the far left fights voter ID requirements in the face of overwhelming evidence that voter fraud is rampant in both Hispanic and Black precincts. It's like this, Pat. The far left uses a binary approach and couch their campaign as the have's against the have not's. They have for over fifty years now managed to coalesce Hispanics, Blacks, gays, aliens, atheists, radical feminists and, some will argue, heavily indebted students. In short, they want to grow the ranks of the have not's with victimization rhetoric."

"What's your take on this, Joan? Is Joe on target here? All this is a little overwhelming for a retired school teacher!"

"For the most part, Pat—ultimately, you'll have to figure out where you stand on all these issues. Joe and I have discussions along these lines about our differences, but I do agree the far left has a long march strategy, and President Haesi is their first big major success. I can also tell you the academic community here and elsewhere couldn't be more pleased."

"Jeez, and I and countless others from the supposedly the' have' camp get caught in the middle!"

"Yeah, Pat, and violent crime is on the rise and institutional standards crumble," interjected Joe.

"The stop and frisk policy so effective in L.A., New York, Chicago and elsewhere is pushed out by the lefties and everybody pays. If current trends continue, Chicago will continue to be the murder capital of the world."

Pat rose from the table, stiff from having sat for so long.

"You know, I should be getting back. You guys got my head spinning."

"One more thing, Pat," said Joan, scraping back her chair. "I'll be sending you a copy of a letter written two weeks ago by four Republican members of the *United States Senate Judiciary Committee* to Jane Bather, Secretary of *Homeland Security*. You will also receive a transcript of Strobe Irwin, the senior Senator from Alabama, railing at Senator Congelosi of Illinois about this crazy ordinance. The letter takes Neapolitan to task because she claims she was not aware of the Cook County ordinance."

"So these Republicans knew disaster was inevitable, Joan?"

"You bet, Pat, and your family paid the price."

Quietly, they headed towards the entrance, past the formidable portraits of past university presidents that hung in the main corridor. The stiff poses and unsmiling faces seemed out of place in the modern setting.

Joan broke the silence.

"Pat, before you go, I think you should know that data going back to the 50's suggests that there have been over twenty thousand felony arrests of illegal aliens in the United States. Now, what's compelling is that many of these arrestees were released on bond and were always presumed to have fled to Mexico. Well, thanks to phony identification schemes, it looks like a good number stayed and are living under assumed names. I'll send you more on that."

"You mean maybe Orizaga's in the States still?" said Pat, his voice trembling.

"Can't rule it out," said Joe. "I guess that's the job of the FBI—at some point they'll get involved, but they take their time, I'm afraid. Pat, I know we've overwhelmed you with different ways of looking at this, but we'll send along all the supporting documents. Please don't hesitate to call—and let us know where all this takes you!"

Joan nodded in agreement.

"My heart goes out to you and your family, Pat. Drive carefully and keep safe!"

"You have both been so kind—I can't thank you enough," said Pat, turning away before they could see the tears welling in his eyes.

"I'll call in a few days, Joe. Oh I forgot to mention that this morning was a scheduled court date and no one expects Orizaga to show."

•

Pat took Lincoln Avenue to the Interstate, figuring he'd be home in time to pick Clare up from the train. As his mind raced over events of the preceding five days, something kept gnawing at him. He had a sense that there were answers to be found, that somehow a weird sort of resolution to this tragedy was possible. While speeding north on I-57, he became convinced that he had to pursue his quest for justice deliberately and tenaciously. Somehow, something positive was down the road—that much he was taking away from his excursion to UIUC. The luncheon with the two scholars had helped shift his perspective. For the last twenty minutes or so, he actually experienced what could only be described as a state of serenity. He reached over to the glove box and retrieved Dion's album and, placing it in the CD drive, located his legendary song, *"Abraham, Martin and John."*

That night, the McGurns watched with dismay a news account that President Haesi had issued an executive order that would provide amnesty to thousands of illegal aliens based on family ties. One commentator referred to critics as "enforcement hawks." Another commentator said, "It's just a matter of time before the President will extend this amnesty to as many as five million."

Pat looked at Clare, his mouth pulled into a forced smile.

"I guess I'm going to become a hawk."

Clare took his hand, her shoulders shaking slightly. Though it was a warm, September night, suddenly, she felt cold.

"Just be careful, Pat—even hawks can get shot down! Please watch your back!"

DAY SIX, FRIDAY, SEPTEMBER 2, 2011

Friday morning, Pat woke up to discover that Clare had decided to take a vacation day. At first, he thought they had both overslept, but then noted she was sporting a white Polo shirt with button-down collar and khaki capris—her customary golf attire!

"Time for some fun!" she had said to him, reminding him that Saturday would be busy with preparations for the traditional Labor Day family gathering. Golf at the *Palos Country Club* was the order of the day and, later on, maybe some "pub grub" at *The Cajun House*.

They played their usual nine holes on the scenic course, followed by an outdoor lunch of spicy blackened chicken sandwiches at the *Cajun House* on 115th Street. They returned home tired but rejuvenated. For a few hours, everything had seemed normal, as if their only care in the world was to play a decent game and share time together. In spite of using sun block and wearing golf visors, both had caught a little sun and looked the healthier for it, though Pat felt more sun burned than tanned. Clare changed into her "gardening clothes" and then started working on the yard in preparation for Sunday's family gathering. For his part, Pat set up his Mac Air on the dining room table to check his e-mail—he'd had enough sun for the day. There was a note from Joan Farnsworth.

"Pat, great to meet you yesterday—I do hope Joe and I were of help. Wanted to let you know that I have a contact at Judicial Vigilance (JV), Charles Foley, who might be interested in your case. I know JV does a

lot of Freedom of Information (FOIA) requests as well as sue different jurisdictions over sanctuary policies. If you like, I'll shoot Charles an e-mail. Let me know if you approve."

Buoyed by the brief exchange, Pat shot her a quick, "go ahead." The meeting at UIUC couldn't have come at a better time, as he no longer had the feeling of utter powerlessness that had been haunting him. He was beginning to doze off when a call came through at around 3:30 p.m. It was from Eileen Murphy who informed him that Orizaga was a no show at court. Based on that and on her testimony, a federal warrant would be issued in roughly two weeks maybe sooner."

"What do you mean, Eileen? Everybody knows Orizaga fled—why the delay?"

"Sorry, that's procedure. Best I could do—the FBI agent will call me for an interview sometime next week and soon after the warrant will be issued."

"Will they call Christy or me?"

"I doubt it—in fact your names never came up. You know the way it works is that the Bureau rarely gets family involved because they think it will be a distraction," said Eileen, matter-of-factly.

"As it turns out, I *don't* know," objected Pat. "Look, I have a lot to think about—I've been trying to make sense of Cook County and now the FBI appears indifferent as well. You know it's a holiday—let's kick back and have a nice weekend."

"You, too—" said Eileen, but Pat had disconnected the call.

Closing his laptop, Pat went out to join Clare in the rear garden. She had already straightened the deck furniture and had set out extra folding chairs. Now she was in the process of pulling out some stubborn weeds from among the day lilies.

"You look angry."

"Do I?"

As Pat went over the conversation, Clare smiled.

"No surprise, Pat—don't take this personally! We've dealt with them at the *Illinois Grievance Commission* and talk about their indifference to anything they consider minor! Look, let's enjoy the weekend and maybe take a long bike ride to *Fredo's* later on."

"You're right, Clare. Let's give this Orizaga thing a rest, at least for the weekend."

"Then beer and pizza it is!"

•

In the middle of the night, Pat woke up in a sweat. He must have been dreaming about Denny because his first thoughts were about his brother. What would Denny have done if it were Pat who had been killed by an alien and Cook County allowed the killer to abscond? The question was so compelling that Pat knew sleep was a long way off. Taking care not to disturb his wife who was sleeping soundly, he got up and went downstairs to the living room. Standing at the window facing Roby Avenue, he gazed out onto the dimly-lit street. There was no traffic and his neighbors' homes were dark, save for a few security lights around their properties. He was tempted to go outside and get some fresh air, but then reconsidered. No point setting off all the neighborhood dogs and awakening everyone …

A few years earlier, he and Denny had read a contemporary commentary on William Graham Sumner's, *The Forgotten Man,* a brilliant essay that railed against progressivism in the 1890's. Graham used basic equation to suggest that when **A** observes that **X** is suffering, **A** then discusses the problem with **B** and subsequently both **A** and **B** propose a law to get **Q** to fix the problem. The simple social equation is that **Q** is **John Q Public** and **John** gets stuck with the bill. Inevitably, years later, **X** still has problems. In the modern day, **X**= the millions of Americans caught in the cycle of poverty, plagued with drug abuse, illegitimacy and criminal records. Yet billions and billions of dollars are just thrown at **X**.

The two brothers had used Sumner's argument on several occasions to critique those mindless "progressive" policies that provided "do nothing" jobs for the unemployable and for politically connected opportunists. Pat would amuse Denny with story after story of any number of foolish central office bureaucrats who would come into schools with asinine solutions for gangs, special education, drugs, violence and scores of school deportment issues. Some had never been in the classroom or lacked teaching credentials! And the bureaucrats were the richer each time … So what about immigration? Pat thought to himself while getting a drink of water from the kitchen. It dawned on him that Denny's take would be that immigration policy was incidental and that the real issue was political power. Most likely, he would have said the ordinance was nothing more than power wrangling.

Cradling the glass of water between both hands, Pat returned to the living room and sat in one of the two Mission-style armchairs that flanked the fireplace. Closing his eyes, he tried to imagine he was having a conversation with Denny.

"D'you really think anybody on the Cook County Board gives a shit about these people being deported or their families? Look, every one of these slimy bastards got elected for money and not a one of them comes close to the so-called underdog. They just use their constituents for political opportunity."

"Are you talking about the five who voted against the ordinance, too?" he might have asked, a tad naively.

"For sure," Denny would probably have said. "The five who voted against it did so for one reason only because they don't want the heat from their 'law and order constituents' in places like Glenview, La Grange, Orland Park and other majority white communities. You see, they knew the vote would be lopsided. Everybody retains power and the Hispanics win more because they now have more illegal votes. The quid quo pro is simple: you get me this ordinance and the emerging Hispanic political block will support spoils for traditional scammer Democrats and, yes, many Republicans."

This was just what Ron Ralston had argued in his columns over the years: that the Illinois political culture is nothing more than a combine. Ralston used a metaphorical farm machine as he considered both Democrats and Republicans to be corrupt. Somehow, the imaginary conversation relaxed Pat, leaving him comforted in a weird kind of way. Picking up a note pad conveniently positioned on the side table next to him, Pat scribbled down his conclusions:

> Preliminary conclusions suggest public policies promulgated by a cabal of unethical elected officials led to Denny's death and the subsequent absconding of the killer.

Well, that's a start, he thought. Back in his school days, he had been trained to define the problem. Now what to do about it? A visit to Wagner— perhaps early the following week—might offer a political solution. Since that was likely to fail, perhaps the Judicial Vigilance Joan suggested might be the way to go. However, that could take years and would likely be filed in a Cook County trial court; given the corrupt political culture, appeals would be inevitable. Then the Muse kicked in, suggesting that sometimes the fight, win or lose, was worth the effort. Pat was ready to enter the ring.

DAYS SEVEN AND EIGHT, SATURDAY AND SUNDAY, SEPTEMBER 3&4, 2011

Saturday was designated for more yard work and preparations for Sunday's barbecue. Clare was out buying last minute provisions for the next day, and since one of her planned stops was Sam's Club, Pat was happy to stay home. Of course, he would help her unpack the SUV when she returned, but navigating through hordes of weekend shoppers and standing in line behind carts overflowing with merchandise was not on his list of favorite things to do. Instead, he had promised Clare that he would boil two dozen eggs for the egg salad—a family favorite. He carefully placed the eggs in a single row at the bottom of a large saucepan of water, added some salt to keep them from cracking, and lit the electric burner. Then he phoned Detective Alphy who seemed to worked alternate weekends. Alphy answered.

"Alph, McGurn here—find out anything?"

"You know we're trying, man. Went over to Roberto's but there was nobody over there, you know."

"Did you get a landline or cell on Roberto and monitor phone traffic?"

"No. We just went over there, you know. Maybe my boss got an idea."

"Help me out, Alph," said Pat, trying to mask the irritation in his voice. "Doesn't your boss know about this?"

"Not sure, man. That sheriff deputy guy called and I says, 'Yeah, I'll go over there."

"Alph, your boss is probably off the weekend, right?"

"Well, yeah, that's right."

"Alph, what about the Feds? You know, Immigration and Customs agents or the FBI?"

"I don't know nothing about no Feds, Mr. Mcgrew," whined Alphy.

"The name's McGurn," said Pat in a decidedly chilly voice. "Look, this is going nowhere—call me if anything pops, okay?"

"No problem, Mr. McGraw."

Pat hit the "End" button on his smart phone. A smell of burning drew his attention to the stove.

"Damn!" he exploded, noting that the pot was completely dry and had most likely been so for at least fifteen minutes. All the eggs had burst, in spite of the salt. Soft mounds of white oozed from the blackening shells and the bottom of the saucepan was now invisible.

"Damn!" he said again, picking up the pot with a pair of oven gloves and placing it in the sink, eggs and all. Just as well they weren't expecting guests that day as the whole house now stank. He opened all the windows and, once the pot cooled down, threw it in the garbage, along with its contents. There were no more eggs in the house and so, for the first time in thirty years, they would just have to do without egg salad at their traditional Labor Day barbeque.

Clare, of course, was not pleased, especially as the ruined saucepan had been her "soup pot"—the only saucepan big enough for the thick vegetable soups she made year round.

"Why did you have to use my best saucepan?" she asked.

There was no mistaking the smell of burned eggs when she returned and, try as she might, she couldn't bring herself to say, "Oh, it doesn't matter, Darling." Silently, Pat helped her bring in the groceries. He hated upsetting Clare and though, in the scheme of things, a burned pot was minor, still he was embarrassed that he had failed in the one task she had asked him to accomplish.

At around 3:00 p.m., his cell phone rang.

"Mr. McGurn, please."

"Speaking," said Pat, not recognizing the voice.

"I'm David Rosen from San Diego. I read the article on line from *The Chicago Globe* and want to commend you for bringing your situation to the light of day."

"Well that's very kind, but forgive me, I'm not ..."

"Please, I'll explain," continued the stranger before Pat could hang up.

"You see, my son Barnett was a twenty-four year old law student here in San Diego. A few years ago, like your brother, he was violently killed by an illegal prior convicted felon from Guatemala. I appealed to my state representatives in Sacramento, but they only listen to the growing Hispanic lobby. I got nowhere—just wasted my time. Here in California there are several grieving families like ours. In fact, I've been working with a Mrs. Lopez in Houston who is gathering the names of grieving families across the country. She's set up a non-profit called the *Remembrance Project* and will soon embark on an informational nationwide tour. She got your name and number from a Joan Farnsworth."

Pat listened in silence. The story was so wrenchingly familiar that it brought tears to his eyes. His grief and David's grief were part of the same narrative of injustice. Both men had tried to seek help from their representatives and both had discovered that those in power were more interested in appeasing voters and lobbyists alike than in safeguarding their own constituents.

"David, my heart goes out to you—by all means give my regards to Mrs. Lopez. And let's stay in touch ..."

Clare grilled steaks outside on the gas Weber grill; they enjoyed stir fry and pretzel rolls, followed by ice cream cones she had purchased at the legendary *Rainbow Cones*, just down the road on Western Avenue. After dinner, they watched *The McGowan Group* which featured a discussion of the upcoming ten year anniversary of the attack on the *World Trade Center*. One of the commentators suggested that the country's new president was not pro active enough in monitoring terrorist activity. Pat thought about the completion of the second tower of the *World Trade Center* that had been dedicated during the summer of 1971. He was stationed at *Fort Hamilton* in Brooklyn that summer and took the afternoon off for the ceremony in Lower Manhattan. After the show, Pat worked on his HO train set in the basement and while Clare put the finishing touches on a receiving blanket she was crocheting for Molly's baby—a girl—scheduled to be born the following week.

The couple retired early.

•

Sunday morning began with mass at *Christ the King Church*. During the short drive home, Pat was unusually silent.

"You're still brooding over Father Dan's homily, aren't you? It couldn't have been easy to hear his message of love and forgiveness," observed Clare, glancing at Pat. His face was set in a grimace.

"Well," said Pat, suddenly smiling appreciatively, "If I didn't know you so well, I'd think you're psychic! But Father Dan missed the heart of today's gospel—it wasn't about love of neighbor at all, but about the fact that all wrongdoing comes from within and defiles us. That's what I needed to hear today, not another damn sermon on love!"

"Easy, Pat—he did his best. We both know he's not much of a preacher. At least he tried—and one can never hear enough about love and forgiveness. At least, I can't!"

"Well, right or wrong, for some odd reason I think I can forgive Orizaga, but forgiving ten Cook County commissioners who willfully let Denny's killer run, that's another story," said Pat as they pulled up in the driveway.

"Okay, enough about forgiveness and defiled hearts! Let's change and then get busy because we've got thirteen or fourteen people coming over in a few hours. Let's see burgers, brats, and potato salad and birthday cake for Aunt Bea …"

The day unfolded more quietly than usual. The adults tried to be cheerful, but it was the first Labor Weekend gathering without Denny. Even Aunt Bea, usually the life and soul of any party, was subdued. Though close with all her nieces and nephews, Denny had been her favorite and everyone knew it. Making sure the children didn't overhear too much, the family spent time reminiscing, sharing anecdotes with a mixture of tears and laughter. Some of the group made a half-hearted attempt to play beanbag toss with the children, but eventually gave up and took them to the park. There, they could chat while the kids amused themselves on the swings and slide.

Pat's, son, Michael, and his niece, Judy, the deputy sheriff, sat on the deck, beer cans in hand.

"Judy, any luck getting more information?"

Pat had not spoken to Judy since the previous Sunday, nor had she left him any messages.

"Well, a weekender signed him out and the word is he had no choice— orders from above!"

"Sheriff Dypsky has part timers working the jail on weekends, right Judy?" asked Michael.

"Oh, yeah, a lot of them are, you know, friends of friends sort of thing."

"You know this person, Judy?"

"No, Uncle Pat—I'm over at *The Daley Center*, so I don't know too many over at the jail. But I got the name of a supervisor, a guy named Tim Joyce who's 'buddy buddy' with Dan Dypsky. I'll text you his number."

"Thanks a million, Judy—I think I'll call this Joyce but I won't mention your name."

"Uncle Pat, you know you're doing the right thing here, getting to the bottom of this."

"I hope so, Judy," sighed Pat, taking a swig of his beer. "There's a lot of unanswered questions here. My guess is that Korshak, Dypsky and Hunter-Goss figure that, after the long weekend, the controversy will fade away."

Michael and Judy shrugged their shoulders as if to say, "Well, maybe." Michael was staring intently at his beer can, watching a wasp walking unsteadily in circles around the opening.

"What *d'you* think?"

"Well, Dad, you're right—they want it to go away, but it looks like they'll be disappointed, thanks to this Ralston at *The Globe*."

"Yeah, he's been great—so did you check out this *Judicial Vigilance*?"

"Yeah, You should call them, Dad—but they will probably only want to file a *mandamus* action to force a change in the law, so don't expect damages. Unfortunately, a legal route could take years."

He tossed his beer can onto the grass below the deck, wasp and all. Reaching for another beer, he popped open the metal tab.

"Dad, you were saying your friends down in Champaign think an amendment is possible?"

Judy listened intently, having come in late on that conversation.

"Yeah, but it's probably a long shot. Hey, I'm retired and I've got time—let's see where it goes, and if that fails I'll call this *Judicial Vigilance*. For now that's what I'm thinking."

"You said something about Congress—what can Congress do?"

"Not sure, Judy—probably try to put some teeth in current federal law that would force states to comply. Look, thank you both for your help. You know I just can't let this go—it's like something is pushing me to do this, and I'm not sure what."

"Yeah, I would keep up the pressure," said Michael.

The park group returned, the children still full of energy, with Molly clearly dragging behind them. Her husband, Frank, had his arm around her waist, as if to support her. With Molly's due date so close, Clare thought it best that they go indoors, out of the sun. Aunt Bea, though sprightly for being in her late 80's, also looked tired. She grasped the deck railing and slowly went up the stairs, one step at a time. The children clambered up the stairs behind her, then ran inside, slamming the screen door behind them, shrieking with excitement in their quest for lemonade and ice cream sundaes. Lucy, the youngest, was glued to her mother's legs, determined to be carried, but Clare was somehow able to take the two-year old by the hand with promises of a visit to the much-loved dollhouse in the basement.

Meanwhile, two of Pat's siblings, Marie and Eddy, had joined the group on the deck, along with Denny's daughter, Christy and her husband Jason. Pat was in the middle of explaining what he had learned about sanctuary cities.

"Got that right, Pat," Marie chimed in, heatedly. "From what Therese says, there are thousands of illegals all over California—she's always talking about their link to crime!"

"You bet, Marie, and it's not just Sis who's saying this. In fact, just yesterday a guy from San Diego called me with the tragic story of his son being killed by an illegal Guatemalan a few years ago. This guy has written articles and testified in Sacramento; he also networks with a gal in Houston who is compiling a list of hundreds of family victims. This morning, my professor friend from Champaign, Joan Farnsworth, sent me two articles—one from L.A. about a Black scholarship recipient shot in cold blood by Hispanic gangbangers and the other about a law student in San Francisco where three illegal gang bangers opened fire on him 'for kicks.' Maybe if I can alert the public somehow, wiser heads might fix this immigration thing and we might all be a little safer. It's one way of returning justice to the family."

"Well, I think that catching this creep is the way to go," said Christy, a tremor in her voice. "If it weren't for him, Dad would've been here with us today ..."

"Well said, Christy, I completely agree with you," Eddy responded gently. "On a different note, I think it's time for Aunt Bea's birthday cake ..."

To the extent possible, the McGurn clan enjoyed their Labor Day celebration. Though they had kept in touch since Denny's funeral, this was the first time all of them were together—all, that is, except Pat's sisters, Catherine and Therese, who lived in San Francisco with their families. Still, some of the Chicago group had reached them by phone and Pat had taken a few minutes to fill them in on all the emerging details regarding Orizaga's release. They had seemed curious, but politely so. Pat got the feeling they were more interested in catching up with news about Molly's pregnancy and the baby shower Clare had hosted for her a few weeks earlier.

"Yes," Pat assured them. "Molly did receive the lovely crib mobile, but has yet to write her thank-you notes."

Later, when their guests had finally left, Pat and Clare began to put away what was left of the food. Much of it went straight into the garbage can—a soggy salad, dried out hamburger buns, a few charred beef patties ... However, they were able to salvage enough food for dinner the following day, with plenty of beer to wash it down.

"I know this is difficult for the family—for that matter, I'm not so sure they understand what I'm trying to do," said Pat, still mulling over his sisters' lack of enthusiasm. Clare, who had been stacking beer cans on the bottom shelf of the refrigerator, straightened up.

"You know, Pat, I think you're being hard on them. You shouldn't take it that way. In good time they'll come to appreciate what you're doing."

"Thanks, Hon—I mean, some of them are with me, but I just get the feeling that, as a whole, the family would rather move on and forget the sordid details. Hey, would you mind if I went over to *Ruth's*? I'm feeling a little claustrophobic—change of scene would feel good right now."

"Sure, I'll be glued to *Masterpiece Theater* for the next two hours."

On the way over to *Ruth's* Pat called Denny's oldest daughter Nataly in Maryland and briefed her on developments thus far. She was grateful for the update and planned to visit Chicago soon. Pat walked into Ruth's and was pleased to see one of his old high school buddies at the bar talking to

Slim, the bartender. There was no mistaking the perfectly round bald spot on the crown of his head—just like a priest's tonsure. Of course, everyone teased him about it, but Rollie took it all in good stride. As Pat sat down, Rollie, a retired Chicago homicide detective, turned towards him.

"Pat, long time no see. Did you go to Mendel's all year reunion last month? Hey, Slim! Give us a couple a'pints!"

"Nope. Too much going on, what with a grandson now and other things. How 'bout you?"

"So a grandson—you know, we have two as well. I'm doing okay—some private work now and again. Wait a second—your brother was killed a few months ago, right?"

"Yeah, Rol—three months now and it's been crazy."

"Sorry about that—Jeez, that must have been awful getting news like that. You know I think it was Mikey Collins who told me about it. Pat, excuse me a second. Hey, Slim get Dooley over there a drink. He doing okay?"

"Not sure," said Slim, looking in old Dooley's direction. The troubled man was sitting alone at the other end of the bar, an empty beer mug in front of him. He was staring into space, completely oblivious to everyone else.

"He's back reliving his Vietnam days and lately keeps playing *Fortunate Son* you know, that old *Credence Clearwater* tune? Quite frankly, it's getting on my nerves."

"Ahh, cut him some slack, Slim. 'Nam kicked his ass going back forty years," said Pat, shaking his head. "The poor devil must have had a major case of post-traumatic stress syndrome—and no treatment from the Veteran's Administration. Of course, forty years ago nobody was talking about PTSS, let alone dealing with it."

"Yeah, Mickey was at the wake—let me give you the latest."

Pat gave Rollie the "Cliff Notes" version of events of the previous week, then handed him a copy of Ralston's most recent article. The paper was badly creased since it had been folded in his pocket, but was still readable. As Rollie smoothed out the creases and began peering at the small print, Pat walked over to Dools.

"Great songs back in the day—I could listen to *Credence* any time."

"You know, Pat—it still gets to me, all these fuckin' draft dodgers or I guess they call these pussies around here draft evaders. You did time, right?"

"Yeah, but not 'Nam, Dools. Got drafted in '71 when Nixon was bringing the boys home."

"What outfit you with?"

"After school at *Fort Hamilton* in Brooklyn I was assigned to the *Second Armor, Fort Hood, Texas*—you know, 'Hell on Wheels.'"

"Good man," said Dools approvingly, smiling a toothless smile. This was a conversation they had on a weekly basis, but Pat didn't have the heart to tell him so. To his relief, Rollie was beckoning him from across the room, waving the article at him.

"Take care, Dools—I got to ask Rollie something."

"Wow, what a fuckin' story, man—like right out of a book," exclaimed Rollie when Pat joined him again.

"Now, let me get this straight—you thinking of making some noise with these commissioners? What about TV? I'm thinking *Wolf News* might be interested."

"I don't know—something tells me to cool it and get some answers first. You know, I really don't like those pretty boy TV types. As for print journalists, I had issues with them ten-twelve years ago when fighting the school board over a couple of rogue principals. So far Ralston's been okay, though."

"Yeah, I hear you, man. I've had problems with the media, especially with that smarmy little asshole at Channel 4. What about these professors, Pat? Sort of out of my league, this academic stuff."

"Well, Joe's kind of an old friend. He's been studying the Chicago machine for years and I think he can be a big help. And Joan? Well, she seems to have a good grasp of the immigration issues."

"Okay, I get it. You want to get them to write something?"

"Well, as a matter of fact, they are collaborating on a big project—or I should say Joe is editing a book on all the problems here in Cook County, and it looks like this whole immigration mess will get a chapter."

Rollie shrugged, but looked generally unconvinced.

"Might help—then again, might not. Tell me about this Murphy at the State's Attorney Office."

"Well, I think she's all right—maybe caught off guard."

"I hear you. The bond was only $250,000—who was the judge?"

"Guy named Santiago from Humboldt Park," said Pat. He drained his beer mug and drummed unceremoniously on the bar to attract Slim's attention. A re-fill was definitely in order, but Slim was busy humoring old Dools.

"I know that idiot—he's Mr. Low Bond guy. His nephew took some convicted alderman's job on the *Chicago City Council* and was appointed by the former mayor a couple of years ago. And you know what, Pat? I think the nephew's involved in some sort a mortgage scam under investigation by the Feds."

"Well, I don't know about you, but I'm thinking why did they send this Orizaga to appear before a low bond guy who's Hispanic?"

"My thoughts exactly," said Rollie, taking a gulp of beer.

"Phone calls had to be made, I figure—happens all the time. So the brother—Roberto—comes up with $25,000.00 cash, right?"

"That's right."

"Well, let's say the brother and Raul are in a gang ... and we know he has a lawyer. You got the lawyer's name? I'd bet he's involved."

"Yeah, Simpkus is his name. My wife is going to look him up—you know she works for the *Illinois Grievance Commission*. She's the chief investigator over there."

"You know that could be a big help if she could get some dirt on this lawyer. Let me think about this, Pat—you know this whole deal with Sunday bail and the lawyer and what's his name, the brother, Roberto ... I mean, I've a whole lot of questions."

"Say, Rol, I'm thinking you want to help," chuckled Pat, still holding his empty beer mug.

"Hey, ole buddy, I'm in if you want me—man, I mean let's make these motherfuckers pay 'cause this is real bullshit. First of all, Murphy should've petitioned for source of funds."

"Source of funds—what's that?"

"Source of funds—you know, requiring the guy putting up the money to show the source of the money before he can bail a guy out. You follow me?"

Pat shook his head.

"Never heard of that. So you're saying the brother should have produced some sort of proof like where he got the dough?"

"Yeah—Murphy should have asked for it—that would have prevented his release as well."

"Well, she was confident the detainer would be the backstop."

"Somebody fucked up, Pat, and you know that idiot Dypsky should have had some procedure in place for notification when releasing an illegal with a federal hold."

"I guess he didn't, Rol—so maybe the talk that he wants to run for mayor in three years offers a clue here."

Rollie took a moment to collect his thoughts.

"Look, somebody came up with 25K or more because the lawyer wants his dough, right? So let's see—the nut to get Orizaga out is 25K bail and 5K for this Simpkus, I'm guessing. You with me?"

"I follow—go on, Rol."

"Well, let me ask you—do you think this Orizaga could get his hands on 30K? Almost impossible, I'd say. I'll bet this fuck head is still in the States, probably under wraps with some gang and given assignments or some other illegal stuff."

"Like where?"

"Well, probably in a sanctuary area like LA—maybe Philly, NY, Brownsville, El Paso, or any number of places where he's not conspicuous. Or maybe right here—say Pilsen, Little Village, South Chicago or maybe Cicero. Western burbs loaded with Mexicans, man."

"You're kidding, Rollie!"

"You ever to those places, man? They're just like Juarez or Tijuana. A guy like Orizaga looks like a thousand of other thirty-something year old Hispanics—can get lost for years, work underground, raise a family and live pretty good with a phony ID. Look, only a theory, but can't rule it out."

Pat was stunned. Until that moment, he had been convinced that Orizaga had skipped the country; the thought he could still be in the States had never crossed his mind. Come to think of it, however, Joan Farnsworth had mentioned that 25,000 or so illegal immigrants had been arrested for murder, posted bail and then disappeared over the course of a few decades.

"You know," continued Rollie, noting Pat's shocked expression. "It's not a piece a cake to cross the border the other way. If this Orizaga did go back, he had to cross illegally."

"I never thought of that—so maybe 50/50 he's still here?"

"Good bet, Pat. Being here illegally, even with a warrant, is better than making a couple a *dineros* a day in Chiapas or wherever the fuck he's from."

"And getting a phony ID's not hard, either …"

"Got that right, Pat. I'll tell you what, why don't you and I do a little digging. I'll start with this Alphy up at Area 3—he sounds like a real whistle-ass. Can't understand why he didn't squeeze the brother like we used to do on the West Side. The shit about a hot plate was all bogus. Give me a day or two and I'll make some calls—maybe snoop around some, as well. If it was my brother, I'd be so pissed and, besides, I like the hunt. Maybe we can find this scumbag. Okay, Pat I got to go, so I'll see what I can learn—and you're going to see Wagner, right?

"Going to try Tuesday and maybe get hold of Riley. Before I forget, Rol, tell Sally that Clare and I wish you guys the best. We'd like to take you out for dinner one of these weekends—that's the least we can do!"

"We'd be happy to join you," said Rollie, making his exit. "But we'll pay our own way!"

•

When he got home, Pat went into the TV room where Clare, already in pajamas, had just finished watching a re-run of *Downton Abbey*. He bent over to give his wife a kiss before sitting down in the adjacent armchair. Pushing the power button on the remote, she cut short the list of donors who had funded her program. She listened in silence as Pat recapped his conversation with Rollie. The smile with which she had greeted him soon faded. Nervously, she twisted the wedding band on her left hand.

"I don't like this, Pat, not one bit. The last thing I need is for you to tangle with a bunch of gangbangers or get in trouble with the police. Rollie's too much of a risk-taker—always has been!"

"Not to worry, Clare. I mean, I know it's a long shot, but it's the best I have right now …"

Sensing her disapproval, Pat went into his study. Sitting at his desk, he closed his eyes, took a deep breath, and exhaled slowly. At one level, he could understand her concern. Rollie had a reputation for ignoring protocol to get results—even if it meant putting his life on the line or getting bad press for overstepping his jurisdiction. On the other hand, he invariably *did* get results.

He decided to call Joan Farnsworth, hoping it wouldn't be too awkward calling on a Sunday evening. She answered and assured Pat the call was welcome. Having given her the updates, he asked if there were any figures on released criminals who were still at large in the United States. Joan, who happened to be at her computer, pulled up the most recent list reported by the *Congressional Research Service*. Extending from 2008-2011, the list showed that during that time span, approximately 159,000 illegal aliens were arrested by local authorities and identified by ICE as deportable, only to be released again. One sixth of these illegals—that is, over 25,000—had been re-arrested. It was therefore not a stretch to argue that Orizaga may have never left the country.

"Joan, I know the FBI is going to get involved, maybe in a week or so—I'll pass this information along. I don't know if I told you, but they're going to get an affidavit from Murphy and go into Federal Court pretty soon to get a warrant."

"Well, that's good but my experience tells me the FBI not likely to call you or, for that matter, even return your calls, but it's sure worth trying."

"You bet I'll try—maybe get Congressman Powers to help."

"I like that idea! Good luck!"

"Thanks, Joan. Sorry again for the late hour," said Pat.

"I'm up late usually—not a problem."

DAY NINE, MONDAY, LABOR DAY, SEPTEMBER 5TH, 2011

On Labor Day, Pat spent the whole day reading the material Joan and Joe had sent him, taking several "mini" breaks to download press reports related to the killing and bail fiasco. Pat also called Rollie, leaving the criminal re-arrest statistics on his voice mail. Meanwhile, Clare visited her sister who lived a few blocks away at 103rd and Longwood, in *St. Barnabas Parish*. She and Pat had agreed to a quiet dinner at *Luigi's* on Taylor Street. They had eaten there from time to time, ever since Michael and Molly attended *St. Peter Claver High School*, more than a decade earlier. It was one of the few restaurants that was open on holidays.

"Nice visit, Clare?"

"Yeah, spent time talking with Tracy and then we took a walk with her grandkids. How's your day? Any calls?"

"Not a one and just as well, I guess—so no news is good news. I had a lot to read—it's like I'm back in graduate school."

"You're probably enjoying reading that stuff—always thought you should have finished your PhD."

"Yeah, Clare, maybe, but I needed to work and get going on life and family," said Pat, expertly twirling long strands of spaghetti around his fork. Clare toyed with her food, pushing the *funghi* in her *risotto ai funghi* to the side of her plate. The sauce was too rich for her and the *funghi* had absorbed too much *vino*. She reached for a hunk of thick crusted Italian bread, dipping it in the olive oil on her side plate.

"Pat, I'm sort of wary about this entire Orizaga deal—you know, the notion that maybe he's here in the United States. I'd hate to see you go on a wild goose chase."

"Don't worry—I'm not going to go hog wild on this. I figure I'll do some preliminary inquiries and see where it goes. Besides, my main interest right now is seeing if the ordinance can be amended."

Clare hesitated, trying to choose her words carefully.

"That, too, Pat seems far-fetched. Do you really think these commissioners are going to change?"

"Who knows, Clare? The idea came up in Champaign and Joe suggested I run it by Wagner. I'm thinking if they don't initially want to consider an amendment, maybe Ralston might write it up and the pressure could make them change their minds. Oh, and Joan Farnsworth sent me some research she did on *Judicial Vigilance*—legal action might be key because, the way I see it, Immigration is federal and the County just thumbed their nose at a federal law."

"Wait a second," Clare said. "Didn't Michael look into this *Judicial Vigilance?*"

"Yeah, we talked about it yesterday at the party—he thought they might be interested. Joan told me she called a contact there named Charles Foley. Apparently, they're a legal advocacy group that issues all sorts of Freedom of Information requests and uses that data to force municipalities and other government entities to follow the law. She said they've had similar cases across the country and thought they might be interested in our case."

"So they *are* interested, it seems?"

"Yeah. Joan sent Foley some of the specifics and I'm to call him in a week or two, when he's had time to go over all the material. Oh and Joan sent me another article that argued that any political change at the federal level will only take place if we elect a Republican President."

They spent the rest of the meal reminiscing about Michael and Molly's years down the street at *St. Peter Claver College Prep.* They chose the school because of its reputation for academic rigor, but, at the time, the Jesuits seemed more intent on enforcing the dress code than on encouraging critical thinking. Both agreed the school left them somewhat disappointed, but it was clearly a better alternative to the other parochial high schools. After *cannoli* filled with sweetened *mascarpone* cheese and *cappuccinos* to cut the sugar, they made it home in time for the evening news. Both were shocked to hear about the killing of two nuns by an illegal alien outside of Baltimore earlier that same day. Pat looked at Clare who was teary eyed.

"I don't know if I told you, but Joan Farnsworth is going to send me information from a gal in Texas who has chronicled all the deaths, rapes and other crimes committed by illegals."

Clare dabbed at her eyes with a crumpled Kleenex.

"You know, with your time and skills maybe you can help. Sorry if I've sounded negative—it's just all been so overwhelming and I'm terrified you'll get hurt in some way."

"Don't worry, Honey—I just *have* to do something. You know I'm going downtown tomorrow. You're taking the day off, so why not join me?"

"That's okay. I need to get materials for Maeve's receiving blanket at the fabric shop."

"Maeve?"

"Molly's baby—remember she told us she's having a girl? She's due any day now."

"So she has a name?" said Pat. "That's the first I've heard of it!"

"That's because you haven't been listening—she's been 'Maeve' for the last month! Don't you remember seeing the photo from the ultrasound?"

"No—can't say that I do. I guess I've been preoccupied," admitted Pat, suddenly realizing how little interaction he'd had with Molly in recent weeks. He would have to make it up to her.

DAY TEN, TUESDAY, SEPTEMBER 6, 2011

Tuesday morning, Clare stayed home and Pat caught the 8:35 a.m. train that he usually took when he needed to go downtown. Since retirement, he'd make the trip once or twice a week, sometimes to attend a class, or, more often, to hear a lecture, go to a museum or attend mass at *St. Peter's* on Madison. Around midday, he always found time to take Clare to lunch. Today was different, not only because Clare hadn't gone in to work, but because Pat's only agenda was to pay a personal visit to the main suite of offices of the Cook County commissioners. If nothing else, he would let someone know that the McGurn family was prepared to get to the bottom of this travesty. He also wanted to get into the County Board Rooms to see for himself the place where ten county commissioners had collectively committed a crime against his family and against all law-abiding citizens.

As he boarded the Metra at 91st Street, he replayed the scene in the Cook County boardroom, as he understood it from talking to Ralston. Let's see, he thought. There were ten for the ordinance, five against, one abstention and a "present" vote from Commissioner James.

Yes, Joe Vanderbiezen had it right—the County and city politicians were all about "ME and MINE" and the commonwealth be damned. Ralston had suggested that perhaps the debate when the ordinance was passed had been staged. Without supporting evidence, however, his editor would not allow for speculation of that sort. Hearing the conductor announce "Thirty Fifth Street, White Sox Park," Pat's thoughts turned to Denny who must have gone to at least a thousand White Sox games in his lifetime. Thank

God, Denny had been alive for the great 2005 World Championship year six years earlier. As the train approached downtown Chicago, Pat thought back to '57 and '58 when Denny had taken him to the school playground at 74th and Dorchester. Pat could still remember how proud he felt to be with his older brother; in those memorable days, younger boys learned from the older boys the joys of baseball—a kind of rite of passage. The tradition continued with both brothers introducing younger brother Eddy to America's pastime, later in the decade when the Sox played the Dodgers for the World Series in 1959.

He got off the train and walked down La Salle Street towards Madison; turning right, he headed towards *St. Peter's Catholic Church*. As usual, there were several homeless men standing on the steps, under the massive stone crucifix above the main entrance, looking for alms. Pat dug in his pockets and gave each a handful of coins. Then he opened the main doors, entering the church itself. Though the predominance of white marble was visually cold and somewhat sterile, the church had an aura of warmth, a feeling of welcome. For a moment, Pat stood in the threshold; then, crossing himself with holy water, he walked in slowly towards the middle of the aisle, away from the street people who were napping in the back with all their bags of belongings. Sitting in his pew, he thought of his dad who went to *St. Peter's* frequently during his life, most certainly to offer prayers for the family. He had worked for the *Chicago Water Department* for twenty five years, having attained his position by scoring high on a civil service exam originating with former Mayor Kennelly in 1952. A reform mayor and successful businessman, Kennelly thought it best to purge the city of the insidious effects of patronage. Pat sat in silence, trying to focus on praying for guidance. Sounds of snoring from the rear pews distracted him and he found it difficult to clear his mind of random thoughts. Still, he took comfort in the fact that God knew his heart and his concerns, even if he himself was unable to pray. Perhaps simply entering the church and making it his first stop was enough for "morning prayer"; perhaps the snores of the homeless were also a form of prayer …

Later, Pat entered the Cook County Building on the La Salle side. On the way down the long corridor first floor corridor leading to the Clark Street entrance, he counted at least twenty police officers who were standing around, doing nothing in particular—hardly representative of the "more police on the street" promised by Mayor Gill. For all their effectiveness, they might as well have been in *Dunkin Donuts*, taking their proverbial coffee break! He took the elevator up to the fifth floor, and turned right into a large reception area. The words, WELCOME TO COOK COUNTY, were printed boldly below a smiling portrait of President Korshak. A middle-aged woman was sitting behind the reception desk, reading *The Daily Sun*.

"Commissioner Wagner, please."

Looking up from her newspaper, the receptionist glared at Pat, as if affronted at having being disturbed.

"He's not in."

"Well, how about Riley?"

"You mean *Commissioner* Riley?" she said, her crimson lips parting in a condescending smile.

"Yes."

"Well, he's not in, neither."

She looked down at her newspaper and turned to the sales pages.

"Are any of the commissioners here today?" asked Pat, struggling to maintain his composure.

"Nope, but I think I saw Commissioner Wagner's assistant."

"That would be great—could you ring her please?"

Without another word, the receptionist dialed an extension, mumbled something into the headset, then returned to her paper. A few minutes passed and out walked an elegantly dressed woman in her early thirties.

"Can I help you? I'm Liz Farmer—I work for Commissioner Wagner."

Pat greeted her with a smile, immediately extending his hand.

"Pat McGurn—I'm here because the illegal alien who killed my brother last June was recently let out of jail. I understand your boss was against the ordinance that somehow allowed this to happen."

Turning her back on the receptionist, Ms. Farmer put a finger to her lips as if in caution.

"Okay, let's step into my office—I think I might be able to help."

When they were out of sight, the receptionist scrolled down her list of cell phone contacts and, in a hushed voice, made a quick call.

"*Ms. Nordquist? This is Rosa. Yes, fine thank you. Just thought someone should tell Ms. Korshak that McGurn's brother—you, know—the one in the paper? Well, he's been here snooping around …*"

The office was down the hall from the reception area. Adjacent to Commissioner Wagner's office, it was a small space adorned with family photos, a framed degree from Bradley University and nondescript office furniture. Opening a multi-drawer steel filing cabinet, Ms. Farmer thumbed through several horizontal files until she found what she was looking for.

"I have a file here, Mr. McGurn. Commissioner Wagner asked me to collect clippings and related documents for him to review because he's taken a few calls from the media. Of course, we saw the paper last week and, needless to say, it sort of shook things up around here and over at *The Daley Center.*"

"Well, I should hope so, Ms. Farmer."

"So no one called you, Sir?" she asked, evidently surprised at the omission.

"No, Ma'am—I guess, since you asked, maybe someone should have. Is that what you're saying?"

Frowning, Ms. Farmer looked down at her notes.

"No follow up calls from the *Witness Assistant Unit* or maybe your commissioner?"

"Not a word, nor did my nieces hear anything—you know, Denny's kids. So you're telling me I was supposed to get a call from my commissioner? Well, all I got was a weird recording from the jail on that Sunday. Look, I'm here to get to the bottom of this ordinance—I just hope Commissioner Wagner can help because he seems to be the only one around here that is likely to do something!"

"Four others voted against the ordinance," Ms. Farmer reminded him.

"I know that. Ralston told me that your boss was the only one he got a quote from—

I gather the others didn't return his calls."

The woman looked uncomfortable, as if at a loss for words. She held the file close to her chest, softly drumming on it with her impeccably manicured nails.

"So you're in touch with the Assistant State's Attorney—Eileen Murphy, right Mr. McGurn?"

"That's right, and the paper stated that I've talked to her. You should also know I called the cop who was supposed to search for Orizaga. Look, I know you're busy, but my family needs answers."

"Well, it's not that easy, Mr. McGurn. I assure you, Mr. Wagner is on your side, but politics are, well, complicated."

"Complicated or corrupt, and, in this case, just plain stupid if you ask me. So back to your boss—and that's why I'm here, Ma'am, because he seems to be the only one that might be straight with me. I just find it strange that the others didn't express outrage."

"Well, I can't speak for the others," she said apologetically. "I'll have Tom—I mean Commissioner Wagner—call you in a day or two. But to save time, let me go over the particulars with you and explain how the proceedings went three weeks ago. It was a hurry up vote without serious deliberation. The chief sponsors rammed it down the opposition commissioners because they knew they had the votes."

"So, you're telling me that your boss was caught unawares that day—is that normal?"

"It happens, Mr. McGurn. Strictly speaking, it should have gone to committee, with testimony from witnesses like yourself and other family victims."

Pat shook his head, the picture becoming clearer.

"Look, before I go, help me understand something. Were there a lot of sponsors?

"Oh yes—maybe eight or nine and President Korshak, even though she is a non-voting member."

As Pat was about to leave, Ms. Farmer informed him that just that morning, Commissioner Wagner had received a call from a professor at the *University of Illinois* suggesting an amendment. Pat smiled.

"Professor Vanderbiezen? We discussed that idea last week."

"Oh, I see—so this professor is a friend of yours?"

"Yeah, an old friend. One more thing if you don't mind. Can I see the Cook County Board Room?"

Giving him a puzzled look, Ms. Farmer hesitated.

"Why Sir, there's no one there!"

"Please, just for a moment …"

Silently, they walked down past the commissioners' offices towards the formidable double doors leading into the Board Room. Just as Pat had imagined, it resembled a regal lecture hall. There, in the front, were the ornate overstuffed chairs for the commissioners, facing an elevated platform where the president of Cook County would sit, flanked on either side by poles bearing city and state flags; behind the presidential chair stood an enormous American flag. For a few moments, Pat surveyed the empty room, trying to picture where each of the supporters of the ordinance had sat. As their faces came to mind, a chill came over him and he shuddered involuntarily.

"Thanks—I just needed a moment."

•

Across town, Nordquist—Korshak's legal counsel—was mulling over Rosa's news. She had figured there might be some flack after the Ralston columns, but never imagined a family member would contact a high profile journalist, a state's attorney and now a commissioner's office. Pretty tenacious for a retired schoolteacher … In less than a week, McGurn had made it to the downtown Loop to track down commissioners, called Murphy and also harassed the cops—what next? He clearly wanted answers and possibly thought all his efforts would get somebody to really work their tails off and find Orizaga. Of course, the felon was long gone, but any more press would be big-time embarrassing for her boss and compromise her own political career. Nordquist re-read Pat McGurn's quote in the Ralston's piece from the week before.

> *"Pat McGurn will do everything in his power to get to the bottom of Raul Orizaga's release If this means reviewing old County agenda, writing letters, going to the press or whatever it takes his family will not rest until those that allowed his brother's killer to flee are held accountable."*

She had to admit it was pretty forceful. Most likely, it had already been read locally by at least 100,000 people; moreover, several on line publications and other conservative blogs had picked up the quote nationally. A search on LinkedIn showed a short biography of Patrick McGurn. Apparently, he had been a presenter at the *Midwest Political Science Conference* the previous spring and delivered a paper entitled, "The State of Civic Education in the United States." He could be trouble for Korshak. Nordquist jotted down in a notebook:

McGurn, a lifelong Chicagoan, knows the political process, seems to have time, retired, tenacious, furious, veteran and a Republican. Somehow he has to be stopped. Calls have to be made. Shouldn't be a problem.

•

Pat left the County Building around 11:00 a.m. and crossed Clark Street, walking past one of Chicago's landmarks in *Daley Plaza*. Foisted on Mayor Daley back in the 60's, the statue had always amused Pat as Picasso was the ultimate art modernist who represented everything the conservative politician despised. Pat recalled how Carl Jung called Picasso a "schizophrenic." He glanced up at the rusty monument with disdain; like many of his peers, he resented having had to look at the "god-awful sculpture" for the last 40 years. A bird? Afghan hound? Baboon's head? What was it newspaper columnist Mike Royko had said at the unveiling? *"Interesting design, I'm sure. But the fact is, it has a long stupid face and looks like some giant insect that is about to eat a smaller, weaker insect."* Heading east, towards Michigan Avenue, he stopped at *Bocci's* for a Greek salad and coffee, and sat at an outdoor table, facing *Millennium Park*. A cool September breeze came off the lake and, for a few moments, he felt completely relaxed. Of course, it would have been wonderful if Clare had been able to join him, but no doubt she was working on that receiving blanket. "Bless her heart, Maeve should be arriving any day now …" he murmured to himself. After ordering and creaming his coffee he looked north on Michigan Avenue and thought of his mother who was raised a mile or so north in the Gold Coast neighborhood and attended *Holy Name Cathedral* parochial school. Jeez, mom would have taken Denny's death so hard. She loved her kids so much. Pat resolved to visit his mom and dad at *St. Mary's Cemetery* soon.

When he had finished eating, he checked his messages, then called Tim Joyce, the supervisor at the Cook County Jail at 26th and California.

"Pat McGurn calling. Got a minute, Deputy?"

"You're the guy whose brother—yes, how can I help you, Mr. McGurn?"

"Just give me what went down, Deputy—I don't need anything else!"

"You know I wasn't there, sir. Roberto Orizaga comes in on a Sunday with 25K in cash, so my guy decided to release him. That's all there is to it."

"So no one thought to maybe call Dypsky or one of his senior people?"

"Well, you know, Mr. McGurn, he *did* have the cash."

"C'mon, Deputy. So no one thought to call the Sheriff, or State's Attorney, or maybe a judge? I mean, a gangbanger walks in with 25K on a Sunday morning and that's routine? Something doesn't add up now—c'mon get straight with me, man! My brother's killer is no Rockefeller."

"You know, you better call Mr. Grodecki."

"Grodecki? The Sheriff's press spokesman? I would prefer to speak to Sheriff Dypsky."

"Sorry, Sir—I was told to give you Grodecki's number."

"Are you telling me somebody knew I was going to call?"

"Well, yeah—I guess so. Mr. Grodecki gave instructions."

"Instructions! Sounds like—" Pat stopped abruptly. "Never mind—I get it. But between you and me, what the fuck happened? You were the weekend supervisor, right? Who was the deputy that released him?"

"I don't know. Like I said, you gotta call Grodecki. His cell is—"

"Thanks for nothing! I got the number Deputy."

Pat pressed "End Call, resisting the urge to hurl his phone into the middle of Michigan Avenue. Catching the startled expressions of some of the other diners, he pocketed his phone, paid the bill and left, too angry to care what anyone had overheard during his testy exchange with Joyce. Rollie was right—the deputy was a real ass kisser. So much for the new day at the Sheriff's office that was supposed to be different than that of his predecessor. First, a prosecutor in the dark, next Alphy Skolickwitcz, the idiot copper, and now this clown, Joyce …

Frustrated, Pat crossed Michigan Avenue and walked briskly towards Lake Shore Drive. Being near the lake always calmed him down, and he needed to collect his thoughts before calling Grodecki. He cut across the rose gardens surrounding Buckingham Fountain, than crossed Lake Shore Drive at the lights, along with the usual assortment of bikers, tourists on Segways, moms and strollers and people with their dogs. Once near the water, he slowed to take in the beauty of Chicago's lakefront. Gentle waves lapped against the rocks and he watched as several ducks navigated the shoreline, perhaps looking for food. In the distance, red vertical banners brightened the façade of the Field Museum, announcing its latest special exhibit—*Ancient Rome: Prosperity and Decline*. He sat on a park bench close to where the Water Taxi collected and off-loaded passengers going to and from Navy Pier. Briefly, he considered going on board, just to escape, but he had promised Clare he would catch the 3:25 p.m. train from LaSalle Street Station. "Might as well get it over with," he said out loud. Taking out his cell phone, he entered Grodecki's number on the keyboard. A recorded message said, "*This is the office of Guy Grodecki, Press spokesman for Cook County Sheriff Dypsky. I am out of the office but will return your call promptly.*"

"Damn!" he exclaimed loudly, turning off his cell phone. He had about twenty minutes to get to the train …

•

Later that evening, he received an unexpected call from Jim Dorsey, a former Sheriff of Cook County. He had heard the news about Orizaga's release and wanted to express his outrage. He and Pat went back many years, having attended high school together.

"Pat, I'm real sorry about what happened to your brother—last week was a travesty. When I was Sheriff that wouldn't have happened."

"You're telling me you would have snubbed your nose at the Cook County Board?"

"Absolutely. They shouldn't have let him out."

"But Dypsky did—didn't you support him and help him get him elected?

"Well, I can't tell him how to do his job now that I'm retired."

"Jim, I just called a guy named Joyce at the Sheriff—he was useless. You know him?"

"No, Dypsky brought in all his own guys. Had it been on my watch, the guy that killed your brother would not have been let go."

"Well, Jim that's encouraging. Thanks for the call."

"Sure, Pat—just thought I'd check in with you."

Clare, who had overheard the conversation, also knew the former sheriff from her youth officer days thirty years earlier. Smiling, she looked up from her crochet work.

"Jim was always a class act and real nice guy. So what d'you think?"

'I guess that's encouraging, but at the moment I'm hoping Rollie gets something going with this Alphy and maybe we'll learn something."

Clare gave her husband a worried look.

DAY ELEVEN, WEDNESDAY, SEPTEMBER 7, 2011

"Hello, Roman Skollickwitcz here."

"I don't know if we met, but I'm Rollie Dufner—used to be with *Area One Homicide*."

"Yeah, I know who you are—say how you get my cell, man?"

"Well, you know, Alphy—," Rollie began in his most collegial manner.

"How you know my nickname?"

"Don't worry about it—I know a lot of things," said Rollie calmly. "The reason I'm calling is that I need to ask a few questions about your assignment to look for Orizaga."

"Look man, I talked to the brother last week and told him we looked for this Orzo or whatever. Say, you retired ain't you, Dufner? So what gives? Maybe this is a private deal—I'm thinking like you getting paid."

"Yeah, I'm retired but I'm doing a favor for a friend."

"Okay, I get it," said Alphy, sounding relieved. "Well, it's all in the report, Dufner."

"Alphy, I'm betting the report contains routine stuff—you know what you saw and all that."

"Yeah, that's about it. We looked for him, Dufner, and he ain't there. I stopped by last Friday, you know, a second time."

"Take it from the start, Alph," instructed Rollie, with a cold edge to his voice. "Like who told you to look and how it went down."

"Hey man, what you mean take it from the start? What's this shit and why are you grilling me? I did my job—besides who the fuck are you telling me how to do my job? I don't need this shit!"

"Hey, ease up, big guy," said Rollie, trying to conceal the amusement in his voice. "I just want to know what went down."

"What you want from me, man? We both know he's in Mexico."

"Do we, Alph?" came the icy reply. "Look, I'm trying to help my buddy out, and you don't seem very cooperative. You know he's got questions—and I told him I'd get the answers. I have my methods, you know."

"All right, all right, I'll tell you what I know, but no more calls after this, Dufner."

Nervously, Alph recounted how he had received a call from a Cook County sheriff's deputy who asked him to accompany him on a warrant to look for Orizaga. They had met up at around 3:00 p.m. at Orizaga's brother's house on the North Side. The brother—Roberto—answered the door but didn't seem concerned to see two police officers standing there. Apparently, he had been the one to post bond and get his brother out of jail. When asked about Orizaga's whereabouts, Roberto claimed he didn't know because Raul lived in the basement and came and went without anyone knowing. He showed them a hot plate that looked as if it had been used recently. There was a pile of bedding on the floor in one of the corners.

"Wait a second, Alph. Didn't Roberto want to know why you guys wanted his brother?"

"No, man, it's like he was cool—like not worried."

"Didn't you think something was suspicious? And was there a john down there?"

"No, nobody by that name there."

"Toilet, Alph! Was there a toilet in the basement?"

"I d-dunno," stuttered Alphy. "We didn't look—well, now you say that, I don't think so."

"You fuckin' idiot, don't you see this was all staged, for God's sake? You should've dragged the brother in and grilled the asshole. Do what good dicks do—scare the shit out of a witness! You know that prick knows more than he's giving up. You two clowns went to the house and obviously didn't give a shit if you found Orizaga."

"You know, Dufner, something told me to hang up earlier 'cause I knew you were gonna fuck with me."

"Thanks for nothing, Alph—and watch your back, asshole."

"Fuck you, Dufner!"

Rollie decided to take a ride up to the house to get a feel for the neighborhood. He drove north on the Ryan X-Way exiting at Fullerton and parked around the corner from the location of the accident that had taken Denny's life a few months earlier. Putting on his best "Clint Eastwood face," he got out of the car, his revolver fully loaded and within easy reach. This part of the Logan Square neighborhood looked pretty rough, and already there were several street people who were eyeing him curiously. No doubt they figured he was a cop. He went into a store and bought a pack of cigarettes—second pack of the week. Not bad, he thought; he'd promised his wife he would quit for good in a month or two. He then strode into the nearest bar; the few regulars sitting at the end of the bar, turned to look at him, then went back to watching Spanish TV. A friendly looking mustachioed man greeted him from behind the bar.

"*Buenos Dias.* Help you, man?"

"Yeah, gimme a draft."

"New around here, Amigo?" asked the bartender, handing him a chilled bottle.

"No—just looking at property over on Corliss but the guy's not there yet," said Rollie, perching on the edge of one of the stools.

"Oh yeah? Maybe I know the dude," said the man, leaning across from him.

"Maybe, but he don't live around here—you know, one of those absentee guys."

"Well, if you buy the joint maybe you'll be an absentee landlord, too," observed the bartender.

"Maybe," said Rollie, noncommittally. "You know the 2800 block on Corliss?"

"Yeah, I know some people over there. Not bad, you know."

"Any drugs, gangs—you know, crime?"

"Shit, Mr. Landlord. No more than anywhere else."

Rollie finished the beer, left three singles on the bar and walked out.

Getting into his car, he drove to the 2800 block of Corliss. The block seemed normal enough. Compared to his special assignment days, the area seemed almost gentrified—"up and coming," in fact, with white professionals and young families very much in evidence. As he pulled up across the street from Roberto's house, he noted several young mothers on their cell phones, pushing babies in strollers. None of the passers-by gave any indication that they were in a dangerous neighborhood or that crime was a possibility. "Oblivious," he muttered to himself. No doubt they had been drawn by lower rentals and cheap property prices. Well, if they could ride out the crime in the area, home purchasers would have a great investment. Still eyeing the street, he called an old buddy still working at the Area *Three Detective Division* in the Chicago Police Department.

"Area Three, Detective Schuster here."

"Schus, your phone presence sucks. You sound like you lost your best friend."

"Rollie, that you giving me shit? Jeez, been a year or so. Hey, how's retirement? You keeping busy?"

"You bet, Schus—had a few private deals looking for runaway husbands, and even got a few private security jobs for VIP's."

"Say good for you, Rol. With your arrest record, I knew you wouldn't be home doing the cross words. So what's up?"

"Schus, remember that Denny McGurn case—you know, the guy who got run over by an illegal in Logan Square?"

"Sure do, Rol—Sheriff Dypsky let the criminal out a week ago, right? Saw it in the paper."

"That's it, Schus—well, I'm helping out the younger brother, an ole buddy a mine from my *Mendel High School* days. Right now, I'm sitting on the killer's brother's house—the one who produced the 25K for bail."

"Where at, Rol?"

"Not far from you—2845 N. Corliss, a dumpy two flat."

"I know the area—sort of transient, you know, with a mix of low lifes and young whites who are in la-la land."

"Well, Schus, I have a hunch that this piece of shit is still in town. Look, I need you to run these Orizaga brothers and see if there's anything that didn't get in the record."

"You got the final report, Rol?"

"Yeah, Shus. I got a guy who works at headquarters bring it to me the other day—not much there. I already talked to this asshole, Skolickwitcz and he's pissed off with me."

Schus laughed.

"Look, Rol, we call him Alph the Goof—he's a clown of the first order, but heavy. You know his uncle, a Deputy Commissioner named Lezniak?"

"Figures, Schus—fucking clout is the ruin of the department, we always used to say."

"Got that right, Rol, but, look, let me send some guys to talk to neighbors and maybe get traffic to pull over the brother."

"No, don't do that—you might spook Roberto. Let me know what you find!"

Rollie spent the next half hour or so watching pedestrians walking to and from stores on Kedzie. In spite of some newly re-furbished buildings and the presence of a few "yuppie types," the neighborhood had seen better days. There were the usual rusted out vehicles sitting on front lawns, as well as boarded up apartment buildings that had been spray-painted with gang tags and graffiti. Several heavily-tattooed young men lounged on a nearby front stoop, sharing a joint. Roberto's place was at least a hundred years old and probably hadn't seen a paintbrush in forty years.

He was just going to call it a day when a Hispanic male, presumably Roberto, emerged from the building, got into an old Ford Windstar and began to head north. Immediately, Rollie pulled out behind him. After some turns and a few lights, the Windstar pulled into *Northeastern Illinois University's* parking lot. Rollie parked in the next row, watching the young man join a few hundred people milling about at the front door to the *Student Center*. It looked like some sort of rally. Putting on a baseball cap, Rollie took out a reporter's notebook and decided he would be on assignment for *The Globe*. He could still see Roberto in the crowd, talking to a few *amigos* and exchanging fist pumps. Suddenly, there was a hush and crowd made way for an older gentleman, none other than Congressman Manny Rodriguez whose thick silver hair and formidable height were unmistakable. Manny was elected eight times from a west suburban district made up of a majority of Hispanics. Before entering the building, Rodriguez singled out Roberto and bent down to whisper something to him. Drawing nearer, Rollie could read the sign announcing Rodriguez's speech which was to be held inside the *Student Center*; it was based on his newly-released autobiography, *Barrio to D.C.*

After working the crowd, Congressman Rodriguez jumped up on the stage and shouted something in Spanish that evoked an enthusiastic response from the audience. Rollie quietly sat in the back, notebook in hand.

Once the crowd settled down, Rodriguez recited his typical inflammatory *"We Against Them"* sentiments, his rhetoric being rewarded with frequent applause. At one point, when the crowd was standing and screaming in support, Rollie slipped out to the parking lot and approached the Windstar. With no one around to observe him, he jotted down the plate and vin numbers. On the front seat, there was a pack of cigarettes and a recent edition of the *SouthEast Observer*, printed in both Spanish and English. Having left the Windstar's plate number on Schus's voice mail, Rollie returned to the auditorium. Rodriguez was still gripping the microphone, stirring the crowd into a frenzy with comments about deportations and racial profiling. Roberto was sitting in the front row, voicing his support along with everyone else.

Later, on his way to Beverly where he was scheduled to meet Pat at *Ruth's*, Rollie thought about the feverish response to Rodriguez's presence. The man was a snake—had been arrested numerous times over the years for his protests and smart-ass remarks with the *La Fuerza*. He was also involved with all sorts of shady real estate deals and irregular campaign finance issues. It was possible that Roberto looked at Rodriguez as a godfather figure; it was also possible that the cabal had managed to manipulate the political process with the fucked up ordinance.

Traffic slowed at 55th Street on the expressway and Rollie called a young marine Iraq vet named Mario of his Veteran's of Foreign Wars (VFW) post. The voice mail triggered and Rollie asked if Mario and his pal Jose might be interested in a few weeks surveillance work. Rollie knew the two youngsters were waiting to be called to the Chicago Police Academy and needed the work. At 4:00 p.m. on the dot, Rollie walked in to *Ruth's* where he spotted Pat at the bar, listening to old Dooley, who, for a change, seemed very animated. As he went to shake hands his phone rang.

"Hey, Marine I think Jose and I interested."

"Good man, Mario, but let me go over the details at the VFW club say about 7:30 p.m"

"We'll be there."

As Rollie ended the call, Dooley shook his hand and patted him on the back.

"Rol, my man, how you doin'? Hey, me and Pat talkin' about Vietnam and shit—wanna join us?"

Rollie grabbed Pat's arm.

"Tell you what, Dools, some other time—we've some business here that's sort of private, see?"

"That's cool but I was just sayin' how in 'Nam—"

"Sure, Dools, later, man."

Pat reached for his bottle of lager, and they quickly retreated to a corner table.

"You first, Pat, and do yourself a favor—keep Dooley at bay," said Rollie, pulling out one of the ladder-back wooden chairs.

"Sure, Rollie. I understand, but he means well. Okay, down to business. First off, I talked to Clare—we got five grand for your time."

"Well, Pat, maybe that dough could come in handy, but what did you find out?"

"Look, Rol—we want to pay you for your time."

"I get it, Pat, I get it, but money's not important right now. Tell me what you learned."

Pat began to recount the details of his day, including his meeting with Wagner's assistant, the call to Joyce, and the attempt to reach Grodecki.

"This Wagner got some fight in him, you think, Pat?"

"Well, he was the only guy who Ralston got a quote from—nothing from the other commissioners. I figure I'll talk to Wagner in maybe a day or two. I gave my number to his assistant."

"So let me get this straight. None of the other commissioners who voted against the ordinance agreed to a quote? You know, this makes me wonder if any of these guys really gives a shit. You try Korshak?"

"Nope. I figure she won't talk. Her assistant left a message. Perhaps I'll write her a letter in a few days after I learn a thing or two."

"Pat, between you and me I don't trust any of these fuckers. What about Jack Riley, you know, our commissioner"

"Nothing yet, but he did vote against the ordinance—I'll talk to him after Wagner."

"What else, Pat?"

"Well, I'm still hoping that my professor friends will help get the law changed. Like I told you, some of the story will get into Joe's book, and Joan Farnsworth will get this before Congress, I guess. You know the Democrats in Washington are talking about this *Good Neighbor Act* that will give several thousand illegal youngsters status?"

Rollie grimaced.

"*Good Neighbor*, huh? Well, Pat, for my money I just want to catch this motherfucker and lock his ass up. And this Farnsworth thinks the guy might still be on this side of the border, like I do?"

"Yeah, Rol—all the more reason to follow your hunch."

"I don't know, man—your brother gets whacked and your family's thinking the piece of shit will be locked up for, say, eight to ten years because of a prior felony but the fuckin' system lets him bolt. So, yeah, as a friend I'm pissed big-time and maybe you're right—the fuckin' County is guiltier than the illegal alien. Pat, I always felt my calling was to get fuckin' criminals, period!"

Pat smiled approvingly. Rollie was not the type of friend he could ever introduce to his more genteel relatives but he admired his resolve. He'd always had gumption, even as a kid.

Pat remembered one day in high school Rollie swung back at a priest who hit him. Somehow he avoided expulsion.

"Let me ask something, Pat—what have these fancy professors got to say about President Haesi? They think he's involved in any of this shit?"

"Funny you ask, Rol. Just yesterday, Joe sent me a paper written by one of the authors talking about Haesi and Senator Congelosi's support of the *Good Neighbor Act*. They think that if it doesn't pass, he's going to figure a way with executive privilege. See, he wants a second term and needs maybe 70-80 % of the Hispanic vote. And another thing, Joe told me that Haesi has been pro immigrant for years—seems he has an uncle from Ethiopia who's here illegally, living in Massachusetts."

"What bullshit!"

Pat shrugged his shoulders.

"He won, so we have to live with it, I guess. So your turn, Rol. Did you learn anything on the North Side?"

Rollie went over his conversation with Alphy, describing how he had followed Roberto to Congressman's Rodriguez's lecture and had managed to take down his license plate. He also mentioned that he saw a copy of a community newspaper on Roberto's front seat from the south East Side of the city. He ended with his call to Schus who would run the plates.

"Schus sounds like a good guy."

"The best, Pat. We go back many years."

"And Alphy?"

"He's a joke—Schus confirmed it. Everybody's on to the idiot."

"So the rally at *Northeastern* might be something, you think?"

"Yeah, Roberto knows Manny, all right, and we always figured Rodriguez and other Hispanic politicians work with gangbangers, especially to rig elections and work the system. That five grand you mentioned—that could fund a surveillance watch. Maybe I could hire some young marines to keep an eye on the brother as soon as possible—I mean like as early as tomorrow."

"That's okay with me, Rol, and I can't imagine Clare would object—but what about *your* expenses?"

"Hey, maybe a dinner or something. Look, run my idea past Clare, will you, because I'm thinking we need eyes on Roberto 24/7 as early as tomorrow night."

"You serious, Rol? Sounds like you talked to these marines already."

Rollie chuckled. Nothing ever got by Pat, even in high school.

"Yeah, left a message with this guy Mario while sitting in traffic and a few minutes ago he and his pal gave it a thumbs up."

"Good guys, huh?"

"You bet—both did two tours in Iraq, but I'll go up once a day to help as well. I think my guy in *Area Three Detective Division*, Schus, will help, too. You know, maybe he'll get his tactical unit guys to support my marines."

"Alphy?"

"You kidding? Look, I'm not sure where this is going, but we got to keep eyes on Roberto. Friday, I'm going to meet with Schus and brainstorm—he'll have to keep this under the radar. You follow me?"

Pat slowly drained his lager, then wiped the foam from his lips with the back of his hand.

"Okay, I'll run it by Clare—if you don't hear from me, it's a go. She'll agree, I'm sure. Something tells me you're on to something."

The two men got up to leave, having agreed to meet in two days. Rollie picked up Pat's empty bottle as well as the one that he had been nursing, and headed towards the bar.

•

"So what if nothing comes of the Roberto surveillance?—$5,000 gets you about three weeks."

As Pat had predicted, Clare was on board with Rollie's plan, but he could hear the reservation in her voice. Sitting out on the deck behind their house, they lingered at the table with their coffee mugs, in no hurry to remove the dirty plates and serving dishes.

"Yep, give or take a week, I suppose," admitted Pat. "But Rollie's convinced he's here or somewhere in the States because he owes somebody some serious money. Maybe Attorney Simpkus is certain to be in on this, too, or maybe this Congressman Rodriguez."

"Well, Simpkus clearly has ethical issues all right—I'd bet he's played these sorts of games before. I guess it's a go, but hold it at $5,000."

"For sure, Clare, that's the limit," agreed Pat, suddenly looking less confident. Five grand was no small sum, especially if it achieved nothing. Handing over the money was a gamble, not much different than playing the lottery or joining some high stake game in Vegas. He added a teaspoon of sugar to his already too-sweet coffee.

"What about the family, Pat?"

"Well, I'll e-mail them on the ordinance strategy and update them about Joe and Joan's involvement, but not about the Rollie thing—not sure how this would go over."

"Well, that, for sure, needs to be kept under wraps. So just you and I are the only ones in the family in on this, right?"

"You bet."

DAY TWELVE, THURSDAY SEPTEMBER 8 2011

Thursday morning brought a call from Commissioner Tom Wagner. After offering his condolences, he got straight down to business. He had obviously done his homework and knew all the details of Pat's visit to the Cook County.

"My assistant, Liz Farmer, went over the particulars, right?"

"Yeah, she was helpful. So this ordinance was sort of rammed down the throats of you and four others, I guess?"

"Something like that, Mr. McGurn," came the guarded reply.

"Well, you were the only one that took issue with the ordinance," continued Pat. There was a pause as the other man chose his words carefully.

"I knew what the majority was thinking and had to say something. But you should really start with Riley, if you're trying to push back."

"The problem is I'm not sure whom to push when and where. So I guess you're telling me that Riley will be the 'go to' guy on this? Between you and me, he never struck me as a fighter," confided Pat.

"Well, he did ask Dypsky's counsel, Paul Nikos, that day if Dypsky helped write the ordinance and didn't seem too pleased with the answer."

"Sorry—you're losing me here."

"All Nikos would say was that Sheriff Dypsky would support whatever the commissioners passed, and felons might be released," explained Wagner. "Let me tell you, Mr. McGurn, those of us against the thing know for a fact that Dypsky was involved. When the measure was getting close, he backed off and let Nikos and his former press guy do his bidding. Then the press spokesman quit a few weeks later."

"No kidding! You know, I talked to the supervisor at the jail and he's been muzzled. I was directed to Guy Grodecki."

"Grodecki's just a kid with no press experience. Trust me, he's part of the Ward organization down there."

"Yeah, I know—he's Dypsky's nephew. I live in that Ward," said Pat, making no effort to hide the disdain in his voice.

"Okay, so that's the way it went down. I don't know how far you want to go with this, Mr. McGurn, but Liz Farmer told me about your friendship with Professor Vanderbiezen. You know he called me?"

"Yeah, it was my understanding when I met with him last week that he'd make the call. Do you think his amendment idea is worth pursuing?"

"Well, first of all, we agreed that an amendment should, for sure, allow the Sheriff to hold any illegal alien charged with forcible felonies and, in Orizaga's case, prior felony convictions."

"That's all I'm looking for," said Pat. "But it will be hard for me to convince my family that an amendment of this kind will return some measure of justice. You see, they want him caught and convicted, and we both know that is a veritable impossibility."

"Not sure if getting an amendment is doable, given the structure of the Board."

"You mean getting enough votes would be tough?"

"Yeah, so I'll talk to some of the other commissioners, but that's all I can do for now."

"Sounds like you're saying to forget about it," said Pat bitterly. "You know I'm getting the impression that there are a lot of two-face types on this board."

"Look, I can't get into those types of characterizations, Mr. McGurn, but I can tell you my constituents are not happy with this ordinance, and I want my people to know where I stand. I think we should move forward, but you need to talk to Commissioner Riley. I'll also suggest a forum of some kind for public input and maybe introduce an amendment that way."

"Okay, I'll follow your advice but he's a Democrat and a Riley—I'm not sure I can trust him. You know he usually gets along with Korshak you know supports her on most things—everybody knows that."

"Mr. McGurn, I can't respond to that," said Wagner, icily.

"I understand, but let me ask you this. There's a Hispanic block, a Black block and a White liberal block, right?"

"So what's your point?"

"Well, you need four votes and who's going to change? Maybe James might, but he's going to get indicted. Korshak controls all the Blacks and that leaves the two white female liberals and Petrutis. Any hope, Commissioner?"

"Mr. McGurn, you sure have been looking at the Board pretty closely, but I can't get into this guessing game with you. Look, all I can promise is that I will at least try to get an amendment on the floor for discussion."

"What's your take on Fanning, Murray or Petrutus?" continued Pat, sensing the call was coming to an end. "They have law and order constituents. Maybe they might get their heads screwed on better?"

"Mr. McGurn, I can't continue this conversation—"

"Yeah, I get it—certain proprieties must be adhered to! You know ten people didn't give a shit when they passed that ordinance and I got a dead brother. Okay, here's my take. Murray's a fool and I've a source that's pretty sure both she and the gal, Boller, had no clue that the ordinance applied to felons. Fanning's a big-time liberal whose old man used his clout to get her elected. Petrutis's just a hack that has figured a way to game the system for a long line of relatives. The others I'll learn more on in good time. I got to tell you, I'm not hopeful."

"All I can say is that I'll make some calls," repeated Wagner, testily.

"Look one more thing, Commissioner. You ever heard of some guy named George Hallet?"

"No."

"My contacts down at the *U of I* tell me this guy's probably behind the ordinance. He's with some outfit called *Immigration Illinois* or something like that and pals with Haesi."

"*Really? The President?*"

"Yeah, and I'm betting he and Commissioner Varbanov worked on this ordinance and you guys got hit with it by surprise."

"Mr. McGurn I really can't comment on someone or something about which I have no knowledge."

"Thanks, Commissioner—I appreciate your candor here. I'm now pretty much convinced this amendment isn't going to happen—maybe the best I can hope for is that it stays in the public consciousness."

"Mr. McGurn, I have an appointment—please talk to Commissioner Riley."

There was a click at the other end of the phone. Pat found himself imagining what Denny's take would have been: "Don't trust any of these slime balls," he would have said.

Maybe Denny was right.

●

The 3:00 p.m. meeting commenced in President Shirley Korshak's conference room with Korshak, her counsel, Inger Nordquist, Sheriff Dan Dypsky, Commissioner Vic Varbanov and State's Attorney Lisa Hunter-Goss. Korshak, anxious to get started, tapped on her coffee mug with a metal teaspoon. The conversations immediately subsided.

"I've called this meeting because we need damage control. I'm assuming you've all seen the Ralston article? Well, as you know, the brother of Denny McGurn is determined to figure out why Raul Orizaga was released from the County Jail ten days ago. Nobody I've talked to expected something like this to happen. So let's start with you, Sheriff."

Sheriff Dypsky stretched out his lanky legs under the table, leaned back in his chair and nonchalantly began shuffling through some papers.

"My people acted by the book. The brother came in with the 25K; paper work was signed and we released him," he drawled.

"Did the deputy who handled it know of the detainer?" Korshak asked.

"Sure, it was there—you know it's on the daily printout."

"Did he call anyone for guidance? I mean 25K for an undocumented Mexican on a Sunday seems sort of unusual, don't you think?"

Dypsky slowly waved a copy of the ordinance in Korshak's direction.

"Didn't need to. The ordinance states clearly that detainers are to be ignored," he said, matter-of-factly.

"So, Sheriff Dypsky," interjected Hunter-Goss. "You must have issued a general order to your staff not to honor detainers—I assume that this was put on some sort of distribution, right?"

"Sure, that's right," admitted Dypsky, looking a little less bored.

"Can I state simply that maybe our office should have been notified? Let's face it, Sheriff, we all look bad when Pat McGurn has to notify my office."

"That was never discussed," objected Dypsky. "And besides, Ms. Hunter-Goss, your second in command was there—I think his name was Sheehan."

Caught off guard, Hunter-Goss said nothing but began jotting down some notes. Clearing her throat, Korshak quickly continued the interrogation.

"Who was the deputy that released him, Sheriff?"

"A part timer that works weekends."

"So you're okay with this, Sheriff?"

"We followed the law, President Korshak, and the record shows my counsel, Mr. Nikos, warned this could be the outcome the day the ordinance was passed."

"But you could have kept Orizaga, right?"

"Sure, but that would have violated the intent of the ordinance and angered everyone who passed it," he said, looking meaningfully at Varbanov.

"I'll be the judge of that, Sheriff," retorted Korshak.

Dypsky stared at Korshak over his reading glasses.

"So let me get this straight—you fight to pass the law and then you want me to break it?"

Ignoring his outburst, Korshak turned to Commissioner Varbanov.

"How about you, Mr. Varbanov? You got me to support the ordinance—

I was convinced this was a Civil Rights issue and that all defendants should be treated equally, including the undocumented."

"ICE screws up all the time," said Varbanov, shrugging his shoulders. "They are constantly grabbing people to deport and splitting up families. I heard they grabbed a guy for a broken tail light."

Dypsky looked amused.

"Really? And *where* was this?"

"I dunno. I heard it somewhere," said Varbanov evasively.

"So far, all we know is that this Orizaga is out, and we think he's gone to Mexico," interrupted Korshak.

"We also know that McGurn is making a fuss over this, and the press is already involved. We *have* to be ready. Now, Ms. Nordquist, we need a defense. I'm thinking of continuing to make this a bond issue, you know—throw the blame at the judges for low bail."

"Well, the judge assigned to the case set bond at 250K—that's real low for someone with a prior felony like Orizaga, but we can't interfere with that," interjected Hunter-Goss.

Looking up from her notepad, pen poised in mid air, Korshak raised her eyebrows in the direction of the woman sitting across from her.

"Lisa, surely your lawyer assigned to bond court could have done something? Who was the judge—or, for that matter, the assigned lawyer?"

"Judge was Santiago from Humboldt Park. The lawyer is new and needs training. Her name is Melissa Rice."

"Santiago? Isn't he related to a former alderman?"

"Yeah, a cousin, I think."

"So couldn't your attorney have objected in bond court?"

"Look, she was brand new, and it's not that easy. You know the judge sets the bail and that's that," snapped Hunter-Goss.

"So new kids are assigned to bond court, typically?" asked Korshak. "I'm no lawyer, Ms. Hunter-Goss, but c'mon—$250,000.00 with a prior felony! Can't we get more experienced lawyers in bond court?"

"Let me remind you that judges are appointed and elected, so that's completely out of my hands," retorted Hunter-Goss. "As for lawyers, the procedure is to have new attorneys for bond court and more experienced lawyers for prosecution—actually, Eileen Murphy was assigned, and she's at least a twenty-five year veteran. However, it looks like she didn't know about the ordinance, because she assured the McGurns the detainer would prevent Orizaga's release."

"Well, she *should* have known, Lisa."

Korshak drummed on the table with her pen, studying the faces of those gathered around the table.

"Okay, so now that we know where things stand, Ms. Nordquist, you can research our options here and call Commissioners Riley and Alport. Apparently, Davida Alport's staff is looking at both legal and political responses to this. Anything else?"

"As a matter of fact, yes," said Ms. Nordquist. "There are some serious legal issues here involving case law. I'm no constitutional expert, but if this Pat McGurn gets the right legal team, we must be ready."

"Any specifics, Ms. Nordquist?" asked Dypsky, looking decidedly uncomfortable.

"Well, my guess is that you, Sheriff Dypsky, would be the likely defendant because it could be argued that Federal authority over aliens is preeminent and that state and local governments must turn over criminals."

"Seems I'm sued all the time, but if someone in the family is a plaintiff, I'm certain standing could be the issue. Don't you think, Ms. Nordquist?"

Inger Nordquist nodded. "Good point," was all she said.

"Ms. Nordquist, you said you talked to Commissioner Alport about another issue," Korshak reminded her.

"Well, yes, Shirley. She spoke with Commissioner Wagner and they discussed a hearing of some sort, I guess, about an amendment. Apparently, Wagner got advice from some professor."

"Look, I know about that advice and, trust me, there may be a hearing but no amendment," chimed in Varbanov, smugly.

"I didn't hear anything about a professor," said Korshak, clearly puzzled. "What are you talking about, Vic?"

Varbanov hesitated, a sheepish look clouding his expression.

"Well, I'm not supposed to say, but this professor phoned Wagner, and I guess he knows Pat McGurn. Best thing is to make it seem like we don't know."

Nordquist shook her head, as if in disbelief.

"I'll look into this and report later," was all she said.

"Oh, by the way," added Dypsky. "A Chicago cop assigned to look for Orizaga—a Roman something—let one of my deputies know that a retired detective, Rollie Dufner, recently gave him a lot of grief. I understand there could be trouble. You know, this Dufner lives in my ward and his reputation is pretty impressive."

"Check on that, Inger," said Korshak. "Okay, so now we know Patrick McGurn has recruited a dream team—this could get real bad for all of us. Ms. Nordquist, what can you tell us about Patrick McGurn?" Inger Nordquist thumbed through a stack of notes, picking out the highlights. She summed up his biography in a monotone, as if reciting a homework assignment:

"Pat McGurn is a life-long Chicagoan and a retired history teacher. He's former military, drafted 1971; married 33 years, 2 adult children, one a lawyer and, the other, a freelance journalist. Somewhat active with the *Midwest Political Science Guild* and has written papers on school reform and civic literacy. Last and maybe significant, thirty-seven years ago, he set up a race relations program while stationed at Fort Hood, Texas, and received the *Army Commendation Medal*. During his Board of Education career, he was a union activist for a time and worked with the *Illinois Manufacturers' Association* some years ago on school reform issues related to vocational training."

"You're kidding! A civic-minded former teacher who sets up a race relations program in the army!" exclaimed Korshak.

"How did you learn all this, Ms. Nordquist?" asked Varbanov, clearly impressed by her detective work.

"He self reported on LinkedIn—but the only thing I confirmed was the medal, and it's the real deal. I got this from his former commanding officer, who is now the head of the NAACP down in Memphis."

"Anything else?" asked Korshak.

"Yeah, married to Clare McGurn who is currently the senior investigator at the *Illinois Grievance Commission*. My source said she knows something about every unethical lawyer in the County."

Ms. Nordquist slowly looked around the table for emphasis.

"Just yesterday I learned she worked with my predecessor some thirty years ago while she was a youth officer on the *Chicago Police Department*," added Dypsky."

Korshak grimaced.

"Just a matter of time before this hits the news again," she said. "Let's adjourn for now, but please keep me posted. We don't want any surprises!"

As the group disbanded, President Korshak motioned for Ms. Nordquist to sit down.

"So tell me more of your conversation with Alport, Inger?"

"She will call it a public Cook County Board hearing and give McGurn the first shot at the microphone—maybe in two weeks, maybe less. Near the end of the public hearing, I'll announce a special task force headed by retired Federal Judge Burns to make recommendations on bail bond procedures."

"Good work, Inger—so Judge Burns is okay with that?"

"Yes."

"Okay, that's good. Look we don't need Vic running his mouth and I don't trust Dypsky for a minute. You know, Inger, just our luck a family member decides to make life miserable for us."

•

After the meeting, while driving from his *Daley Center* office to his home on Hoyne Avenue, Sheriff Dypsky called his legal counsel, Paul Nikos, another South Sider. He listened attentively to Dypsky's synopsis of the meeting.

"I'll get all the facts that I can and let's meet at the Ward office tonight. Should I call Guy?"

"No, he's tied up with more scuffles at the prison in D wing. You know, more gang shit—I think a couple got sent to Stroger hospital. Better we meet at *Muldoon's*—I need a drink."

"No problem, Dan. Remember like I said the day of the ordinance, we will follow the law and you did, man."

"Hope you're right. I've got bad vibes about all this. How about 8:00 p.m.?

"I'll be there."

•

Meanwhile, Rollie had received a call from Detective Schuster who was eager to meet with him. They agreed to meet at *Heffernan's* in Bridgeport at 4 P.M. As he made the trek down Western and down Garfield to Halsted, he recalled his childhood days in the 50's, going to visit relatives at 51st and Peoria; later, in 1965 and 1966, as an Andy Frain usher, he had taken the same route to what was then called *Comiskey Park* to make $7.00 a game. But that was a lifetime ago, when he was young and green, and still believed the world was the Garden of Eden. Clearing his mind of memories, he called Mario who was scheduled to start the Roberto surveillance at the Corliss house at 6:00 p.m.

"Rollie, here. Look, I'll be up there maybe a half hour late. I gotta meet a guy. You got the address, right?"

"You bet Rol. Traffic could be problem on the Kennedy Expressway."

"Yeah, that's what I'm thinking."

When Rollie walked into *Heffernan's*, he had to smile as he looked at all the autographed *Chicago White Sox* photos hanging on the walls. They went back at least sixty years. He loved the Aparicio and Fox ones in particular, perhaps because these players were the key to the '59 World Series which he still remembered, even though he was little more than a child at the time. *Heffernan's* had been one of his favorite haunts for the last thirty years or so, sometimes to meet buddies before games and, later, in the early 90's, to take his son there as well.

He sat at a corner booth and ordered a draft beer. Across the street were the 11th Ward headquarters, a center of political power for roughly the last five decades. He wondered if Pat had talked with Jack Riley, the former governor's nephew and the Cook County Commissioner that represented Pat and his district.

Schuster, sporting a summer plaid jacket and a broad smile, walked in and sat down in Rollie's booth.

"Hey, Rol! Long time no see! Retirement suits you well, pal."

"Got that right, Schus. The ghetto can wear you down, man."

"Hey, I hear you! I got five more years and, you know, you begin to get jaded. So you're back in the hunt—you got that look!"

"Yeah, like I told you yesterday on the phone, I just want help this guy and something tells me the bastard's here—maybe not in Chicago, but still in the United States."

"You're not planning on going out of town, are you?"

"No, no, Schus. If our investigation leads that way, it's officially in the FBI's hands and they won't do shit. Both McGurn and I got confirmation that it might be two weeks before they do anything. My involvement ceases if Orizaga left town for sure, but something tells me this creep's still in town. So what have you got for me?"

They were interrupted by the waitress who took their order for two blue cheese burgers—a house specialty—and the inevitable beers.

Schuster studied a crumpled sheet of paper.

"Where was I? Oh yeah. Alphy's blaming everyone, mainly the sheriff's deputies. I guess he took some heat from the top because your guy, McGurn, made some noise. A big mess, I got to think. Everybody's covering ass, Rol."

"Screw Alphy—he's useless" said Rollie contemptuously. "Ass covering is a high art in this town. I see you've got a lot of notes—go ahead."

"Well, first of all that Windstar is registered in Roberto's name—no traffic warrants, but no insurance. I could get traffic to pull him over, but you told me you don't want to spook him."

"That's right—so what else, Schus?"

"Well, back in October, 2008, when the cops nabbed Orizaga for driving on sidewalks, knocking over signs and scaring the bejesus out of a hundred people or more, you wouldn't believe what he told the coppers back at the station!"

"He admitted he was illegal, right?" asked Rollie, already knowing the answer.

"You got it, Rol, all in upper case. The report read that Orizaga said, "I NO HAVE PAPERS.""

"So you got the 2008 police report?"

"You bet! It says a lot about how fucked up this town has become."

"Unbelievable! Ralston and the prosecutor told Pat about the prior felony, but they didn't have the quote, and that's important, don't you think?"

"Yeah, and not a one of these assholes in the *Cook County State's Attorney's Office*, Chicago cops, Sheriff's shop and the judge up at Skokie Branch called *Immigration*!

"Hey, the coppers could have called *Immigration*—you know I did a few times—but I know guys that didn't bother."

"Same here, Rol. You know, I asked around and some of the guys tell me word is out like no one's to call ICE. It's sort of unofficial kind of thing." Rollie shook his head in disbelief.

"Pat's brother, Denny, would be alive today if the fuckheads in charge of the arrest or the ding-a-lings at the State's Attorney called the Feds. What he get, Schus?"

"Two years probation, Rol, and released from probation February 2011."

"Who was the judge?"

"It's in the report—a real moron named O'Fallon, up at Skokie Branch."

"Schus, that asshole could have picked up the phone or directed someone to call the Feds. What about Roberto? Oh and before you answer, you know after we talked the other day, I followed Roberto and saw him talking to Manny Rodriguez at *Northeastern* at some pro immigration rally."

Schus smiled wryly.

"Not surprised—Manny's been gang banging most of his life. Last twenty years or so sort of a godfather in the collar suburbs and gets gangbangers to hustle votes. Okay, here's what I got on Roberto. He looks legal and the Windstar is his for sure—just some minor arrests for battery with no convictions."

"Hmm, work history, Schus?"

"Not that we could find, but a lot of these guys work off the books—lawn jobs, dishwashers, you know, shit jobs. I'm thinking Roberto's income now must be gang related.

This connection with Rodriguez could mean he's part a one of these Hispanic political organizations. You know, the bangers hide behind so called front groups like *United Community Organization*. Rodriguez's certainly involved with that bunch, Rol. That I know for sure."

"Good thinking. Yeah, for sure Rodriguez got to be connected to gangbangers. Look, I owe you, Schus."

"So what next?"

"Well, we hired a few vets. I got two guys who did time in Iraq to sit on Roberto's house for ten-twelve hours a day, starting this evening. Pat came up with 5K for starters. In fact I'm heading up there after our meeting here to set up the surveillance routine."

Schus whistled softly. "No shit, Rol. You're going to have to introduce me to McGurn. I mean, going all the way to get his brother's killer like this is really something and to come up with 5K to boot!"

"Yeah, good guy," agreed Rollie, nodding his head.

"You know, we went to *Mendel* together—graduated in '67. I don't really see him that much—he's a retired teacher and me an ex copper. I got to tell you, Schus, he's going after the whole bunch—Hunter-Goss, the commissioners who voted this thing and Dypsky."

"And, with your help, maybe Orizaga as well, huh Rol?"

"Hey, with a little luck, Schus, anything's possible."

"Look, Rol, send me the make and plates of your lookout cars and maybe I or one of my guys can, you know, give your guys a break."

"I was counting on your offer, Schus," said Rollie, smiling appreciatively. "I got the information right here, along with their cell numbers."

"Hey, hope I can help. You go after Orizaga, McGurn goes after the County and who knows—something might pop."

"You got it, Schus, and if we're lucky we can tie the two together and expose a whole lot of assholes."

"Unbelievable! You guys got the makings of a fuckin' movie—hope you pull this off, man. Look, I know you have to run—I'll get the check. Oh, I almost forgot—here are photos of Roberto and Raul."

"Thanks, man! I'll get copies made later on—got a guy to take care of this."

•

Rollie reached the Corliss watch at 6:30 p.m., as planned. Mario, the first vet on duty, was parked down the street of Roberto's building, with full view of the front door. Though he was tuned into his headset, he was clearly focused on his mission, his eyes never wavering. Rollie knocked on the passenger window, and Mario released the security lock. Wise move in this neighborhood, thought Rollie, especially at nighttime … He slid into the front seat and went over specifics with Mario who continued to stare out of his window. It was going to be a long night, as the next shift wouldn't start until 5:00 a.m. the next day, with Jose, Rollie reminded him.

"Hope you have some food with you," he added, realizing that the area was pretty much a food desert. Mario gestured to a large paper bag containing his lunch.

"Great—not the healthiest but it will get you through the night. Just be careful if you need to use the alley—don't get jumped or nothing."

Mario grinned, pointing to a switchblade lying next to him on the driver's seat; glancing down, Rollie could also make out the distinct outline of a hand gun in Mario's pocket. He was not a man to be messed with. Relieved, Rollie explained there would be other guys helping out and that he would work on a schedule as soon as he knew their availability. Never taking his eyes off Roberto's building, Mario thanked him in Spanish and Rollie exited. He could hear the sound of the door locks behind him.

•

At home in Beverly, Pat continued his education in immigration trends. Apparently, there was a lot going on with the pro-enforcement people, whether border advocates or anti-sanctuary folk. He had the feeling that both Joan and his old professor were grooming him for political activism, perhaps at a national level. Joan had sent him some congressional testimony that he found especially interesting. *The U.S. House of Representatives* was now controlled by Republicans, while the *Judiciary Committee* was chaired by a representative named Reece from Austin, Texas; he not only stood against liberal immigration policies like the *Good Neighbor Act* but also supported increased deportations for felons and other questionable illegals. Pat continued to read testimony from the *Chair of the Immigration Subcommittee*, Representative Sutton from California. It looked as though Sutton had brought any number of police chiefs before the committee for the express purpose of demonstrating support for ICE initiatives to deport those illegals deemed dangerous. Perhaps it would be a good idea for the Judiciary Committee to subpoena some Cook County Officials, particularly Dypsky or Korshak, he thought, jotting down a reminder to contact Joan about this possibility.

Pat was impressed with the efforts of the *Judiciary Subcommittee on Immigration* and its efforts to pass legislation that would remove illegal convicted felons within thirty days, while prohibiting probation or suspended sentences. Had that legislation been in place, Pat concluded, Denny would be alive. Reality set in and Pat realized President Haesi sure to veto any enforcement measure. Maybe things might change in 2012.

•

Paul Nikos and Dan Dypsky ordered a pitcher of beer and sat at a table in *Muldoon's Saloon* at 112th and Western. It was a quiet Thursday night, with all the college kids gone and just a few die-hard Sox fans at the bar.

"Thanks for coming out, Paul," said Dan nervously. "So look, I don't want to get caught off guard here, but I got to tell you this McGurn seems like he's not going to fade away. You know anything about him?"

"Nope. He's just a regular guy in the neighborhood I see at church—seems harmless enough."

Someone once said, "Beware the fury of a patient man," said Dypsky, between gritted teeth. "There's talk of an amendment and you know it won't go anywhere with Korshak, Varbanov and Alport running the show. So here's the deal. As I see it, the amendment gets discussed at a Cook County Board meeting, the press plays it up like they have already, and I look stupid because we let this Orizaga out."

"So more bad press but that will peter out, Dan. What's eating you?" Nikos studied his cell phone, scrolling down an assortment of text messages.

"What worries me is a lawsuit filed by some big name outfit looking for publicity—that could ruin my reputation."

"Dan, you didn't pass the damn ordinance, so forget about it," came the irritated reply. "You asked me to look at the standing issue and I asked around—and let me tell you, there's no way in hell McGurn or anyone else has standing to file a law suit."

"So if he files, then what?"

"I guess minor publicity that's short lived—I can't think of one judge that will give him the time of day."

Dypsky still looked concerned. He looked across the table at Nikos who was tapping out a reply to one of the texts with a thin stylus.

"Paul, you know and I know I didn't have to follow the ordinance because federal law on immigration trumps local laws. The publicity will kill me. I'm thinking they're going to have me at the next *Cook County Board* meeting and I need you to get me the right talking points."

"Not a problem, Dan. I'll have it for you by Monday," said Nikos in a tone that suggested he had no sense of urgency about the matter.

"I don't have a good feeling about this," continued Dypsky. "McGurn has recruited a retired homicide detective and some professor. What's more, his wife has investigated high profile elected officials at the *Illinois Grievance Commission*. Now I got this to worry about."

Nikos casually topped up Dypsky's drink and then emptied the pitcher into his own glass.

"I wouldn't worry—I mean what can they possibly do?"

"Probably nothing, but what really concerns me is this retired detective Rollie Dufner helping him. He lives in Mount Greenwood. Ever heard of him?"

"Nope."

"He's a tenacious hard ass. I made a few calls, and there's maybe thirty or more guys in Menard Prison because of him. Oh, and one more thing. Did you know that Orizaga had a prior felony conviction back in 2009 and no one contacted ICE? Orizaga drunk as a skunk and with no license wiped out half the neighborhood near where McGurn got killed."

"No. First I heard of this—so what happened?"

"Judge O'Fallon up at Skokie Branch gives him two years probation and, four months later, he kills Denny McGurn. So Pat McGurn is really pissed!"

"So what can he do, Dan? I mean give me a break—this Orizaga's in Mexico!" Nikos leaned back in his chair, hands clasped behind his head.

"Hope you're right. It's just that with this Dufner stirring things up, I'm worried. Let's get out of here. I've got to call Guy and see if anybody died at *Stroger Hospital.* Maybe you haven't heard but one of the combatants in D Wing got clobbered with some kind of metal object—someone snuck it in to the jail."

DAY THIRTEEN, FRIDAY, SEPTEMBER 9, 2011

Rollie worked on the spreadsheet, providing schedules, compensation, procedures, and time lines. Mario would work ten hour shifts from 6:00 p.m. to 4:00 a.m., while Jose would cover 6:00 a.m. to 4:00 p.m. Schus would do his best to cover the two- hour afternoon window and get tactical unit guys he could trust to cover the 4:00 a.m. slot. He had assured Rollie he could pull this off for at least two weeks. If there were a conflict, Rollie said he would cover and maybe even get Pat to help. Next, he got out his notes and saw he had entered, "*Southeast Observer*, September 7, 2011." A Google search to see if there was anything of import there brought up the community paper's simple website, providing local news and ads in both Spanish and English. Across the top it read, "*For Community Minded Residents of South Chicago, Irondale, Vets Park, South Dearing, Hegewisch and East Side.*"

The issue contained the usual community reports on high school sports' programs, meetings for *United Community Organization* (UCO), *La Fuerza*, *Local School Council* meetings, as well as want ads, personals, and so forth. Pretty typical community newspaper stuff, thought Rollie, identifying the publisher as a Senor Max Orana. The paper circulated on Tuesday, September 6th and the very next day he had gone to the rally—that could mean something and, that, in police work, qualified as a lead.

Following his instincts, Rollie left home and headed east on 103rd Street, towards the *South Chicago, Fourth District Police Station*. On the way over he called his old friend Watch Commander Frank Higgins and set up a lunch appointment. As he pulled into the *Fourth District* parking lot, he recalled his uncle telling him when he was a kid that the district headquarters had been built there because of the riots that had taken place in nearby Trumbull Park fifty years earlier. Probably still a lot of racial tension in the area, he thought. Walking in, he saw his old friend, Frank Higgins, in a starched Lieutenant's uniform, talking to the desk sergeant.

"Rollie, good to see you! Say, Ralph, meet a buddy a mine—Rollie Dufner," said Higgins, evidently pleased to see him.

The burly desk sergeant pumped his hand enthusiastically. Wincing, Rollie forced out a "Good to meet you," and, with bruised hand retrieved, turned his attention to Frank Higgins.

"You goin' crusin'?" he asked, and Higgins, hearing a hidden agenda, immediately agreed.

"Okay, Ralph—you know how to reach me if all hell breaks loose! Might stop at *Jimmy's* for lunch."

"Best place in town for greasy burgers," quipped Ralph. "Nothing like them in Chicago, even if I say so myself!"

They walked over to Commander Higgins' squad car and sat with the engine running for a few minutes. After Rollie outlined his involvement with Pat McGurn's quest for justice and his hunch that Orizaga might be in the city they started cruising the district. The Commander gave him the hard facts: the area was 75% Hispanic, crime was way up, schools were overcrowded, and there was major gang infiltration.

"Pretty big district, right, Frank?"

"Yeah, Rol. The 10th Ward and Fourth District pretty much overlap in an area five miles long and three miles wide. Let's go over the bridge on 106th Street and I'll turn north on Ewing."

"Sounds good. What about the Blacks, Frank?"

"Nothing but problems at both high schools because those idiots at the Board of Education keep sending black gang bangers to *Jefferson High School* on Wolf Street. You see, they keep closing the real bad high schools in Englewood and Woodlawn and then send the worst actors to us."

"*Jefferson* used to be a pretty good school by reputation, as I recall," observed Rollie as they drove by one derelict building after another. All the stores seemed to have security gates and barred windows; here and there, groups of Hispanic males huddled on street corners, boldly passing joints from one to the other, too "cool" to hide their activities.

"Sure was," replied Higgins. "And so was *Rowan*. The school board managed to ruin that place going back twenty-five years or so."

Higgins continued down Ewing and crossed the Calumet River, his eyes taking in every detail, every movement, and every person on the road.

"Look, about your hunch, Rollie—talk about a long shot finding this Orizaga, but I guess you thought this through."

"Look, Frank, I don't want to brag, but hunches are what got me a whole lot of convictions for twenty-five years. Look I forgot to mention that I saw a copy of the *Southeast Observer* on the brother's front seat after I tailed him."

"Oh, now I get it, that's your lead. So you're thinking if a Hispanic gangster from the North Side has the *Southeast Observer* in his car there's a connection. Look, if your man's in the Fourth District, it's a good bet he'll be on the north end of the ward. My guys tell me some of the time they think they're in Tijuana! I'll drive around a few blocks before we stop."

"What's your take on the gangs here in the 10ᵗʰ Ward?" asked Rollie. "Well, everyone reports to a guy named Archuletta, a real bad ass and deeply connected to cartels in Mexico."

"Feds got to be looking at him, right?"

"Oh yeah, but sometimes I don't know about them—seems like they don't give a shit. We think this Archuletta is involved with this Samienga Cartel gang in Nuevo Laredo. Gang crimes sent two guys down there to investigate and they came back empty."

"Help from the mayor, Frank?"

"You know, I'm not sure because there's talk he wants to, you know, kiss the Hispanics ass just like Korshak did with that ordinance and, besides, I don't trust that asshole Gainer who heads up gang crimes. Oh yeah, get this—I heard from Deputy Duggan the other day that the City Council, with Mayor Gill's support, is going to vote on an open city ordinance that I guess shores up the County ordinance that your guy McGurn's pissed off about."

"You know he's trying to get the ordinance changed," commented Rollie.

They turned down 90ᵗʰ Street, driving past another stretch of boarded up buildings. The only viable businesses seemed to be a Currency Exchange and a laundromat. There was not a convenience store in sight, let alone a grocery store.

"Yeah, saw that in *The Globe*. He got a chance, you think?"

Rollie shrugged.

"I don't know—I get justice done the old fashioned way, not by changing ordinances! You know what, Frank, the more gangs the better, these idiot politicians must be thinking. Jeez, I wish this Gill would wake up and get real about crime. So tell me about this alderman here."

"Well, the Dukavich family ran this ward for forty years, but they are pretty much out of it after big shot Milan's health problems. Now a guy named Kruse runs it. He knows he has to cater to the Mexicans. Most of us think he's likely to lose next time because of *The Hispanic Community Organization* aka *HCO*. Look, here's *Jimmy's*—he's a cousin of the Dukavich family yet, for some reason, he's estranged from the politicians in the family. Jimmy just always wanted to run a restaurant, and he's got a pretty good read on all the craziness going on in the 10th Ward."

The two men got out of the car and walked across the parking lot towards the entrance. A waitress escorted them to a booth next to a window looking onto 92nd street. At first glance, Rollie thought she was in her thirties, but the grey roots to her platinum hair suggested otherwise.

"You asked about Kruse," murmured Higgins. "Well, I'll tell you, Rol, between you and me, a lot of the guys think he's all bullshit—you know, tied in with the old political machine. Now he has to kiss this new mayor's ass, and my guys have no use for Gill. Like I told you, Rol, the connected folks around here are looking to run the Ward, but they got a problem—their leader, Park District boss Hal Rojas, just got put in jail by the Feds because he skimmed federal grant money."

Rollie smiled, as if to say this was nothing new.

"Fuckin' city never changes. First the Wasps, than the Paddys, next Dagos, Croats, Serbs, Pollocks, Lugans, Jews, Czechs, Slovaks, Brothers, Hispanics and now Islamists. I could go on and on—they're all on the make."

"Sounds like you read the famous author Nelson Algren who coined the phrase *City on the Make* in an essay written maybe seventy years ago. It was his take on the city back in mid century that it was run by hustlers, con artists and corrupt politicians."

"I ain't much of a reader, Frank, but maybe I'm gonna get this Algren's book."

"Here comes Sophie, our waitress. How about if we both order the bacon cheeseburgers and cokes?"

"Sounds good, Frank, but black coffee for me."

"Regular, Commander?" Asked Sophie, twirling a blonde lock between long, fake fingernails.

"You got it, Sophie, and same for my friend. Oh, he wants coffee."

"You here to help clean up all the garbage around here, mister?" she asked innocently.

Without answering, Rollie stood up and bowed. "Glad to meet you," he said.

"Commander, your friend here's got manners. I like that—he's good looking, to boot. None of these bums around here ever greet a lady proper."

She patted her hair self-consciously, then smoothed down her apron. Rollie shot her his most charming smile and winked at her before she took off for the kitchen with their order.

"She's a real character, Rol—been with Jimmy from the start. Real neighborhood gal. Doesn't look her age at all—she must be on the wrong side of fifty!"

Looking around, they took in the bustle of noontime South Chicago. There was an unending line of people waiting for take-outs while thirty or more patrons scarfed down the famous burgers. A man right out of the 50's with a ducktail haircut played Dion's, "*The Wanderer*," on an old fashioned jukebox. Stanley, a beer-bellied former steel worker asked Sophie to dance.

"You kiddin'!" exclaimed Sophie, a look of outrage clouding her face.

"So much for customer service!' laughed Higgins.

Ignoring his comment, Sophie, disappeared into the kitchen, her ample hips swaying; she returned a few minutes later with their order. The greasy burgers were served with fries and draped with bacon. Higgins was just explaining how Jimmy claimed he was the first to sell bacon cheeseburgers, when Jimmy himself walked up to the table, extending a handshake to Rollie.

"Say, Jimmy, this here's an old buddy a mine, Rollie Dufner, retired homicide detective."

"Oh yeah? How you doing? Retired you say? Ever work around here?" asked Jimmy.

"No, most of the time I locked up the bad guys on the West Side," said Rollie, keeping explanations to a minimum.

Placing his hands on both men's shoulders, Jimmy bent down, into the gap between them.

"Say, listen you guys," he whispered. "I got to tell you I'm going to sell this joint—the fuckin' Mexys are crazy 'cause they're fighting out front here. There's been gang shit at Jefferson High and Rowan—I mean nothing but constant gang wars between the *negras* and *mexys*."

"*Negras* and *Mexys*, Jimmy?" asked Rollie, raising his eyebrows.

"That's what we called them at Fort Polk in the seventies," said Jimmy,

"That's not what they were called at Camp Pendleton back in the day. Say these high schools, Jimmy—a lot of gangs, right?"

'Hey, Frank can tell you—lotta gangs, man! My oldest works at both schools—teaches a class at Jeff and one at Rowan; the rest of his day he's sort of a troubleshooter working with the gangs and helping the better kids."

"Yeah, my guys work with Mike all the time," confirmed Higgins.

Jimmy nodded, smiling broadly.

"Sounds like a good kid, Jimmy," said Rollie. "You've got to be proud!"

"He's a do-gooder with balls—like he cares about these kids, but won't take any shit, you know what I mean?"

"Gotcha Jimmy. I'd like to meet him."

"Tell you what—he's stopping by about 3:00 p.m. to kill some time before a football game at Eckersall. I think Rowan's playing Jeff and there could be trouble, Frank."

"Yeah, Jimmy, we got guys on overtime for that. Remember, last year we had to lock up twenty-five kids and the cheerleaders went at it, too. One girl put a Rowan kid in the hospital, I remember."

"Look, Jimmy, you say your boy Mike's coming by at 3:00 p.m.?—I'll stop and have a short chat," said Rollie, standing up to leave.

"Say Rol, I got some time—let me show you some more of the district."

"Appreciate it, Frank," said Rollie, leaving twenty bucks on top of the check.

"Thanks, Jimmy—I'll be back in a few hours. Can't wait to meet this son of yours!"

The two old friends walked out of the restaurant and headed towards Higgins' unmarked squad car, across the parking lot. Within a few minutes, they were a block east of Commercial Street, an area notorious for criminal activity, run down apartments, transients and gang turf wars.

"So what do you figure, Frank—how many in this square block are gang-banging?"

"Maybe a hundred or more and that includes girlfriends, wives, kids—and the main ones are the so-called enforcers."

"That figures—who are the beat cops?"

"Well, they're not the best—mostly guys on days ready to retire."

Out of habit, Rollie peered left and right out of the window, taking in every detail of street life. After years on the force, he had learned to be vigilant at all times and to miss nothing.

"So what's the money source of these gangs?"

"The usual—drugs, protection and, occasionally, prostitution. Lately, we had to deal with phony identification papers, but that was stopped by the Feds. Of course, we helped, but I think another operation has started on the North Side."

"Really"

"Yeah, it was in the papers. There was this old guy who ran the racket out of his printing company at 92nd and Commercial. He's the father of an alderman from the 51st Ward on the North Side."

"I remember that—the Feds ran a sting, as I recall."

"Yeah we had a joint task force set up. I had two of my best guys to work with the FBI."

"Old guy named Ramon Castro—his kid, Sammy the alderman, claims he knew nothing."

"Lying sack a shit, this Sammy Castro—don't you think, Frank?"

"You got it, but the ole man's doing time at Marion downstate. Hey, the printing company was in that boarded up storefront, kitty-corner from us."

Rollie leaned into the passenger window, pressing his forehead against the glass. He could make out the faded signage above the main entrance to the building, still displaying the name, "Castro."

"So the kid knew the score but didn't want the ole man's shop in his Ward?"

"That's what the FBI told me."

"Unbelievable, Frank. These assholes come here illegally and then get slimy politicians to front for them to get phony papers. You know, maybe there's a connection for my buddy Pat."

"Could be and like I said, we think another one is operational probably on the North Side. These ID's look real and the illegals pay through the nose."

They continued cruising south on Commercial, with Rollie scanning each street with radar eyes. It was pretty quiet as neighborhoods go, but he knew that nighttime would bring out all the undesirables just spoiling for a fight. Higgins pointed out an old building that was now a block of apartments but had clearly seen better days. It turned out that his grandfather had lived in the building when the neighborhood was more genteel. That would have been around 1900, when it was a boarding house.

"No kidding, Frank."

"Yeah, he was a pipefitter and helped build those refineries across the border in East Chicago. Back in those days, a fella could hop on a train and get to work at the refineries and on weekends catch another train to go downtown Chicago take in a show and get a meal."

"That's really interesting," said Rollie, momentarily distracted from his street surveillance.

"Yeah, that's how he met my grandma at some function in the South Loop; they got married at Corpus Christie in 1910, we think."

"Tell me about the rest of the district. What's the deal with Hegewisch?"

"Well, that's far south and pretty quiet—mainly white—Serbs, Croats, Poles, few Irish left and Hispanics moving in. Lot of city workers and retired displaced steel workers kind of area, Rol. You know, sort of like Mount Greenwood in a way. Guys I know hang at Club 91, and, in the summertime, they fish and play bocce ball along *Wolf Lake*. Some of my guys hang out there after the second or third shift to shoot eight ball"

"What about the East Side?"

"Well, mixed. Whites moving out and Mexicans moving in. Otherwise pretty quiet. It's just that *Jefferson High* is seething with crime and they can't seem to get a decent principal. Gang fights all the time—I send as many as ten or more uniforms over there every day at dismissal. The incumbent principal doesn't have a clue."

"What about the school officers?"

"Political hacks, Rol. One guy's tied in with the Petrutis political family and weighs about 300lbs, to boot, a real dog ass."

"The department still not enforcing weight requirement?"

"In all my years, Rollie, they never did because of clout. Look, the real gangbang stuff, you know, the heavy-duty rackets, are in the area between 87th Street and 92nd Street. On Commercial like I said, not south."

They drove back to the *Fourth District* near Trumbull Park. When they pulled up, Higgins looked distinctly uncomfortable. He hesitated a few moments.

"Rol, I wish you well, and you know I'm ready to help but …"

Rollie turned toward Higgins and patted him on the shoulder.

"I know, Frank, sure you got doubts—I know that, but it's in my gut that this piece of shit is here in town, maybe in Little Village, or Pilsen, or even in your neck of the woods. I just know he didn't run to Mexico and I got to believe Roberto will fuck up."

Opening the car door, Rollie handed him a picture of Orizaga and his brother that Schus had given him the day before.

"If you hear anything—"

"Sure, Rollie, I'll pass this around at roll call, but one more thing—"

"Yeah, Frank?"

"I know this is premature, Rollie, but if by some chance this Orizaga is here in the Fourth District—"

Rollie interrupted "Frank, I can tell you one thing—my guy, Pat, don't trust the County after what they pulled. I'm telling you, he's convinced Denny'd be alive if the County and city didn't fuck up two years ago and would have this punk Orizaga if they didn't let him loose two weeks ago."

"I get it, but don't go crazy on me, Rol, and get McGurn to do something he'll regret."

"No, no you don't understand. That maybe me, but that's not Pat. I may have another idea," laughed Rollie.

"That's what I'm afraid of. You always were a little over the top."

Rollie gave a quick salute as he walked to his car.

"Not to worry, Commander," he called out.

When Rollie walked back into the restaurant, Jimmy gestured towards a corner booth where a man in his middle thirties was bent over a stack of papers. He looked up as Rollie approached and stood to greet him.

"Mike Dukavich, Sir. My dad told me you were coming in. I've got, oh, maybe twenty minutes because of this game. You're a retired detective, right?"

"Yeah, sure am, Mike—the name's Rollie."

Rollie gave Mike the "in a nutshell" account of the Denny McGurn case. Mike listened quietly, sipping a root beer, until Rollie brought his story to an end.

"So I think Roberto, the brother, has been down here in South Chicago," Rollie concluded.

"I'm sure you ran these two on some police database, right?"

Yeah, sure did. Roberto's sort of under the radar up north—nothing serious that we can think work with. Raul the killer illegal for sure has a prior felony. Oh and one more thing. Roberto's a pal of Rodriguez the congressman from the western burbs."

"Really, that could mean something—can never tell."

Mike shrugged.

"Is Roberto a citizen?"

"Yeah, my guy Schuster confirmed that with the immigration people."

"Well, that tells me that this Roberto is more than a brother—I'm guessing he recruited brother Raul for some reason and the twenty-five or thirty grand tells me something. So you got police reports on Raul, too, huh?"

"We got police reports and all that, but I'm thinking if we watch Roberto we might get somewhere. In fact, I set up a 24/7 watch that started last night."

Mike looked at his watch.

"Well, let me think, Rollie. All the Mexicans do read that paper you mentioned—it's free you know. As you suggest, this neighborhood might be a good place to hide, because there's always a lot of strangers in and out—you know families doubling up."

"How many illegals, Mike?"

"Oh yeah I'll bet there are well over 400 in each of my schools—you know, the law says we can't check. Last year some census takers came in the area and they were completely confused, because they knew many of the residents lied. What would stop him from going right back to Mexico?"

"Well, Mike, in the first place, getting out is pretty difficult. Besides, my theory is that he owes somebody because some serious money got him out."

"Hmm, Rollie, I'm no cop, but what you're saying sure makes sense."

"You got it, Mike. I know it's a long shot, but we detectives operate on hunches and this one sticks with me."

"Even in these high schools, we've got some of the enforcers—I mean real bad asses who are smart enough to keep their noses clean. The good news is that we've got an eye on them. There's also the *wannabees* and they're just a nuisance—girls *and* guys. Our problem is mainly the fighting between the rival Black and Hispanic gangs. Occasionally, I talk with what's his name in *Gang Crimes*."

"Gainer's head of *Gang Crimes*, Mike."

"Yeah, that's him but I'm not too keen on him—sort of a braggart type. Gives all these clichés like, 'I got a guy' or, 'we'll take care of it' and nothing really happens."

"Look, I know him and you're absolutely right. Between you and me, he's a real asshole because his uncle's an alderman. Anything else come to mind? I'm fishing here."

Mike glanced down at his watch.

"One more thing and I gotta go—there are two kids who would have been seniors at *Rowan* that I got out of the gangs and got them enrolled downstate at a boarding school in Murphysboro. Well, they're both smart as whips and were enforcers, I mean high up for eighteen year olds and tied in with the Samienga gang. They were leaders at the school in a bad way but, over time, I got into their heads. In short, they wanted out."

"So you got them out of the gang and installed downstate?"

"Yeah, when you leave a gang serious trouble follows."

"Sure, Mike, I understand, so tell me how did you swing getting these kids downstate?"

"I got some wealthy folk to underwrite this and convinced them that the kids were worth it. My guys were a special case because I thought they might get killed."

"I'm impressed. Is the school working for your guys?"

"So far. They've been there eleven weeks now and no problem. This place has a summer arrangement with *Southern Illinois University* in neighboring Carbondale, so it worked out. These kids know everything there is to know around here, and I'll bet if either of those Orizaga brothers gang-banged around here, they would know them."

"Really? You been down there to visit?"

"Not yet, but I plan to."

"Do you call them?"

"Sure—maybe once every two weeks or so. I check in with Headmaster Shryock."

"What's he say?"

"Well, as you might guess, there aren't too many Hispanic gang enforcers in Murphysboro but it sounds like they're fitting in. Shryock arranged for a couple of Mexican students at SIU to mentor the kids and that helps."

Rollie pulled out a photo of Roberto and Raul and handed it to Mike.

"Here's a photo of the brothers—and here's twenty bucks for you to overnight it to these guys. Just tell them you're e doing me a favor."

"Sure—there's a *Fast Trak Express* down the street. I'll take care of this after the game.

Gotta go—just got a text that the brawling has already started!"

"Thanks a lot for your time, Mike, and good luck at the brawl!"

"You know, a few years ago, Rowan lost the game and won the brawl and the former principal had a prep rally."

"You're kidding!"

"Can't make this stuff up. See you!"

●

Rollie decided to take an alternate route to *Ruth's,* but getting stuck at the 106th Street Bridge had to wait for two international cargo ships to be guided by tugs into the harbor. He was always fascinated by the freight traffic and usually wouldn't have minded the delay. Today, however, he was in a hurry to meet up with Pat McGurn. He turned off the engine and wearily got out to light a cigarette. Leaning against the car door, he closed his eyes and exhaled slowly. Strains of Gordon Lightfoot's hit ballad, *The Wreck of the Edmund Fitzgerald*, began to play in his memory. When was it—1975? The freighter had gone down on Lake Superior, all souls on board. Yes, the crew must have heard that wave break over the railing, and every man knew, *"as the captain did, too, T'was the witch of November come stealing* …" By the time he opened his eyes again, the ships had made it into the harbor and the bridge was open to traffic once more.

When he arrived at *Ruth's*, Dooley was over by the jukebox fumbling for money and four or five of the regulars were watching a high-speed car chase on the enormous flat screen TV. Pat was sitting at the bar, a big grin across his face. Rollie looked at him quizzically.

"Hit the Jackpot?" he asked.

"Sort of," said Pat. "It's a girl! Maeve, clocking in at 8lbs. Mom and baby doing just fine!"

"Congrats, Pat, now you got two grandkids I'm happy for you! Hey, how about moving to a table? Some of the stuff we're into here best kept quiet, you know what I mean?"

They carried two beer mugs and a pitcher over to a quiet table next to one of the windows.

"You first, Pat."

"Well, I don't know if I can trust this Wagner. I just got some bad vibes like nothing's going to change."

"Well, Pat, I guess if you get the County to change the law and none of these other bad ass illegals get loose, you and the family will feel like you won a battle. Well, I gotta tell you, in my business the only justice is for this punk to get locked up and for a long time at that. Some guys I know would kill him."

"I know, Rollie—some of my siblings and nieces feel the same way, but they're beginning to see what's really at stake here. If I can make the ten clowns who voted for the ordinance—as well as Hunter-Goss, Dypsky, and Korshak—look like the fools they really are, well, that's something."

"Talk to Jack Riley?"

"Not yet, but Wagner said he talked to him and Riley left a message, so I'll call him."

"So, Pat, you're telling me you think these commissioners are going to change?"

"Probably not, but, hey, maybe Jack Riley might have something. But the more I think about it, it's a real long shot because I don't get the sense these people try to persuade one another on hot button issues."

"So what else?"

"Joe had me contact this guy, McLaughlin, at *Southern Illinois University.*

His take was really pessimistic—suggested that even the five that voted against it only did it for political cover."

"What d'you mean?"

"Well, he's said they're all bullshit—Riley's close to Korshak, Googan's in financial trouble as is Wagner, and the other two represent heavy non-Hispanic white districts. McLaughlin figures they're looking out for their own skins."

Rollie shook his head.

"So it sounds like you're 'pissin in the wind' as we used to say in the marines."

"That's one way to put it, I guess. I don't know if I mentioned it before, but this McLaughlin has research from 1972 that lists all the political crooks that have been convicted. In Cook County and Chicago, if memory serves, the number was seventy-nine. I'm talking judges, governors, state officials, state legislators, congressmen, city officials and aldermen."

"I'd like to buy this McLaughlin a drink. About time somebody got those numbers out," said Rollie.

"Yeah, good guy—told me on the phone he's from the South Side. Went to *Bishop Stritch Prep*. I think and graduated late 70's. Grew up in *Saint Thomas More Parish*. You know probably ten years younger than you and I, Rol."

Rollie looked up at the *Ruth* regulars who were still mesmerized by one movie chase scene after another. The sound of screeching brakes and high pitched sirens created a surreal backdrop to their conversation.

"You know, it's no wonder there's so many bad drivers out there with shit like this on the tube," he observed. "Okay, second day of surveillance and all seems okay. Schus texted me to let me know his guys will do the best they can to cover that two hour window in the morning and afternoon. I'll go up to from time to time to give breaks and maybe you can help, too."

"No problem—just call. Lately, I'm home reading stuff from my friends downstate. So your guys okay with the watch?"

"Oh yeah, good guys just waiting for the call from the Academy. That won't happen for at least a month."

Rollie pulled out a sheet of paper from his pocket and handed it to Pat. It was the two week surveillance schedule, outlining hours to be covered and the rate of pay. So far, there was nothing to report. Mario had followed

Roberto to a taco joint around midnight, but he had returned immediately. It looked like Roberto stayed home a lot. He then went over his time in the 10th Ward, describing his field trip with Higgins and and the meeting with Mike. Pat listened attentively.

"So what d'you think?"

"I gotta tell you, I like this connection with the kids downstate."

Rollie took a long pull on his beer and watched as Dooley joined the bar flies in front of the TV.

"Well, if these two kids see a familiar face in those pics, we have a Samiega gang connection and that's a start. If not, we keep a watch on Roberto and if he's connecting with Raul, he's bound to fuck up, I got to believe. Look, I know what you're thinking, but I must tell you, we've started investigations with a lot less."

"No, Rol—I'm with you 100%. Don't know how to thank you."

"Look, pal o' mine, I love getting these creeps and putting them away. It's like I always felt I was put here to clean up all the shit I can in this fucked up, crime ridden town."

Pat took a long pull on his beer.

"I was thinking earlier about this Manny Rodriguez and you following Roberto two days ago. I mean a marginal character like Roberto hanging with big shot Manny should mean something."

"Manny's always been slick and he's got cover from political machines in DuPage and Kane counties, plus Mexican cartels. Anyhow the speech at *Northeastern* got me the South Chicago lead. Manny won't dirty himself with harboring a fugitive, but I wouldn't rule out a gang connection. Important thing is we got what I think is a good lead with the *Southeast Observer*. Let's hope Mike has some luck with the kids downstate. Look, Pat, let's talk tomorrow—I got to go. Sally wants me to look at refrigerators somewhere."

"I'll give you a call Rol."

•

That night, Pat was preoccupied and avoided talking about his recent activities. Before bed, Clare, ever observant, asked him if everything was all right. For the last two weeks, all Pat could talk about was getting justice for Denny and holding everyone accountable, from the Cook County Board commissioners down to Alphy, the asinine detective at the bottom of the totem pole. He had briefly asked about the new baby, smiling in response to her gushing description of Maeve, but seemed very detached. He said little during their evening meal and there was an aura of heaviness around him. Of course, she knew he was delighted to welcome a new grandchild but Maeve was not his focus. To her surprise, he had admitted he had not yet called Molly to congratulate her—and had forgotten to send her a text!

Clare changed the subject.

"Oh, I forgot to mention—we got a memo at work today that there's going to be a ten-year, 9/11 memorial of some kind at the Mars Building Plaza on Randolph. Why don't we go down and pay our respects? Might give us a more global perspective if we spend some time remembering that awful day."

"Good idea—ten years ago was like the baby boomers' Pearl Harbor."

Pat sounded more upbeat, but privately, felt troubled, almost uneasy as though he were about to receive some unpleasant revelation. Around 3:00 a.m., he woke up suddenly and realized he had been communing with Denny. As he struggled to recall specifics, he remembered his readings of Carl Jung and the importance of writing down what you remember in a dream. That required getting out of bed, finding pen and paper and following the dream backwards. He had actually done that a few times in his life, particularly when struggling with issues in the military and during his teaching profession. Quietly, he slipped out of bed, found a legal pad and began the backward spiral of his dream conversation. The setting was in a gazebo-like structure on the banks of a wide river; everything was covered in a heavy mist and Denny himself, except for his smile, was more of a shadow than a flesh and blood presence. He did indeed have something to say, and Pat wrote:

"Amendment a waste of time … *Rollie* …"

Pat stayed up the rest of the night.

DAYS FOURTEEN AND FIFTEEN, SATURDAY AND SUNDAY, SEPTEMBER 10&11, 2011.

The next morning, Pat spent a few hours poring over more of the documents that his *University of Illinois* friends had sent his way. Since he had not managed to sleep the night before, it was difficult concentrating; however, black coffee and sheer determination sharpened his resolve. He was particularly interested in some of the transcripts of earlier U.S. Judiciary Committee testimonies—the ones that outlined the many issues related to implementing the *Secure Communities Program*. After reading the documents, he could see how difficult it was for *Immigration and Customs Enforcement* to get local cooperation. Border enforcement was difficult, to be sure, but internal enforcement was even more problematic, given the laws and policies. He had just decided to take a break when Clare returned from running the usual Saturday errands. Finding Pat in the library, she suggested they take the 10:30 a.m. downtown to make the noon 9/11 Memorial. Pat, too tired to think of driving, readily agreed. They just made the train at 91st Street, climbing into the empty carriage at the rear just as the conductor was about to flag the "all clear" to the engineer.

During the twenty-minute ride, Clare went over a conversation she had had with co-worker, Bonnie Risk, the day before. Pat leaned back in his seat and closed his eyes; fighting off sleep, he listened as Clare explained that Bonnie had worked for ten years at the State's Attorney's office as an attorney but had left abruptly because of her dislike of State's Attorney Hunter-Goss. Apparently, Bonnie wasn't surprised at what happened—in fact, she had known the County was considering the ordinance for some time, and had personally contacted ICE on the quiet at least twice; however, she hadn't received much of a response. When she learned the ordinance had been passed, she figured Hunter-Goss was behind it from the beginning.

"People over there are getting real disillusioned but are too timid to speak up," explained Clare.

"Bonnie also suggested that Simpkus probably knew that the ordinance was likely to pass and, for that reason, kept getting continuances. We looked him up and saw that he has a pending complaint for stealing a client's retainer fee."

"Does Bonnie have the Simpkus file?"

"No, some new guy does, but they have the same investigator, Rick Jensen. As you know, I have the upmost respect for Rick. He said sleazy lawyers like Simpkus always insisted on cash retainers and didn't care if it was dirty money."

"So let me get this straight—it sounds like your pals, Bonnie and Rick, are convinced Simpkus knew all along what was going on behind the scenes and that he could get Orizaga out."

Clare nodded.

"Bonnie also said that all those continuances last July were bogus. Efforts should have been made to expedite the conviction and sentence Orizaga."

"Well, that explains a lot more, I guess. So I'm also thinking that Hunter-Goss's number two man, Sheehan, was indirectly complicit because he knew the ordinance was forthcoming."

"Absolutely! And they all have cover. As for Murphy, well I'm with you on that, Pat—I think she was blindsided."

"What about the judges—you know, Martin and Santiago?

"She said she had no use for either of them—just political hacks. If you're thinking of a disciplinary complaint against either, forget about it."

"Funny you mention that because I thought it would be interesting to file a complaint against that fool judge at Skokie Branch that removed Raul from probation."

"Oh, you mean that O'Fallon from the previous deal in 2009? No, Bonnie wouldn't know him because he's at Skokie Branch. When I told her about the prior conviction, she just shook her head in disgust."

The conductor announced 35ᵀᴴ STREET WHITE SOX PARK and, as the train slowed down, Pat opened his eyes, anxious for a glimpse of his beloved stadium.

"Remind you of Denny?" asked Clare softly.

Pat turned his back to the window.

"Yeah. So let's see—elected officials, prosecutors, defense attorneys, county staff attorneys, commissioners … I mean nobody's to be trusted, I'm thinking."

"I hate to see you so cynical, Pat. Now didn't you tell me that this McLaughlin down at Southern even thinks your so called commissioner supporters are guilty bystanders in all of this as well?"

"Yeah—Joe says the same thing and Denny agrees."

"*Denny?*"

"Yeah, I talked to him last night. I know it sounds nutty. Hey, it was a dream," said Pat defensively, noting Clare's visible shock.

"Give me a break, Pat—there's a fine line between sanity and madness!"

"Is there? Look, I've heard you and your pals get mystical—I think your pal, Lois, claims she and her sister talk to spirits or something. Hey, you told me you saw a psychic once, right?"

"Yes, and she told me I'd marry you," admitted Clare, a half smile playing on her lips.

"Okay, then—there's more to life than meets the eyes, right? I'm telling you I communed with him. Sure it was weird and he sort of told me not to trust any of the bastards. When I mentioned Rollie, he nodded with a reassuring smile that suggested, 'Go for it.'"

As the conductor announced LASALLE STREET DOWNTOWN, they stood up and made the way towards the exit. Once on the platform, they walked towards Van Buren. An "EL" train rumbled overhead, and Pat instinctively covered his ears, unused to the screeching of metal on metal. Van Buren always felt seedy to him, what with the homeless folk who congregated there, the pigeons, and the nearby pawn shops.

"So what were you all engrossed about this morning?" asked Clare, once the tracks above them were clear.

"Well, I spent time reviewing Joan's recent Congressional testimony and it looks like there is convincing evidence that deportation numbers don't add up."

"*Really?*"

"Well, she's convinced there are two sets of numbers. The implication is that President Haesi needs to increase the vote totals in the Hispanic community while at the same time trying to convince voters he's cracking down on illegals."

"Pretty clever, it seems to me, trying to have it both ways."

Pat nodded, slowing down his pace.

"There's this congressman from some Midwestern state—Kane, I think his name is—who introduced a resolution, *National Day of Remembrance*, for November 6th, starting this year and every year after. Joan told me he's taking the lead in trying to bring this to the attention of the nation. He managed to get the non partisan *Policy Foundation* to report on illegal alien crime. Early reports indicate over 10,000 homicide arrests of illegal aliens since 1955."

Clare stopped to catch her breath. They were drawing close to Michigan Avenue where they could stroll at a more leisurely pace. She, like Pat, was anxious to leave the darkness of Van Buren Street behind them, but they had walked a little too fast for comfort—and certainly too fast for anything more than a casual conversation.

"You alright?"

"Will be, in a moment, Pat. Just give me a few moments."

"Now let me go over what Joe's guy, Professor Jones in California, came up with. Remember, I mentioned this Hallet character from the *Illinois Immigration Coop?*"

"Yes, but let me catch my breath—we need to slow down. All this rushing isn't good for either of us."

They stopped for a few moments, then continued on. Clare, feeling more rested, recalled that Hallet had left a message and that Pat's downstate contacts knew something about him.

"Well, Clare, I haven't returned the call, but I will now that I've learned more about him. Jones shows that a guy named Chambliss, a protégé to the infamous Shelton Lalinsky. Yep, mentored this Hallet. Lalinsky started—oh, back in the late 40's in the Back of the Yards community."

"Well, that's interesting urban history. Lalinsky was that crazy radical that everybody hated back in the 60's and 70's. Right?"

"Yep. Now bear with me, will you? I'll connect a few dots. So this Hallet trained in the Lalinsky tradition and gets to be pals with none other than a young kid named Haesi back in the 80's. The two of them join this community organization to empower black people in neighborhoods like Burnside, Roseland, Grand Crossing and more. Haesi gets trained, too, and they both become part of something called *Industrial Social* something or other. Long story short, there's this vast network of people of all stripes trying to save the inner city and this Hallet moves in the direction of Hispanic causes and stays in touch with Haesi who was working the Burnside and Roseland neighborhoods. Hallet remained loyal to Haesi as his political career climbed the ladder right up to the White House."

By now, Clare was looking skeptical. She wasn't sure whether it was the heat of the day that was getting to her, or the content of their conversation. She understood Pat's interest in details but by now her mind was spinning. Fortunately, they had reached Michigan Avenue and were walking on the east side of the street where they could feel more of the breeze from the lake.

"Earlier you were dreaming about conversations with the dead, and now you're tying the President in with conspiracy theories," she remarked.

Pat frowned.

"I'm not blaming Haesi—he's just part of a larger picture. But for some reason more and more sanctuary cities are coming on line since he was elected. Look, I'm not going to dwell on this, Clare, but facts are facts. These people know one another and their goal, according to Jones, is to move the country to the far left. He cites all sorts of evidence supporting his views, and perhaps the most convincing is their support of open borders and amnesty, coupled with lack of immigration enforcement. He also gets into questionable voter registration campaigns. At the beginning of the book, Jones flirts with some serious philosophy type stuff that goes back to Marx and, later, to some guys named Lucas and Gramsci. This Gramsci—an Italian—came up with the idea that there are haves and have-nots. For him, the haves are bad, rich white guys while have nots are Blacks, immigrants, homosexuals, you know all sorts of marginal people. Jones suggests that this cabal of far lefties is determined to get as many people as possible dependent on far left government entitlements and supportive policies. He even suggests that these people are determined to destroy Christian families."

"You going conspiracy nutty on me?" said Clare, checking for traffic before the two jay walked across the street.

"Hey, Clare, *you* asked me what I'd been reading! I'm trying to make sense of all this.

Oh yeah, then we get to the 60's and these people or Gramscians are starting all this crap on college campuses. Here we are, forty years later, and they're pretty much taking over universities and promoting neo Marxism.

"So now you're blaming the hippies for letting Orizaga go?" asked Clare, with a sardonic smile.

"Real funny, Clare. Now c'mon, this stuff makes some serious sense, you got to admit. Oh yeah, this whole philosophy is known as the *Frankfurt School*, but I don't have time to explain that."

"Okay, it all could make sense, I suppose. Please be careful—you know with the Rollie connection, these professors, talking to your brother … It's like you're obsessed."

"I am," said Pat. "Damn right, I am!"

The McGurns arrived in time for the 9/11 commemorative, which was conducted by a contingent of Chicago Police and Firefighters. The Mayor and Governor gave emotional speeches; the plaintive wail of bagpipes brought many in the gathering to tears. Pat and Clare stood silently, shoulder to shoulder with other Chicagoans who had come to remember and honor the dead. On the way home, a somber Pat wondered if 9/11 it might have been prevented had the immigration authorities had been on the ball ten years earlier. He recalled that three or four of the hijackers were illegal aliens who had been stopped by law enforcement and let go, just as Raul Orizaga had been let go. If it weren't for corruption, wouldn't Denny be alive, together with 3000 plus 9/11 victims? The couple arrived home and ate a late lunch, after which Pat watched the Wisconsin-Oregon State game.

During half time, Rollie called to provide a surveillance update.

"So this is the fourth day and Roberto has just gone in and out to eat, you're saying?"

"Maybe that's his orders, Pat. Hard to say. We gotta be patient, you know—surveillance takes time."

"I hear you, Rollie. Let's talk tomorrow," said Pat, wearily.

"For sure—hopefully I'll hear something from my guy, Mike."

"Yeah, I like that lead. Take care. Bye."

After dinner Pat got the coffee and went over Rollie's earlier report with Clare.

"So they'll work ten-hour shifts?"

"Yep, and this guy Schus has tactical unit guys giving breaks to the surveillance team. So far, coverage has been good. These guys are supposed to call Rollie on his cell if anyone enters or leaves the house, giving him a full description. Next, if the brother leaves, they are to tail him and follow prescribed procedures. Also record plate numbers."

"An interesting way to spend $5,000!" observed Clare, with almost imperceptible grimace. "Still, I suppose we could have blown it in Vegas, right?"

"I don't believe we're blowing it, Clare—don't think we'll regret this at all."

•

That same afternoon, Raul Orizaga was getting antsy stuck in an airless basement. He had spent almost two weeks in the hole, but that was the deal. He had agreed not to leave the basement until the club gave the okay, and only then with an escort. He also worried about his assignment and wished he could see his brother. Lou, the club contact, informed him that Robby would be allowed to visit soon, maybe in a week. Meanwhile, Orizaga had a small fridge and some canned goods. There was a toilet by the furnace and an old TV, so all he did was sleep and watch a couple of Spanish stations with bad reception. However, that was preferable to the jail on 26th Street and, for sure, to spending five to seven years in prison, followed by deportation. He understood he had to lie low because his brother told him the Feds would be looking for him, along with the Chicago cops.

What kept him going was the promise that if he did all the jobs they assigned him, he would get a new ID and phony papers. On the other hand, Lou had warned him that if he tried to sneak out, the club would immediately know about it and either call the cops or kill him. Raul hated that he couldn't use the cell phone they gave him for any outgoing calls; the club's orders were only to take calls. Later that day Raul's cell rang.

"Raul, Baby—Robby here. You okay, dude?"

"Shit, bro—sucks here, man. When I get out?"

"Soon, Baby—I call soon but remember, no calls. Only answer if you see Angela's name."

"Got it! Sure no one checking, Robby?"

"I sure, bro. *Yo tengo que ir ahora, sólo tiene que hacer lo que te dicen!*"

"*Si, si --Entiendo lo que estás diciendo!*"

Yes, he understood everything and his brother had to go. Yes, he would follow orders—after all, he had no choice. At least they hadn't forgotten him and the old man put the food out every day.

●

The next day, Sunday, the McGurns attended Mass as usual, then drove to *Little Company of Mary Hospital* to see their new granddaughter, Maeve. Clare, of course, had already met her, but Pat had been too preoccupied with his paperwork. He hugged Molly who was sitting in an armchair, nursing the baby, and shook his son in law's hand and gave grandson Matt a big hug.

"So happy for you guys," he said, watching little Maeve tug greedily at her mother's breast.

"A strong little one!" he remarked, quite surprised at the baby's personality. Not even two days old and she was already asserting herself in this world.

"No doubt about it, Dad," laughed Molly. If she had been disappointed at his lack of interest in her pregnancy, she didn't show it. She exchanged looks with Clare, as if to say, "This will be good for him!"

Maeve pulled away and gave an unmistakable burp.

"Here," said Clare, passing a cloth diaper to Molly. "Put this over your shoulder and pat her back like so—that will help with indigestion! Don't let her lie down right after feeding—keep her upright!"

Maeve let out a few more noisy burps and a trickle of milk appeared on the diaper.

As the baby began to nod off, Molly passed her to her father.

"Here, Dad—why don't you hold her for a few minutes? That way you can introduce yourself properly."

Nervously, Pat reached out and took the infant from Molly. His hands were trembling but miraculously, Maeve lay still, as if aware that he was afraid of dropping her. Looking down at her tiny face, Pat marveled at how perfect she was—soft strands of light blonde hair framed her round face. She had the tiniest of noses and dimples in both cheeks. And her eyes—for a few seconds, Pat's eyes met Maeve's blue eyes, piercing like Denny's.

"Here, you'd better take her," he said, hastily giving her back to Molly.

"What's wrong, Dad? Did something upset you?"

"No, no—she's beautiful! Just feel a little emotional, that's all ..."

•

Rollie's phone rang at 9:30p.m.

"Rol, Mario here. A chick just went in with an overnight bag and carry out. I figure she's staying the night. She parked a beat up Ford Taurus down the street. Oh, and I just saw a light go on."

"Just the broad, food and a light. That's it Mario?"

"For now, Rol, and oh she's a fox. Not sure if that means anything."

"Could mean something. She's dressed like a hooker?"

"Nope. Sort of regular, I guess. Hard to say, nowadays."

"Good work, Mario, get the plate and call right back."

"Got it right here—the plate is KA 11776."

"Mario, I'll get back to you in a few." Rollie immediately called Schus to give him the plate number.

"Schus? Yes, I know it's Sunday night. Look, I'm sorry man, but I need a favor, tonight if possible."

"My guys giving your guys the breaks, right, Rol?"

"Oh yeah, they're helping when they can. I'm calling about a plate I need a fix on."

"Not a problem, Rol. Give me the number. I got a pen handy."

Within minutes, Schus called back. The car was registered to an Angela Montoya, age twenty. Angela had a few tickets, but no warrants. Her address, at least at the time of registration, was 10901 State Line Road.

"Fourth District. Schus, that could mean something."

"That's right—you saw that paper—*Southeast Observer*—I remember."

"Yeah, it was in Roberto's car. I think I told you I met with Higgins in the Fourth District."

"You said you were going over there. So this Angela's connected, maybe?"

Rollie described his meeting with Mike Dukavich, and how the teacher had his pulse on gang activities in the neighborhood.

"When you going to hear from this teacher?"

"Any day—but now I'm thinking of calling him to look into this Angela girl because she could have gone to *Jefferson High School* over there."

"Good move! Oh, before I forget, Rol—I got a call from a copper named Kopko who heard I was asking around. He told me this Roberto is pretty slick prick—his street name is Ozzie, short for Orizaga. He said the word on the street is he's a bad ass."

"Anything recent?"

"Nope. Kopko said he hasn't heard a thing in maybe two years, so maybe he's operating elsewhere."

"Elsewhere, huh? Well, maybe I know where, Schus. I owe you, man— you know, helping me out on a Sunday night."

"Anytime, Rol. Hey, let me know what you learn about this Angela. See ya."

•

Rollie knew it was late, but instinct told him to act quickly, so he called Mike Dukavich. Mike was home, watching the Bears; fortunately, he didn't seem to mind the interruption or, if he did, he was too good natured to let Rollie sense this. He himself didn't recognize Angela's name and wondered whether perhaps she had attended *St. Columba*, the local Catholic school. Putting Rollie on hold, he called a friend of his who was Senior Counselor over at *Jefferson*.

"Got lucky, Rol. Yeah, my guy at *Jefferson* is Brian Raferty and he remembers her. She was a math whiz, and damn near maxed the ACT. Get this, though—she dropped out and hung around with the wrong crowd. Liked the boys, too," he said.

"I guess Raferty didn't mind the late call, huh Mike?"

"Not at all—he's another hopeless Bear fan. Both of us continued watching the game while we talked. He remembered her well. You know, Brian's the kind of guy that will go the extra mile for a deserving kid. Look, he suggested we take a ride over there tomorrow and maybe learn some more. You know he can pull the records and ask around."

"I'd love to, Mike, but your schedule!" objected Rollie.

"No problem. I've just got a morning Criminal Justice class at Rowan and there's a guy who owes me a favor—I'm sure he'll cover for me. I told Brian 10:00 a.m. sharp, so just park in the west lot. Say, why not bring the guy you're helping along?"

"Yeah, you read my mind. I'll call him in the morning and thanks again. For sure, I'll be there."

DAY SIXTEEN, MONDAY SEPTEMBER 12,2011

Pat had planned to spend the day writing a letter to Cook County President Korshak. The idea was to copy all the commissioners and selected media so as to keep pressure on the political front. After hearing from Rollie, however, he welcomed the shift in plans. For a change, he would be at the forefront of the investigation rather than waiting to be briefed! While waiting for Rollie to collect him, he decided to look at the 2010 *Jefferson High School* State of Illinois Report Card in order to get a handle on the place. He always figured it was like his old school up north, the John Dewey, where he had taught for twenty-five years; the stats proved him right: 2000 students, low ACT scores, most teachers with advanced degrees and a female principal named Cilla; equal numbers of Hispanics, Blacks and Whites.

At 9:20 a.m., Rollie pulled up as scheduled.

"Well, let's hope for the best, Pat," said Rollie as Pat strapped himself in. "You'll like this kid Mike, you guys being teachers and all."

"For sure, Rol. In my thirty-three years in the business, I never heard of a Chicago teacher lining up fat cats to subsidize tuition for troubled kids."

"Yeah, and a real neighborhood guy as well. Dukavich is a Croatian name—I think there's a Croatian church over there named *Sacred Heart*."

"Yeah, I figured that since he was related to big shot Milan who I think went to *Chicago Vocational High School*," said Pat as they drove over the 106th Street Bridge.

"Yeah, I forgot about that. Jeez, those were the days when he was giving old Arnett a rough time in the city council."

A commercial freighter had just passed under the 106th Street Bridge, briefly delaying them at the Calumet River until traffic was moving again. They drove down Wolf Street, passed the old rusted hulk of *Wisconsin Steel*, and into the *Jefferson* parking lot. Walking into the office, Rollie loudly announced their presence.

"Mr. Dufner and Mr. McGurn to see Mr. Raferty and Mr. Dukavich!" he said.

"What's this—the Irish Mafia?" joked one of the clerks looking up at them through her bi-focals.

"Best looking boys I seen in a long time, Esther," observed the other clerk, pouting her red lips suggestively. Esther smiled.

"Welcome to Jeff High, Sirs—Mr. Raferty and Mr. Dukavich are waiting in the Social Room down the hall."

"Appreciate it, ladies," said Rollie, flashing his most charming smile.

As they walked into the Social Room, Mike introduced them to Brian Raferty and then, excusing himself, left the room to make some rounds. After expressing his condolences to Pat, Brian opened a file that was sitting on his desk.

"Look, guys, between us here, Angela was a project—I mean here's a kid who maxed math on the ACT but just mixed with the wrong group. Let's see, she was born in 1991—left two years ago, with a year to go. Quiet kid and a few of us worried about her—well, you know, she liked the boys. Always with a rough looking character."

"Not sure how much Mike told you, Brian, but we think Angela's the girlfriend of the brother of the guy that killed Pat's brother."

"Yeah, he did, but I'm not sure where you're going with this."

"Let's just say a few of us are trying to get justice because we think the official criminal justice system really doesn't give a shit. Appreciate it if you keep our investigation to yourself."

"No problem," said Brian, closing the file. "After speaking to Mike, I did call her home on State Line Road, but the family hasn't seen her in a year and doesn't seem to give a shit. Look, the only other information I can share is that her family's—excuse my French—all fucked up. Not sure, but I thought there could be abuse going on, perhaps with the daddy. The kid didn't have much supervision—sort of did what she wanted. However, she was gifted, you know—scores off the charts. One of our teachers gave her an unofficial test that suggested she could be another Einstein. In fact, when she was in Eighth Grade, we let her take Algebra here with the Advanced Placement kids."

"So what you're saying is she's a bright kid, running with a tough crowd, who drops out," said Rollie.

"Yep, that's about it."

"And now sleeping with an older dude who is likely a ranking member in a Hispanic gang," added Rollie. "So what d' you think, Pat?"

"Well, I've seen this sort of thing before," said Pat, caught off guard. "We had all sorts of gangs, including Asians, and almost everyone was from troubled families. I guess my hope is that this Angela can help us, but I got to tell you, my heart goes out to these kids who get caught up with assholes like this Roberto."

"Yeah, I agree, Pat—seems like a tragic waste," said Brian. "We have a teacher in our Math department, a Ms. Ruchka, that worked with Angela, but the problem is that she and I don't get along. She hates cops and probably all men but she might have something."

Rollie smiled.

"A nut-crusher and cop hater. My kinda girl."

"Who's this?" asked Mike as he entered the room again. *"You're not talking about Angela?"*

"No way," laughed Brian, explaining how Ms. Ruchka had come up in conversation.

"That's right—she's Ms. Math Whiz. So she was tight with this Angela kid, Mike?"

"Yeah, I guess a mentor- mentee deal for all three years Angela was here. She taught her AP Calculus."

"You know, I stay away from her," admitted Mike. "She's sort a weird— you know, maybe too much acid in the 60's. I heard she was a former radical or something. Is that right, Brian?"

"Yeah, that's the word."

"I know the type," Pat interrupted. "We got a few at Dewey. There's one named Phyllis who tells her kids about Woodstock every day, like she's in a time warp. Say, maybe I can help—I've been around eccentric teachers for thirty plus years."

"Well, it will have to be you, Mike, you know, to introduce Pat to Ruchka," said Brian.

"Sure, nothing to lose—and it's part of my job. But are you suggesting this because you think she might know more about Angela than her math ability?"

Brian glanced at the wall clock.

"Maybe, but it's worth a try. Let's see her lunch fifth period which starts in a half hour—she eats alone in her room and listens to public radio, I hear."

"Look, I got an idea," said Mike, turning towards Pat. "Here's what I'm thinking. Rol told you about my raising money from money guys for these scholarships, right?"

"Yeah, you mean with those kids downstate?"

"That's right. I want you to be an agent for some hypothetical fat cats by telling this Ruchka that you screen candidates for these awards—you know, you being a former teacher and all. So what do you guys think?"

"Hmmm, well I can play that game," said Pat, "Provided there are no formalities and we keep it anonymous. What do you guys think?"

"She just might buy it," said Brian. Rollie nodded in agreement.

"Worth a try, I guess, you know using a ruse was part of our training in the academy."

"Brian, are you sure you're okay with this? I mean, it could backfire and you're in big trouble," said Pat.

"Hey, boys, I know nothing. Never heard this conversation. All I know is that you guys wanted to talk to Ruchka about a former student."

"What about you?" said Pat, looking squarely at Mike. "You could get your ass in real trouble."

"Hey, I always stick my neck out around here so not to worry."

"Well, I guess I'll get lost then, since she hates cops," said Rollie. "I'll take a ride over to the traveling Vietnam wall—great exhibit, I hear. It's only a mile away. Anything else?"

"I better use an alias with this Ruchka. How about Pat Dunleavy, Mike?"

"Sounds good."

"Okay, boys—then we have a plan!" said Brian. "I need to meet some kids now—hope this helped."

"Trust me, Counselor," said Rollie, "My gut tells me this old hippy got something to say."

The group split up, with Rollie and Brian going their separate ways while Mike escorted Pat down the hall. It was a rough scene, with kids shouting obscenities at each other and flashing gang signs. Pat couldn't believe the conduct or the language, let alone the apparent indifference of the staff who seemed oblivious to what was happening right in front of them. Mike stopped to reprimand at least six or seven students, cautioning them to watch the language. Calling them by name, he seemed to get both their attention and their respect. Outside the main office, there was total chaos, with a kid in cuffs while the cops were yelling not at the kid but at some harried, middle-aged teacher.

"Sir, you got to come to the station and file a report," said an older cop with a beer belly who was evidently enjoying the teacher's distress.

"I don't want to—I just want him out of my class 'cause he's mean."

"What he do?"

"He hit me."

"You have to fill out forms at the station, Mr. Boynton," said the cop, his ample belly shaking from suppressed laughter.

Mike walked over to the cops.

"Charley, Joe, take them in—I promise you, I'll get Boynton over there before 3:00 p.m. today to file charges."

"Okay, Mike, for you I'll do it, but you know it's against protocol," said Beer Belly.

"Charley, screw protocol. I'll be over with Boynton later—just keep the kid in the lock up."

Pat was aghast.

"Jeez, Mike I've seen some crazy stuff here—does the principal know about all this?"

"Oh yeah, but she couldn't give a damn," said Mike bitterly.

"A teacher getting hit and the principal indifferent!"

"You got it! I could write a book on this useless lady, but, like I said, she's connected.

Don't get me wrong, Pat—this Boynton's a problem, too!"

"Where is she—the principal, I mean?"

"Hiding somewhere—no one ever sees her. She takes tons of days off and the Assistant is probably out recruiting basketball players. Most of the time, no one's in charge around here."

"This place is a fucking joke, Mike!"

"You're telling me. Look, with a little luck and twenty grievances pending, we might get the attention of downtown and get rid of her, but she's got clout,. C'mon, Pat. Let's get to work."

By now they had reached the Math Department and were standing in front of Ruchka's door. Hearing the radio blaring out national news, they knocked loudly. There was a shrill, "Come in! Door's open!" and they walked in. A gaunt woman with her hair tightly knotted into a gray bun, swiveled her desk chair to face them.

"Ms. Ruchka, Mr. Dunleavy and I would like a word," said Mike in as friendly a tone as he could muster.

Ruchka waved them to stand to the side of her desk as she turned the radio down.

"A word? You and I never talk, Mr.—what's your name?" She glared at Mike, as if intent on staring down her worst enemy.

"Dukavich. Mike Dukavich."

"Well, what about your friend. I've never seen him, so what is this? Is he a cop?"

"Well, Ms. Ruchka—oh, can I call you Ethel?"

"No!" she spat. "So what do you want? *Is* he a cop?"

"Not to worry, a former teacher," said Mike, forcing a smile.

"Good, I hate those fuckin' cops. You a Republican mister?"

"No Ma'am, independent."

"Good, they just had that racist billionaire fool on the radio who wants to deport people."

"Ms. Ruchka, we're here about a former student of yours, Angela Montoya," continued Mike, seemingly unruffled.

"Angela, you say? She left us two years ago."

"Well, let me explain. Mr. Dunleavy here represents, shall I say, several people who are interested in helping gifted students, particularly in Math and the hard sciences. They've established an award precisely—"

"*Really?* You're telling me rich people give a shit about little brown people?"

"Well yes, brown, black, and white—you name it. You see, they look for gifted future leaders."

"So you think Angela's a candidate? You know she dropped out—this sure sounds strange and you, Mr. Dunn or whatever—a former teacher. I don't get it."

"Let me explain, Ma'am," interjected Pat. "You see the people I represent are aware of familial and social issues that plague the inner city, but they are also aware that out of the urban weeds, there are scores of really gifted students with technical skills."

"So you're for real about Angela?" said Ruchka, eyeing them both suspiciously.

"Well, based on what we learned from Mr. Raferty, you're the key for Angela Montoya to get the award," said Pat, feeling his cheeks burning.

"Raferty, huh? Well, he doesn't like me, so I don't know."

"That may be, Ms. Ruchka, but I think you will agree he has the upmost respect for your teaching abilities," said Mike smoothly.

Her face more relaxed now, Ruchka looked from Mike to Pat.

"Well, now that you put it that way, I *do* talk to her from time to time. In fact, I finally managed to talk her into taking GED classes at one of the YMCA's on the North Side. I believe she might wrap it up by the end of the year."

"Commendable, Ms. Ruchka," Mike gushed.

Ignoring the compliment, Ruchka stared at Pat.

"Exactly *who* are these benefactors?"

Squirming under her sharp gaze, Pat tried to keep his voice steady.

"Well, we can discuss that later, but first, if you don't mind, we need to talk to her. Do you know how she can be reached?"

"She seems very guarded, but I do know she lives north and, oh yes, she is estranged from her family, that I know, but I do recall her fondness for her grandparents, the Delgados. She always talked about them."

"Mr. Delgado have a first name, Ma'am?"

"Ignacio, as I recall. They used to be pretty close because Angela stayed with them quite often—you could say she lived with them, off and on, because of her family problems. I don't know anything else about them."

"Do you have her number?"

"No, she only calls me—usually once a week, after GED Classes on Wednesday night."

Pat handed Ms. Ruchka a piece of paper on which he had scribbled his cell phone number; again, he was conscious of his cheeks burning.

"I appreciate your time, Ms. Ruchka. Please be so kind as to call anytime if Angela calls and simply tell her about our conversation. Oh, and kindly write a letter addressed TO WHOM IT MAY CONCERN recommending Angela for a four year college scholarship—just put it in Mr. Raferty's mailbox."

"Give me a day or two," she said with a strained smile.

"Thank you—and one more thing. Why do you hate cops so much?" asked Pat, truly curious as to what she might say.

"You mean "pigs"—I was at the *1968 Democratic Convention.*"

"So was I," smiled Pat. "So was I ..."

•

In the parking lot, Mike informed Rollie and Pat that he would be going down to Murphysboro in the next few days.

"So the boys haven't called, Mike?"

"No, I'll get to them tonight—there must be a reason for the delay. I sent the photos last Friday. I'll call you, Rol, after I get through to them."

After Mike left them, Pat, somewhat proudly, handed Rollie a piece of paper on which "Ignacio Delgado" was written.

"This might be key. Ignacio Delgado and his wife are Angela's grandparents and they live around here somewhere. She's real close to them."

"Good job, Pat," said Rollie, "I'm impressed! I got to believe we'll have no problem running this lead down."

On the way home, Pat looked at Rollie who seemed lost in thought.

"You okay?"

"Oh, yeah, you guys did good. This Ignacio connection's a big- lead. It's just that the traveling Vietnam wall gets me down. This time they had recordings of patriotic hymns playing in the distance. I sort of broke down and then I got really pissed thinking of that asshole who desecrated the Star Spangled banner when I was in Vietnam in '69."

"You mean that guy Hockley at Woodstock with that weird guitar?"

"Yeah, that's him. My pals in our squad wanted to break his fuckin' head."

As if for emphasis, Rollie whistled a few bars of the *Colonel Bogey March* from *The Bridge on the River Kwai.*

"Okay, back to business," he said abruptly. "We both got work to do today, so *Ruth's* tomorrow to compare notes. 4:00 p.m."

Getting out of the car, Pat noticed tears running down Rollie's cheeks.

●

After lunch, Pat decided to take the rest of the day to write a letter to President Korshak which he would copy to all the commissioners. He started writing, but had a hard time moving beyond the opening lines. Damn Writer's Block, he thought to himself. After an hour of struggling, he telephoned Eileen Murphy to see if she had any further information—it had been several days since their last conversation.

"Eileen, Pat McGurn calling. I thought I'd see if you learned anything new before I send out a letter to Korshak."

"Well, I did learn something, but I'm not sure if I can discuss this."

"C'mon, Eileen. My brother's killer fled and my family wants answers."

"Okay Pat, but this is just between you and me. Well, I had a meeting with my boss, Lisa Hunter-Goss and she really wants to put the lid on this whole matter, so I need to be low profile."

"So I guess conversations with me and the press are off limits, huh?"

"Please understand—I'm trying to help."

"So what can you tell me? Anything new?" asked Pat, trying not to sound irritable.

"Well, yeah, but I have to ask that you keep my name out of your letter."

"Not a problem, Eileen," said Pat, drumming his frustration onto the edge of the kitchen counter. He paced up and down the kitchen, waiting for her to continue.

"They're going to use the bond court as their defense, Pat, and blame the judge. Now, the judges are pretty independent and can pretty much set bond as they choose."

"Eileen, everybody agrees that the bond was low, but the issue is the detainer, for God's sake!"

"That's the point! My boss wants to get the heat off her and, by extension, the Cook County Board, President Korshak and the Sheriff. They want to put the blame on this new gal, Rice, who represented your family in bond court before I got the file."

"So what you're saying is they just want cover," said Pat, his anger mounting.

"Okay, so this Rice kid screws up and Santiago, a low bond guy, and Hunter-Goss try to sweep it under the rug. Well, what about this scenario, Eileen? Maybe Orizaga's lawyer, Simpkus, got to a political friend of Santiago's to keep the bond low. An illegal with a prior felony conviction kills a guy and gets 250K bond—sure sounds fishy to me."

"Well, Pat, I could have gone back into court and challenged and increased the bond."

"So you didn't know about the ordinance, but knew of Orizaga's prior felony, right?"

"Yes, Pat, yes—we went over that before."

"But why didn't Judge Martin expedite this, given the fact of a prior felony and overwhelming evidence of guilt. I mean, Eileen, it was almost three months!"

"Well, the plea was not guilty, so the court must allow the defense time to prepare for discovery proceedings."

"Oh, yeah? Maybe some people got to your judge too and maybe he knew the ordinance was in the works!"

"Whoa, Pat! Please don't go there—any implication that includes me is disturbing."

"I'm not blaming you, Eileen, but your judge and maybe Hunter-Goss, and certainly Varbanov and others. Plausible, right?"

"No comment—I've nothing further to say."

"I understand, Eileen—and I know you're busy. Is there anything else you *can* tell me?"

"Just one more thing—I spent a few hours with a guy named Bruce Horsefal at the FBI who is assigned to this. He's preparing an affidavit for a federal warrant and he thinks a warrant will be issued this week if he can get it before a federal judge."

"Well, I guess that's good news, but c'mon—sixteen days lead time for slick little Raul doesn't get my hopes up. So is this Bruce going to give me a heads up?"

"I doubt it, Pat."

"Eileen, I'm not hopeful, but thanks anyway. I'll wait a few days and maybe call this Bruce. Look, the real reason I called as I told you earlier is that I'm working on a letter to Korshak, which I will copy to the commissioners, press and others. You and two of my advisors will get the letter via e-mail."

"Thanks, Pat, I'll look forward to reading your letter."

If there were chilliness to her tone, Pat did not notice.

After a few hours of writing and proofing, Pat printed twenty copies of the Korshak letter, addressed twenty envelopes and overnighted the letter to all the commissioners, President Korshak, State's Attorney Hunter-Goss and Sheriff Dypsky. This is what the letter said:

President Korshak
Cook County Board
118 N. Clark Street
Chicago, Illinois 60602

Dear President Korshak,

My brother was killed on June 8, 2011, by an illegal immigrant who had a prior felony conviction and was subsequently released from Cook County prison on account of a wrongheaded ordinance sponsored by you and others.

The Assistant State's Attorney assigned to this case, unaware of this ordinance, assured my family that the killer would never be released because of a federal detainer or hold that had been placed on him. My brother's killer, one Raul Orizaga, was released on August 28, 2011, after he posted the $25,000.00 bond. The United States Federal requirement of holding him for an additional forty-eight hours was ignored.

I have brought this issue to the attention of the *U.S. House of Representatives Judiciary Committee* and the *Immigration Customs Enforcement* (ICE) for consideration. Finally, this killer admitted he was illegal at the time of a prior arrest in 2008; I will argue that had Orizaga been deported at that time my brother would be alive.

I would appreciate your considering a revision of current policy to protect the six million citizens of Cook County from illegal alien felons.

Sincerely,

Patrick McGurn
Chicago Illinois

•

Pat decided to send copies of the letter via e-mail to his relatives, Joe, Joan and Rollie. He wasn't sure how the extended family was reading his political efforts and hoped they understood the pushback. So far, they hadn't taken much interest in his quest for justice. Dinner at home was quiet. Clare listened as he went over the events of the day.

"I guess it's wait and see on this Angela lead, but be ready for commissioners' calls—and for anyone else's call, including the family. All I'm saying is be civil—sometimes, your anger gets the better of you!"

"How do you expect me to be? All the politicians are two-faced liars who thrive on obstructing justice and are being paid to do so!"

"I'm just letting you know you can attract more flies with honey than vinegar," said Clare calmly, dabbing at her mouth with her napkin.

"All these sons of bitches are vinegar in my book!"

"Just don't use this language when the grandchildren are around, please—it's really uncalled for. You've been hanging out with Rollie too much! And one more thing—let Rollie do the detective work. I'm not happy at all that you went to *Jefferson High* and spoke to that Math teacher—what's going to happen when she finds out that *you* lied to her, speaking of liars?"

"She won't find out because I used an alias."

"Doesn't sound too undercover to me. And the girl—don't you think she might figure something out? Bright kid, certainly capable of adding things up!"

"C'mon," said Pat. "The neighborhood's beautiful and it's the perfect night to go to Rainbow Cone for hot fudge sundaes. Let's give all this a rest!"

"Best thing you've said all evening!" said Clare.

DAY SEVENTEEN, TUESDAY SEPEMBER .13, 2011

The next day, Pat called Vanderbiezen at *Serendipity Place*.

"Joe, Pat here—thought I'd call. You got my last e-mail, didn't you? The letter?"

"Sure did, and talked to Joan about it as well. We both feel you made your point clearly. When are you coming down, Pat?"

"I don't know. Now that this letter went out, I thought the three of us could stay in touch by phone and e-mail for the next week or so."

"You bet, Pat—I understand. Some of your callers could be angry and well …"

"I know that—in fact, I'm expecting it."

"Good. If I were you, I'd also send it to as many people you can. Trust me, the bloggers will pick it up and, with luck, in a day or two maybe a few thousand will read it. Some of the conservative on-line media will run it to *The Daily Crier*. I don't know if you're aware but their publisher, Buck Holmgren, is a real pro immigration enforcement guy."

"Good idea, Joe—no, I didn't know that."

"Now, it might get rough, Pat, so be prepared."

"What do you mean?"

"Well, people like Varbanov, Hallet, Rodriguez's people, *La Fuerza* people—you know, any number of pro-immigration folk will try and get you to back off. Say, Joan and I were wondering if you spoke with Riley yet?"

"No, not yet—maybe today."

"That should be an interesting conversation! Look, Pat, I also want to tell you I started working with a graduate student, and we are finishing up a three-page profile on all seventeen of the commissioners. This student—Hinton—is working on a dissertation on county government. He's looking at voting records of what he calls 'rubber stamp' commissioners in Cook County, Harris County (Houston) and San Francisco. Cook County, for example, has mostly 'do nothing, go along' commissioners who are only interested in protecting their political careers. Most of the ten that voted for your ordinance fit that description, according to Hinton. I'm helping him on the draft and I'll get it out to you tomorrow. Should give you a bit more perspective."

"You know, Joe, that will help. Talking to Wagner was pretty disillusioning. Moreover, your guy, McLaughlin, at *Southern Illinois University*, seems to think any amendment proposition is nothing but smoke."

"He told me the same thing, but there's always hope. Now, you didn't get the impression that Wagner would withdraw the amendment, did you?"

"No, I guess they want to have this hearing and listen to both sides. My guess is they'll simply table it."

"You know, when I talked to Wagner all he really said was that he's sure he can get an amendment on the floor. So I guess we'll have to see what happens. One thing, however, is that it will keep the issue in the news and that can't hurt."

"Right. I'll talk to Riley soon and maybe learn something about this hearing. I got to trust him, after all, because he's a Riley and up here in Chi-Town that always means something."

"Okay, Pat, but keep in mind the key word here is veracity. You deserve forthrightness from these commissioners, nothing less."

"I like that Joe, but I'm skeptical."

"And with good reason! Oh, and let me know what you think of Hinton's work."

"Will do, Joe. I'll touch base when I get a chance."

Later, while he was in the middle of preparing supper, Pat received a phone call from Commissioner Riley who had just read the letter. Wedging his cell phone under his chin, he poured a generous amount of poultry seasoning on a plump chicken in a roasting pan, and wiped his hands on his apron. The timing was not good, as he was scheduled to meet up with Rollie at *Ruth's* in less than an hour.

"Well, I figured friends and enemies should know where I stand," said Pat, making a half-hearted attempt at humor.

"Well, Pat, no one is your enemy here at the Cook County Board. I can speak for all the commissioners and President Korshak that we are deeply sorry for your loss."

"*Really!* Ten voted for an ordinance that let my brother's killer abscond. You're telling me they're sorry?"

"You know that I and four others voted against it."

"Commissioner, believe me, I've done some homework here and I'll take five condolences from you and the others that voted no but not the others. Look, Korshak, Hunter-Goss, Dypsky and ten commissioners are not my favorite people! So tell me about your Cook County Board! I'm asking if there's a realistic chance of an amendment of some kind?"

"I can't promise anything, but it looks like an amendment will be presented."

"Well, tell me this, Mr. Riley, would you bet on an amendment passing?"

"Why is this amendment so important to you?" asked Riley, avoiding the question.

"This is the best way to seek justice because you know and I know no one will ever find my brother's killer. The coppers fucked up the search after I had to alert State's Attorney Murphy. Did you know that?"

"Well, I do now."

"And, get this, the useless FBI won't get involved until maybe two weeks!"

"Well, I'm not sure about that—I'll check."

"I already checked! The County, the coppers, FBI—you name it, they screwed up and all I get are hollow condolences. Look, you get the votes to change that ordinance and maybe, just maybe, some semblance of justice will be returned to my family. That's all I'm asking—just so that this will not happen to another family. You know, I wish the powers that be could do more to get rid of *all* convicted illegals. I understand there are thousands of American citizens out there who have fallen victim to these outrageous sanctuary policies. Look, sorry for the rant …"

"Pat, sometime next week, maybe Tuesday, there'll be a public hearing in the County Board Room—might be a good time for all sides to say their piece," said Riley, soothingly.

"Wait a second! I mean, c'mon, the other side already had their say and got an ordinance passed, right?"

"Well, that's one way to put it but maybe wiser heads might encourage an amendment."

"Commissioner, I've been consulting with Joe Vanderbiezen at the *University of Illinois* and Professor McLaughlin at *Southern*—they tell me an amendment's a good idea, but that it's a real long shot. Moreover, I didn't get the impression Wagner is hopeful when I talked to him."

"*Really?* That's surprising. We discussed the logistics of this public forum and looks like you're going to be up first, but the formal invite will come from Commissioner Alport."

"What's with Alport?" countered Pat, suspiciously.

"She's chair of public meetings. Her office will line up public speakers."

"How many speakers and will it be balanced?"

"Well, I'm not sure what you mean," said Riley.

"Davida Alport's pro-ordinance, so she's not impartial yet she's running the show!" objected Pat.

"She's a good lady, Patrick, and she's truly sorry."

"Look, I'm game, you know, to keep this in the public eye but my gut tells me this is going to be all bullshit."

"Excuse me?"

"Commissioner, the ordinance was 10 - 5. It wasn't a close vote—there's a Korshak block, Hispanic block and a progressive liberal block, so who's going to change?"

"Well, I can't speak for the others, Pat, but I'll bring your concerns to them. Do talk to the Commissioner. If there are any other developments, I'll keep in touch."

"There's one more thing," continued Pat. "You read my letter, you say—did you know of Orizaga's prior conviction? My position is clear that had the County contacted *Immigration and Custom Enforcement* in 2008 or 2009, my brother would be alive."

"I can't respond to that," said Riley. "Please understand."

"Unfortunately, I do understand. Thanks for the call."

What a joke, Pat thought to himself. He put the chicken in the oven, along with two foil-wrapped baking potatoes, and set the timer for 5:30 p.m. With a bit of luck, supper would be ready when he returned, and he would just have time to prepare the salad before Clare got home. At 4:00 p.m., he walked into *Ruth's*. Rollie was waiting for him and already had a pitcher and two glasses on his table.

"Sometimes I'm thinking why bother?" said Pat, sitting down heavily.

"Cheer up, Pat—I got some more information."

"That's good, because I may be chasing my tail with these commissioners. I just got off the phone with Riley and I smell a rat. This amendment discussion might very well be all bullshit."

"Riley, huh? Screw him and screw that whole bunch of crooks down there. Try to calm down. Listen, Mike finally talked to his guys in Murphysboro and he thinks they're spooked, you know, pretty scared about Roberto."

"What about Raul?"

"Didn't recognize him, I guess. Roberto's a different story because one of them said 'real violent' in Spanish while the other kid just sounded scared. Mike's convinced the two kids are scared shitless of this Roberto."

"When's he going down?"

"Tomorrow—he'll go down early and return late. Also, Schus ran Ignacio Delgado on all the databases and located him near the intersection of 88th and Commercial Avenue right in the heart of gangbanger territory in the *Fourth District*. He also learned the guy is behind in his real estate taxes and got his pension whacked down some years ago because of financial problems at the old *Republic Steel* on Avenue O."

"Wow, cops can get all that from data bases?"

"Yeah, no secrets anymore, Pat. He's seventy -five and his ole lady's seventy- nine. He's hurting, and he's certain to be the grandpa of our girl, Angela. As Mike says, it's like a barrio in that area with lots of guys under the radar or in the shadows."

"So grandpa's broke and may need some extra cash, you thinking?"

"Good bet, Pat—you thinking what I'm thinking?"

"I don't know, Rol—you're the detective, but it's got me thinking."

"If he's hiding in the dump, he's probably in the basement so maybe a pair of eyes are needed over there."

"What about your guys up north?" asked Pat.

"Well, all they report is that Roberto and Angela are in and out and a few times they both went to a local taco joint on foot. Oh, and sometimes they stop and get some *cerveza*.

She's there three nights now, so maybe she's a permanent live in or needs to be close for something to go down. Pat, I'm going to change the watch and see if I can get Schus to do the best he can to cover Corliss."

"Sounds good, Rol. How about same time tomorrow?"

"You got it!"

Pat picked up Clare at the usual time and they enjoyed a quiet evening. Pat thought it best to avoid the topic that so preoccupied him and worried Clare. He suggested they go to the show and see *The Bounty Hunter and Enforcer* released a year earlier and featured at the Mount Greenwood Art Center. On the way home Clare said,

"So you think Duke the bounty hunter and ex cop another Rollie?"

"Maybe. Don't forget we want justice not money."

DAY EIGHTEEN, WEDNESDAY, SEPTEMBER 14, 2011

After a morning run and coffee at the *Moonscape Cafe*, Pat turned on his computer and found an e-mail from Joe, with two attachments. The first was the three page PDF giving background on the commissioners, and the second was the draft elaborating on Schwab and Cook County. Pat began with the second document, which contained some of Joe's academic musings. The e-mail explained that this document would give some insight into Joe's chapter entitled, *Born to Hustle*, a monograph on how generation after generation of Cook County families were socialized to view political operatives as elites worthy of unwarranted deference. Joe explained that such socialization allowed thousands of elected and appointed officials to accumulate vast amounts of wealth. The majority of the electorate in Cook County were perfectly willing to view elected officials as feudal lords rather than servants of the people, he concluded.

Pat smiled. He had always thought that academics were in a world of their own, always trying their best to get to the truth. Joe was right up there with the best of the ivory tower crowd. There were at least twenty families that fit Joe's profile right there in the 19th Ward. He knew of one couple that would go to political events just to be in the presence of an alderman. They were no different than a Hollywood groupy who would strain to see some marginally talented celebrity. Thomas Jefferson would not have been happy with the clout-crazy electorate in the neighborhood.

Next, Pat looked over the Hinton biographical sketches of the commissioners, noting that Fanning graduated from *Lynwood Academy*, as did Googan. Fanning's biography showed she was once a community organizer in New York City. So now we have President Haesi, George Hallet and now this Fanning girl who were all community organizers, thought Pat. It was no coincidence that the last two were directly involved with the passing of this foolish ordinance. In a moment of cynicism, Pat concluded that one way to organize communities was to make them unsafe. Hinton confirmed that Korshak controlled all the Blacks with the exception of the gambler, and womanizer, James. What with the five other progressive liberals plus Chico, there wasn't a snowball's chance in hell that the law would be changed. Why, then, did Wagner and Riley even proffer such an idea? Hinton really hit hard on what he called the "do-nothings": Fanning, Petrutis, Murray, Mayfield and McAbee. According to him the five simply did as they were told.

Looking ahead, Pat noted that Hinton wrote unflattering sketches of county officials in the other counties as well. As he was paging through the document, the phone rang. It was Inger Nordquist, Chief Counsel for President Korshak.

"Hello, Ms. Nordquist, I gather you're speaking for President Korshak. Oh and forgive me I failed to return your call last week."

"Well, yes—she asked that I contact you."

"Sure," said Pat in his most affable voice. "But I sent the letter to President Korshak and would like to talk to her. I just have a question or two."

"Well, I speak for the President," came the steely reply. "First, we are deeply sorry for what happened—"

"Really?" interrupted Pat. "I'm confused because you must have known a guy like Orizaga would be an absconder. You're telling me Korshak and you are sorry?"

"Well, yes, Mr. McGurn. You see we think the bail bond system is flawed and are going to sponsor a commission to try and fix it."

"*Really?* So my brother's killer flew the coup because of the bond?"

"Well, yes—perhaps a higher bond would have been more appropriate."

"This is nuts!" exploded Pat. "If this creep raised 25K, who's to say he couldn't raise 50K and still run, so don't give me that crap!"

"Mr. McGurn, I must ask that you refrain from—"

"Look, I'll refrain when my family gets some justice. Dypsky had him in custody in compliance with federal law. Your boss, in cahoots with ten other commissioners, railroaded this thing through and we now have felons running the streets. That's the cold hard truth and take that to your boss. Next time I want Korshak to call."

"Mr. McGurn, President Korshak is going to--"

"Going to what? Carry on about her silly bond argument? Let me tell you, she came up with that as a cover and you know it. You're a lawyer—you should know a recent Supreme Court case stated clearly the U.S. Government has broad, undoubted power over the subject of immigration and the status of aliens. Now, let's get busy and amend this ordinance to make sure illegal felons stay locked up, prosecuted and deported! Your boss knows for damn sure my brother's killer should still be in custody. Please tell her that Cook County has no business pre empting federal law. And one more thing—Orizaga had a prior felony conviction in 09 and was released from probation February 2011. Four months later, he killed my brother and, to my knowledge, no one contacted *Immigration Customs Enforcement.*"

"I'll have to look into this, Mr. McGurn."

"Ma'am, you already know President Korshak is well aware of this," said Pat, straining to stay calm. "It was in the papers, and I mentioned it in my letter."

"Like I said, Sir, I'll look into it."

"Hope you do, Ma'am. A full copy of the 2008 arrest can be found at Police Headquarters on 35th Street—Orizaga even admitted that he wasn't a citizen!"

"Sir, I will take your concerns to President Korshak—"

"Thanks!" snapped Pat, pressing the "End Call" button.

He was still seething when the phone rang yet again. This time, it was a Father Sean Ryan from San Francisco parish in Little Village. He was the pastor of a Mexican Catholic church and was calling to express condolences and to promise his prayers and those of the parish for the McGurn family. Remembering the priest's name, Pat thanked him, apologizing for not returning his phone call from a few days earlier.

"Father, please understand that I've been very busy trying to make sense of a lot of things lately," said Pat.

"I understand, Patrick, but I also see another side to the story—the devastation of deportation to families. You see, my parish has felt the effects of what we think are unfair deportations because most of these men support families."

"Fair enough, Father. Look, I'm trying to find out why the County Board passed an ordinance that ignores federal law and allowed my brother's killer to flee. Did you know this guy had a prior felony conviction?"

Father Ryan hesitated. "Patrick, if this ordinance is repealed or amended, we think many more innocent families will get caught in the web and be deported."

"*Really?* Look, Father, there is another web and my family and hundreds of other families are in it across the country because of these so-called sanctuary ordinances and policies in scores of jurisdictions. These other families also had loved ones who were killed by illegal alien felons."

"I'm so sorry, Patrick," said the priest. "I just—"

"Look, Father, I get the church's side and know something of the church's social justice tradition, but my family was hoping for justice of another kind and this ordinance snatched that away. I guess I'm supposed to understand your support of a measure to protect aliens, but I'm having a hard time with all of this. Tell me, Father, did you know this measure would allow criminals like Orizaga to post and flee?"

"That's not quite fair, Patrick. You must understand my concern is with families."

"Father, give me a break. How can punishing a felon who is illegal with priors hurt families? I asked before, did you know about Orizaga's prior felony?"

"No, Patrick, I did not."

"Yeah, he was taken off probation four months before Denny was killed and should have been deported!"

Father Ryan sounded shocked, not so much about Orizaga's release as about Pat's vehement support of deportation.

"I know families, Father, and trust me I'm all about families, too. Raised two kids, got a grandson plus a new granddaughter, am happily married, and have an extended family of at least thirty. And the one thing always on my mind all these years has been safety for my family. Let me tell you, Father, this ordinance endangers the community."

"Well, Patrick, we think that the undocumented are also at risk because they are afraid to call the police."

"Well, that's their problem. Father, you can assure your flock—and I know a lot of coppers—and they don't check for citizenship on a domestic call. If a bad guy gets pinched and he's guilty, he should do the time and get deported. Mind if I ask you a question?"

"Please go ahead, Patrick."

"I'm wondering if you work with NGO'S—you know non-governmental agencies?"

"Well, we work with the *Illinois Immigration Cooperative* or IIC, and I'm an active member of *Clergy for Immigration Justice* here in the archdiocese. Why are you asking?"

Ignoring the question, Pat went on.

"*Illinois Immigration Cooperative*, you say, Father? I'm not comfortable with their political agenda. I've learned they played a major role in drafting this ordinance that is in violation of federal law."

"So you know about IIC, Patrick?"

"Yeah, I do, Father, and like I said, I've been busy lately trying to make sense of all this. Look, please understand there is a man on the run who killed my brother, and I'm getting the sense that somehow people seem to be defending what any reasonable person would view as outrageous."

"Patrick, we certainly don't think Mr. Orizaga should be free."

"Well, he is free and your *Illinois Immigration Cooperative* is largely responsible. I don't know what else to say, Father. Oh, one more thing—are you aware that the *Illinois Immigration Coop.* is in partnership with the *American Islamic Mediators* (AIM)?"

"Well, yes. I'm told they're moderates."

"Check again, Father. My sources tell me otherwise. Think about the object of their fund raising."

"Very interesting, Patrick, I must go now. I'll be praying for your family."

"Thank you, Father—and please forgive my tone. I appreciate your prayers."

Though he had stayed calm throughout the conversation, Pat was livid. Instead of feeling spiritual solace, he felt manipulated. Father Ryan sounded sincere enough, but he had certainly not called for Pat's benefit, nor for that of the McGurn family. Intuitively, Pat knew that Hallet and his *Illinois Cooperative* had used the priest to persuade him to back down. Fuck Hallet, Pat thought. He was now more determined than ever to return justice. He walked onto the back deck and gazed into the sky, trying to find some peace. There was comfort in the fact that Rollie's efforts over the past twelve days were beginning to show some promise.

The phone rang once more. This time it was Irv Haussman from *Wolf News* who wanted to stop by with his cameraman. Apparently, he had a letter Ms. Korshak had written to *Immigration and Custom Enforcement* Director. Pat thought for a moment.

"You know I read Morlan's letter to her about a week ago, I think. So Korshak gave you her response did she?"

"Yeah, so if you look at it maybe we can go from there."

"Look, give me some time to read it over and then put me on camera. I'll respond to Morlan's letter to Korshak, for sure, and will reserve judgment on any response to Korshak's letter."

"Fair enough, Mr. McGurn—so I think we can be at your place by, say, 3:00 p.m."

Joan Farnsworth had sent Pat a copy of Morlon's letter the week before. She said that Morlan consulted her because he knew she was in touch with the McGurn family. His letter offered three suggestions: 1) that Cook County simply allow two ICE officers in the jail to determine who should be deported; 2) that Cook County should notify ICE when the County was going to release an alien because he/she posted the necessary bond money; 3) that ICE would reimburse Cook County to the extent that the law allows. Having read Joan's comments endorsing Morlan's letter, Pat decided that his strategy would be to ignore any response to Korshak's letter while endorsing Morlan's three points. Cradling a cup of coffee, he stared out of the kitchen window, glad for a few moments of peace. His reveries were interrupted when Haussman pulled up in a *Wolf News* van.

"Hello, Pat. I'm Irv Haussman and this is Sungren, my camera man," said the TV journalist, jabbing a finger in the direction of a slight man with Asian features. The three men shook hands, and Pat led them into the living room. He and Irv sat in the Mission-style arm chairs on either side of the fire place, while Sungren set up camera equipment in the background.

"So," said Pat cordially. "Why don't you explain what happened today before you came here?"

"Well, Inger Nordquist—President Korshak's chief counsel—called and asked me to stop by to show me a copy of a letter to *Immigration and Custom Enforcement* Director Morlan. I then figured I'd get your response."

Eyebrows raised, Pat leaned back in his chair, arms folded against his chest.

"That's funny," he remarked slowly. "Strange none of the other news outlets called—I'm guessing she gave you the exclusive. You represent the conservative voice here in town, right, Irv?"

"What are you getting at, Pat?"

"Well, it's all staged," said Pat, taking his time with his response. "Korshak debunks Morlan's arguments and—by the way, have you read Morlan's letter, Irv?"

"Well, not exactly."

"So you're going to report on Korshak's letter without having read Morlan's letter? Tell you what—why don't you read Morlan's letter and I'll read Korshak's letter. Then you and I can have a discussion."

"Well, I'm on deadline you see, and we need to speak with Sheriff Dypsky," said the newsman who by now was beginning to look quite flustered.

"Irv, gimme a break," drawled Pat. "It's so obvious what's going down here—you don't have to tell me. I'll bet Korshak just refuted everything Morlan asked for and played her silly bond argument. Am I right?"

"Well, yeah, that's sort of the gist but you know I got a job to do."

Pat looked steadily at Haussman.

"So I get shot gunned by you on her behalf and *Wolf* gets a good segment tonight on the *Nine O'Clock News*. Look, Irv, tell Sungren to turn on the camera and I'll give a response to the Morlan letter and more."

By now, Sungren had finished setting up his equipment. He handed a portable mic bearing the *Wolf News* logo to his boss, then took his place some eight feet back from where they were sitting. With the exception of the fireplace area, the living room was a mess of lights and cables. Sungren nodded in Irv's direction, giving him a "thumbs up."

"Fair enough, Pat—you ready to go?"

"First tell me your opener," said Pat.

Somewhat perturbed, Haussman informed him that his segment would follow Korshak's and maybe Dypsky's. This sequence, he explained, would prep the viewers.

"I'll say something like, 'Mr. McGurn has pushed back in support of an amendment' and then I'll introduce you."

"Well, I can't control the others, but I want everything I say to be included in this piece," insisted Pat.

"Pat, I'll try. It's just that we can't control these things given time constraints," said the now flustered Haussman.

"Ok Irv, do your thing," shrugged Pat.

Sungren snapped his fingers to signal the camera was running and that the mic was live. Haussman began:

"We now go to Pat McGurn, brother of Denny McGurn who was killed by an undocumented person named Raul Orizaga last June. Mr. McGurn believes that his family fell victim to what he calls a misguided ordinance that most believe allowed Mr. Orizaga to flee the country. Mr. McGurn, we have a letter here that Cook County President Korshak addressed to Ice Director Morlan about your situation and the thrust of her argument points to the low bond Mr. Orizaga received."

Clearing his throat, Pat leaned toward the microphone.

"Mr. Haussman, you misspoke. Korshak can write all the letters she wants. Look, first of all, the correct phrase for Orizaga, my brother's killer, is 'Illegal Alien,' not 'undocumented.' Next, yes, the Cook County Board did pass an ordinance that allowed my brother's killer to flee and I hope, with help, to amend this ordinance. Any discussion that points to a low bond argument is nonsense. Quite frankly, President Korshak is hanging her bonnet on that foolish argument. Furthermore, I support Mr. Morlan's recommendations that include granting access and workstations to ICE personnel—that should have always been the case. The fact of the matter is that Sheriff Dypskey should have ignored the ordinance and complied with federal law."

"What do you mean?" interjected Haussman, his face expressionless. Pat shook his head, and continued.

"Look, I don't know what Korshak told you but here's the deal: the Feds had a detainer on Orizaga and Korshak and her pals at the County Board conspired to circumvent federal law. Now they are trying to cover themselves, pure and simple. The detention and deportation of illegals with a prior felony is a federal responsibility, and ICE must have local cooperation. Let's not forget that Orizaga should have been deported two years earlier, because he had a felony conviction from 2009. Not one Cook County criminal justice official contacted the immigration authorities back then."

"Thank you, Mr. McGurn," said Haussman, motioning to Sungren to stop the camera.

"I want all that in there, Irv—every single damn word!"

"Pat, I can't promise that," said the reporter, standing to leave. "Of course, I'll do what I—"

"Will you, Irv? I thought *Wolf News* was truth always, so I got our conversation recorded," said Pat, pulling out his iPhone.

Haussman stormed out without so much as a "goodbye," leaving Sungren, who was chuckling to himself to gather up his equipment.

"Good luck, man," he said, winking at Pat as he left.

"Thanks," Pat replied, smiling for the first time that day.

Once both men had closed the front door behind them, he surveyed the living room. There were a few pieces of furniture that needed to be pushed back into place—the couch was at a strange angle and the coffee table was behind the couch instead of in front of it. A few framed family photos had been knocked over on the bureau, but there did not seem to be any damage. Satisfied that the room was straight, Pat made his way to the kitchen. By now his coffee was ice cold, but it tasted good, all the same and gave the day a semblance of normality.

Feeling more relaxed, Pat called Clare to go over the interview with her.

"Did you comb your hair?" she laughed.

"Nope, I looked like a wild man. Next time, I'll don the Unabomber look! Look, pizza night—I'll pick you up at the usual time. See you— Rollie's waiting."

On his way out the phone rang and, recognizing Eileen Murphy's cell phone number, he answered. She was much more distant than usual and was clearly not interested in providing any more information than was necessary. Apparently, the FBI warrant would be coming out that Friday. She promised to send him a copy and then quickly terminated the call.

Now running late, Pat drove the ten blocks to *Ruth's*. There were only a handful of patrons at the bar, which seemed odd for a Wednesday. Pat walked over to a corner table under a poster of the Chicago Bears. Rollie had already ordered a pitcher of Molanger.

"I bet you're wondering why so few regulars?" observed Rollie. Before Pat could answer, he added, "Well, they all went to a Sox game on a coach bus. So we got the joint to ourselves."

"You know, Rol, I'm a fair weather fan. I mean going to a game when your team is ten games out in September makes no sense but I'll tell you, Denny, no matter what, he'd go to thirty maybe forty games a year. He loved it, Rol!"

"You think of Denny a lot, don't you?" observed Rollie.

"Yeah, I do—but, hey, good to see you! Everything okay?"

"Sure, Pat, grandkids doing good and—let's see, oh, birthday celebration for my son Robin on Saturday."

"Sounds like a good time—you go first, Rol."

Taking a long pull on his Molanger, Rollie described the phone call he had just had with Mike Dukavich. As he had surmised, Roberto was a character to be reckoned with.

"He's one mean motherfucker! Remember I told you his nickname?"

"Yeah, I remember. Ozzie, right?"

"The kids confirmed that, so we know for sure who this guy is; now we must figure his next move. First, I should tell you his profile. For initiation into the gang, Roberto forces kids to witness real torture and maybe death. Mike said they were freaking out just to talk about him—one of the kids was actually crying. If anyone rats, he's a goner."

Pat was visibly shaken.

"Wow! This is like something out of a violent flick! Rol, you ever hear of anything like this before?"

"Well, I knew of initiation rites, but never had the pleasure of interrogating anybody like this. Look, I'm thinking this supports the theory that Raul has a gang connection and gang money very probably got him out, follow me?"

"Yeah, I follow—so where're you going with this, Rol?"

"I figure Raul owes somebody for his release—and for sure a low skilled illegal ain't got 25K or 30K, so there's must be payback."

"Like what—rob a bank?"

"Maybe some kind of a big job—I'm thinking maybe a hit, and it was all part of a deal worked out ahead a time. Think about it, you're a lowly illegal sitting downstate in prison for eight years and upon release you get deported. For sure, you're motivated. You got nothing to lose and everything to gain. More on that later. So, look, I set up a new watch with my guys at the 88th and Commercial Place. You okay with that?"

"No problem, but if this Roberto is such a bad ass, why don't the cops know about him?"

"Well, they do somewhat, but he's slick—I mean no record. Schus got a guy up north that had an unofficial file on him, but lost track a few years ago. I'm thinking Roberto operates in the Fourth District, probably with this Samienga gang, and uses an alias. The kids only know him as Ozzie, with no last name. Remember, phony ID's are a piece of cake these days."

Pat looked up at the TV screen. "Boys are having a good day. Sox winning in the 8th. What else?"

"Well, I rode around a bit yesterday and today and spent maybe two hours or so in a meter reader uniform with flash light and hand held device. While walking the neighborhood, I saw a *bodega*—you know, a mini-mart, a couple of gin mills, a Catholic church, and, not far from the Delgado place, maybe a half block, I found a Polish deli. Few Poles left, I guess, from the old *U.S. Steel Mill* days. Anyhow, I go in and chat up a late 40's guy named Wally and tell him I'm a meter reader and we get talking. His old man owned the joint for forty years. Now Wally keeps it open for five hours a day because old timers keep coming back for what, back in the day, was considered the best Polish sausage. Forgive me I digress."

"Hey, no problem Roll—I love Chicago history trivia. Did you buy some sausage?"

"You bet—having some tonight with sauerkraut. You want some, Pat?"

"Naw, Clare would kill me. She hates that stuff. Thanks anyway. So, tell me, did you read Wally's meter?"

"Yeah, I went down and wrote some numbers and Wally bought it. So I tell him somebody on the next block told me that our subject's house maybe for sale. Wally says he didn't hear anything like that, but he did say he heard the ole guy's wife is pretty sick. She used to be up and down the block, but now he hasn't seen here in a year or so. So I grab the bag of sausage and head toward the house, pretending to be a meter reader, and go in the back yard. There's no back door, but there's a side door and, of course, a front door. Also old lace curtains on the basement window so I'm guessing people enter either door. The good news is our guys can spot anyone entering and leaving and not have to worry about a back door. Just a little more intelligence gathering might help."

No longer interested in the game, Pat looked at Rollie.

"Okay, so we have a rough neighborhood and a destitute older couple, related to Roberto's girl friend. Our watch needs to monitor comings and goings. That's why we need to switch the watch."

"For sure, Pat," responded Rollie. "Oh, and this Officer Relinski who Frank arranged to drive by reports lights on in the basement. That's another piece to the puzzle. So let me go over the new watch, and what I'm trying to set up at Corliss."

"When is the change, Rol?"

"Way ahead of you, Pat. Jose starts at 6:00 p.m. tonight and goes all night to 6:00 a.m. when he'll be relieved by Mario tomorrow morning. You and I got to provide spells—I'll do an 11:00 p.m. break for Jose tonight for an hour. Hopefully, my guy will confirm the lights on in the basement or, with luck, Angela or Roberto paying a visit. Meanwhile, Frank will get this Officer Relinski to help and both my guys on the watch and have exchanged cell numbers with him."

"This Relinski's been watching this place for a few days now—has he reported anything or maybe heard of Roberto aka Ozzie?"

"No, just the basement lights on but Frank's high on this kid and if something weird's going on there this guy should notice. Besides, we got to understand he only drives by there from time to time—he's got a pretty active beat. Oh, and I'm in touch with Schus up north and there's going to be coverage of some kind with some Tactical Unit guys Schus is working on."

After listening to Rollie's updates, Pat went over his phone calls with Joe, Nordquist, and Father Ryan, before describing the Haussman interview.

"I'm pissed because it looks like Korshak used Haussman to get her point across," said Pat, feeling the anger rising.

"You see, Korshak fed Haussman this letter that refuted this guy Morley who's the ICE director. Morley wrote her a letter a week ago or so trying to work something out so that his agents can do their job—you know, like deport bad news illegals. Morley's on my side, you might say. Now get this, Rol—Haussman wanted to give me like a minute to read the fuckin' letter and I would have looked like an idiot trying to rebut her claims. Luckily, I smelled a rat and told him all he gets is my rant."

"Did he go for it, Pat? You get to say your piece?"

"Yeah, I said a lot so we'll see—watch *Wolf @9* tonight. Oh, speaking of news, Murphy told me this FBI guy spent an hour or so preparing an affividavid and looks like a federal warrant will be issued Friday."

Rollie pulled a face.

"Fuck the FBI! All those pretty boy types will just send out the paperwork and won't do shit. We're going to get this gopher—I'm pretty sure he's in that basement."

"Rol, you're serious?" said Pat, incredulously.

"I'm telling you, my friend—it's in my gut. We're going to get this fucker, but there's a lot of planning yet and for now we need more validation. One more thing, Pat—we may need more help."

"You mean the cops helping unofficial like they have been, Rol?"

"For sure they're with us, but I'm talking the big dog here and I know just the guy, but he lives in DC. I haven't talked to him in a while. Maybe Jake Hawk will help us out."

"Rol, I got questions, but I won't say a word until you talk to this guy. When you going to call this Jake guy?"

"Day or two, I'm thinking, Pat," said Rollie, suddenly glancing at the large wall clock. "Look, I gotta run."

"So do I," said Pat, suddenly remembering his promise to collect Clare at the 91st Street train station. Within minutes, both men were in their cars, hurrying to their respective destinations.

As planned, Pat and Clare headed out to *Rossi's* for pizza. They split a small sausage pizza and ordered drinks. For an hour or so, they enjoyed relaxing, avoiding any heavy topics. Molly had sent some photos of baby Maeve and they enjoyed studying each one, marveling at how quickly their newest granddaughter was growing. They got home just in time for the news.

The opening segment reported on the Republican candidates' debate down in Tampa, Florida. Clare thought all the candidates looked pretty good.

"Gingrich sure doesn't pull any punches going after President Haesi," she remarked. "Perry doesn't seem to want the nomination that bad and Romney's clearly in the hunt—God knows he's raising some serious money. What do you think, Pat?"

"Yeah, Romney all the way, but when nominated the left will try and crucify him with lies and more lies. I'm convinced after reading some stuff lately that they will stop at nothing in order to retain power. Gingrich was spot on talking about the illegal immigration crisis. I didn't know that there's a likelihood of thousands upon thousands of illegal kids getting in."

"Neither did I," agreed Clare.

After the commercial, Irv Haussman opened his local news segment. The couple was astonished that the producer played all of Pat's rant. All Haussman said at the end was,

"Stay tuned."

"You need a haircut," said Clare, fondly stroking Pat's hair. "Just kidding. That was pretty good."

"I was angry but somehow I kept a cool head. Well, I guess it came out the way I wanted."

"You were terrific!" Clare affirmed. "Look, I know it's late, but we didn't go over your conversation with Rollie."

Pat summarized the Mike Dukavich report, Rollie's walk about at Angela's grandparents, and the fact that Relinski saw the basement lights on. After a few brief comments about the Riley call and ended his summary with the watch change, but deliberately left out details about his own involvement.

"When?"

"Tomorrow, and Rollie's North Side guy is going to get some coppers to keep an eye on Roberto and Angela."

Clare smiled.

"I don't know. Too many moving parts and one thing for sure, your TV rants won't sit well with all sorts of people."

"I know, but I got a dead brother who fools let loose."

"Denny would be proud," Clare said.

Clare for some odd reason did not feel the same level of concern that she felt the day before. Maybe it was the lighthearted conversation earlier while viewing Maeve's photos or maybe the resolve her husband demonstrated with the Haussman interview. The glass of white wine helped.

DAY NINETEEN, THURSDAY, SEPTEMBER 15, 2011

Inger Nordquist, Commissioner Vic Varbanov, Sheriff Dan Dypsky and States Attorney Lisa Hunter-Goss had gathered for a 9:00 a.m. emergency meeting in President Korshak's conference room. They were joined by George Hallet, head of the *Illinois Immigration Cooperative*. The mood was subdued. Recent news reports put the County in a bad light and each person in the room stood to lose face–or worse!

"We have a problem," Korshak began. "Pat McGurn was pretty convincing last night on *Wolf News* and my guess is that the blogs, phone calls and letters will come to his support. We have to be ready. Mr. Haussman told us and—correct me if I'm wrong, Ms. Nordquist—that he was only going to get McGurn's reaction to my letter to ICE Director Morley, right?"

"Yes, that was the understanding, Shirley."

"Well, evidently he had a change of plans. I just learned the interview was on a few cable channels," snapped Korshak.

"Well, cable outlets like Wolf and TNN frequently run local stories with national interests," countered Nordquist.

"Let's face it," said Dypsky, "immigration has national and international interests. Europe has a huge problem with illegals getting into Greece, Spain and Italy."

Varbanov looked at the group.

"I only care about what's happening here in Chicago. This McGurn went after all of us—the guy's gonna be a problem."

"The more I think of the prior felony, I don't blame McGurn for being really angry," said Dypsky.

"Look, he's angry with a whole lot of people, Mr. Dypsky, and you're included," observed Hunter-Goss.

Dypsky shot Hunter-Goss a contemptuous look.

"Did you know that Phil Regan picked it up last night, too? I don't know about the rest of you, but last night my press guy gave me a heads up from the Regan show, and it sure looks bad for us. He invited some legal types and they suggested a law suit."

Korshak cleared her throat.

"Look, we have already discussed a strategy to kill this. Before I go on, Mr. Hallet, Mr. Varbanov assured me that you would keep this meeting in the strictest confidence."

"Most certainly, Madam President. Commissioner Varbanov has brought me up to speed and I think I can help."

"That's why you're here, Mr. Hallet. You worked with President Haesi, I understand."

"Yes," acknowledged Hallet. "We served on the *Tomes Foundation*. I also did some community organizing work with the President on the South Side in Roseland and other communities years ago."

"So you have met with the President on this subject?"

"Yes, President Haesi and I have looked at immigration. I have moved him in the non-enforcement direction, and he and his staff are now working with *Homeland Security* Secretary Tyrone Jackson on this. We are trying to get him to back off on internal enforcement by getting rid of *The Secure Communities Program*."

"Is he going to get rid of it?" asked Varbanov.

"Well, it's been here since 2008 and got ramped up pretty good in over forty states. For some odd reason, the President allowed a bunch of deportations, but now he realizes he's shooting himself in the foot by losing the support of the Hispanic base. I read just the other day that Hispanic eligible voters are well over 20 million and our efforts hope that number will grow. Aside from lobbying the White House, my role at the *Cooperative* is to get local jurisdictions like Cook County to thumb their noses at *Immigration and Custom Enforcement*—which is precisely what Cook County did last month. Oh, and I might add, others are likely to follow because you guys are high profile and Chicago is the President's home. Our goal is to get two or three hundred more jurisdictions to follow what Cook County did. All I can say at this point is that the President might try to issue an executive order to deep six the *Secure Communities Program.*"

"This is all well and good but we didn't know this Denny McGurn would get killed or that his brother would make life miserable for us all," said Korshak.

"Look," interjected Dypsky, "I'm confident this is a news cycle that will dissipate in a week or so."

"Anything to add, Ms. Nordquist?" asked Korshak, looking somewhat more assured.

"Well, I spoke with the President's Chief of Staff, Bolevsky, just yesterday and brought them up to speed. That's all I can say for now—"

Varbanov cut her off.

"They going to do something?"

"I believe so," said Nordquist. Hallet nodded and winked at Varbanov.

"Right," said Korshak. "Now, Inger, please go over important developments since the last time this group met. I think you mentioned something about more bad press."

Ms. Nordquist looked at her notes.

"The story has gone across the country. We already discussed Regan and Wolf. *The Daley Crier* had a piece yesterday and Sonny and Rhoda had a national feed this morning on their radio show, with the phones ringing off the wall. They even got a hold of this African American guy in L.A. whose football star son was gunned down by an illegal. The McGurn story will have legs along with similar cases and you can bet there will be letters, blogs and books."

Korshak seemed unimpressed.

"Okay, so we know it's gotten big but what about specifics?"

Nordquist hesitated for a moment.

"Well, first and most important is that our friend, McGurn, is going to fight. We all know he won't win on an amendment, but we must keep in mind that he has conservative media supporters. The reason is clear—Raul Orizaga had a prior felony conviction and these news reports keep pounding the idea that Denny McGurn might very well be alive today had ICE been informed during the first felony arrest in 2008."

Varbanov banged his fist on the table.

"Look, this was the right thing to do! Screw the talk shows and blogs—they nothing but racists. You know, we got all kinds of people fighting back on blogs—ain't that right, George?"

Hallet nodded.

"Yes, I set up a blog strategy a few years ago, and we have methods to debunk anti- immigration bloggers. We're also pretty good at undermining Tea Party groups. The racism strategy always works."

Varbanov jumped to his feet.

"See! We're going to fight back, not let some goddam prick—"

Pointing a finger at Varbanov, Korshak yelled at him in disgust.

"Hold it, Vic, and sit down, for Christ's sake! Damage control is why I called this meeting so please calm down! Now let Inger finish."

With an eerie silence in the room, Nordquist continued.

"Well, we know Pat McGurn is talking to this Professor Vanderbiezen down state—I think that came up last week, right?"

Everyone nodded in agreement.

"Okay, well I've discovered that there's a visiting female professor named Farnsworth down at the U of I. She's an expert on immigration enforcement and has also been talking to McGurn. I learned just this morning that she works for the *Center for Immigration Analysis*, the leading think tank on immigration enforcement. She and several others have published papers making convincing arguments for enforcement. She is also routinely invited to testify before the *House Judiciary Committee*."

"Whose side are you?" Varbanov interrupted. "You agree with this Farnsworth lady, you telling us?"

"No, Sir," said Nordquist calmly. "I'm trained as a lawyer first and a partisan second and all I'm saying is that if you look at their work, it is careful, thoughtful analysis."

"Is that clear, Vic?" asked Korshak, her icy tone suggesting that it had better be.

"Perhaps—I guess so."

"Okay, so now we know why this has gone national in a big way," said Hunter-Goss.

"My deputy, Mr. Sheehan, phoned me on the way over and said people calling into these radio shows want me to resign."

"Welcome to the club!" said Dypsky, smiling sarcastically.

"Let me continue," said Nordquist. "You all heard McGurn on *Wolf* last night. It's clear he doesn't buy our bond argument for a minute. My guess is that the professors prepped him. He's not going to roll over on this."

"My guess is that there may be more than we know in his corner," observed Korshak. "Okay, Vic, your turn."

"Well, my amigo, George, here and I thought Father Ryan might help us out. He's real pro-Hispanic—you know he's a pastor in Little Village. So we had him call Mr. McGurn. George, what did Father Ryan tell you?"

"First off, Father Ryan is pastor at San Francisco parish and real active in *Clergy for Immigration Justice*. We learned McGurn was a practicing Catholic and thought he would see the social justice angle."

"Whose idea was this might I ask?" interrupted Dypsky.

"Both of us," said Varbanov smugly. "Father agreed because he thought he might know people McGurn knows in that Beverly neighborhood."

Ignoring Varbanov, Dypsky looked at George Hallet.

"Any luck, Mr. Hallet?"

"No, not really, Sheriff. All the Padre said was that McGurn knew all about *Illinois Immigration Cooperative* and more or less suggested it was a rogue group. He even went after our partner, *Arab Immigration Mediators* (AIM). He also debunked the families' pitch—you know, deportations hurting families."

"Hold it!" said Korshak, a look of disbelief clouding her face. "Arab-Muslim partners—What are you talking about?"

"Oh, I thought you knew we partner with AIM."

"No, Sir, I did not and had I known, I would have thought twice about getting involved with your organization. I'm telling you, I don't trust Muslims! And you, Commissioner Varbanov, why did you not tell me this?"

Varbanov shrugged but made no comment. Hallet quickly tried to smooth things over.

"Please, Ma'am let me get you some literature. If I may, Arab and Muslim are not the same."

If Hallet intended to be helpful, his efforts backfired. Ignoring the correction, Korshak turned to Dypsky.

"You've been quiet—you got something to say?"

"I'm guessing he's getting more information than all of us know from Vanderbiezen and some woman downstate."

"Well, I don't know about a priest or professors but let me ask you, Sheriff. What about reimbursement?" asked State's Attorney Hunter-Goss.

"Yeah, we get full reimbursement from the Feds and it's called *State Criminal Alien Assistance Program* or SCAAP."

Pointing at Varbanov again, Korshak looked as though she was going to choke.

"You know, Mr.Varbanov over there had me and ten commissioners convinced we don't get reimbursed, so what the hell is going on here? What was it, over three million last year, Mr. Dypsky?"

"Yes, that's right, give or take."

"Well, Commissioner Varbanov," said Korshak, looking at her fingernails. "I'm listening."

"Look, I was misunderstood," protested Varbanov. "Besides, we went over this days ago. I knew the Sheriff here got some money, but George and I thought it didn't cover all the expenses."

Looking exasperated, Korshak turned towards Hunter-Goss.

"What's more, this prior conviction of Orizaga's is sure to haunt us, right Ms. Hunter-Goss? Let me ask you this, did you in-service your people on the ordinance?"

"It was under review, Shirley."

"Under review! Well, surely someone must have known an Orizaga type release would hit the papers. I'm asking, did your three or four hundred attorneys know about the non-detainer enforcement ordinance?"

"Look, please don't tell me how to run my office. We all supported this thing and maybe we didn't think things through—now you are trying to make out like it was not your fault."

"I'll pretend I didn't hear that, so let's move on," said Korshak.

"Let's see, Ms. Hunter-Goss, who was assigned to prosecute Orizaga?"

"A veteran named Eileen Murphy. I told you that two and a half weeks ago."

"Well, excuse me, counselor," came the testy response. "Now the way I see it, this Murphy had no knowledge of the ordinance and, if she did, she could have made a request to increase the bond, right?"

"That's my understanding," said Hunter-Goss, wearily. "And, no, she did not know. I met with Ms. Murphy just yesterday for damage control and she told me that McGurn doesn't really blame her, but seems to really have it in for all of us at this table."

"Well, we have a perfect storm," said Korshak, looking around the table. "Anybody have any ideas?"

"Well, one more thing—Eileen Murphy told me that a federal warrant is likely to be issued tomorrow. I spoke with my deputy, Mr. Sheehan, but he doubts it will amount to anything."

"I agree," interjected Nordquist. "The FBI won't really look for him but it might quiet McGurn."

"That's all we need—for some loud mouth Tommy Lee Jones type hauling Orizaga before TV cameras and making us look bad."

They all smiled politely.

"McGurn won't be fooled by an FBI warrant if he has Dufner helping him," said Dypsky. "Besides, Cook County has a warrant and, trust me, McGurn knows that's a joke, too."

"So you know this Dufner, right, Sheriff?"

"Met him once or twice—you know he knows people I know kind of thing. He's older—maybe 10 years or so."

"Well, what sort of help are we talking about?"

"I think I mentioned at our meeting last week that he verbally roughed up this Chicago detective Skolickwitcz pretty good, and I'm guessing he's got his eyes on the brother. The detective was assigned to look for Orizaga."

"How do you know all this, Sheriff?" asked Varbanov.

"My deputy was with the Chicago detective they call Alphy. And let me tell you, Alphy was really pissed off after Dufner reamed him out for not grilling Orizaga's brother. I also asked around—you know Dufner's from my ward in Mount Greenwood."

"Don't mean nothing, Why worry about some retired cop?"

"Hope you're right, Commissioner," said Dypsky with a smirk.

"George and I are thinking of maybe calling this McGurn," said Varbanov, casting an angry look at Dypsky.

"Really! Think that's a good idea, Mr. Hallet?"

"Sure, the man is educated, so at least he should be polite enough to listen, Ms. Korshak."

"Earlier you said he gave a priest a hard time," objected Nordquist.

"Why don't I have my new press guy, Grodecki, call him? I think McGurn knows him or his family from the neighborhood."

"Well, I suppose a friendly phone call can't hurt, so I guess you all have my support. Oh and Mr. Dypsky, it's been close to a month since the ordinance was passed—do you have any numbers? I mean how many other illegals with detainers have been released?"

"Well, my staff is working on this," replied Dypsky. "I can tell you that about a hundred have been released and at least six have been arrested since they posted and have been charged with felonies including a rape in Kane County."

"What about the ninety-four others or so?"

"Well, when they're released it's the State's Attorney who monitors their process through the system."

"Well, Lisa?"

"I don't know off hand. I guess I'll look into it."

"Lisa, this is a matter of urgency—we *need* to know. Will your office get a warrant for Orizaga?"

"Already did—I told you as much. I don't know about the others."

"You can bet Pat McGurn or conservative media like Wolf will ask. Maybe do a Freedom of Information request," suggested Dypsky.

Hunter-Goss gathered her files and rose to her feet. With a dismissive wave, she walked out.

"Well," said Korshak. "I guess this meeting is adjourned. I suspect you'll hear from Ms. Nordquist soon. Mr. Varbanov, please stay back a moment and you, too, Inger."

Once the other attendees left, Korshak gestured to Varbanov and Nordquist to sit down.

"Vic, between you and me, do you have any connection with these Orizaga brothers or their lawyer, Simpkus?"

"President Korshak, please don't insult me! I never heard of the Orizaga brothers!"

"Okay, how about Simpkus?"

"Yeah, I know him. He's helped a lot of people and works with a firm in Pilsen."

"How about Congressman Rodriguez?"

"What do you mean?"

"Well, does Rodriguez know the brothers?"

"Not that I know of, but you know anything is possible."

"Simpkus has likely represented gang bangers and drug dealers, right, Vic?"

"I think so," said Varbanov cautiously.

"These people in gangs, Vic?"

"Probably," he conceded.

"Oh, that's great—do you know if this Simpkus contributed to Hispanic politicians?"

"Well, I know his law firm has and maybe he has. Not sure."

"Did the firm contribute to Alderman Castro, former Commissioner Ruiz or maybe Judge Santiago?"

"Why you ask about these people?"

"Sammy Castro's father, Ramon, was convicted of a phony ID ring last year and, to this day, I can't believe they didn't go after his Alderman son. You know the Feds have their eyes on the other two. My problem, Vic, is that Ralston or someone else and maybe even McGurn might connect some more dots."

"Madam President, I think you exaggerate—there's nothing to worry about!"

Exasperated, President Korshak stared directly at Commissioner Varbanov.

"God help us, Mr. Varbanov, if this gets out! I wouldn't be surprised if McGurn does find this out! I wish you had never approached me for support of this ordinance. Now tell me what you know about this Islam thing? McGurn sure knows about this we just heard."

"George says they're okay and that McGurn got it all wrong."

"That worries me, Vic. Anything more I need to know?"

"Nothing for now."

"I heard that Chicago ICE Director Yu said Cook County is now more dangerous because of the ordinance," Korshak continued.

"Surely we got some leverage here, you know, with the President being a Chicagoan to maybe get this Yu to watch what he says," said Varbanov, pushing his chair back from the table.

"I also asked Rodriguez to call Senator Congelosi on this Yu," commented Nordquist. "I also learned that the Republicans on the *Senate*

Judiciary Committee have been making a lot of noise because of what they say is poor immigration enforcement and border control. In fact, Senator Irwin from Alabama was railing against our ordinance the other day on the Senate floor and really pissed off our pal, Senator Congelosi. Rodriguez's staff sent me the link to watch it in C-SPAN

Varbanov made no comment but stood up and extended his hand to Korshak. There was a strained look on his face.

"You know you made me look bad," he said.

"Wasn't my intention, Vic."

After Varbanov left, Korshak suggested that Nordquist look into Simpkus.

"Start with the *Illinois Grievance Commission*, Inger, and see if any complaints have been filed. Also let's have a meeting at my house Sunday at 10:00 a.m. and issue formal invites for a brunch so we don't get accused of violating the *Open Meetings Act*. This McGurn thing is worrisome."

"Who do we invite?"

"Let's see. Varbanov for sure and invite Alport and Houma—they can bring us up to speed on this forum for next week. Oh and get George Hallet here as well."

"Good idea, Shirley. I understand that Alport's got this forum down pat. I think she sent a registered letter to McGurn just today."

"Inger, you know, I may invite Dilbert and Bernice Redstone."

"*Really?* You know if that gets out you're finished politically. The right wing press refers to them as the satanic siblings because they're brother and sister."

"I know it's risky, but I need them. Besides, this controversy may shorten my political career. You know what Dilbert told me?"

"What? I'm afraid to ask!"

"Between you and me, Inger, President Haesi said at a private dinner last week that the Hispanic caucus in Congress has been bugging him to do something about this mess here and he wants this to go away."

"Yeah, this could hurt his re-election next year. You know when I talked to his Chief of Staff Bolevsky he mentioned that as well."

"You know, Inger, Dilbert is a genius and his concern for the oppressed second to none. The President privately will tell you he owes most of his political success to Dilbert and Bernice."

"Well if you insist on inviting them, just but be careful—you know as well as anybody that the right-wingers are constantly dragging up the Redstones' past because they got off on a technicality twenty-five years ago."

"Yeah, Inger, that worries me and I try not to think of their radical past. So many of us owe them a lot. Let's see, we'll get calls into Special Assistant Jahnna Suhud and Chief of Staff, Bolevsky. Next we'll get this Cook County forum finalized, and Hallet will continue undermining the conservative bloggers. What am I missing, Inger?"

"We got ten iron clad Cook County commissioners that will never change their vote. Oh and one more thing, Alport told me she thought a rally on that day might be something to think about."

"I like that idea—we can discuss this on Sunday. Anything else, Inger?"

"Well, yeah, now don't laugh, but my secretary, Joelle, overheard Mona, the receptionist down the hall, talking about some planning meeting to have Varbanov running for your job next election!"

"You're kidding!"

"Nope—I guess he's serious and they're thinking of the slogan, *Vic equals Victory.*"

●

That same morning, Rollie spent time at the new watch with Mario and made calls to Schus, Pat and Frank Higgins to ensure that all bases were covered. With a little luck, he hoped something might pop. Pat agreed to cover the house on Commercial the next day, so Rollie could brief Jose, Mario, Higgins and patrolman Relinski. Later in the afternoon, Rollie spent an hour or so with Schus and a tactical patrol team (TAC) at a restaurant up north near *Clemente High School* that specialized in Puerto Rican chicken. The TAC police agreed to drive by the Corliss property from noon to 4:00 a.m. The team was on a special sixteen hour shift ordered by the new police chief because of increased gang activity and murders in both the African-American and Hispanic communities. Schus had arranged for the TAC teams because they would blend right into the neighborhood, what with their plain clothes and the old cars repossessed from convicted drug dealers. He cautioned Rollie that this was the best he and the team could do—and for no more than two weeks, given the irregularity of the detail. Rollie understood.

The four men enjoyed the meal and made small talk about the city in general and the measured increase in crime. They all agreed that the jury was still out on the new mayor and his choice of the new Police Commissioner, Chang. Rollie mentioned how Chang had responded "irrelevant" when asked about the citizenship status of the killers of several black kids in a city in New Jersey.

"Are you telling us that he said that after these kids were gunned down for no reason by illegals?"

Rollie nodded.

"Yeah, and get this—their mayor backed him up. So what Pat figures is that the whole lot of them—you know county and city big shots—are just bending over to help these illegals while the coppers gotta clean up the shit."

The TAC guys shook their heads in disbelief. Before they could express their views, however, the radio squawked.

"Trouble in Humboldt Park—we gotta go!"

"I owe you, guys," said Rollie. "And, hey, call the Police Union and tell them what I just told you about this Chang!"

"Hope you get this asshole, man—we're proud to help!" said the team leader as they headed for the door. "I'm calling the *Chicago Police Brotherhood* first chance I get!"

Schus looked at Rollie with a mixture of admiration and shock.

"Rol, I gotta tell ya I'm more convinced than ever that rule breaking is the only way to get the bad guys."

Rollie smiled.

"C'mon, Schus, you know all kinds of crazy shit went on like that back in the day. Remember when we were rookies and Commissioner Condon had undercover guys checking on those fuckin' radicals in the early 70's?"

"Yeah, I remember. I wish someone would a write a book on that. Okay, Rol, I got to go—I'll call tomorrow."

"Your guys know to keep this on the quiet, right, Schus?"

Schus smiled.

"Not a problem. I'll leave you to cover the check and tip."

●

Meanwhile, Pat had a series of phone messages to return. First, Joan Farnsworth said she was going to testify in the *House Subcommittee on Immigration* at 2:00 p.m. ET and that her testimony could be accessed on the *Judiciary Committee* web site. The McGurn case would be part of the record, she assured him. She also congratulated Pat on his remarks the night before on *Wolf News*.

There were also calls from three commissioners—Julie Googan, Lori Fanning and Vic Varbanov. George Hallet also asked for a return call and mentioned that this was his second attempt. All left cell numbers except Fanning who had voted for the ordinance; a big-time liberal, she represented a multi-cultural district up north. Googan, a Republican, had voted against it and lived in Alsip. Pat started with Varbanov.

•

While driving to a meeting of the *Minority Construction Consultants,* Vic Varbanov answered his cell phone.

"Hello, Commissioner Vic Varbanov speaking."

"Pat McGurn, returning your call."

"Oh, thanks, Mr. McGurn. You know we are really sorry about your brother."

"Sure you are," said Pat sarcastically. "What about Orizaga getting out of jail? Say, can I call you Vic?"

"Well, I don't know—I mean my people call me by my title."

"Good, so I'll call you Vic. Say, Varbanov, isn't that a Slavic name?"

"Yeah, my father is Bulgarian. Why you ask?"

"Curious, Vic, that's all."

"My mama from Argentina, so I'm Bulgarian and Argentine. Look you sent me and the other commissioners a letter."

"Sure did, Vic, I'm listening—so what's on your mind?"

"Well, it's like this—we think the bond was set too low and that's the problem."

"I think you know my position on that argument."

"Well, you might not know all that's involved."

"Vick, I know exactly what I'm talking about and the bond issue is just a cover. Look, the Assistant State's Attorney told us not to worry if Orizaga posted bail because the Feds had a hold on him."

"Well, I think she was wrong."

"What the fuck are you talking about? You know damn well a detainer was issued."

"Detainers are just bad."

"Bad, Vick? It's federal law, man! So you got nullification rights now?"

"Look, Mr. McGurn, I'm acting in good faith here—now don't get ugly!"

"Vic, this is unbelievable! You sponsor a fucked up law that lets my brother's killer skip and I'm ugly! You know damn well that you and nine others were out of line and I'll bet most of your fellow commissioners didn't know what the fuck they were voting on!"

"Okay, okay, Mr. McGurn. How about you coming down here and we'll have a chat, you know what I mean?"

"I don't think so, Commissioner. I think this is all bullshit and nothing will change my mind. The way I see it, you somehow got to Korshak who got her people to vote—I'm still trying to figure Petrutis, Houma and Fanning and some of the others. Look, Vic, I got other calls to make, so you got to do your thing and so do I."

"Let me tell you, Petrutis, Houma, Fanning—all of them cares about the people."

"Sure they do, Vick. All they care about is lining their pockets!"

Next, Pat called Commissioner Julie Googan.

"Julie Googan speaking."

"Pat McGurn here—you left a message."

"I just wanted to extend my condolences and remind you I voted against the ordinance."

"Appreciate that, Julie. Thanks for voting the *right* way. Let's see, five no votes—do you think we can change the vote?"

"I doubt it," said Googan. "With President Korshak on Varbanov's side it would be tough. I think Wagner's trying to get a hearing scheduled with Davida Alport."

"Yeah, that's what I hear. You know, Julie, I just got off the phone with Varbanov."

"*What?* Varbanov called you, Mr. McGurn?"

"Yeah it was a return call, and I just hung up with him. I mean, he had the audacity to give me a load of crap about bond court," said Pat bitterly.

"Interesting is all I can say, Mr. McGurn. It looks like this committee meeting will be next week or so, and my guess is Alport will invite you."

"So tell me, Julie, what's with the bond argument?"

"Well, President Korshak argues that, as far as she is concerned, it was the bond court that's the issue."

"Maybe you can help me with this. I'm thinking Korshak came up with this silly bond argument just in the past couple a weeks for cover. You agree?"

"All I know is what she said, Pat," said Googan hesitantly.

"So you won't go any further than that?"

"I gotta be careful."

"I understand. Do you think an amendment has a shot?"

"Not enough votes, Mr. McGurn."

"So a hearing is a waste of time, Julie?"

"Well, I don't know, Pat. I wouldn't get my hopes up and, well, Wagner's not liked by the—well, I better not say."

Pat gave a muffled laugh.

"Okay, I get it—the minorities don't like him and you have to be careful."

"You see the issues are complicated," said Googan slowly. "Like each commissioner may need another commissioner down the road."

"Okay, Julie, not hard to figure where you stand. You're right—no point getting hopeful, but you know what? I'm not going to give up, damn it! Look, thanks for your time."

Pat got off the phone and watched Joan Farnsworth on C-SPAN testify before the *House Subcommittee on Immigration*. He spent the next half hour taking notes, listening attentively as she documented the issues concisely and coherently. Her starting point was economic. She argued that in the current climate, immigration regulation should be enforced more rigorously because the jobs illegal workers would obtain were the same jobs that underemployed or unemployed U.S. citizens could hold. She pointed out that the decade was the largest period of immigration in American history. Over 13 million immigrants had entered the U.S.—millions of them, illegally, with no record as to how many were criminals. Examples in her testimony included the death of a ten year old boy who was mowed down by an illegal; the murder of a mother and son who were shot by a released illegal; and the senseless death of Pat's brother, Denny.

By the time Farnsworth's testimony had come to an end, Pat was livid. The "bare facts" hit home hard, especially in the wake of his conversations with Varbanov and Googan. He was just contemplating whether he should pour himself a drink, when yet another call came through.

"McGurn speaking."

"Sir, this is Jill Jacobs, associate producer from *Wolf in the Morning* TV talk show in New York. We would like for you to appear this weekend—Sunday, perhaps. No need to travel to the Big Apple—all you need to do is go to our studio in downtown Chicago."

"Really?", responded Pat with suspicion.

"Yes, we know about your situation and perhaps you can share your concerns and how you feel."

"Feel, you say? Look, I don't want to be some grieving subject to appeal to your viewers' emotional brain on a Sunday morning! Please understand my fight involves rational policy—I'd be happy to debate any number of pro-immigration, beltway think tank types."

"Well, Sir, I'm not sure if that's possible."

"Look, Ms. Jacobs, I don't think I'm a good fit here. Besides, I got a lot on my plate. Thanks anyway."

Having terminated the call, Pat found himself wondering whether perhaps he should have just politely declined the invitation. The morning talk shows always irritated him with all their silly, lightweight, happy talk. How seriously would viewers take him, if he went on TV as a grieving brother surrounded by smiling blonds? He thought about having a drink again, but then decided against it. Instead, he got an early start on supper, preparing pork chops, dressing and peas for dinner that night. After dinner Pat suggested that he and Clare should go to see the movie *True Grit* about a young girl who embarked on a courageous journey to avenge the murder of her father in the 1870's. The couple remained silent for the ride home.

DAY TWENTY, FRIDAY, SEPTEMBER 16, 2011

On Friday morning, Pat put in a one-hour spell at the Commercial Avenue watch, conferring with Mario by cell phone when he pulled up. Mario had nothing to report other than the usual hustle and bustle of a working class community. Old man Delgado went out each morning for what appeared to be fresh bakery goods, and today he purchased a newspaper.

"What time?" asked Pat.

"Same time as yesterday—around 7:00 a.m. Pat I'm going to take off and meet Rollie."

"Okay, take whatever time you need."

Sitting in his SUV, Pat stared at the building. From the light that was still shining through the broken blinds covering the basement windows, it was clear someone was down there. The odds were pretty good that it was Orizaga. Of course, it would be so much easier to let the *Fourth District* coppers get him, mused Pat, but then the criminal justice system had failed the McGurns twice before. Even if he did tell Murphy of his suspicions, chances were nothing would happen because of some legal silliness. Who was to say that someone might actually alert Orizaga so he could abscond again? Tension rising, Pat called Rollie.

"It's me, Rol. Mario's on his way to your meeting. Everything's quiet and the old guy went out for food and a paper earlier."

"Good, Pat. Be patient—this stuff takes time. Yesterday, Mario told me about the old guy's morning schedule. Might mean something."

"Call your 'Nam pal yet?"

"I'm thinking tomorrow, but I wish we had more confirmation."

"I hear you. Will this guy come on short notice, Rol?"

"Oh, yeah, not to worry. He'll be here in less than forty-eight hours or more like twenty-four. He told me, off the record, that most operations in East Germany back in the day were with short notice. So what do you have going today Pat?"

"Just more reading and phone calls. I gotta keep on top of this political stuff even though it's probably a waste of time with Cook County. I talked to Varbanov yesterday—he's a real piece of work. You know he tried that bond bullshit and I sort of went off on him."

"Good for you *Mendel* man. Fuck Varbanov! What else?"

"I also told a kid from *Wolf in the Morning* who wanted me on early Sunday 'thanks but no thanks.' They just wanted an angry family victim and that's not a role I aspire to! These TV people just don't get it."

"Good for you, Pat. I hate those phonies myself, and, besides, I'm thinking we're going to be busy this weekend. I gotta tell you, for some reason I'm thinking something might pop."

"Hunch, Rol?"

"Yeah, maybe more. Look Mario just walked in—let's talk later."

After Mario returned from his meeting with Rollie and Higgins, Pat headed home to Beverly. When he arrived, Leroy, the mailman, was standing in the driveway with a registered letter. It was an invitation from Commissioner Alport for Pat to give a four-minute presentation before an open forum on Tuesday, September 20, 2011, at 10:00 a.m. The R.S.V.P was no later than the following Monday at noon. Pat had expected the letter and decided he'd wait until Monday before replying. He had barely entered the house when Ralston phoned him from *The Globe*.

"Hey, Pat, I'm learning something about the commissioners!"

"My favorite people! Make my day, Ron. Oh I just got a registered letter invitation for the Tuesday forum."

"I guess they really want you there, Pat."

"So what did you learn, Ron?"

"Well, it looks like at least three of them had no idea that this ordinance would release felons."

"You know, I pretty much came to that same conclusion, Ron. So who's your source?"

"Can't say—promised anonymity. So Murray from the south suburbs, McAbee from the West Side and Rucker from the South Side didn't know the ordinance would apply to convicted felons."

"They had no idea, huh? They told you that? You know, I figured as much."

"Yep, me, too, Pat. Both McAbee and Rucker confirmed a few minutes ago while Murray said 'no comment.' McAbee and Rucker said they were misled and thought it applied only to misdemeanors. Korshak controlled their vote for the usual favors. I talked to Wagner earlier and he would neither confirm nor deny it. He just said that he couldn't speak for other commissioners."

"So you figure Wagner's bullshit, Ron?"

"I don't know."

"I don't know, either," admitted Pat. "Wagner seems sincere some of the time, but now I figure these fuckin' commissioners look out for one another because, in the end, it's all about a pretty cushy part time job and political hustle."

"Pat, I'm not sure what to do about something else I just learned. I have a source in the jail—you know, someone with an axe to grind against Dypsky—who told me that since Raul was released at least fifteen more illegals with prior convictions have also been released and at least a hundred with detainers. I have to get confirmation from Dypsky or his counsel, Nikos, or maybe his new press guy, Grodecki. Short of that, I have to do a Freedom of Information (FOIA) request. This source told me one's a convicted rapist and two others damn near killed a couple of cops in Frankfurt Park."

Pat whistled softly.

"Sounds like a story, if you get confirmation, Ron."

"Well, I think they'll confirm this because Dypsky would look stupid if he stonewalled. That's not all. Get this—McAbee and Rucker both e-mailed me that they'll deny they said what they said."

"You got to be kidding! I bet Korshak or Nordquist must have called them."

"Yeah, I'm sure of it."

"Unbelievable! And to think we spend millions on these people's salaries! Well, I'm thinking you can go with the commissioners not knowing what they voted on. Maybe break down the blocks on the board and show how Korshak controls minorities."

"Only problem is my editor probably will want another quote. I'd like to comment on the felony thing, but I better be careful."

"Here's a quote, Ron," said Pat, feeling a sudden burst of inspiration:

"Good public policy is always compromised when racial politics and 'cover your arse' are the trump card. Cook County citizen residents continue to be unsafe because of this inept Cook County Board. The McGurn family is hopeful wiser heads will surface and amend the ordinance that allows convicted felons to abscond and commit more crimes."

"I may have to contact some others because of your statement, Pat. May call later."

"No problem. I'm home tonight."

"Thanks—by the way, Kelly Sorich from Hunter-Goss's office told me the Feds have a warrant. Do you know anything about it?"

"Yeah. Murphy told me that would be out today. I doubt that will amount to anything. I'll call the Chicago FBI and get confirmation. I'll look forward to your piece."

"Okay, Pat—if you get anything before 6:00 p.m., let me know and I'll include it in my story."

"For sure, Ron. Take care."

Pat tried Eileen Murphy to see if she could confirm and, since there was no answer, left a message. Next he Googled the Chicago FBI and got the number. The receptionist put him through to an on duty agent.

"Agent Bodenhamer. May I help you?"

"I need to talk to Bruce Horsefal."

"He's on vacation. May I take a message?"

"Well, put me in touch with whoever is managing his caseload while he's away."

"I'm not sure that's possible. Maybe I can help."

"I need to confirm there's a warrant out for Raul Orizaga," said

Pat, having explained the situation in as much detail as he thought was necessary.

"Mr. McGurn, we cannot give out information on an ongoing investigation."

"Mr. Bodenhamer, all I want is confirmation—yes or no."

"Like I said, we cannot give information on an ongoing investigation."

"Look, I'm not asking for agents' notes, for Pete's sake—just a yeah or nay. I know Horsefal prepared the affidavit and I want answers. Please put me through to your supervisor!"

"He's gone for the day."

There was a loud click and Pat found himself staring at his call log. What a fuckin' idiot, he thought. He then called Congressman Tom Powers from the *Third Illinois District* and reached his Washington Office. The receptionist immediately connected him with Larry Lormer, the congressman's Chief of Staff. Pat went over his exchange with Bodenhamer and his conversation with Eileen Murphy concerning Agent Horsefal. Lormer put him on hold for a few minutes. When he returned, he promised to do what he could to help, but warned Pat that the FBI could be difficult.

"Sure, but I think you'd agree I deserve an answer. You know I was the intake guy for congressional inquiries down at *Fort Hood* thirty-eight years ago and we had commanders respond ASAP to a congressional investigation. I doubt things have changed."

"I'll get right on it and you'll have an answer no later than tomorrow, Mr. McGurn."

Aware of Ralston's deadline, Pat called him at *The Globe*.

"Ron, I'm not sure there'll be any developments before 6:00 p.m. but here's what I'm thinking. Look, if you don't hear from me by 5:30p.m., why not write something like this: 'the Chicago FBI office stonewalled Mr. McGurn when he asked for confirmation of the warrant. He was forced to go to Congressman Powers and was still waiting for a response at the time of this writing.'"

"I like it, Pat. Hope my editor approves. Oh, just before you called I got confirmation on releases from the jail."

"This article's certain to piss off a whole lot of folks, Ron."

"The more the better," said Ralston.

•

There was one more call—George Hallet from *The Illinois Immigration Cooperative*.

He began with the usual condolences, explaining that Commissioner Varbanov had given him Pat's phone number. Wearily, Pat listened to the opening remarks, but also knew that Hallet was probably more of a force to deal with because of his long-standing friendship with President Haesi.

"Okay, I got a few minutes, but before you go on, I hope Varbanov told you that we want that ordinance amended."

"Well, he told me that and more."

"I'm sure he did," said Pat testily.

"I understand your anger, Mr. McGurn."

"Of course, I'm angry. Look, call me Pat and you're George. Go ahead."

"Okay, Pat. We agree that certain illegal criminals should be deported."

"Stop right there! Like Orizaga?

"Well, yes we do but—"

"Yes, you say? Hold on, George—it looks like you helped write the ordinance and now someone gets killed and you're telling me my brother's killer should have been deported. My sources tell me that your buddy, Commissioner Varbanov, pushed this by conning President Korshak, and the rest of the board, that the Feds were unduly harassing Mexicans. So, all of a sudden, ten dimwits on the board decide to give the finger to the Feds. What's more, you knew that Sheriff Dypsky would comply because of his political ambitions. All of you knew that convicted felons would get 'out of jail cards.'"

"Who told you I helped write the ordinance?"

"You expect me to tell you my sources, George? You're all over the country involved in this madness. I'm telling you there's a whole lot of American citizens that have lost loved ones because of sanctuary laws you had a hand in. Am I right or wrong?"

"I don't write laws, Pat."

"George, no more bullshit. I've learned quite a bit these past few weeks. In fact, we even checked White House logs and know exactly when you were visiting your buddy, President Haesi, this past year."

"All right. Fair enough—I admit I supported the new ordinance."

"And you supported similar measures across the country, right?"

"You have to understand that our mission is to help families."

"*Really?* Look George, I'm getting a real education here. I'm convinced you and your pals use the family to play on emotions and that your real agenda is far left control of the Democratic Party. You know what, George? I just learned a few hours ago that the Sheriff has released more illegals. Did you know that?"

"Who told you that, Mr. McGurn?"

"Read *The Globe* tomorrow morning. Like I said, I'm getting an education. Let me ask another question—are you involved with all the illegals sneaking across the border from Central America recently?"

"Many of them are just children, Mr. McGurn."

"I guess you don't want to answer that question, George. Look, this is going nowhere. Before I forget, did you consult with Father Ryan in the last few days?"

"He's a friend of mine."

"I think you answered my question—it looks like the old 'let's get the church on our side' strategy in play."

"I don't understand."

"Mr. Hallet, I learned recently your cooperative and another outfit named the *Association of Community Assistance Now* or ACAN are off shoots of the old Shelton Lalinky strategy to install radical lefty policies all over the country. The latest is your Hispanic empowerment strategy to establish sanctuary jurisdictions here and elsewhere and get millions more illegal aliens on the dole and voting. Lalinky was a master at duping the clergy to support these lefty goals and even got money from them as far back as the 60's. You also got President Haesi to persuade Democratic House members to fund part of your operation under his stimulus package. And that was why you were hanging around the White House.

"Your facts, Mr. McGurn, I must—"

"You *must* what? *Con more churches and hustle the President and Congress?*"

•

After the call Hallet sent emails to Varbanov, Nordquist and Alport stating that he would feed blogs and media with suggestions that McGurn was supported by any number of white racist groups. Because of his vast network of contacts from coast to coast and right up to Pennsylvania Avenue, Hallet was confident he would succeed in damage control. He re-read Shelton Lalinsky's rule #5 **Target your opposition and destroy it by any means necessary.**

A call to Haesi's Chief of Staff, Bolevsky, confirmed that Secretary Bather would be on board; he also agreed to check in with Illinois' Senator Congelosi to make sure he was supportive. Bolevsky later sent Hallet a confirmation e-mail that read:

"George, this crisis soon will pass because you have followed #5. This County Board Forum I promise you sits well with the Big House."

●

That evening Pat and Clare strolled over to *Frigo's* on Western for pasta. It was a cool evening for September, and recent rains meant there were hordes of mosquitoes to contend with. Still, Pat was glad they had decided to walk as it gave him the opportunity to talk to Clare in private.

"What really angers me is Hallet's connection via this *Illinois Immigration Cooperative* with this Muslim organization or AIM," mused Pat, swatting a mosquito that had viciously attacked his neck.

"You know what, I hear there's a huge problem of border Security in Texas, Arizona and California," said Clare. "The news reported that residents are finding literature in Arabic on the border."

"Hopefully, our efforts will bring some of this madness to the light of day—if Rollie's hunch is right, Clare, and somehow Orizaga can be apprehended, maybe, just maybe, Congress might wake up and begin considering comprehensive immigration criminal enforcement—"

At that moment, his phone rang; this time it was Derrick Schroeder, Supervisor of *The Fugitive Unit of the Chicago FBI*. He had called to apologize for the way Pat had been treated on the phone, but also informed him that Federal Magistrate Roberts had issued a warrant around noon that day. Relieved, Pat requested a copy of the federal warrant and of the affidavit that had been used to secure the warrant; however, he was disappointed when Schroeder warned him that the FBI probably would not search for Orizaga for a few more weeks. He also said that their first step would be to get the Mexican immigration authority to issue a warrant as well. Apparently there were hundreds of these warrants issued by U.S. federal judges and Mexican authorities rarely acted upon them. Pat asked if President Haesi could help and, needless to say, Schroeder avoided that question.

Dinner was enjoyable. Both agreed to turn off their cell phones for the duration of the meal and only discuss lighthearted subjects. For a change, they spent time reminiscing about the many weekend trips they had taken with the kids while living in Karlsruhe, Germany in 1986 and 1987. They ordered their favorite pasta entrées and shared a bottle of wine. Then, on the way home they walked past their first home at 9917 South Talman. With much laughter, they recalled the extensive remodeling they had undertaken, marveling at how they had managed to complete a 270 square foot addition on a shoe string budget. Of course, they had managed by doing most of the work themselves, including digging the foundation!

They got home around 9:30 p.m. As they reached the driveway, Pat stopped for a few moments and squeezed Clare's hand.

"Hon, I know I've been a bit crazed lately over all of this. Something is driving me like I have never experienced before, but I just know it's for the best."

"God, I hope so!" said Clare, anxiety clouding her face.

Pat was getting ready for bed when the phone rang around 11:30 p.m. So as not to disturb Clare who was already asleep, he grabbed his cell phone and went down to the kitchen.

"Pat, Rollie here. Look, one of the TAC officers watching Roberto just called about two minutes ago. He's following Roberto in the Windstar and, get this, Roberto took the Dan Ryan X-way, got off at 87th Street and is heading east. Chester, the TAC officer, is updating me every block on his cell. I'm calling you on my landline."

"Yeah, Rol. I think I just heard him say 'Jeffrey.'"

"Look, call Jose will you? Tell him I'm on my way over there and that a TAC officer in an unmarked car is tailing the beige Windstar."

"Gotcha, Rol! I got his cell number."

"Stay up—I may need you," instructed Rol.

•

"Just went underneath the Skyway," reported Chester calmly.

"Good! Now, in a few minutes you'll be at Commercial. I'm betting he will park in front of an old frame house right on 88th Street on Commercial. We have a guy on watch there in an old black Chevy and we gave him a heads up."

"10-4, Rollie, I'm still with the Windstar."

Sure enough, the Windstar parked eastbound about a third of a block down; Chester parked on Commercial, leaving himself good sight lines for observation.

"He's walking west toward the corner with what looks like two plastic grocery bags. Yep, he's walking up the stairs of an old frame house and now he just entered. An ole man let him in."

Rollie, racing eastbound in his own vehicle, turned left on Jeffrey to go down 87th Street.

"Good work, Chester! Now keep your eyes peeled and your phone on. I'll be there in five minutes. When you see my blue Honda pull behind you, just take off. See the black Chevy?"

"Yeah."

"Good, he's been instructed to sit tight. I owe you, Chester. Give Schus a heads up for me. Take care."

Slowing down, Rollie called Jose, then pulled over in front of the frame house.

"McGurn called you, right?"

"Yeah, Rol—the dude went in with two bags. That this Ozzie guy?"

"Yep. Look, I'm across the street now and for sure it's Roberto. I'm 90% certain his brother's down in that basement hole."

"You think they going to run like tonight?" asked Jose, evidently thinking it was a possibility.

"No, I just think it's provisions for the bastard, but anything might happen. Here's the plan—we'll both stay and if Roberto leaves solo, I'll follow him and you stay on the watch."

"What if they both leave?"

"Plan B. We both approach and I'll play cop and accost them and you cover. You okay with that? It could get nasty, but I can handle it. You got to understand, I need cover."

"You sure about this? Maybe we may need some help?" said Jose.

"Look, my gut tells me we gotta go alone on this, with no cops. Don't worry, Jose—like I said, I doubt they will split tonight and, if they do, well it's their loss. I'm certain I can take them down."

"Okay, Rol, I got your back. *Semper fi*, man."

Around midnight, Roberto left the Commercial building empty handed. Rollie followed the Windstar for the forty minute ride back to Corliss address. On the way, he called Pat to update him on developments.

"So what next, Rol?"

"You relieve Jose at 5:00 a.m. I'm thinking we gotta get ready. I'll tell Jose you're coming to work the watch for an hour until Mario shows at 6:00 a.m. I'll have Jose brief Mario."

"No problem, Rol. Okay, let me get a few hours' shuteye and we'll talk tomorrow. You okay for tonight?"

"I'm certain Roberto's just going home, but I got to tail him to be sure."

"Okay, Rol. I'll wait for your call when I get back home tomorrow."

"I'll check with Jose for the next hour or so and go home. I'll try to grab maybe four or five hours of sleep and give you a call."

"Sounds good—let me get some sleep!"

As expected Roberto went back to the Corliss place and thirty minutes later Rollie was heading west on 111th Street to his house in Mount Greenwood. Getting off at 111th Street, Rollie knew it was time to call Jake Hawk. He last saw Jake down in Key West for a reunion of the whole 'Nam gang from back in 1969. Tears came to Rollie's eyes as he remembered that awful night in Vietnam.

DAY 21, SATURDAY, SEPTEMBER 17, 2011

Raul Orizaga was really getting frustrated and could not understand why he still had to stay in a smelly basement. He figured three weeks was enough. After all, that lawyer man told Robby maybe a week in this hole and no more. He was tired of the shitty instant coffee he had to make on the hot plate and of the footsteps he heard all day long upstairs. The sheets were starting to smell and all he could take was "bird baths" in the sink near the toilet. He didn't appreciate Robby holding his nose the few times he came to visit. The only company he had was the screeching of alley cats fighting off and on. Fortunately, the TV reception was okay and the Spanish channel kept him current on the *tele-novelas* in Spanish.

Roberto had made it clear the night before that no orders had come down yet from the man.

"Maybe something real soon, bro, and when they come, you got to deliver or you're fucked!"

"I know, I know, bro—I do anything to get out."

"Well look, this guy McGurn on TV last night, he pissed that you got out, bro, so heat's on. Maybe you here long time, man. This dude may know the mayor or something."

"Fuck! I'm goin' loco here, bro."

"Look, Rauly, you need to watch *Telemundo* every day. This new mayor might get the cops to start looking—Senor Simpkus tell me the immigration motherfuckers got a federal warrant so folks looking for you, bro. I figure another week or so and things get cool, man."

"And I get my job and new papers, Robby?"

"Well, job first, bro."

"And you know nothin', Robby?"

"No, but it be big, Raul, like you know."

"I kill some motherfucker, right?"

"I don't know, man. I don't know, but serious shit. Well, you know the deal—you were headed for eight-ten years, man, and those motherfuckers were going to fuck you big-time in the prison, dude. You gotta understand, bro—ain't nobody know shit about you being in this hole 'cept me and Simpkus."

"Okay, so what happens after I does this?"

"Well, the lawyer, Simpkus, says he don't know 'cause he don't want to know, man, but he set it up."

"With who, bro?"

"I don't know, but I'm the one who's gonna get the word, man."

"You trust these fuckers, bro?"

"Man, I've got to—no worry. Ole man's no problem—he's okay, right, Rauly?"

"Yeah, the only time I know he's alive is when I hear him walking and his ole lady mucho sick like she gaggin' all day. Yeah, he put note on the steps with the food so I know you was coming, bro."

"Okay, I gotta go, Raul. Now, in one of those grocery bags is a piece—you used a .38 before right?"

"Yeah, many times—never killed nobody, man. Maybe winged a dude in Laredo once, but, yeah, I can shoot Robby. So looks like I gotta big job, huh, bro?" "That's right, Rauly, but like I say before, ain't nobody gonna know shit—that's why it's shush, shush. When I get the word, you go, bro."

"Soon I hope," said Raul.

"Me, too, man—maybe next week."

"Adios."

●

At 5:00 a.m., Saturday, September 21, 2011, Pat pulled up on Commercial and called Jose who was parked a little ahead of him on the same side of the street.

"Hey, Jose, Pat McGurn here. Everything okay ?"

"Good to see you, Sir. I just had to lay low all night. There was nobody in and out of the house. About three hours ago, some cop drove by and gave me a half-hour break," said Jose, stifling a yawn.

"Thanks for helping us out, Jose. It's that old grey house on the corner, right?"

"That's the house. I'm pretty sure someone's living down there because when the lights went out at maybe 1:00 a.m., I saw like a faint flicker as if a TV was on."

"Tell me, Jose. You get a good look at this guy who went in last night?"

"Yeah—mean looking Hispanic dude. Had a tough walk—maybe six foot tall."

"Yeah, Jose, I think we got something to go on. Okay, I got it covered here, so get some sleep."

"Thanks, Mr. McGurn. Mario should be along in an hour or so. I got a hold of him an hour ago before he hit the shower and told him what went down last night. He knows to look for you."

"That's good, Jose, and thanks again."

Pat's thoughts turned to Rollie. How amazing it was that he had found guys willing to work the details and to sit for hours. 5K was a stretch to the budget; however, if they could get Orizaga it would certainly be well worth it. The next half hour was uneventful, but at 5:30 a.m. a newspaper truck pulled up and loaded a stack of papers in the machine down the street. Pat searched his pockets for quarters, then got out and headed to the machine. Having pulled out a copy of the Saturday morning *Globe*, he returned to his car. A teaser read below the fold on page one: MCGURN FAMILY CONTINUES THE FIGHT WITH COOK COUNTY. Turning the page, he noted Ralston's piece started with another headline that read: COOK COUNTY COMMISSIONERS RESPONSIBLE FOR LETTING OUT CRIMINALS. Ralston's editor must have approved the story after all.

Ralston reported that several more illegal felons had been let out since the story broke twenty days earlier. One of Dypsky's people—probably Grodecki—confirmed the massive release of alien criminals. Two weeks ago, a rapist had been released and was now thought to be in the western suburbs committing more rapes. Ralston quoted the mayor of another suburb who said he had in custody two illegal gang members caught selling drugs. They, too, had been released under the provisions of the ordinance. The mayor from Frankfort Park railed against Cook County because recently released illegal felons from Dypsky's jail had savagely beaten two of his police officers. Ralston reported that at least three commissioners didn't even know what they were voting on when they approved the ordinance. Pat's quote had made it in and, by the end of the article, the ten Commissioners and President Korshak looked like fools. Before closing, the journalist included a prepared statement from Dypsky's press spokesman, Grodecki:

"Sheriff Dypsky says the ordinance applies to everybody who is charged with a misdemeanor or felony who posts bond or has his or her case adjudicated.

The article was followed by an invitation from Commissioner Alport's office for the public to attend an open forum on the ordinance at 10:00 a.m., Tuesday, September 20th, sponsored by the *Cook County Board*. It included a statement from Commissioner Alport who hoped to make the public aware that "all human beings on Cook County soil will be given due process."

Disgusted Pat threw down the paper. With such short notice, it was likely few citizens would show in support of an amendment. Moreover, Alport's statement was a giveaway that no one with political clout had any intention of passing an amendment. It was appalling that both Wagner and Riley would allow this so called travesty of a forum to proceed knowing full well it was a joke. At 6:10 a.m. Mario pulled ahead of Pat's car and waved. Pat checked in with him by phone before heading back to Beverly.

Entering the house, he was surprised to find Clare already up, working a crossword puzzle in the living room.

"Someone from *Judicial Vigilance* named Charles Foley called and left a message. He's in town visiting relatives and would like to meet with you this weekend," she said.

"Jeez, I can't take the time now, so maybe I'll call and tell him I'm tied up. You know Joan mentioned this Foley."

Clare put the crossword down and stared at her husband.

"At the rate you're going, you're not going to be tied up but locked up.

Where have you been? You never told me you were taking off in the middle of the night!"

"South Chicago over at that Commercial house' said Pat, nonchalantly. "Had to cover for an hour."

"*Cover?* That's what we're paying Rollie's crew for! For God's sake, Pat, you're a retired teacher, not a cop! Your pal Rollie's got something in the works and you're going to get in big trouble. So what's going on over there in South Chicago?"

"I thought you were with me on this," said Pat, startled by Clare's outburst. "Sorry I didn't tell you, but I got the call after you went to bed and saw no point in worrying you. All I did was sit in the car for an hour until Mario showed up."

"*Sat in the car? On Commercial Avenue?* I hope you stayed in the car the whole time and were fully alert," she exclaimed, noting the newspaper under Pat's arm. Slowly, she shook her head.

"You weren't sitting there reading *The Globe*, were you? You're lucky someone didn't put a bullet in your head. You don't even look as though you belong in the neighborhood—at least Jose and Mario blend right in!"

"Look, you've got a point, Clare, but something's going down soon. Orizaga's brother went in that house late last night so we got confirmation. In fact we're going to talk to this Jake guy in a few hours."

"I'm scared for you, Pat, and for us," said Clare, standing to give him a hug. So what's next?"

"I guess we get him somehow. Rollie's going to arrange for Jake to help."
"When?"
"Probably this week."

"Look, call this Charles and see what he has to say. At least with them you'll have legal protection. Running around with ex marines bent on pulling off crazy schemes is going to get you killed!"

Pat's arms tightened around her; for a few minutes, they held each other in silence.

"I must see this through, Clare," said Pat. "I want you to look at this morning's *Globe*."

Clare read the Ralston piece while Pat checked the college football schedule for the day.

She looked up in disbelief.

"I can't believe *The Globe* editors let all that in. This could cost Korshak's ambition to be Mayor."

"Maybe get a few commissioners in trouble, too. Immigration reform is not on the average voter's mind and when word gets out that Korshak put the arm on some of these goofy commissioners who knows what could happen."

"Maybe that's all the justice you need," said Clare.

"I want more," said Pat.

•

Rollie got up at 9:00 a.m., checked in with Mario and then began to read Ralston's article in the morning paper. He was barely half way through when the phone rang; he saw on the phone ID that it was his old partner.

"Boz, what's happening man?"

"Rollie, ole buddy, just thought I'd check in—maybe go out for one or two and watch the *Notre Dame* game."

"Look, Boz, I was thinking of calling you but I'm tied up for now. Did you see the paper this morning—the story about this guy, McGurn?"

"Yeah, Rol, about that illegal Mexican who skipped?"

"Yeah, Boz, I'm working it."

"You're kidding, Rol! All the retired coppers at my coffee hang out were buzzing this morning about it."

Rollie told Boz about his investigation and his hunch that Orizaga might still be in the country; he went over the Corliss watch, the Commercial watch and events from the night before.

"This is getting pretty heavy, Rol. So you got some serious 24/7 coverage it seems?"

"Yeah, my guys are both former marines waiting to get called to the police academy. Listen, Boz, there's a whole lot I must tell you if you're interested—we might need your help."

"Hey, I think I'm interested."

"Tell you what, later around 3:30p.m., we're going to meet up at *Ruth's* and go over a whole boatload of shit, so if you're interested why not join us? If we got time, we can watch the second half of the Notre Dame game."

"I'll be there, Rol. Let me tell you, this is some pretty heavy shit you're talking, 'ole partner."

193

"Boz, I want this prick bad. Remember back in the day when we went after that piece of shit that killed one of our guys and it took us a week?"

"How could I forget? You damn near killed the little fucker when we cornered him in that gangway on the West Side!"

"Good memory, Boz, and I got the same fire in the belly, man. Look, I got to make a few calls. I'll see you later. *Ruth's* 3:30 p.m. Not a word to anybody."

Rol got into his SUV and headed towards Pat's house where he had agreed to pick him up. On the way over, he called Fourth District Watch Commander Higgins.

"Hey, Rol! Thought I'd hear from you. So what's up?"

"Well, something interesting at that Delgado House. We saw Roberto enter with two grocery bags around midnight and then exit empty handed. Schus's guy followed him and my guy and I took over. Almost certain he went in the basement and our guys see lights flickering late at night."

"You're certain now, right Rol?"

"Hundred percent. Look, I'm gonna recruit an ole 'Nam buddy who's the best at grabbing undesirables—and no one will be any the wiser. He did this kind of work for years in East Germany as a contractor. Now trust me, Frank, you and your guy, Relinski, will never get mentioned."

"Rol, not a problem. All I ask is that you keep me posted."

"For sure, Frank, and please give my guys those half hour breaks for a few more days. One more thing, I'll go over all of this with McGurn because he may want you guys to get the arrest, Frank. What I have in mind could be shaky for McGurn."

"Rol, I knew days ago you wanted this your way and I guess I'm nuts for going along, but if McGurn's not game for your big show, we stand ready and willing to take this guy down."

"Thanks, Frank."

When Rollie picked up Pat at his Roby address, he told him about his conversation with Boz whom he said he was "in."

"What are you talking about, Rol?"

"I think we need a fourth, maybe for back up."

"Jake's idea?"

"No, mine. Boz is the best for this type stuff."

"Okay, whatever," said Pat with a shrug of his shoulders.

"Hey, Pat, you okay? You sound like you're getting shaky."

"Rol, look, I got to tell you this whole thing's got me nutty. And, yeah, Clare's really worried."

"Hey, I get it—so, look, let's call my man Jake and you be the judge. I'll put a call into him now so you can hear him over speakerphone. I talked to him earlier and he's waiting for our call. Fair enough?"

"Go for it, Rol."

Rollie activated his hands free speaker system and got through to Jake in D.C. After he introduced the two men, he gave Jake a brief run-down as to what had been going on. Jake took notes while Rollie provided a chronology of events.

"Jake, we need your help like real soon."

"Been waiting, let's see, almost forty years to return a favor and the time is right—my next job is in the Big Easy next weekend."

"Good, I'm thinking maybe two or three days for our project here in Chicago.

Right now, we're on our way to the subject's house for surveillance."

"Well, I already figured you're in a car, near water and you got abduction in mind," said Jake.

"Right on all three, marine. How'd you figure water?"

"C'mon, marine—I heard two horn blasts."

"McGurn and I just pulled up so give me a second."

Rollie parked behind the black Chevy and gave two quick hand signals so Mario would know he could take a thirty-minute break.

"So you're sure this Angela is one and the same—you know, grandchild and girlfriend?"

"For sure, Jake."

"On a scale of 1-10, what's your take on Orizaga being in that hole?"

"Nine, maybe ten."

"Who's watching Roberto?"

"Shus, my buddy in Area Five, checks while on duty and has TAC guys help."

"TAC—*what's that?*"

"Tactical Unit—you know, plain clothes in unmarked cars."

"Think that's enough?"

"Best I can do, Jake."

"What about the subject's house? You got help from that precinct?"

"We call it 'district' here and, yeah, I'm a pal with the watch commander and he's got a guy helping, you know, unofficial."

"What else?"

"Just this—Roberto uses torture to train new recruits in the gang."

Rollie went over the connection with Mike Dukavich and the kids in Murphysboro. A recent conversation with Mike had revealed that they were terrified Roberto would go after them, even though they were three hundred miles away from Chicago. Apparently, his violent reach extended way beyond Northern Illinois.

"Good work on that one, Rol. Now, we must get a clear picture on this asshole—this gang got a name?"

"Samienga and the leader is an hombre named Archuletta from Nuevo Laredo in Texas."

"Connected to some big-time cartels, don't you think?"

"Good bet, Jake."

"Good work! Look, I'll need Roberto and Raul's dates of birth and the exact address of the target. I'll have my contacts here in the beltway patch me in their mapping system.

Oh, yeah, you mentioned in your narrative that you used a meter reader cover for foot surveillance, right?"

"Yeah, Jake just last Wednesday to survey the house," said Rollie.

"Which utility?"

"Electric."

"I prefer Gas companies as a cover for this type operation. Let me see, I'm checking my computer—your gas utility is called *Chicagoland Energy*, I see."

"Yeah, that's right."

"Okay, I got a supplier here and I'll come with emergency gas company paraphernalia and signed uniforms for three guys. Rol, the cops must have a sheet on this bad boy Roberto, right?"

"Jake, somehow he's clean. Minor stuff, you know, misdemeanors but no record of felonies or convictions. My guy Schus knows coppers who say Roberto's really slick—he's bad news."

"Okay, that helps. This Roberto must have been active up north and moved his operation far south."

"Yeah. I'm also thinking the Commercial house may be used for other operations as well and the old man goes along with it because he needs the dough."

"Okay, so my guess is you guys want to grab this punk pretty soon."

"You bet!" said Rollie.

"McGurn, what say you?" asked Jake.

"Got my vote," said Pat.

"Rollie, I bet you got some kind of crazy plan to need some crazy fucker like me," said Jake. Rollie chuckled.

"You know me too well! Yeah, I got a three phase plan, Jake—that's why I need Pat here because he's got the final word. But first let me talk to my surveillance guy because he just came back from break. Back in five minutes."

"So you guys go way back, Jake?" asked Pat while they waited for Rollie to return.

"Yeah, we do and watched one another's back in 'Nam. I guess you call it a pact we made and it looks like my turn to deliver. Say, McGurn, you're nervous about this, right?"

"Yeah, I guess I am," admitted Pat.

"Hey, you got a good man with you on this—I can promise you we'll get this punk and, if I know Rollie, he's got a fool proof plan. Look, being nervous a good thing."

"So far I like what I'm hearing," said Pat. "The rest got me a bit worried."

Rollie re-entered the car and said, "Sorry about that—just had to brief Mario. Well, Jake, what d'you say?"

"Okay, I can be there tomorrow afternoon—I'm guessing *Southern Fly* will get me into *Midway* between 4:00-8:00 p.m. Now, tell me about your house survey. You already did that, right, Rol?"

"Yeah. We got a break because there's no rear exit either by window or door, so we only need to be concerned with east and west side windows and west side door and front door. Surveillance team has eyes on exits 24/7."

"So tell me this, Rol. You're thinking the front door will do the trick?"

"Yeah, and I'm certain the basement entrance is right there as well because we know Roberto went in that way last night."

"Great! On a different note, Pat, has *Immigration and Custom* ever contacted you?"

"Not a word, Jake. I called once and the Chicago or Midwest Director just said Cook County was less safe because of the ordinance."

"So you don't think they are doing anything like working with the FBI on this?"

"Nope. Not according to the agent I talked to."

"Your going congressional will get the FBI off their duff, but don't get your hopes up. They'll probably give you a line of bullshit because they hate congressional hassles. Say, what's the agent's name?"

"Schroeder's the supervisor and the other guy, Bodenhamer, is on vacation."

I'll check because if the FBI got eyes on your house, all bets are off. Follow me?"

"Jake, we been at this dump for three days now and, trust me, the Bureau hasn't got a clue."

"No surprise, Rol. Let me ask you this—really important. Are you sure your police pals will give you full cooperation and no interference?"

"Guaranteed."

Jake thought for a moment and said,

"Now, Pat, my plan is going to be a seizure and I'm out of there once you two have this guy in that van. You understand?"

"Yeah, Jake."

"Okay, so by the time I get there, you guys will have to know exactly what to do with this creep, so as not to draw attention to your operation. All I'm gonna do is snatch this fucker and bring him to a vehicle. Believe me, this asshole will be as meek as a scared child. So you guys work on that. One last thing, Rol—get a grey windowless panel truck with bench seats front and back. I'll text you the flight information in an hour and set up a meet tomorrow evening at your place, Rol. Okay, if I crash there?"

"Attic bedroom is yours, marine."

"Good—see you tomorrow, team."

In a daze, Pat stared at the subject's house. The conversation and lost sleep had left him exhausted. He felt as if he were in the middle of some bad action movie.

"Your guy Jake doesn't pull punches, man."

"That's Jake, Pat, and, believe me, it's a done deal. Sometime this week—I'm thinking Tuesday, Wednesday or Thursday—we will have our man," said Rollie, making a U-turn.

"Ok, now for Phase Two. First answer me this—are you certain this county forum meeting is on for Tuesday?"

"Yeah, but what's that got to do with Jake?"

"Well, let me finish. Here's what I'm thinking. Let's say we get him in the next few days and install him in a safe house for the final act."

"Sounds like you know the place—what d'you mean by the final act?"

Rollie smiled secretively.

"I'm still working those details, but, yeah, I got a place. I'll get to that.

So let's say it's real early in the morning on Tuesday and Jake does his thing and we whisk him to a safe house nearby—"

Pat shook his head in protest.

"Whoa! Tuesday, I'm on stage at the Cook County Building at 10:00 a.m."

"I know, Pat, that's why I asked about Tuesday. Let me finish! Here's the plan and we can tweak this. You, Raul and me walk into the County Building say about 10:05 a.m. You know, sufficiently late so that the meeting has already started and everybody's seated and listening to some bullshit, probably from some commissioner or maybe even Korshak. We three walk in, leading in a compliant Raul—they're looking for you because you're first up, right?"

"I think so—I'll know for sure when I RSVP Monday with Alport's office."

"Well, even if you're not, we can still pull this off. After we get in, we stand near the back until *The Pledge of Allegiance* is over. Then you yell at the top of your lungs:

"COMMISSIONERS OF COOK COUNTY, I HAVE HERE MY BROTHER'S KILLER, ONE RAUL ORIZAGA. I HAVE MADE A CITIZEN'S ARREST."

Pat was aghast. Never in his wildest imaginings would he have envisioned an outcome like this.

"What the fuck are you suggesting? Are you nuts? You really think we can drag this guy into Cook County Board chambers without being noticed?"

Rollie took both hands off the wheel and gestured wildly. The car veered to the right and then stabilized its course.

"Pat, I know this sounds crazy, but after Jake has finished dealing with him, trust me, Raul will be compliant. The only thing we got to do is cuff him in a discrete manner. I can arrange to get us through Security. Look, after I drop you off, I got to run to the safe house and let's talk later on with Boz. I'll give you all the details."

"Rol, look I need time to wrap my head around this," said Pat who by now had developed a full-blown headache.

"Look, I get the impression your guy, Jake, doesn't know about this citizen's arrest, does he?"

"Nope, why should he? You heard him—he's all about the seizure and then he bolts. That's his *modus operandi*—always has been, Pat. You see he is paid well to secure the subject and turn him over and fade away. I bet he's done at least forty of these. You see, Jake trusts me for the rest."

Pat continued to look worried; he still couldn't believe the plan that was unfolding. Not what he had signed up for at all!

"Okay, I accept that Jake gets our guy, but I gotta tell you—"

"Well, I know this is tough stuff to ponder but you have the final say— we can cancel anytime. It's up to you. Just let me go over the rest with you and Boz and then you can decide. You know, I talked to Commander Frank Higgins about this and, trust me, he'd love to get the prick. Once we give him the word we want out, his guys would swarm that ole man's house with everything they got."

"I get it, Rol, and for this guy, Higgins, to let us conduct a rogue operation is hard to believe."

"Let me tell you, with over thirty years on the job, there were more than a few off the books operations, but I'll concede this is a new one. You know what, though, Frank will see the political advantage that sends a message to those commissioner creeps that passing unlawful, stupid ordinances just ain't gonna fly."

"Higgins doesn't know about a lot of this, does he?"

"No, not yet."

"All right, tell me about this safe house."

"Well, I'm going to finalize that after I drop you off. It's the horse stables at the old South Shore Country Club. A buddy of mine is in charge over there and on the far end of the complex we can secure our guy without notice after the abduction."

"I've played golf over there," said Pat. "The stables are right there when you drive in, I'm thinking two miles or so from the house."

"You got it, and at the crack of dawn when I'm guessing the abduction goes down we are good as gold. This guy, Sergeant Clancy and I, are going to go over details in an hour or so. Later, at *Ruth's*, I'll go over the plan. Tying in the grab with the safe house should be pretty easy."

"Rol, I'm with you, but I must tell you the last phase has got me worried. I need to run this by Clare or I might end up single again!"

"Tell you what, Pat, let's take five and try to relax. Later, at *Ruth's,* we can go over it again and maybe watch the Notre Dame game."

"Sounds good, Rol."

The two classmates were silent for the long haul going east on 87th Street. Pat closed his eyes and tried to clear his head. They passed *Chicago Vocational High School*, crossed Stony Island, and a few minutes later crossed the Dan Ryan Expressway. In no time they entered Brainerd, Clare's old neighborhood. Pat broke the silence.

"There's Justine Street—Clare grew up two blocks north, right near Foster Park."

"No kidding, Pat. I didn't know that. When you guys get married?"

"We had to wait till we finished college and my army hitch. The happy day finally came June of 1973 at St. John Fisher where we bought our first house. Speaking of Clare, I think I'll take her out for coffee and go over our plans."

"What parish was she from, Pat?"

"St. Ethelreda—you know the neighborhood changed and her family moved in 1968 to a split level in St. Cajetan's."

A few minutes later, Rollie turned into North Beverly and pulled up at Pat's house.

"Pat, I know from working with you these past few weeks that you and Clare consult on everything. Please don't think for a minute I'm going to push something that would cause problems for you guys."

Pat turned toward Rollie, giving him an appreciative look.

"Thanks, Rol—look I'll be at *Ruth's* later."

"Sounds good, Pat—we gotta lot to cover."

•

Over coffee on Longwood Drive in Beverly, Pat and Clare sat outside on the sidewalk patio, facing the Irish Castle at 103rd and Longwood Drive. Built in 1886 by the Givens family, the structure was Chicago's only authentic castle. Now a Unitarian Church, the building had once housed a thriving pre-school where their children had spent many a carefree hour. As Pat went over the tentative plan, Clare listened attentively, looking anything but carefree.

"Are you out of your mind, Pat? What if there's a mix up and I'm bailing your Irish arse out of the hoosegow!"

Frustrated, Pat repeated Rollie's sales pitch.

"Jake never fails from what I understand, and he's done this many times under contract in Europe."

Clare threw her arms up in the air.

"Everybody screws up once in awhile and what's with this compliance? Will Orizaga know who you are? This is all crazy! Did you ever think that if there is a trial and you're under oath what could happen to a perjurer?"

Pat looked around anxiously, hoping that their voices were not carrying to adjacent tables. The last thing he needed was for their plans to be the talk of the neighborhood.

"I'll get more details later—all I know is that this Jake and Rollie are like really confident. Look, Clare it's my call but I want it to be *our* call."

Clare took a sip of her latte.

"Well, if you're so determined, I guess I can't stop you, but on two conditions—first, once this is all over, let's take another trip to Ireland and forget all this for awhile. Now that I think of it, Pat, does Sally know about all this craziness?"

"I doubt it. You know coppers like Rollie rarely bring work stuff home. Look, I can't tell you how much your support means."

"Support is tepid—I just can't help it. So you're off to *Ruth's* for more planning or, should I say, crimes?"

"Now that you mention it, I thought you could be my Bonnie and I'll be Clyde."

Clare shot him a sarcastic look.

"And look what happened to them! Okay, Clyde Barrow, take me home—I'm going to check your life insurance."

"You mentioned two conditions, Clare."

"Well, I was going to wait to tell you. I'm thinking of calling our lawyer, Josh Jordan, but not to tell him too much, but to at least get him to agree to be available."

"Why Josh? I mean, he's a lawyer and officer of the court; we can't make him privy to this abduction."

"I know, but I'm thinking I could run a hypothetical scenario by him to give him cover and maybe get some worthwhile advice. After all, he's one of the top criminal defense guys in town. Some of us at work did him a big favor a few months ago on a criminal case that helped his client—he owes me a lunch."

Pat nodded.

"Now that I think of it, that's a good idea, especially if there's a trial possibility."

"That's what I'm thinking, Pat."

"So drop me off. I'm going to make a reservation at *Sylvano's* for say 7:15 p.m. so we can watch *The McGowan Group*."

"Ask for a rear table. I don't want to meet any nosy neighbors," said Pat.

●

After Rollie had dropped Pat off, he sped back east to *South Shore Country Club* and finalized details with his old buddy, Clem Clancy, a veteran Chicago Police Officer on the horse detail. Rollie had called Clem a few days earlier and had run the idea by him. Clem was a rule breaker and saw no problem with using the stables as a safe house for a few hours.

Rollie left the stables at 3:00 p.m. Heading west on 71st Street, he called Jake who picked up immediately.

"All systems go, marine. I'm getting the uniforms and other stuff in a couple hours. I examined the area in some detail on our map system and not to worry about the FBI."

"Not even close, Jake?"

"You know the Bureau, Rol—they could give two shits about average citizens. I checked on this Schroeder who has the file and my source tells me the guy's a dumbfuck. So what you got? First, is your guy McGurn on board for sure?"

"Should be, Jake. He's probably going over everything with his wife, Clare, as we speak. I think she'll go for it. I know *he's* on board."

"Sounds good, Rol. Look, I 'm on *Southern Fly's* web site and the flight gets in at 3:10 p.m. Pick me up and set the meet for 5:30 p.m. See you tomorrow and remember I'm bringing *Chicagoland Gas Company* uniforms. I also got a portable mars light."

"How's that going to work, Jake?"

"The old man will smell non-toxic gas everywhere the morning of the pinch. I'm thinking two of us—maybe three—will be emergency responders, and I'll bring three gas masks as well for dramatic effect. Does McGurn carry?"

"Yeah, I think so or at least he used to because years back I'd see him at a range in Blue Island."

"Better check. All of us need to be armed, Rol."

"Gotcha. *Semper Fi,* Jake."

Rollie entered *Ruth's* and, spotting Boz at the bar, handed him a twenty to get a pitcher of Molanger beer and three glasses. Meanwhile, he secured his favorite table in the corner. Pat spotted the two men immediately and walked over to the usual place. After introductions, Rollie looked at Pat quizzically. Pat gave a thumbs up, and Rollie broke into a grin. After he had given Boz the run down on Jake's involvement, he outlined Phase One in more detail.

"Okay, fellas. I pick Jake up around 3:30 p.m. in a rented grey panel truck tomorrow and we all meet at my house at 5:30 p.m. He just told me it would be best if he and I recon the house before our meeting. Now Jake's bringing gas company paraphernalia for three, so that means one or maybe two of us stay on the panel truck. Target day is Tuesday real early. All I know for now is we will have the one vehicle and maybe a second. Any questions?"

Pat and Boz shook their heads and took advantage of the pause to sneak a look at the TV screen. As the Fighting Irish kicked a field goal, Boz clapped with the assembled *Notre Dame* fans.

Rollie shrugged and continued.

Good. Now for Phase Two. The safe house is the former *South Shore Country Club*, which houses the Chicago Police Department horse stables. I got a sergeant buddy over their named Clem Clancy who will set aside an unused rear room for us. It's adjacent to his office and there is a toilet there for our use. In short, no one will figure something strange, because Clem arranged to take the night and day shift that day and the six coppers assigned Tuesday won't show until 7:00 a.m. They'll be out of there by 8:00 a.m. with their horses and trailers. Oh, a horse trainer will show around 7:30 a.m. but that's not a problem as he works in the arena, a good one hundred yards from where we will be holding Orizaga. We will have time to prep Raul with some food and maybe clothes for the County presentation at 10:10 a.m. I see you guys have questions—Boz, you first."

"Rol, what's the procedure to keep Raul, you know, cooperative?"

"Not sure, but Jake has a few tricks up his sleeve and even though he will be gone, I'm confident his measures will keep our prisoner compliant. Pat, what's on your mind?"

"C'mon, Rol—the obvious. You know, bringing this guy to South Shore's one thing, but Phase Three still got me worried."

"Okay, take it easy, Pat—remember Boz and I will be with you. So here's the deal. I drive the van to the stables with Pat and a blindfolded Orizaga in the back seat. Remember, Pat, you're the arresting officer. Jake fades away and, Boz, you need to get to *South Shore* on your own—we will go over that tomorrow. At the appointed time, Boz, you drive the van to the County Building, I ride shotgun and you, Pat, are with our boy in the back seat. After the drop off, Boz, you'll bring the van back to the rental agency near the airport. I escort Pat and Orizaga to the County chambers. Look, by tomorrow I'll have this planned out in considerable detail. Trust me, Pat, we will pull this off and you have to come up with a plan once you turn your guy in. I can't help you there, so you gotta get a lawyer."

"Clare is already working on that," said Pat relieved that Clare was behind him.

"Good. Raul will be booked, charged, you know the whole nine yards. My guess is that a couple of detectives will ask you questions for sure, so you gotta have a lawyer at the ready."

"I figured as much."

"Will I be carrying?" asked Pat, again looking concerned.

"That reminds me—Jake wants to know that. I told him I thought you had one and are probably still licensed."

"Yeah, I trained on small arms at *Fort Hood* and I keep the permit current. If this goes down as a solo citizen's arrest, I gotta be carrying, right?"

"Good point. Let me think on that."

Rollie wrapped up the meeting.

"Okay, boys, tomorrow at my place, so let's now watch the second half of the *Notre Dame* game."

•

Meanwhile, back at the Roby house Clare made a cup of tea and called Josh who was also watching the Notre Dame game.

"Everything, okay, Clare?"

"Sorry for the Saturday call—it's just that I wanted to take you up on your lunch offer on Monday, if you're free."

"Sure, love to Clare. Sure you and Pat all right?"

"We're fine, Josh, but there's this situation that could be problematic and I need to run something by you relative to something I'm working on."

Aahh, spoken like a veteran legal investigator, thought Clare, feeling a tinge of guilt.

"Let me think, how about *The Stage* on Michigan Avenue at noon?" suggested Josh.

"Say, Clare, Peggy and I are behind Pat's effort with the County."

"Oh, you've seen the paper?"

"Oh, yeah, and the TV interview on *Wolf* a few days ago. He was impressive."

"Yeah, Josh, he's trying and really thought an amendment would return justice. Well, let's just say he doesn't think it will happen and some of these commissioners have been less than honest."

"No surprise there, Clare—so look, Monday noon I'll be there for sure."

"It's a date, Josh. Thanks a million. See you Monday."

After the call, Clare couldn't get over the fact she was somehow supporting what was probably an illegal escapade so her crazy husband could avenge the death of his brother. She thought back to the couple's "outside of the box" adventures over the years, usually spearheaded by her imaginative husband. There was the year long trip to Germany to teach army brats in 1986, when Michael was only eight years old and Molly, six.

Seven years later, they bought a ninety-year-old Arts and Crafts house for the purpose of restoring it to its original glory. There were other projects, perhaps not as ambitious, but nonetheless stressful, but this new one took the cake, as they say. As her mind wandered over the years, Pat interrupted her reveries by parroting the familiar, *"Hi, Honey, I'm home!"* greeting so familiar to the tens of millions of baby boomers who faithfully watched *Father Knows Best* from 1954 to 1960.

Clare smiled.

"About time, Bub—reservations at *Sylvano's* at 7:15 p.m."

Pat looked at his watch. There was plenty of time to get ready and watch *The McGowan Group*. Two hours later, just as they were getting ready to leave the house, Rollie phoned. Clare shot Pat a meaningful look as if to say, "Not again" and pointed to the clock. They did not have much time.

"Pat, Rollie here, sorry to bother you but I just got a call from my brother-in-law, Sonny, who's a retired Chicago copper."

"Oh, so what's up?"

"Yeah, well he's got this cushy retirement job in the Cook County Building, you know walking around as a weekend watchman see and ... Well, he has access to all the offices, because Korshak's paranoid about terrorism. In any case, he spotted a memo on her desk that said "Sunday 10:00 a.m." Get this, Alport, Varbanov, Hallet and Houma were on the list with check marks after each name under a heading that said, 'confirmed.'"

"I don't get it," said Pat, suddenly feeling irritated. "How's this guy know you'd be interested?"

"Sally must have said something to him. He's okay—I mean he won't give us up. For brother and sister they're pretty close," said Rollie, clearly embarrassed that Sally had been discussing the McGurn assignment.

"Well, what d'you think?"

"Well, Pat, you got these commissioners on your radar and this forum is on Tuesday, so I'm thinking that Sunday morning group probably has something to do with your situation. Don't you agree?"

"Good bet, Rol, but I still don't get where you're coming from," objected Pat. By now, Clare was motioning him to get off the phone so they could be on time for their dinner reservation.

"Pat, look, if I were you maybe it's a good idea to tail one of these jokers like Houma because he lives sort of close to you. Maybe you might want to do a little gum shoe."

"I like it," said Pat, rallying to the idea. "Yeah, I'll get Clare and we'll go to the 6:30 a.m. mass at *St. John Fisher*, then head north and sit on Houma. So you know his address?"

"I'll e-mail you by tomorrow morning."

"Well, Rol, I guess a diversion like this is a good idea to kind of get my mind off Tuesday."

"One way to think about it I guess, Pat, so good luck—I'll see you at my place at 5:30 p.m. I'll get that address to you in a few hours."

As they headed out the door, Clare anxiously looked at Pat.

"*Now what?* Has there been a change in plans?"

"No, hon, just what looks like some sort of commissioner meeting tomorrow that I think we should monitor because this Hallet's involved."

Pat went over the specifics and the plan to follow Houma and see if he could learn anything.

"Want to join me?"

"Sure, why not?" said Clare. "Now trespassing, next abduction—hey, we'll both go to jail together!"

"C'mon, be a sport. Rollie will text me Houma's address and we go from there. No way we're going to snoop around on private property!"

"I don't get it," said Clare. "*Why Houma's house?*"

"Well, all we know is that he's invited to a meeting somewhere at 10:00 a.m. tomorrow with Korshak, Alport, Varbanov and this Hallet character. So I'm thinking it's got to be related to this Tuesday sham meeting at the County."

"So, early mass and then we tail some fool commissioner around. My kind of Sunday! I thought about visiting Molly, Frank and Matt and the new baby."

"Next week—promise you! Hey, when's the last time we took a Sunday drive around town?"

Clare smiled and said, "Let's go! I'm ready for dinner."

DAY 22, SUNDAY, SEPTEMBER 18, 2011

As planned, the couple attended the 6:30 a.m. mass at *St. John Fisher* the next day. After church, Pat figured they had better get a spot in front of Houma's place in Portage Park by 8:30 a.m., so he and Clare got coffees "to go" at *The Beverly Coffee Shoppe* and were heading north on the Dan Ryan Expressway by 7:50 a.m.

"I'm guessing Houma will get in his car and go have breakfast," said Pat. "All we have to do is follow him and see what happens."

"My kind of day," said Clare good humoredly. "Hey, what else would I be doing? You know I always wanted to be a spy! Seriously, Pat, what do you think this meeting is about?"

"Well, like I said last night, it's gotta be about Tuesday. A meeting on a Sunday with these four elected officials who are pro immigrant along with this Hallet must mean something. So I'm thinking they don't want other commissioners to know about it. Beyond that, Clare, I can only guess."

"So you get confirmation of this secret meeting and so what? Lots of people have brunch gatherings on a Sunday."

"Who knows? We might be surprised," said Pat.

"So you're convinced they won't vote this amendment on Tuesday?"

"Well, if we pull this stunt off, they will have to adjourn the meeting. If, by some chance, the meeting proceeds, the best we can hope for is a vote at a regular County meeting in a few weeks. I got to tell you, though, from talking to Joe, Ralston and this McLaughlin at Southern, it's next to impossible this thing will go anywhere."

"I'm thinking James might change."

"That's just one vote, Clare, and he's going to get indicted anyway. Forget about the two white women, Fanning and Murray. Most of the other ten who voted for the ordinance do what they are told and Petrutis is just gaming the system. Never speaks up at meetings and just follows the Democratic line. No, it's hopeless—all the more reason to grab our guy and shove him into Korshak's face."

Clare shook her head in disgust.

"So this whole amendment thing is just a joke and our guys Riley and Wagner must know—it's a sham, right, Pat?"

"Sad but true—all the more reason I'm in for this crazy citizen's arrest. I mean Riley and Wagner and maybe the other three—Giglio, Guest and Googan—were against the ordinance. This McLaughlin explained that all five of them see their job first and foremost as a pretty good part time pensionable gig."

"What's that mean?"

"That they're not boat rockers. We heard nothing in the press from any of them accept Wagner. You know they might want a favor down the road. That's how the game is played."

"Well, Wagner will continue to be outspoken, won't he?"

"Hope so, but don't hold your breath. Look, here's Barlowe Street. Here we are—see the house across from the church? 5111 Barlowe?"

"Why not park along side that Lutheran Church? Looks like there's a church service taking place."

"Good idea—I see a space. Look, 5111 has a side drive and garage so with a little luck Houma will launch any minute."

"You know, Pat, I've got to admit this gumshoe stuff is kind of fun."

Pat smiled.

"We have done some crazy stuff together, haven't we? Look, can you get the binoculars out of the glove box—I want to have them at the ready."

At about 9:20 a.m., the garage door opened and Commissioner Houma drove out in a late model Lincoln and headed toward Milwaukee Avenue. The McGurns followed closely in their Ford Explorer, trailing Houma onto the Kennedy Expressway. After roughly twenty minutes, Houma got off at 55th Street and headed east. Clare got a pretty good picture of the Lincoln with her phone.

"Looks like Hyde Park or Kenwood, Pat, don't you think?"

"Yep, and Korshak's got a big house near the university in Hyde Park."

"Remember, Korshak was a former school principal at *the Oliver H. Perry School* in nearby Burnside. I think she graduated from *Brandeis* and worked in a kibbutz in the 70's."

"Well, there is a social swirl of liberals here in Hyde Park. I'll bet Hallet is right in the middle of this as well. You know what? It just occurred to me—Joe or one of his sources told me Hallet spent a few years here doing graduate work here at the *U of C* in Sociology. Come to think of it so did Shelton Lalinsky back in 1940's."

"Who else is part of this fraternity do you think?"

"There's a lot here, but many elsewhere, too. Oh, yeah, that new Secretary of Education lives around here. He's a basketball pal of Hallet's and about the same age. When I was at the *Board of Education*, he was the CEO and he kept pushing all sorts of reforms that never worked. The guy, like his predecessor, would listen to foundation types, academics, and guilt ridden CEO's but never listened to those of us slugging it out in the trenches. Enough of that—let's see where our friend, Houma, is headed."

The Lincoln sped through Washington Park. All was quiet on a Sunday morning and Pat was able to stay back a good distance because traffic was light. Houma turned right on Woodlawn and drove two blocks to a large Chicago bungalow and pulled into the double circular driveway at 5916 where there were already three cars parked. The McGurns drove around the block and found a good spot alongside a corner play lot to get a fix on the Korshak house. They had to be careful because a Cook County police squad car was parked nearby as well. A few minutes later, a Mercedes pulled in and out came Hallet and Alport. Five minutes after that, Commissioner Varbanov parked behind the Mercedes in his Honda convertible. There was one of those weird Smart cars there as well.

"So now what?" Clare asked.

"Well, let's sit a few minutes, and get the plates for confirmation in case we need this info later for something."

While Pat was writing, Clare nudged him excitedly.

"Two sixty-something walkers are headed toward the house, Pat."

Pat took the binoculars from Clare, and stared hard at the two figures.

"Clare, get this! I'd bet my life I just saw Dilbert and Bernice Redstone. Brother and sister terrorists back in the 70's."

Clare took back the binoculars and focused on the couple.

"That's Dilbert alright—can't say about Bernice because I don't think I've seen her mug in years."

"I have, Clare. Trust me, that's them—the question, is what's going on? I know one thing—they're perhaps the two slimiest Americans to ever live. They are responsible for at least three deaths we know of, and could very well have killed scores of Americans. They skated because because the FBI screwed up and the government had to drop charges. They turned themselves in the early 80's because their lawyer had an angle to let them skate."

"Weren't they the chief organizers of that radical 60's group called—I can't remember the name."

"*Port Huron Underground*, Clare. You know I could have been a victim because I was on temporary duty at Fort Dix in New Jersey when these criminals planned to blow up the NCO club. The joke of it was that some of the fools blew themselves up in a New York City townhouse a day earlier."

"You mentioned that years ago, Pat. So no jail time at all huh?"

"Nope. Brother and sister Redstone had a rich daddy who was, I think, a big shot with the *Illinois Metals Corporation*. No sibling rivalry with those two because they both wanted to terrorize as many Americans as possible forty years ago. The Redstones have had our Commander in Chief's ear from day one. It's been documented in a book written by a guy named Wirtz. And he even argued that terrorist Dilbert ghostwrote President Haesi's autobiography. Okay, Clare I think the breakfast club's got a quorum, so let's sit awhile just in case some other radicals show up."

"You know, Pat, I'm thinking Haesi will be a one term president."

"Roger that! His numbers are sliding big-time with this health law that seems doomed to fail. Pretty soon, according to Joan, his numbers will fall even further with this foolish *Good Neighbor Act* on immigration. You know, Clare, it was astounding that the 19th Ward went for him—what was it? About 60%, I think. You know most of the people in the Ward did so grudgingly. I'll never forget what old Ray Sheridan, who had a succession of do nothing, scam type political jobs said to me once:

"You know he ain't my kind of guy but the guys by the Ward Office tell us like we could get stuff because he's a Chicago guy."

Another common line bandied about the 19th. Ward went something like this. *"You know this Haesi maybe like you know different but he's real smart so our guys think we should give him a shot."*

Clare smiled.

"Sounds like the 19th Ward philosophers—keep spoils, secure cushy jobs, get the wife and kids do nothing jobs, claim multiple pensions and the beat goes on. Another thing that bothers me is that the local politicians support Democratic leaders who are pro abortion."

At about 11:30 a.m., seeing that no one else had shown up, they headed home. Pat decided to take Stony Island home. They crossed 71st Street and made their way south.

"The more I think of it, even if the amendment fails, you will win in the court of public opinion. Everybody I talk to at work and all our friends support the amendment for sure."

"I agree, Clare, and I'll continue because of that support, but if this Jake character can pull this off and Rollie's plans work, it will make a big splash on the national scene. Look, here's 73rd Street—let's see what the old house looks like at 73rd and Dorchester."

The couple drove west on 73rd Street, stopping at 7367 Dorchester.

"You told me your grandfather bought the house in 1920 or something."

"Yeah, Grandpa bought it in 1926 and we moved out of there thirty years later. Down the street there's the Madison School where I went to kindergarten. Two blocks the other way is *St. Laurence* where I went to school for three years."

"It's fun to go back and cruise around. Remember when we rode around *St. Ethelreda Parish* for my reunion a few years back and took photos of my old house?"

Pat laughed.

"Sure do—that black guy in your old house had a real attitude when he spotted us pointing a camera at the back of his house."

Pat recalled some Chicago history research he did a few years back by perusing old newspapers and discovered a list of 1942 conscripts from *St. Laurence Parish* that included his dad and several of his friends who served honorably for three to four years. Before they continued driving home, Pat put on a CD of patriotic songs and on came *"When Johnny Comes Marching Home Again."* Clare knew the words.

"When Johnny comes marching home again
Hurah! Hurrah
We'll give him a hearty welcome then
Hurah! Hurah
The men will cheer and the boys will shout
The ladies they will all turn out
And we'll all feel gay when Johnny comes marching home."

Pat feeling a surge of sadness, nostalgia and patriotism looked at Clare.

"Sometimes I try to imagine those days when millions of young guys went off to war from neighborhoods just like this and the joy when they came home in 1945 and 1946. Let's see you had you had cousins and uncles in the war right?"

"Yeah, Uncle Ray and Tom in North Africa and Europe. Cousins Jim and Leo were flyboys and a sailor Jack was at Iwo Jima."

The couple arrived home at 1:00 p.m. Pat would meet Jake later.

•

At the Korshak residence, the assembled guests helped themselves to generous portions of scrambled eggs, sausage, grits and coffee cake, all presented on an elegant cherry-wood buffet table in the dining room. Prominently displayed above the buffet was a large, hand-signed print of Nelson Mandela; in the center of the room was a matching table, set for brunch, with all its extension panels in place. There were eight chairs which could only be described as "shabby chic" that seemed to belong to the set, as well as a couple of mis-matched chairs. Having introduced her surprise guests, Bernice and Dilbert Redstone, Korshak invited everyone to be seated; when there was silence, she convened the meeting.

"Thank you all for taking the time to be here, today. Before I proceed, no one—not even the other commissioners—knows about this meeting. Is this understood?"

Looking around the table to assure that all were in agreement, Korshak turned to Alport.

"You're going to take the lead as we discussed on the phone last night. I'm depending on you to get us out of this mess and somehow silence this McGurn. I never figured on all this bad publicity. I invited Bernice and Dil because they have access to certain people, as you are aware. Okay, Commissioner Alport, the floor's yours!"

"Look, I know it's my job to settle this problem, but I got to tell you—and no offense—but Dil and Bernice are not exactly without controversy. Before I go on, we must be very careful here because if *Wolf News* gets even a whiff of what we are trying to do our political futures are in big trouble."

Dilbert Redstone waived his hand in protest.

"We are old friends going back many years—you know Bernice and I can be trusted. I'm not sure if Shirley discussed our conversation, but I do have a few ideas that might help this situation."

"Thank you, Dilbert," said Korshak, "but let's save your input later in our meeting. Please continue, Commissioner."

"Here's the deal," said Alport, clearing her throat. "The public got *The Globe* story and the *Wolf news segment*. The topic's been bandied about in barrooms, stoops, water coolers, barber shops—you know, all over the place. As might be expected, people form opinions. Let's face it, the ten of us commissioners who voted for the ordinance are getting heat while the North West and South West Sides of the city, are already with McGurn. My plan is we have a public meeting with our kind of media and orchestrate this thing in such a way that McGurn is quickly forgotten. Ms. Nordquist and I went over the meeting you held last Thursday and her notes made it real clear that Dypsky, Hunter-Goss, you, President Korshak, and Mr. Varbanov seem to be the most worried over this. Forgive me, but I think you'll agree your concerns have something to do with your political ambitions."

"Hey, man—all of us are political here!" objected Varbanov.

"So I understand—that's why the goal is to get rid of this. Let's face it, we look bad when McGurn keeps pounding 'the brother would be alive' theme if the County had not embarked on lax enforcement policies. Recently, the media is reporting other released felons, so we got our work cut out for us. The key is for us to play our best cards and that is family victimization, unfair deportations and civil rights. My staff, together with Vic, will line up twenty or so families backed up by Mr. Sheehan in Hunter-Goss's office for the legal deal."

"What's the legal deal?" asked Varbanov.

"He will argue that if you're on Cook County soil, regardless of citizenship, you have constitutional guarantees and I know the Cook County State's Attorney agrees.

"We are certain there's no chance of an amendment, right, Commissioner Alport?" said Korshak.

"That's right. At best, it will get introduced and I won't even allow an up or down vote. However, there are a few possibilities we should consider—like McGurn going off on us and spellbinding the crowd in front of the entire media."

"Well?" asked Korshak.

"It's a chance we gotta take, but if he goes on too long, I'll cut him off. The forum should take care of any political issues, but we're taking this one step further. My staff, George and Vic have been working on a large demonstration in Daley Plaza, complete with speakers, music, placards and, hopefully, three thousand or more people. It will be similar to what George and Vic did last month in the west of downtown at that Secure Communities thing to include traffic tie ups, right, Vic?"

"You got it, man and I got two dudes from the *Association of Community Assistance Now* flying in to teach the kids how to tie up traffic all day. I also got maybe 200 signs, too.

Korshak smiled approvingly.

"*Okay, Mr. Hallet, tells us about your conversation with McGurn. You spoke with him* Friday, I think."

All looked towards Hallet attentively. Wiping his mouth with his napkin, he pushed his plate aside.

"Well, first you should remember McGurn put a damper on that Secure Communities Demonstration a few months ago with that speech at Haymarket Hall. Anyhow, my conversation didn't go well last Friday—I mean this guy is furious with us. He knew about a lot of stuff including my visits to the White House and other things that shouldn't go public."

"Like what?" asked Alport, leaning across the table to make sure she missed nothing.

"Well, he seems to have figured out that at least three of us conspired to get this ordinance through. He didn't mention you, Commissioner Alport."

"What else?"

"Well, he knew about other illegal felons getting out of jail and accused me of conning Father Ryan. Oh, and he said Dypsky was malleable."

"Well, I agree with that," sneered Alport.

"Did he sound—you know, like crazy?" asked Korshak, a light gleaming in her eyes.

"Oh, no. He was measured and yes, angry. Look, he's as committed to changing this ordinance as we were to passing it, and the more he fights the worse we are going to look. I think we all agreed a few days ago he was pretty good in front of the camera. His words are clear as a bell, he looks sharp and, above all, he's got time. Oh, and he has an advisor named Joan Farnsworth—I think someone mentioned this other day. Well, I did a bit of research and she's from the *Center for Immigration Analysis*. It's real pro enforcement on K Street in Washington D.C., well funded, too. She and others have testified numerous times in both Houses of Congress. Oh, and they partner with some outfit called *Judicial Vigilance* and they love to sue everybody."

"Well, let's keep her away and fuck that *Judicial* whatever," interjected Vic.

"Too late, Vic," said Hallet. "I'd bet my life she's prepped him now for these past three weeks or so and there is this Vanderbiezen character as well."

"McGurn may want her to appear with him—then what?" asked Korshak.

"Not to worry," said Alport reassuringly. "With our majority, she'll never get a hearing or even be invited. George, tell us more about the priest you mentioned a few minutes ago."

"Oh yeah, that didn't go very well according to Father Ryan. McGurn took shots at our *Cooperative* and somehow knew Ryan and I are affiliated. Involving the priest backfired, but Father Ryan will show for the forum Tuesday and represent *Clergy for Justice*. That should help."

"What about the President?" asked Korshak. "Are you going to reach out?"

George looked at Dilbert and his sister.

"Well, I went over what I did last week and Haesi is ready to move closer to our position.

In fact our situation came up at Friday's White House press briefing and the spokesman endorsed our ordinance. Frankly, this whole Cook

County controversy needs to be resolved and, above all, we have to make sure we don't damage the President politically."

Korshak looked at the Redstones, trying to read their reactions.

"Bernice, Dil—*what do you think?*"

Dilbert finished slathering a bagel with lox and cream cheese, then put down his knife.

"Well, as you know, for the last few years the right wingers have tried to discredit the President by tying me in as a close confidant. My communications always go through a third party or other secure methods and George and I coordinated with the President.

"We're aware of that," said Alport impatiently. "So please go on. Who's that guy on *Wolf News* that always demonizes you? I just hope he doesn't get wind of your involvement here."

"Rory Hanratty—let's forget him. As I was saying, we always supported your views on immigration and I have a memo here that we will send out by secure e-mail today. We have a special server for these communications. We suggest a telephone conference for tomorrow morning at 10:00 a.m., CST, with the White House Chief of Staff, Marvin Bolevsky. In short, we will request that he call Senator Congelosi, and the Democratic leadership. We also got word to the *Congressional Hispanic Committee* led by Congressman Rodriguez—he assured us that all eyes will be on Cook County next Tuesday. Oh, and Manny plans on attending the rally in Daley Plaza on Tuesday because he can rev up the crowd. That was George's idea."

"So you and George worked on this?" said Korshak, smiling.

"Yeah, over the phone yesterday. If I may have a minute to simply say that we must all be mindful of the big picture here and that is progressives must always be ready to exploit opportunities. The Hispanic population will approach 50 million and if we play our cards right they will become our loyal progressive supporters for generations."

Smiling enthusiastically, Bernice was next. "Dilbert's point about opportunities is key to place America on the right side of history. Our biggest success is in the White House and that was handed to us on a silver platter and we simply must see that he is reelected."

The assembled group nodded their approval.

"I like it. You two always put everything in the right context. If there are no questions I say this strategy is approved. You know Haesi's Senior

Advisor, Jahnna Suhud, and I are old friends. Maybe I should call her as well."

"Sure, why not Ms. Korshak?" said Dilbert.

"I would!" echoed Hallet.

"I'll call her at home tonight. I knew we could count on you two. The President has a lot of leverage for sure and I like the idea of Congressman Rodriguez flying in for this. Okay, Vic—give us your take here, as you're the chief sponsor of the ordinance."

Varbanov adjusted his tie nervously.

"I'm going to join George at the rally as soon as I can get out of the chamber. Ms. Alport, here, is going to run the show and I'll sneak out and fire up people outside after an hour or so. Look, can I ask the group here something?"

"Sure," said Korshak, but with little enthusiasm in her tone.

"I'll bet McGurn approached some of these racist Tea Party groups out there or they recruited him," said Varbanov breathlessly.

"I doubt it, Vic," responded Alport. "Demonizing McGurn as a racist would backfire and, from what I gather, he has too much class for that and wants a fair fight. However, he might go off on the political machine angle."

"Don't forget he's got those *U of I* contacts and they hate us up here," cautioned Inger Nordquist.

"Getting back to Vic's take that McGurn may be a tea partyer—you know, perception is everything, my friends," said Hallet slowly, measuring every word.

Alport shot him a suspicious glance.

"What are you getting at?"

"Hey, it's certainly plausible that McGurn would join up with that tea party spin off. Like I said, the public is free to believe whatever they want, you know what I mean? I guess what I'm saying is that racists could have got to him."

There was a murmur of agreement as those gathered exchanged comments. Korshak looked at her assistant, Inger, and instructed her to contact the media. She then turned to Houma who was sitting on her right, seemingly disengaged. He was toying with his food, as if forcing himself to eat. Most of it had not been touched.

"Mr. Houma, you have not said a word. Is something the matter?"

"I got a call last night—I can't say from where that Denny McGurn's daughter lives in my district."

"Oh, I get it," said Korshak. "You feel bad you didn't call or go to the wake?"

"Not only that. I learned Denny McGurn was killed in front of *Hacienda Leon* and that he was the owner's insurance agent. Denny lived two blocks from there, this caller told me. I also learned that the owner donated to my campaign."

A weary silence descended on the gathering. Korshak glanced at her watch and then asked Alport to take a few minutes to wrap up the meeting. Everyone left with an assignment, including Hallet who agreed to work with Father Ryan to line up more victims of deportation whose cases were especially heartwrenching.

"I'll call McGurn on the way home and confirm for Tuesday, 10:00 a.m." Alport concluded as the group prepared to disperse.

•

At 2:30 p.m. Pat and Clare were home reading *The Sunday Globe* when the phone rang. It was Cook County Commissioner Alport. Pat put his phone on speaker so that Clare could hear the exchange.

"So what's with a Sunday call—is this urgent or something? I got your letter yesterday and planned to RSVP tomorrow. Saw the announcement in the paper today as well."

"That's good, Mr. McGurn—so you will be there?"

"Sounds like a few of you just had a meeting or conference call," said Pat, grinning at Clare, as if to say, "Let's have a little fun here!"

"To contact me on a Sunday afternoon seems odd from my perspective, but go ahead, Commissioner. Let's see what's on your mind."

"I'm not interfering with a family function, I hope," said Alport .

"No, no just preparing for some important things I have to do this week. So say, what's on your mind?"

"Well," said Alport, sounding flustered. "You got my letter and it sounds like you're coming. I'm calling to see if you have any questions."

"That's very considerate of you, Commissioner," drawled Pat in his most nonchalant manner.

"Hmm, Riley said something about the process last week. So let me get this straight—I say a thing or two for about three minutes, followed by speeches from pro ordinance people and maybe a handful of anti ordinance people?"

"Yes," said Alport quickly, sounding relieved. "And one or two amendments will be introduced. I understand Commissioners Riley, Wagner, Googan and I think Giglio are working on at least one amendment."

"So what about you and this amendment—maybe you might support it?" asked Pat, feigning innocence.

"Well, Mr. McGurn, I supported the ordinance, so I will be on record to vote against any measure to change it. You see my call is merely a formal invitation to you."

"Oh!" said Pat. "Now I understand. Please forgive me it's not everyday I get a call from Cook County Commissioners."

"Certainly, Mr. McGurn, I understand. Now, if you don't mind—"

"If you don't mind, Commissioner, I have a couple a more questions. Is Dypsky going to speak and for how long?"

"Sheriff Dypsky will state his position and he may be for or against these amendments. I don't know his views."

Really? said Pat, seemingly surprised. "Well, I got to tell you I went over the transcript the day the ordinance passed and Dypsky's guy, Nikos, apparently was sent there to be non committal—just said that his boss would follow the letter of the law. When pressed, the kid would not say one way or the other if his boss agreed or disagreed with the law so I'm not encouraged."

"Well, let's see what happens at the forum," said Alport. "Look, I—"

"Commissioner, I got a sneaking suspicion you and the rest of the commissioners know exactly what's going to happen at this forum," said Pat, winking at Clare who was by now trying to stifle her laughter.

"Excuse me?"

"C'mon, Commissioner, be straight with me," drawled Pat in his "best buddy" voice.

"I don't agree with your assessment, Mr. McGurn," said Alport coldly.

"Hunter-Goss showing?"

"She declined but will send a representative as will President Korshak. The suggested length of the presentations no more than three minutes. Now I—"

"You know I'm thinking this is going to be a stacked deck, Commissioner." Alport's voice sounded strained.

"As you know, an announcement was published today and will be tomorrow as well. We will accept speaker requests all day today and my staff expects twenty to forty applications. We will probably hold the speakers to no more than that."

"Whoa, wait a second," objected Pat. "You're telling me potential supporters of my position get just today to make arrangements to go downtown on a work day. C'mon, Commissioner, I'll bet your side has been lining up speakers for a week or more already while my side gets one work day!"

"Mr. McGurn, we realize this is short notice, but our calendar is such that we decided it had to—"

Pat cut her off.

"Commissioner, don't bullshit me—this is nonsense, for Pete's sake. C'mon, like I said your side planned this days ago and figured you'd spring it on my family and public at the last minute. You've seen the survey data and know full well an overwhelming majority of Americans support vigorous border and internal enforcement."

"Sir, I'm not aware of that," said Alport indignantly.

"Okay, I get it—I guess that's half the battle dealing with the likes of you, Korshak and nine others."

"Mr. McGurn, I'm telling you—"

"No, you listen to me. I get it now! I'll be there and I'll take as much time as I require at the mic to say my piece. You know and I know the overwhelming respondents will be pro-ordinance. In fact, the more I think about it, this sounds like a classic set up."

"Mr. McGurn, you're first up."

"Always liked it when I was the lead off man. Look, Commissioner, I have no control over this other than to snub the invite, because you all are going to go through with this, regardless. If I decline, my family gets nothing and you all have the pleasure of saying 'we invited the family and they could have made their case but didn't.'"

"Mr. McGurn, it's really not like that I can assure you."

"*Oh, no?*" responded Pat sarcastically. "I'll be there 10:00 a.m. sharp with a few other people. I've one last request and that is I want a copy of the amendment."

"Well, this is irregular but if you insist, Mr. McGurn, I'll ask Commissioner Wagner to send you a copy. When you get to the County Boardroom, just provide identification to the deputy and he will escort you to the rostrum. If time permits I and other commissioners will offer our greetings. May I have your e-mail address?"

"Sure—patmc@burnside.com. Okay, see you, Commissioner. I'll be there with one or two others."

"Got it, Mr. MGurn. I'll have my staff get the document to you as soon as I receive it."

Clare wasn't sure whether she was more amused or outraged. Pat's performance had been masterful, but Alport's duplicity was disgraceful. She dabbed at her eyes with a Kleenex.

"You crying, Clare?"

"I don't know!" she said, blowing her nose loudly. "What nerve! Now we know what the meeting was all about at Korshak's this morning."

"Got that right and with the Redstones at that meeting, it's anybody's guess what plans they've hatched! I guess it's safe to say their bombing days are over," remarked Pat.

"You don't need to blow people up when you've got your guy in the White House."

•

Meanwhile, Jake Hawk's plane landed on time at 3:30 p.m. Upon disembarking, he called Rollie to let him know that he had checked three pieces of luggage and that it would therefore be at least twenty minutes before he finished with baggage claim. Since he was already close to the airport, Rollie turned onto a residential side street and parked at the first available spot. He then called Schus.

"Hey, Schus! Rollie here—we're going to roll on Tuesday so you might as well ditch the surveillance."

Schus was on the 17th Green at the Billy Caldwell golf course with his Sunday foursome when his phone rang. He was half expecting that Rollie would call.

"I'm sure Frank Higgins has everything set for the arrest."

"Yeah, Schus we're working the details and final plans will be completed tomorrow. You know I probably shouldn't tell you this, but Frank's not involved."

"What are you talking about? You're not going to grab this guy on your own, I hope?"

"Nope, McGurn is."

"What? Are you nuts, Rollie?"

"Look, Schus, take it easy. You know me—a little drama can help. I got most of it figured and, look, mum's the word."

"When are you guys going to take this guy down?"

"Like I said Tuesday. Look, I said too much, but I know I can trust you. I gotta go."

"Me, too. I can't believe what I just heard."

●

Hawk got in the grey van at 3:50 p.m.

"You looking good, Rol. The van's just what we need."

"You, too, Jake. What's with the tattoos? I like the gold chain."

"Hey, I've always had tattoos, Rol—forget? Just a few more, that's all. As for the chain, jewelry's big these days for senior citizens—you should try it."

"Not a chance on da South Side of Chicago, Jake. Can you see me with a diamond stud earring? You can get away with it, perhaps, but that would make me a fuckin' target! How was the flight?"

"Sucked—felt like a fuckin' sardine and I had to sit next to two slurpers. Nicknamed them Drippy and Droopy. Get this—Drippy was a talker so I played deaf."

"Always ahead of the curve, Jake. As a man of your talent, why not get an aisle seat?"

"Not possible on short notice, Rol. Look, the van's perfect—we use these adhesive logos to represent firms like your *Northern Illinois Energy*. Never had a problem. I also have phony IDs with the firm's logo on them, uniforms some other paraphernalia and, oh yeah, a Mars Light."

He craned his neck so as to survey the back of the van.

"Looks good. You got a door-locking device?"

"Yeah."

"I like the bench seats front and back. Hey, we'll need to use your garage to give the van a new look."

"Not a problem, Jake."

"Good! We don't need your nosy neighbors knowing anything and when we go Tuesday it will be dark. You follow? Sorry, I'm all business, but you know me."

"No problem, Jake."

Rollie turned left on 87th Street, heading toward the Commercial house in South Chicago.

"We got about eight miles of city traffic before we get to the subject's house, so we've time to go over details."

"Good. Let's go over the players here, Rol. Tell me about these guys."

"Okay, about the team. Well, as I said on the phone it will be McGurn and this guy Boz. McGurn's aged sixty-two like Boz and I'm a year younger—we're all in pretty good shape."

"Rol, what about your surveillance guys?"

"Nah, I don't want them to get involved with the abduction, Jake. They're just starting out."

"Fair enough. So here's the plan: the two of us will grab this Orizaga while McGurn stays in the van or just outside the van."

"All in uniform, Jake?"

"For now, you, me and the third guy. Look, I'll go over this when we get to your house. There's a lot to go over, since we got only thirty-seven hours, give or take."

They passed the *Beverly Country Club* at Western and sped down the hill, crossing Ashland.

"Going through some great neighborhoods here, Jake. When we were kids, a lot of guys caddied at the club we just passed. Within a three mile radius, there must have been seven, maybe eight, Catholic schools in the 50's and 60's—twenty, maybe thirty, thousand kids were educated for a couple a bucks a month by Catholic nuns."

Jake smiled.

"You mackerel snappers sure like big families, Rol. Hey, just kidding. Must have been a lot of fun, you know, with a bunch of kids to play with going back 50 years."

"Yeah, sure was, Jake. You know every year at the *Beverly St. Patrick's Day Parade*, there must be two or three hundred house parties all over the 19th Ward. Story after story gets told and re told about those magical days. Forgive me, Jake, I'm getting up there and the past kind of gets me sometimes."

"No problem—back to business. How far now?"

"Let's see, we just went over the Dan Ryan expressway so maybe ten minutes before we get there. I'll park behind my guy Mario's car on Commercial and get a report while you look over the site."

Mario had nothing much to report—apparently, even gangbangers tune it down on Sundays. The old man had gone to the local gin mill a few hours before and, in the morning, he may have gone to church because he left the house wearing a long sleeved shirt and bolo tie; when he returned, he was carrying what looked like a parish bulletin. During Jose's evening watch, the TV could be seen flickering through the basement window again.

"Thanks, Mario. I got my pal Jake here and we're going to reconnoiter for about thirty minutes or so. You can take off now for your break—unless you hear otherwise, tomorrow will be your last shift."

While Rollie was speaking to Mario, Jake's eyes combed the area.

"You're sure there are only those two exits?"

"Yeah. Here, let me show you on my iPhone. You know I did a 360 a few days ago."

Slowly, Jake scrolled through the images, studying each one carefully.

"The old man and Roberto are the only people you guys recorded going in and out—it's always which door?"

"Front door."

"Okay, then—we'll go in the front door. I see the mailbox there as well, so Delgado and his wife are front door people. Okay, let's look at the street."

"Well, I walked the area and across 87th Street it's light industrial and a used car lot."

"What about going east on 88th Street?"

"Let's see—there's an empty lot next door and three old two flats before you get to Houston Street; it's pretty quiet between 5:00-6:00 a.m., Jake."

"South on Commercial looks like maybe there's some activity there, right?"

"Yeah, the Polish deli, tavern and the *mercado* I told you about. Also, there's an upholsterer, hardware store, and a real estate agency—maybe three or four storefronts across the street."

"So no residential on Commercial Avenue?"

"Nope."

"Okay, that's good, Rol. We don't need prying eyes. Now, you're 100% sure the cops won't bother us, right?"

"Guaranteed, Jake. I'll give Frank a call tonight with a follow up on Monday night with specifics. His beat guy on duty will be apprised."

"Look, I'm comfortable with the setting. This should be a no brainer."

"I like the confidence, Jake. Mario will be back in a few and we'll be right on time getting to my house. So what have you been up to?"

"I do these under the radar operations maybe once every two months."

"Love life, Jake?"

"Zip for a year or more. Seeing a babe in Georgetown. Time will tell."

"Hanging out in Georgetown, huh?"

"I don't know if I told you, but I help out at the *Foreign Service School* from time to time. A couple of professors invite me so these graduate students can pick my brain about the Cold War. I can give them some insight into special operations contract work."

"Tell 'em your secrets?"

"Wish I could. I keep it simple, you know, focusing on all the paranoia that went on. I'm still governed by my clearance. I do tell the kids it was easy to get in those countries. Security was far more lax than most people knew in the West. These seminars are at night and the one professor holds court in the back room of a popular joint called *Zeta's*, a short walk from the *Foreign Service School*."

"You and Zeta an item, Jake?" asked Rollie, following a hunch.

"Mind like a steel-trap, marine. By the way, I'm thinking 5:30 a.m. Tuesday for the grab."

"That sounds about right. What about the weather? Oh, wait a second—let me give Mario a thumbs up—I see he just got back from break."

"Checked last night the 60617 zip and two sources report it will be clear as a bell, maybe 70oF. Say, Rol I see you're taking another route."

"Yeah—this is faster, maybe more scenic."

"Scenic! I probably counted thirty, maybe forty, run down shacks—who are you trying to kid?"

"Yeah, Jake—old South Chicago's seen better days. At one time there were maybe twenty-five to thirty-five thousand steel worker jobs in the region back in the 60's and that's just in the city limits."

Jake shook his head.

"So the area never rebounded, I'm thinking? Poverty makes it ripe for gangs."

"Yeah, that's what Mike, the high-school teacher, struggles with. I owe him a lot.

"Well, if you guys get this creep before all these two-bit politicians on Tuesday, your buddy Mike will certainly be amused. Say, I see you just entered an expressway."

"Yeah, this is a spur that takes us on to the beginning of I-57—the third exit or 111th Street takes us to my domicile."

"You mean the high rent district?"

"Not too many people would call Mount. Greenwood that, Jake, but, hey, we like it—it's sort of like Staten Island in the Big Apple, you know, all cops, firemen, teachers, and city workers."

"My kind of neighborhood, Rol—so looks like we're here. Say nice place—let me guess, ninety years old?"

"Close, Jake—built in 1934. We rebuilt the front porch a few years ago. That's my hang out in warm weather for listening to White Sox games, having a few beers and bullshitting with the neighbors. Here we are—I think the boys are waiting."

Sally greeted them at the door and the two ex-marines entered, hauling the luggage across the threshold.

"My goodness—it's almost thirty years since we met at the opening of the *Vietnam War Memorial*," said Jake, kissing her lightly on the cheek.

"I remember like it was yesterday, Jake—almost thirty guys from your company showed."

"Yeah, a few of them have left us but the rest of us still get together."

Rollie introduced him to Pat and Boz who were sitting in the living room. They then examined the uniforms, gas masks and van insignia while Sally served ice tea.

"Okay, guys—here's the scoop!" said Rollie. "Jake and I did a little recon and, as far as we can see, all systems are go for Tuesday morning. Now, before I turn it over to Jake, I want to make absolutely sure we're all on the same page—by that I mean you're in."

Pat and Boz nodded.

"Let me be clear," Jake interjected. "I'm only the first phase and that's the grab. My flight is not until later in the day and I'll find my own way to the airport. The way I see it, there are three phases and I'll give you guys a break-down of Phase One tomorrow morning when we all reconnoiter the joint. Phases Two and Three I'm not part of and hope that's clear."

"Jake, I can speak for the team—they understand. On a different note, I forgot to tell you, there's a Metra station nearby."

"That's great! Pat and Boz, you see the van out front? That's our vehicle—it will be adorned with *Chicago Land Gas* signage. Okay, now let's walk through the grab, starting with our staging area and that should be here."

Rollie nodded.

"I'm thinking 4:30 a.m., Jake."

"Yeah—sounds good. I want to reconnoiter the place tomorrow morning with all four of us in the van. I might want a closer street level survey, but probably a drive around might be good enough. First, we'll watch the joint between 5:00-5:30 a.m. Rol, you can send your guy home when we get there and make sure you tell the next guy what we are doing."

"My guys will know the score, Jake."

"So here's the deal—we meet here at 4:30 a.m. tomorrow and by noon the plan will be committed to memory. Tuesday morning, Rol and I will do the grab and our target will not recognize anybody until he's at the safe house at approximately 5:45-to 6:00 a.m. Pat, you will be the final act and I'm thinking a lawyer would be a good idea. I mean one you know well."

Pat nodded and gave thumbs up. Jake looked at Rollie.

"Safe house?"

"Safe house taken care of. Less than two miles away."

"Okay, see you guys in the morning. 4:30 a.m. sharp!"

•

Clare was watching PBS when Pat walked in. Muting her program, she gave him the familiar 'eyebrow raised concerned look.'

"Well?"

"All systems are go; we reconnoiter tomorrow morning."

"Tell me about this Jake," she said.

"Seems competent, I can tell you that. Pretty much all business. Certainly not a typical neighborhood guy, you know what I mean?"

"No—have no idea. What are you talking about?"

"I'm talking gold chains, left earring, slick dyed black hair, arm tattoos—you know the works."

"Yikes! He really looks like that?"

"Hey, you get used to it," said Pat, shrugging his shoulders.

"Well, is he going to look normal for your escapade?"

"Probably not, because he said Orizaga will never see him I'm telling you, the guy's a pro. Not to worry."

The couple watched a BBC murder drama set in the Cotswolds.

"You really weren't watching this, were you?" said Clare with a sigh.

"Not really. You know how my mind wanders. Let's go upstairs and watch the news."

About half way through the news, there was an interview with Commissioner Vic "Charo" Varbanov. Pat and Clare were astonished to hear the radical Varbanov dismiss interviewer Roger Dunn's question regarding public safety and Cook County's refusal to honor detainers. Varbanov claimed the ordinance would not result in the release of criminals and that detainers were too expensive to implement. Dunn was evidently not expecting this.

"What about the McGurn case?"

"I don't know what you are talking about," said Varbanov testily.

Somehow the interview ended and the producer or Dunn let Varbanov's comment go.

"Please, don't let that get to you," said Clare, grabbing Pat's hand.

"God help us! Lying is routine for these sons a bitches' said Pat.

"I just thought of something," said Clare. "I think I can get a copy of the warrant that Eileen Murphy got three weeks ago."

"How?"

"Well, we have ways," said Clare evasively. "If you're going to make a citizen's arrest probably best to have a warrant. I'll have Ricky get it tomorrow."

DAY 23, MONDAY
SEPTEMBER 19, 2011

The team met at Rollie's in Mount Greenwood at 4:30 a.m. as planned. Pat and Jake got into the grey van with Rollie at the wheel, while Boz followed in his pick up truck because he had agreed to give Mario a break later that morning. As they headed east, Rollie gave Jake a running narrative on the various neighborhoods. They passed Morgan Park, Fernwood and Rosemoor. When they stopped at the light at 103rd and Doty, Rollie pointed to *Olive-Harvey College*, explaining how Olive and Harvey had both been killed in Vietnam; Harvey had gone to Jefferson High School.

"Good thinking, naming the school after heroes. I like that," said Jake appreciatively.

"I think about the guys that bought it every day, man."

The van crossed the Calumet River and Pat mentioned that he had read something about a massive plan to improve the port facilities in the next ten years.

"Good idea, seems to me," said Jake. "Say, did you know my grandfather was a longshoreman at the Dundalk port in Baltimore in the 30's?"

"No kidding! You're full of surprises, Jake."

"Yeah, he got my father and aunt out of the dust bowl in Oklahoma and found work at the Baltimore Harbor. Look, enough of my history—how about coffee?"

Rollie looked at his watch and then suggested an all night diner on Torrence Avenue.

"Go for it—I'll buy!" said Jake.

With coffees in hand, the team drove to the Delgado house, arriving at 5:10 a.m. Rollie signaled to Boz who was waiting on Commercial to join them. He clambered into the back of the van.

"Coffee on Jake, Boz."

"Appreciate it—so now what?" said Boz, reaching out for the paper cup. Jake flashed him a "wait" sign while Rollie called Jose.

"Hey, Jose, pretty quiet it looks like last night?"

"Not a thing and our boy's still up late watching TV. I see you got a few hombres."

Yeah, we recon this morning. Look, this detail will be closed in twenty-four hours so you got one more shift and tomorrow is the big day. When you see us pull up about 5:30 a.m., just take off."

"Ok, no problem—good luck with the recon. You know, I'll hang around for back up if you want."

"No, man, you guys already stuck your necks out. I'll call Wednesday, so get some sleep," said Rollie, ending the call.

All eyes fixed on Jake.

"I checked the weather and maybe there'll be a shower later today, but tomorrow's perfect. Let's sit here and collect our thoughts. I always figure if the team's got the time to ponder an operation that's good, so let's go over what we'll be doing in twenty-four hours. As soon as the next watch shows and Rollie briefs his guy, we'll take a ride around the perimeter just to get more acclimated. I'm guessing there'll be a few early bird types walking to busses about now."

"Not this early, Jake. I doubt there'll be anybody near our subject's house."

"Okay, listen up you guys," said Jake, giving each man a sheet of paper. "The abduction will take place at approximately this time, give or take a few. Okay, here it is 5:35 a.m. and this should be the time we go in. Now I want you three to read this one sider and in five minutes I'll take questions."

NOTE: ROLLIE, JAKE AND BOZ WEAR GAS COMPANY UNIFORMS, GAS MASKS AND HARD HATS.

- **5:30 a.m.** GREY VAN AND FOURSOME ARRIVES. ROL SIGNALS MARIO TO LEAVE.
- **5:34 a.m.** JAKE ISSUES SILENT ORDER FOR DURATION.

- **5:35 a.m.** JAKE AND ROL EXIT VAN. JAKE SPRAYS NONTOXIC GAS AGENT AROUND FRONT AND SIDE OF HOUSE.
- **5:40 a.m.** JAKE AND ROL KNOCK ON THE DOOR AND RING THE BELL AND YELL "GAS, GAS! PELLIGRO, PELLIGRO!"
- **5:41 a.m.** MR. DELGADO APPEARS AND JAKE YELLS, "PELLIGRO, FAMILIA, SENORA!"
- **5:42 a.m.** DELGADO TURNS TO GET SENORA AND JAKE CROW BARS BASEMENT DOOR, DESCENDS STAIRS, NEUTRALIZES, CUFFS, BLINDFOLDS THE SUBJECT AND SECURES ID'S. BOZ ESCORTS DELGADOS AROUND THE CORNER, DOWN THE BLOCK. JAKE ESCORTS SUBJECT TO THE VAN.
- **5:45 a.m.** SUBJECT INSTALLED IN GRAY VAN BY JAKE.
- **5:46 a.m.** PAT TELLS SUBJECT HE'S UNDER ARREST FOR FAILURE TO APPEAR IN COURT ON SEPTEMBER 1st, 2011.
- **5:47 a.m.** JAKE LEAVES AND WALKS SOUTH TO THE METRA STATION.
- ROL GETS IN THE DRIVER'S SIDE OF THE VAN
- **5:48 a.m.** ROL DRIVES VAN AND HEADS NORTH ON 41 TO SAFE HOUSE. SUBJECT IS NEUTRALIZED, CUFFED AND BLINDFOLDED IN BACK SEAT NEXT TO PAT.
- **5:49 a.m.** BOZ ESCORTS DELGADOS BACK TO THE HOUSE. TELLS THEM,"SEGURA CASA" (SAFE HOUSE)
- **5:50 a.m.** BOZ RETREATS AND HEADS NORTH ON FOOT.

For several minutes, Pat, Rollie and Boz studied the plan.

"Neutralize! Jake, what do you mean?" asked Pat.

Jake smiled.

"Trade secret, fellas—it never fails and the subject is guaranteed to be compliant, lucid and maybe a bit stunned for seven hours or more."

"What about toxicology screening? I'm thinking there's got to be a blood test when we turn him in?" said Rollie.

"Glad you ask—first, there may not be and, second, in my experience nothing ever shows."

Pat continued to look worried.

"You said secure ID—what d'you mean?"

"Locate his wallet or equivalent."

"Okay," said Pat. "So who will the subject think you are, Jake?"

"He will think you and I are the same people and that you, Pat, a lone Chicago detective, made the arrest. He will never see me because of a non-toxic screening agent I use that looks like smoke—he won't know the difference. You will be the only voice he hears. Remember, he'll be cuffed and I will use a full head blinder."

"Look, Pat," added Rollie, re-assuringly. "Everything goes super fast—remember, Jake and I never say a word, so he'll only recognize your voice. He will believe you are the arresting officer. Boz, you're the last to leave the scene and you're on foot. You okay with that? It's a little over two miles."

"Sure, Rol, piece of cake and with the uniform I got perfect cover."

"Now, listen carefully. I need you to walk to South Shore but take your time and arrive at 9:00 a.m. I located an all night coffee joint at 79th and Exchange where you can kill some time because it's only about a two-mile walk. Later, I'm going to tell you what you should do when you arrive. Okay, Pat, remember Orizaga only hears your voice. It's imperative that he believes the citizen's arrest is solo. You follow me?"

Pat nodded.

"Good. So I drive the van and you're in the back with Raul. Maybe it takes ten minutes to get to the stables. We turn left on US 41 and pull into the old *South Shore Country Club*. The horse detail's Sergeant, Clem Clancy, will be waiting and he'll direct us to the far south end of the stables. Time will be 6:05 a.m. or thereabouts. The eight or ten guys from the horse patrol won't see us when they show up for work an hour later. Oh, and get this—they got an assignment for Tuesday to show up on Clark Street for street demonstrations at the County Building. I'm certain this detail's related to your county meeting."

Pat smiled.

"Small world!"

"Okay," continued Rollie. "So you escort Orizaga into the sleeping room, sit his ass in the chair and place ankle restraints on him. It's real easy and I'll show you how—remember, I'll be real close just in case but keep in mind that our boy will be compliant. If he gets feisty, I'll take care of it. Clem will have left coffees and egg sandwiches in the room for Raul and us. At that point you remove the blindfold and place sight impaired glasses on him—the type used for the visually impaired. Questions, Pat?"

"I'm still worried about convincing this guy there's only one abductor."

"Look, Pat, he will be interrogated and his lawyer may want to make life difficult, so we're taking these extreme, silent measures. Yeah, he might say there was more than one abductor but, remember, he only hears one voice and he's blindfolded. So if the interrogator asks about a second guy, Orizaga won't be convincing because he only heard one voice."

Boz pointed out the window to a grey Ford.

"I think your 6:00 a.m. guy just pulled up, Rol."

Rollie waved at Mario and gave him a quick call to let him know that this would be his last shift; Boz would give him a break in a few hours. Then he continued explaining the plan.

"Okay, back to the stables. The horse detail gets their mounts into the trailers and they're out of there by 8:15 a.m., heading toward downtown. A half hour later, you, Boz, will arrive at South Shore on foot and will assume the role of 'cabby.' Get in the driver's seat of the van and wait. So, Pat, I'm like your guardian angel—you know, close but invisible. Remember, Raul won't see a thing."

Pat nodded.

"So far I follow."

"Great! So at 9:07 a.m. you remove the ankle restraints, stand him up and place one of these portable nylon wrist restraints on him. Next, wrap this three quarter light trench coat on him, so he'll look like some sort of eccentric and, yeah, weird but, trust me, we will get him in. Next, escort Raul to the van; get him in the back seat, and simply say, 'police station.' So all our boy thinks is that he's been arrested and he's going to the police station."

"I guess that's good," smiled Pat. "What do I tell the creep if he asks while we are in this room by the stables?

"Just tell him you're waiting for a driver to take you in—remember he's still pretty dazed right, Jake?"

"Sure, that's right—like I said, this compliance agent we use is fool proof. Let's see—we're talking six hours plus and for sure he's in a conscious state but barely functioning. Look, it's tantamount to someone who suffers from severe depression. That's the best I can describe it—in fact, that's what he really will be. If you have ever seen a real depressed person you'll know what I'm talking about, so not to worry. Say, Rol, let's get back to your house—I got to take care of a few things and we got to dress the van."

"Good idea, Jake. Boz, you're okay with giving my guy a break in a few hours or so?"

"Sure thing—maybe I'll ride over to the stables and introduce myself to this Clancy guy."

Rollie nodded.

"My thoughts exactly, I'll give Clancy a heads up—don't forget to check out that coffee joint on 79th Street."

Rollie pulled away, heading east.

"Okay, where was I?"

"Boz will be driving. You ride shot gun and me with Raul in the back, at 9:10 a.m. give or take."

"Yeah, yeah, okay. Boz takes off, takes a right, gets on South Shore Drive, heads north. Traffic that time would give us an estimated time of arrival I'd say 9:55 a.m. If early, we'll drive around and then get out on the LaSalle street side of the City/County Building. Okay, you get out first with Orizaga and I follow. We walk in the revolving doors and you head for an elevator on the right side."

Pat shook his head and grimaced. "Okay, I'm standing there with a supposedly blind Hispanic who's cuffed and dazed—this doesn't look weird?"

"Hey, Pat, take it easy—there's all kind of weirdoes' going in that building all the time and, trust me, the coppers on that detail do nothing but kibbutz all day or read the papers. Besides he's got a three quarter trench coat draped over him."

Pat still looked skeptical.

"So what next?"

"Oh, before I forget, Pat—you and I should dress like we're aging liberals—you know, sort of like, you know, guys in older flannels, blue jeans, walking with a casual shuffle."

"What are you getting at with this dress code?"

"Look, we got to look like we're pro-immigrant, liberal and part of a cause—Raul's our guy. I'm going to wear one of Sally's ear rings."

"Okay, I got a flannel shirt and blue jeans so I'll look like Pete Seeger. Wait a second, aren't I supposed to look like a cop to Orizaga?"

"Remember, the guy's blindfolded, but if by chance he sees you he'll think you're undercover. Besides, Raul will be out of it. Oh, and that reminds me, before going into the Cook County Building, you gotta ditch the holster and piece in the van. Boz will take care of it."

"What next?"

"We walk down to the elevators, get on, get off on the fifth floor, take a right, walk maybe ten paces, take another right and our Security guy's waiting. We get a pass and in in we go. You do your thing, the place goes up for grabs, you and Raul get escorted—probably behind the podium—and the newsies will be on their cells."

Pat looked perplexed.

"Our Security guy—what d'you mean, Rol?"

"Oh, I forgot this part. You know after 9/11 everybody gets scanned and pockets emptied in these places, you know, like at the airport but not as thorough? So I made a few calls and the scanner detail will let us by."

"Oh, yeah, Rol? So you got a guy on that detail tomorrow?"

"Yeah, there's nothing to worry about. We play the game and go in."

"Why don't you go over this again when we get to your house?" interrupted Jake. "Training in a moving vehicle's not the best, Rol."

Five minutes later Rollie pulled into the alley opened the garage door and the three men got out. Rollie pulled down the overhead door, while Jake got to work on affixing the gas company decals to the van.

"Okay, back to the plan," said Rollie.

"I'm with you, Pat, and of course with Raul. When we enter the County Chambers, we stand in the back. I'll slip our boy out of the restraints and take the blind man glasses off. Next, you issue your proclamation loud and clear while I cut out. You got to understand, Pat, for this to work the detective and attorneys on both sides, I mean the Assistant States Attorneys assigned and Orizaga's guy, if he has one, have to be convinced you did this citizen's arrest on your own."

"I know, Rol, we went over that, but I'm still shaky about Orizaga's interrogation. He will probably say there were two of us."

"Pat, it's your word against his and, remember, he will only hear your voice and he's blinded."

"What if they ask me why I blindfolded him?"

"You just tell them you read that somewhere and it looked like a good idea. Old man Delgado will never say a word because he gets pinched for accessory for harboring a fugitive if he opens his mouth."

"Let me think about this a minute, Rol," said Pat, slowly pacing up and down the garage.

"Sure, take your time."

"The cops are going to want to know how I knew where to arrest this guy."

Jake looked up from his decorating work and smiled.

"I was waiting for that question for the past half hour, but my ole buddy got that nailed down—it's about time you gave Pat that part, Rol."

"I was going to get to that," said Rollie, "but we got bogged down in all that other stuff. So, here, read this piece of paper back to me."

He pulled a typed sheet from his pocket and handed it to Pat.

TO: MR. PAT MCGURN
FROM: ANONYMOUS
Mr./Senor Raul Orizaga goes for a walk just before dawn around the block in the vicinity of 107th and Ewing.

"You found it in your mailbox last Friday," explained Rollie.

"I give—now what the fuck do I do with this?" asked Pat, somewhat dumfounded.

By now, Jake was placing a Mars light on the dashboard.

"Rollie, this is your show but go over this part slowly. Pat has got to nail this down."

Rollie nodded.

"Pat, you just said the detectives are going to ask how you knew where to go and you must give them something that can't be traced like a phone call. So you carry this piece of paper with you and when your lawyer is okay with interrogation proceedings, you go with this unless your lawyer guy has some other angle."

Pat looking at the paper.

"I better get a hold of my lawyer but I guess I can't tell him any of this for now. I don't think I told you, but Clare's having lunch with him today to make sure he's available."

"Who's the lawyer, Pat?"

"Josh Jordan."

"*You're kidding?* He's the best in town—you know him?"

"Somewhat—I guess it's more Clare and her work at the *Illinois Grievance Commission*. She helped him a few times. This cryptic note foolproof, you think?"

"I typed it and it came out of my printer. You don't want it to be your computer or printer. Okay, Pat, so you can continue by telling them you went to the 107th intersection the next day and figured out a way to monitor this morning walk. You found a spot on Ewing that was inconspicuous and decided to check it out the next day, Saturday. Sure enough, at 5:15 a.m. on both Saturday and Sunday, Orizaga came out of an alley and walked south on Ewing to 108th and turned east. Fortunately, he walked under rather bright street lights so you could confirm his identity."

"What you think, Jake?" asked Pat.

"Rollie ran this past me this morning and I like it. There's no flaws in the scenario, Pat. Sometimes in this kind of work you must stretch the imagination. Get to your lawyer as soon as possible after you turn him in and don't tell the cops shit. Initially, you got legal rights that need to be protected in case the County gets nasty. Your lawyer may have another angle, so for sure don't give the authorities anything until you meet with him."

"The cops are going to ask me where our guy lives, I'm thinking."

"Rollie showed me on Google maps that block and there's an alley. Like I said, with your lawyer's approval, just tell the detective he went in and out the alley between Ewing and Avenue Y at 107th Street. The anonymous note never gave an address—just says he goes for morning walks on the East Side. Don't worry—before the interrogation phase, if there is one, you'll have time to prepare."

Jake had finished detailing the van.

"Looks authentic, Jake—so the Mars light goes on right before we go, in I guess?"

"Yep, when that's on no one will question our authenticity."

"How is it powered?" asked Pat.

"Six batteries."

"Well, I think that's it for now so if you want to join us, Pat, Jake and I are gonna hang out and get some lunch. Oh, before I forget, Jake told me last night he'll take the Metra downtown and, you know, just be available. Right, Jake?"

"Yeah, I can take what you call the Orange Line to Midway around 3:00 p.m."

"You gonna join us for lunch, Pat?

"Thanks, but I'll skip," said Pat, still looking agitated. "I need some time to screw my head on right. I'll call if I have questions."

●

Ten minutes later, Pat was home. His first stop was to check his e-mail. The amendment from Commissioner Wagner was in the "Inbox," sent as an attachment." The accompanying e-mail read:

> Mr. McGurn, attached is a singular amendment sponsored by myself Riley, Googan and Giglio. Note the key to this amendment, if it passes, will improve public safety and create some form of justice for victims of crimes and their loved ones.

The wording sounded promising, but the phrase, "if it passes," confirmed what he suspected days before: that the committee hearing was nothing but a big sham. Pat carefully read through the document. The key language clearly would give the Sheriff discretion to honor detainers as long as undocumented felons were either listed on a federal terrorist list or on a list of inmates charged with felonies that included bodily harm or death and certain drug offenses.

A second e-mail was from Commissioner Alport and read as follows:

> Good to speak with you yesterday. Just a reminder that tomorrow morning you will have four minutes to comment on the amendment at approximately 10:00 a.m. Commissioner Wagner assured me the amendment would be sent a.s.a.p.

What confusion, Pat thought to himself. Sure, Wagner made a lot of noise but to what end? This was not a serious attempt to change the ordinance or Riley or maybe Googan would have said they were working on the others to change their minds. If they were at all serious, they would have issued a press release.

"They know damn well it won't change so this whole meeting tomorrow is a joke!" he said out loud. Well, if all went well, the joke would be on every one of them and the whole lot of them would be wiping egg off their faces.

Pat sent a copy of the amendment via e-mail to Professor Vanderbiezen in Champaign; in the header he wrote, *Let's talk later*. He then called Clare to see if her lunch arrangement was still set and if she had secured a copy of the arrest warrant.

"Yeah, I had Rick pick up the warrant this morning. Josh is a real pro—always returns calls and honors appointments. More I think about all this, the less I worry now that we have Josh involved. I'm going to type up this memo and head on out in twenty minutes."

"Look, Clare, I don't know how your conversation is going to proceed, but tell Josh that this citizen got an anonymous tip in writing."

"Sounds like you guys nailed this down."

"Yeah, we did," chuckled Pat.

"Thank God Josh is a good listener and good at figuring things out. I got to go. I'll call later."

"You're the best, Mrs. McGurn."

"Mister, I just want to keep you out of jail. See ya!"

Deciding he needed to unwind, Pat got out his shag bag and headed out to hit golf balls for an hour or so at the Dan Ryan Woods Forest Preserve. This time, he just took his new wedge to practice closed and open face shots. He walked down Roby, took a left on 90th Street, then proceeded a few more blocks to Leavitt where the cross country skiers commence their two mile runs in the winter. Finding a log, he sat down and gazed across Western. As his thoughts turned to Denny, that strange mystical feeling came over him again. He had no words for the experience any more than parents have words to describe their love for their children. Feelings of warmth washed over him, but the warmth also filled his heart with happiness. There was no audible message from on high, but the conviction came upon him that the crazy plan that would begin to unfold in twenty hours was certain to succeed. Buoyed up, Pat proceeded to go through his golf drills; he couldn't remember the last practice session that had been so productive.

●

At noon, Clare entered *The Stage Restaurant* on Michigan Avenue across from the Art Institute. She sat in a booth and checked her e-mails, noting messages from Molly and Michael asking about the County Board meeting the next day. If the kids only knew what their crazy dad was up to, they would be shocked to know that she approved. She was about to send a message in reply, when she looked up and saw Josh waving at her through the window.

"Clare, so good to see you—somehow your call seemed urgent so I hope you, Pat and the kids are all right."

"Oh, we're all in good health and all that, but there is an issue with which I thought you might be of help."

"Sure, Clare—first let's order," said Josh, noting a waiter hovering next to their table.

They both ordered Cobb salads, iced water and coffee.

"You know, the owner is an important immigration advocate and belongs to *Cook County Business for Immigration Reform* and something called *Gaels for Immigrants Rights.*"

"Really? How interesting, Josh—so you know this guy?"

"Well, I met him once at one of those business meetings a while ago and he was the speaker. But enough of that—is Pat still pursuing the County and maybe trying to get them to reconsider the ordinance?"

"Glad you asked, Josh. Yes, he is—in fact he's scheduled tomorrow to give the opening statement on behalf of an amendment that would give the Sheriff Dypsky discretion to comply with federal detainers."

"Good for him! So is that the issue you wanted to talk about, Clare?"

"Well, no—there's this other issue and if you got a minute—"

"We're on lunch, so the floor is yours!"

Clare proceeded to relate a situation involving a "hypothetical" abduction and citizen's arrest and the apparent justification for such an act on the part of one Joseph Cruice; he had supposedly "arrested" a man named Ross.

"Was there a warrant?" asked Josh.

"Yes, Mr. Ross missed a court hearing and Mr. Cruice had a copy of the warrant."

Josh looked quizzically at Clare.

"Why not go to the authorities?"

"Mr. Cruice doesn't trust them and I can't say why."

"I understand," said Josh, signaling for more coffee.

"I feel like we are writing a script," he said.

"Well, it's hypothetical, so maybe it is."

Josh added cream to his coffee.

"Does this Mr. Cruice know anything about citizen's arrest, Clare?"

"Not sure—in fact, I doubt it."

"How did your Mr. Cruice know where to find his arrestee?"

"Anonymous tip in the form of a note dropped off at his house."

"Hmm. Well, as you can imagine this part of the law is not something I or anyone else I know practices. However, Clare, I can promise you there's case law here and it has been done in the past. If my memory serves from my law school days, there's a history of this sort of thing. Beyond that, I can only offer to look into it and, that is, of course, if hypothetical Mr. Cruice so desires."

"I would think Mr. Cruice might be very interested, sooner rather than later," said Clare, trying to keep a straight face. Josh smiled.

"Mr. Cruice, you know, sounds familiar—like I might know him," Josh smiled.

Clare returned the smile.

"Wonders never cease and you know a lot of people."

"Well, Clare, I promise I'll have something for you say before 4:00 p.m. today."

Putting aside the hypothetical Cruice/Ross scenario, the two lunch companions enjoyed the next fifteen minutes discussing family and current events.

•

Meanwhile, Jake and Rollie had taken a ride to the new brew pub on Western. Both ordered pints of Labor Ale and burgers.

"Rol, you can't imagine how grateful I am to be able to finally return the favor after all these years," said Jake, his eyes growing moist.

Rollie grinned.

"You know, Jake, probably not a week goes by that I don't' think of that awful night in Vietnam."

"Me, too, Rol—you saved my ass dragging me thirty forty yards under enemy fire."

"Look, Jake, there were a few times I thought of calling you over the years, but with marine training I could handle stuff. This McGurn thing really gets under my skin and I like this guy, you know. He's got spunk and he really wants to show the world how slimy these fuckin' politicians are."

"I'm glad to return the favor. Say, let's take a walk—you can show me around this Beverly neighborhood."

As they took a long walk through central Beverly, Rollie pointed out some of the historic Queen Anne and Prairie Style homes. Jake, it seemed, was awestruck at the sheer beauty and magnificence of the neighborhood.

"Some pretty nice digs in your part of the world, Rollie. If I were you, I'd buy one of these places."

"Not for me," laughed Rollie. "You know, I'm not looking for that much work fixing up an old house. Besides, I feel more at home with the coppers and firemen west of here."

"What are you saying, Rol? A lot of liberals in these big old houses?"

"Yeah. You know, a buddy of mine showed me Haesi's numbers in the 19th Ward in 2008. The precincts around here east of Western are full of liberals. Now they're probably thinking, 'oops!'"

"'Oops—huh, I like that. The whole fuckin' country is saying the same thing as far as I'm concerned. The guy doesn't have a clue and how he came out of Chicago is a mystery."

Rollie shook his head.

"He might win again, Jake, don't you think?"

"Perish the thought, marine. Let's go back. I want to run this abduction over in my head and get some rest. What's on your mind, Rol?"

"Sort of worried about Pat."

"Well, you know him better than I, but for what it's worth, for a former teacher this guy seems to be pretty resolute, if you know what I mean. Prior military and small arms training got to help, don't you think?"

"Yeah, but he really seems worried."

"Rollie, of course he is for God's sake! He should be and that's a good thing, man. Just remember our night patrols back in the day. One thing, though, I just hope he's got a good lawyer."

"That won't be a problem. This Jordan's the best."

•

Pat ate a light lunch around noon and checked his financial portfolio. The market was flat and a handful of e-mails from friends and family would have to wait. For some odd reason, he decided to prepare a four-minute speech even though he had no expectation of delivering it. He wondered whether the Cook County Board would agree to enter it into the official Cook County Board proceedings. The speech focused exclusively on Orizaga's prior felony conviction in February 2009 and release from probation two years later. Four more months after that and Denny was killed. The final sentence read: COOK COUNTY'S FAILURE TO CONTACT IMMIGRATION AND CUSTOM ENFORCEMENT DURING THAT TWO YEAR PERIOD CAUSED THE DEATH OF MY BROTHER.

He had just finished writing the speech when Vanderbiezen called.

"Pat, I just read the amendment and it's good. Some might question sheriff's discretion, but in law enforcement discretion is generally inevitable from the arresting officer to the judge. The theory in a democracy is the electorate, in its collective wisdom, will endorse competency and if the elected official's discretion is poor he or she gets the boot."

"Yeah, Joe. Clare and I think it's good, too, but are troubled with Wagner's 'if it passes' remark."

"Me, too, Pat. This was always along shot, but if the press picks it up maybe something might happen. Say, remember when Joan and you discussed the possibility of Orizaga still being in the U.S.?"

"Sure do, Joe," said Pat, smiling to himself. "But I'm still waiting on the FBI."

"Yeah, Pat, even if he's still in the States, he's long gone, I guess."

"Joe, maybe something might surprise us. Say, are you coming up tomorrow? Might be worth your while."

"We were going to, Pat, but we're putting up five professors from *Berkeley* for a philosophy seminar on Jean Paul Sartre,"

"You attending, Joe?"

"Not in a million years. As far as I'm concerned Sartre and the modern political correctness crowd are the reason this country is in decline."

"Whew, you're going to have to send me more on that, Prof. I gotta go so thanks for the call, Joe—I'll get back too you maybe in a day or two. Be sure to watch the news and best to Judy."

"Good luck. I'll be seeing Joan later on at a faculty meeting and I'll give her copy of the amendment."

"Appreciate that, Joe. Give her my best."

Pat had wanted to share the "Great Plan" with Joe but suspected that his academic advisors might find this abduction strategy in poor taste. Academics viewed the world as a challenge to attack with sound reasoning and empirical research, not with madcap escapades. In their wildest imaginings, the two professors would have never dreamed that a radical solution would soon unfold. Pat smiled to himself. Ironically, because of this escapade, all their academic research and legal reasoning would garner more support. Needing a change of pace, he made himself a cup of coffee and began reading the paper. NATO was all set to continue bombing in Libya while the *Occupy Wall Street* movement was growing by the day. As usual, there were foreign and domestic challenges on every front—nothing unusual there. Discarding *The Globe*, Pat went down in the basement and retrieved his licensed revolver from its safe. He checked it over and was satisfied it was in working order.

No sooner had he made his way up to the kitchen again when Clare called.

"Pat, I spent forty-five minutes on citizen's arrest over lunch with Josh—he just e-mailed me some comments."

"You're kidding, Clare! Now, he doesn't know?"

"No. He's an officer of the court so we talked in hypothetical terms—I'll forward his comments. Of course, I'm certain he does suspect something's in the wind. I also have his cell number."

"Okay, Clare something to discuss tonight," said Pat as they ended the call. Nervously, he opened the e-mail from Jordan.

Dear Pat and Clare,

Glad to see all is well with the McGurns and glad to do a bit of legal research, so here goes. States look at citizen's arrest or warrantless arrest generally by allowing said procedure if a person arrested has committed a felony and the citizen believes the person arrested committed the felony. In Mr. Cruice's case, given that there is a warrant it could be more problematic. Beyond that, a citizen contemplating such a move will be well advised to have a responsible lawyer who can advise the citizen during interrogation procedures after the arrest. Last, the citizen should not answer any questions until his lawyer is present. I hope this helps. If you have further questions, please do not hesitate to call at either my cell or office number listed below. I will be at my desk all day tomorrow.

Pat heaved a sigh of relief and turned his attention to supper. Time to put on the chicken wings and peel the potatoes.

At 5:10 p.m., Pat picked Clare up at the train station and drove directly home.

"I read Josh's e-mail and I think he's going to be our guy tomorrow and keep me out of trouble."

"God I hope so. Let's talk about that later. So what's on the menu tonight?" asked Clare.

"Chicken wings, mashed potatoes, peas and ice cream."

"Your wings are better than those Buffalo ones everybody goes on about."

"Secret recipe, I guess—so how's the day?"

"Pretty good, but glad to be home. I think maybe another year and I'm going to hang it up."

"Works for me, Clare—let's travel. I'm thinking Australia next winter or maybe Ireland like next week."

"You're playing with me, Pat—you know we can't afford that."

"Maybe I am, but, hey, if the market rallies maybe we can. Look, dinner in ten minutes. We can watch the news in the sunroom."

The couple ate a sumptuous dinner followed by ice cream cones and coffee. At 6:00 p.m. they watched local news on Channel 3 and the second segment announced a *Cook County Public Forum*, chaired by Commissioner

Alport. The smiling TV anchor apparently read from a press release that said:

> **Regarding the matter of undocumented foreigners, Cook County Commissioners will solicit comment from the public and select public officials on the subject of federal detainers. Interested persons can e-mail forum@cookcounty.gov**

"Smiley," the TV anchor, never mentioned crime victims and their families or the increasing numbers of criminal aliens released. In fact, she gave viewers the impression that the whole forum was about the plight of illegal aliens and never mentioned crime statistics.

"Sons a bitches—now I know this is a set up."

"Calm down, you have too much on your plate, so let me give you my updates. You read Josh's e-mail, right?"

Pat nodded.

"Yeah, I like it, so let's talk strategy about your role tomorrow. I'm thinking you'll take the day off."

"Already did—my boss, Gregor, knows about the *Cook County* hearing and he understood. I'll take the 8:30 a.m. train and tell Christy and her husband to meet me at that coffee shop down the street from the County Building on Adams Street. Oh, and I e-mailed your brother Eddy and he's coming."

"What about Josh?"

"Well, you know he knows the score. Like he said, he'll wait for the call—I'll phone him once you are escorted wherever."

"He won't know where to go right? So when I do get moved and they want to do a Q&A I'll make a call."

"That should do it and wherever you are, Josh will find you."

"What about Christy and Jason, you know after the meeting?"

"I'll take them to lunch, text Michael and Molly and wait for your call. Look, let's leave the supper things and take a walk."

"Sounds good," said Pat.

Before they left, there was a brief call from Rollie.

"You okay, Pat?"

"Yeah, kept myself busy and I'm now going for a walk with Clare."

"Good—but let me quickly go over tomorrow and see if you got questions."

"Don't bother, Rol—I got it. I'm ready."

"Talk to a lawyer?"

"Clare did—he's on call, Rol."

"Great. See ya in the morning—remember, we're now meeting at the *Agricultural School* on 111th Street, not at my place. And dress like a middle age liberal political activist. That reminds me, Pat, I briefed my two pals— Schus up north and Frank in the *Fourth District*—and they're cool with everything. I assured them their names never get mentioned."

"Sure that was the thing to do?"

"Yeah, I thought it best. Okay, time for shuteye."

"Jake okay, Rol?"

"He's up there listening to Buddy Holly or Jerry Lee Lewis. I forgot the guy listens to 50's oldies all the time."

"Goodness gracious—*Great Balls of Fire!*" said Pat.

Rollie laughed.

"Okay we're all set and I'll confirm with Boz. Oh I can't remember if we told you that after the grab, Jake will walk the few blocks to the Metra and go downtown. See ya."

DAY 24, TUESDAY, SEPTEMBER 20.2011

Pat got up at 3:45 a.m., took a shower, shaved, and dressed in old denim shirt, jeans and work boots. With his drab olive baseball cap, flannel shirt and faded jeans he was all set. He went downstairs and found Clare waiting for him in the kitchen.

"I can't sleep—you might be locked up tonight!"

"Real funny—hey, not to worry. For some odd reason, I'm feeling relaxed."

Clare sat in the breakfast nook, on one of the stools overlooking the back yard.

"I know, I know—Jake never fails and Rollie's the best detective ever! I just want you to know I'm scared, so I'm running over to *Christ the King* to attend the 6:30 Mass."

Pat walked up to her and put his arms around her.

"Thanks, I need all the help I can get. So I'll call you and you'll call Josh."

"That's the plan, but who knows what might happen and where? I mean your Phase One seems ironclad, but, beyond that, who knows?"

"I know this is crazy but we came this far and I gotta do this."

"Okay, so I'm meeting Christy, Jason and Eddy at the *Chicago Java* on La Salle—we will go into the County Building at 9:50 a.m. to try and get a seat. You know they are going to be shocked—I'm going to have to tell them, right?"

"Yeah, give them all the details, but don't mention Rollie, Boz, Jake, the two marines, Schus or Higgins by name."

"Not to worry—besides the only names I can remember anyway are 'Rollie and Jake' because they sound like a Vaudeville act."

Pat squeezed his wife tightly.

"Gotta go. Love your sense of humor."

"Please be careful, Pat."

"Promise."

At 4: 10 a.m., Pat went into the all night *Coffee'n Donuts* on Western, ordered four large coffees to go, got back into his car and drove slowly to Mount Greenwood. He was about ten minutes ahead of schedule. He pulled into the *Agricultural School* parking lot and waited. For a few moments, he thought about the odyssey of the last twenty-four days. Initially, he had attempted to learn the particulars of Orizaga's flight; this goal led to press reports, conversations with academics, disturbing interviews with commissioners and perhaps the most significant was entering into the political world of George Hallet. No matter what happened later that day Pat knew he would likely spend years into the future fighting these progressives who were hell-bent on destroying the United Sates he so loved. The last three weeks could only be described as bizarre, given the behavior of the cast of elected officials and their surrogates, none whom could have cared less about the sensibilities of the McGurn family. Joe and Joan's input had been invaluable because they provided an understanding of the big picture. And Rollie—well, returning justice with this Wild West caper was certainly unorthodox. Who would have thought a former high school teacher would partner with the likes of two former marines and pull off something like a citizen's arrest? His musings brought a sense of calmness, and he felt assured that on this day September 20, 2011, a clear and convincing message would be sent. Jurisdictions adopting sanctuary policies might now realize that federal cooperation with respect to criminal aliens was critical and that their policies should be repealed or amended.

The grey van turned into the *Agricultural School* parking lot at exactly 4:30 a.m., with Jake, Rollie and Boz already on board. Pat gave the men their coffees and climbed in the back. Then the van took off west on 111th Street. Jake turned around and looked at Pat and Boz.

"You guys all set?"

Both men nodded.

"Pat, you look like a something out of central casting. I like the look and the rest of us look pretty good in our uniforms. Oh, when we are done, give the paraphernalia to Rollie and he'll put it in the back of the van. I don't know about you guys, but I'm going to discard the uniform shirt as I'm wearing a polo shirt underneath."

While they headed towards the Delgado house, Jake went over the plan for Phase One for the last time. It would be sun up in two hours, so the operation from the grab to the safe house was going to be in the dark. The van stopped at the 95th and Stony Island red light where they had to wait momentarily for an emergency vehicle to pass. At 4:55 a.m., the van turned right at 87th Street and continued east. They were a few minutes early, but Jake told Rollie to signal to Mario to take off. Then Rollie went over Phase Two, with Pat and Boz listening attentively.

"Looks good," said Jake. "Everybody keep your eyes peeled. In seven minutes, I'll turn on the Mars light and we go."

At exactly 5:30 a.m., Jake and Rollie exited the van with gas masks on. Jake discharged the first canister and the two men pounded the door and rang the bell, yelling, "Gas! Gas!" After about thirty seconds, the old man appeared at the door, his frail wife peering anxiously over his shoulder. Terrified, the elderly couple allowed Boz to escort them away from the building and around the street corner. As planned, Jake used a crow bar to open the basement door, discharged the smoke canister, ran down the stairs and grabbed Orizaga from his bed, stuck a needle into his arm and secured his wallet. Within minutes, the felon—fully dressed, handcuffed, and blindfolded—was in the back seat of the van, as docile as an infant, babbling incoherently. Rollie monitored the street for potential problems. Pat said,

"SENOR ORIZAGA, YOU ARE UNDER ARREST FOR FAILURE TO APPEAR IN COURT ON SEPTEMBER 1, 2011."

Slumping over, Orizaga whimpered softly, but had nothing to say for himself. Anxiously, Pat looked at Jake who handed him Orizaga's wallet and signaled a "thumbs up." Apparently, this was to be expected.

Boz returned the old couple to the house, indicating it was now safe. Jake shut off the Mars light and placed all the paraphernalia in the rear of the van. Then, silently, he signaled Rollie before taking off down an alley on foot. Meanwhile, Boz waved to his comrades as he crossed the street heading north for the long walk to the stables. Rollie, behind the wheel, with Raul and Pat in the back seat, headed east to U.S. 41, and then north for the ten-minute ride to the *South Shore Country Club Stables*. Then, at precisely 5:50 a.m., the van entered the South Shore complex, making a hard right to the far end of the stables.

Pat clambered out of the van and grabbed Orizaga's arm. He had some difficulty getting him out of the back seat, quickly realizing that his prisoner was quite disoriented. Eventually, with a little help from Rollie, he succeeded in getting him to step down on to the ground. Placing an arm around Orizaga's waist, he led him into what appeared to be an old office, complete with a shabby oak desk, table and chairs. Rollie followed quietly. Pat pulled out one of the chairs and gently sat his charge down. From the threshold, Rollie gestured to Pat to remove one of the hand restraints and affix it to the chair. Next, following Rollie's silent directions, Pat took off the blindfold and placed sight-impaired glasses on his charge. He then put the coffee and an egg sandwich on the table, within Orizaga's reach.

"Disfruta tu desayuno," said Pat, trying to keep his voice as neutral as possible. By now he was feeling a surge of emotions—rage, pity, disgust. The time was 6:10 a.m. Pat and Orizaga sat in silence, but Orizaga had begun to take small sips of the black coffee, slurping noisily. Pat looked at him with loathing. Some men in this situation might have returned justice the old fashioned way and no one would be any the wiser. Most guys in his old Burnside neighborhood would have easily resorted to that option. For a minute, he found himself thinking of Clare. She supported him making a citizen's arrest, after some difficult moments. Perhaps her prayers and the grace of God were enabling this bizarre vigilante option. Pat was convinced this plan was certain to return broader justice by spitting in the face of ten Cook County commissioners and the scores of political hacks that supported sanctuary policies for illegal aliens. If all went well, this bold act would send a message across the country. Pat continued to stare at his brother's killer. To his surprise, he felt a tinge of sadness for this pathetic figure that, in some ways, was nothing more than a pawn in the evils of the far left political agenda.

Meanwhile, Rollie had changed shirts and put on an old sweatshirt and blue jeans; he now looked like any other run of the mill middle-aged leftist activist. He and Pat would appear to be two guys escorting a blind amigo to a County Board meeting. The cover should work. Rollie gestured to Pat that he needed a smoke and that he would be back in ten minutes. The time was 6:45 a.m.

Rollie, enjoying a Marlboro Light behind the stables, saw Clem come out and light up a cigar.

"All set? Your guy doing alright in there?"

"So far so good. I think McGurn could have been a cop, Clem."

"Gotta give the guy credit. Been on the job thirty years and I thought I seen it all."

"I better get back—so the horse patrol guys are here at around 7:10 a.m. or so, right?

"Yeah and like I said, you won't see them and the trainer over in the arena. I'll make sure the whole detail is out of here by 8:30 a.m."

"Clem, we owe you for this. You know we could have been stuck waiting in the van for three hours over at Rainbow Beach or somewhere with no telling how this guy would react. Your stables are perfect for this operation."

"Hey, I'd do it in a heartbeat again. What happened to McGurn's family is pure bullshit and these mealy-mouthed phonies that run this county should be run out of town."

"Couldn't agree more, Clem, but I better go."

Back at the office, all seemed quiet. Orizaga was still slumped over but was now fast asleep. He had drunk half the coffee but ignored the egg sandwich. The glasses were still affixed to the bridge of his nose and his mouth gaped wide. Arms folded, Pat sat watching him, fascinated by the range of his own shifting emotions. Rollie, returning from his smoke break, was startled by Pat's expression of hatred. For a moment, the thought flashed through his mind that Orizaga might be dead rather than sleeping. To his relief, their charge began to snore loudly.

Glancing at his watch, Rollie walked across the room and told Pat to take fifteen minutes to unwind. Clem had brought in two morning papers and so Pat took *The Chicago Sun*, the more liberal paper, and made his way to a bench facing the ninth green of the golf course. Below the fold, a headline read: **CONROVERSIAL COOK COUNTY FORUM TODAY**. The article quoted George Hallet extensively. He went to great lengths to defend the controversial ordinance, arguing that the detainer-ignoring policy was not to blame for the disappearance of Denny McGurn's killer. He continued with the bail bond argument, which the author supported with a quote from Cook County President Korshak. She said her counsel, Inger Nordquist, was going to set up a task force headed by retired Federal Judge Burns. What a joke! Nothing but smoke, Pat thought to himself. Burns had been recruited to provide political cover for the ten lawless Cook County commissioners. The only pro-amendment argument came from Commissioner Wagner who stated that there might be lawsuits.

There was nothing from Pat's commissioner, Jack Riley. The most disturbing piece was a three-paragraph article as a sidebar suggesting Pat McGurn belonged to an anti immigrant Tea Party off shoot. The implication was that he was a racist, anti-immigrant activist. Two anonymous sources were used. Pat was seething. He had to remind himself that the editorial board at *The Chicago Sun* had always supported progressive causes and candidates. Another organization called the *Prairie State Roundtable*, made up of prominent private sector businesses, was also quoted as endorsing the ordinance; it was clear that they were against the amendment as well.

Pat walked back into the office. Orizaga was still snoring, though it looked as though he had drunk some more of the black coffee and sampled the egg sandwich. Rollie, gesturing excitedly to something he had just read in *The Globe*, handed the paper to Pat who, in turn, handed *The Sun* to Rollie. To his surprise, Pat saw in the **LETTERS TO THE EDITOR SECTION** that good old Joe Vanderbiezen had been given some ink. Joe made a brilliant argument supporting the detainer policy in general and the amendment in particular. He reported that, as of August, 11, 2011, there were 278 detainers issued by *Immigration and Custom Enforcement* in Cook County and over one-third were accused of either murder, criminal sexual assault or other felonies. Pat was stunned to read that in addition to Origaza, there was another illegal alien charged with manslaughter as well a rapist who had been released. Joe reminded readers of the clear responsibility of the federal government to enforce immigration laws with the help of local jurisdictions. Pointing to Joe's piece, Pat gave a "thumbs up." Raul remained slumped. The time was 8:00 a.m.

Clem Clancy was at the departure staging area working with the detail and going over prescribed procedures for downtown demonstrations;

meanwhile, the civilian trainer was preparing the horses in the arena. The detail would include six horses, three trailers and six police officers. The trailers would park on the north side of Washington Street, facing Daley Plaza. They would leave at 8:30 a.m. After the briefing, Sergeant Clancy's phone rang.

"Clem, Liam Lannigan here—look I'm here in *Daley Plaza* and the boss assigned me as supervisor for this demonstration. I need your guys like now. It's getting pretty crazy down here, man."

"Take it easy, Liam—we are going to load the trailers now. 9:00 a.m. is the earliest my guys will be there."

"Okay. I'll keep Washington open. They know the drill, right, Clem?"

"Yeah, they've had that detail before so no problem. We always use Washington Street as a staging area for demonstrations in the County-City Building and *Daley Plaza*. So it's getting a little nutty down there?"

"You got it. There's some whack job stirring up these Mexicans. They got signs and we just broke up a 'Lie-in' on Clark and there's another traffic tie up on Randolph. Intel texted me—they figure maybe three thousand by 10:00 a.m."

"Yeah, I hear there's some kind of controversial County Board meeting," said Clem. "Something about some Beverly guy who's all pissed off about his brother's killer running to Mexico."

"So that's what this is all about! Say, Clem you still got that horse Silver with that Navajo copper called Tonto who can do that '*Hi Ho Silver*' routine like the Lone Ranger?"

"Yeah, in fact he's loading Silver now. His name is Hokee—don't call him Tonto. He don't like that. He's on the detail."

"Good. I may assign them to the Picasso because these assholes are climbing up there and waving the Mexican Flag and some other fuckhead is waving the U.S. flag upside down and pretending he's going to torch Old Glory. Maybe I can get Silver to scare the shit out of them. You know what I mean?"

"Hokee's the man, Liam. I'll brief him before he takes off. I see him horse-whispering Silver now."

"Clem, four more bus loads just pulled up and they're getting off, already frenzied!"

"Liam, half an hour, give or take, the detail, will be there."

Back in the rear room, Pat wondered if Orizaga could hear the horses neighing in the distance. The subject remained slumped, however, and made no further efforts to reach either the coffee or the egg sandwich.

•

At 8:45 a.m., overlooking the demonstration from President Korshak's conference room window on the fifth floor, stood George Hallet and Vic Varbanov.

"Nice of Ms. Korshak to let us in here to watch," said Hallet. "You know, there must be two thousand here already. I'd be pleased if we got two maybe three times that, Vic. Far more than we had last July at *Haymarket Hall* for that *Secure Communities* meeting."

Vic looked down on the Plaza.

"Violence you think, George? I see cops busted a few already, man. That ain't cool."

"Maybe, maybe not—can't say for sure. I hope nobody does something stupid like mess with a cop, you know what I mean? I tell you what. If we get enough people down here my plan is to instruct our street supervisors to block Randolph, La Salle, Clark and maybe State Street. You know, we had trainers fly in from LA from ACAN over the weekend to show us how to obstruct traffic. If we build momentum, I'm going to order a Kennedy expressway strategy at 3:30 p.m. to block rush hour traffic. Say, Vic, you all set for this meeting?"

"Oh yeah, the amendment's in the trash already, so we listen to this McGurn, vent a few minutes and the rest is all taken care of. Between us, man, we got at least twenty-five people going to stand up for us."

"What about Wagner, Vic?"

"Naw, Alport told me Wagner, Riley, Googan, Giglio and Guest know there won't even be a vote."

"You promise them something, Vic?"

"George, I can't talk about details, but, yeah, three of them will be taken care of. So who you line up to speak in the Plaza, George? I see a stage set up."

Hallet glanced at his notes.

"I got a new hire from our *Cooperative* to pick up Manny and a few others at Midway Airport. They're flying in from Washington DC this morning and he's bringing one or two from the *Mexican Legal Action Group* and Congressman Sanchez from Texas to speak. Oh and our favorite trouble-maker Zorrow from ACAN will do his thing. I want you up there after the meeting adjourns to tell the crowd the amendment measure was killed. Oh, and I got Sergio Chavez from *The Hispanic Community Organization* to be the master of ceremony. Okay, let's get to work—it's 9:00 a.m. I'll look for you near the stage around 11:30 a.m. I'm guessing the committee will get through most of the speakers by then and, like I said, Alport won't allow a vote. My goal is to make our rally the main event so as to marginalize any noise McGurn makes. That way, we'll turn the bad press into an opportunity."

Commissioner Varbanov looked down at the swelling mob in Daley Plaza.

"You know, this McGurn was really pissed off when I talked to him, you know what I mean?"

"Hey, forget about McGurn. Sure, I kind of feel for the guy. Trust me, after today he will just fade away. The beauty of our strategy is that we let him think there could be a change so all he got left is to bug those Immigration cops or maybe the FBI. See *The Daily Sun* this morning, Vic?"

Varbanov shook his head.

"Maybe read it later, man—we got good press there."

"For sure, Vic—they made it clear they're against the amendment and pro ordinance. The Sun's always on our side."

Vic gave George a fist pump.

"I learned a lot when you trained me in community organizing ten years ago. You're a good amigo I always say, Senor Hallet and you trained President Haesi as well, right?"

"Not exactly, Vic—I had a lot of help from Roy Chambliss who was a protégé of Shelton Lalinsky who founded the *Industrial Areas Project* back in the 60's. Yeah, I was Haesi's field trainer twenty some years ago in Roseland. We did a good job in those days raising awareness in minority communities. Look, we better get out of here and get to work."

As Varbanov and Hallet were about to leave the conference room, in walked Cook County President Korshak. She didn't say a word but gestured for the two to follow her to the window.

"Why are these people climbing on the Picasso and waving those flags like that? I think one of them is shredded. And some fool's pretending to light the United States flag. Did you two authorize that?"

"No, ma'am, just part of the demonstration, I guess."

"Well, it looks like these people are starting a revolution. Look, I'm all for, stopping deportations and all that and both of you got me to support the ordinance, but this doesn't help. Can you get them off the Picasso statue? What if they start spray painting? Mexican people love to do that."

"Well, I'll try Madame President."

"What about you, Mr. Hallet? I should hope these demonstrations don't tax the police too much. Look, the horse patrol just showed up. What does that mean?"

"Probably routine, Madame President. The city assigns the horse detail for public assemblies."

"Sir, I'm aware of that—now I want this demonstration out there to be orderly."

"Yes, Ma'am."

Turning her back to the window, Korshak shook her head.

"Well, you two better go—I have calls to make."

Varbanov and Hallet left the room in silence. Once out of earshot, Varbanov turned to the older man.

"Hey, I gotta meet with Commissioners Alport, Houma and Chico and make sure everything's set. So you going to try and do something about the dudes on the Picasso?"

"Nope, Vic. Besides, I like the message and Korshak will get over it. Reminds me of an American flag burning we set up at the Los Angeles Coliseum last year."

•

Meanwhile back at the stables, Pat, with Rollie looking on, took off the other cuff, got Orizaga to stand up and escorted him to the john. He then placed a three quarter length trench coat over him to hide the new nylon hand restraints, before slowly escorting him toward the van, which was parked in front, with Boz at the wheel. Rollie quietly slipped into the front seat next to Boz and issued a 'shush' reminder. Thirty seconds later, Pat opened the door for his arrestee, sat next to him and said, "Police station!" They began the eight-mile drive to downtown. It was still rush hour and the time was 9:07 a.m. Orizaga hunched forwards, head down.

The van crawled along Lake Shore Drive and as they were going by the *Museum of Science and Industry*, Rollie handed Pat his iPhone; there was a text from Jake that read:

In the plaza—maybe four thousand rowdies be careful. Cops on horses. Kinda crazy!

Pat nodded and returned the iPhone. Looking at Rollie, he pointed to his watch. It was now 9:35 a.m. Rollie got out a pen and paper, scribbled a note and handed it to Pat: *I'll have Boz drop us shortly on the La Salle side of the County-City Building.* By then, they were heading west on Madison and were making good progress.

●

Earlier, Clare got off the Metra at the La Salle Street station at about the same time that Christy and her husband got off the train at Ogilvie Station. Pat's brother, Eddy, had also agreed to join the group. The plan was to meet at the corner of LaSalle and Madison at 9:15 a.m. for coffee at a place called *Chicago Java*. All assembled at the appointed time, exchanged greetings, found seats and ordered lattes. Jason mentioned that he had overheard people talking on the street that *Daley Plaza* was loaded with demonstrators. Some were blocking traffic and there had already been arrests.

"I walked down Washington from the underground parking lot and it's bedlam over there," said Eddy. "There must be hundreds of cars just stuck because these idiots are blocking traffic. Cops on horses are trying to remove people from the streets—I didn't think this meeting was that big a deal."

"I can't explain the size of the crowd," said Clare, "but if I had to guess, I'd say this demonstration has been in the works for several days. You know, for the three weeks or so one of the professors sent Pat all sorts of material. It looks like professional trouble makers are brought in to organize these demonstrations."

"Well, I remember when Uncle Pat was on TV last month at some meeting, the demonstrators tied up traffic on the Kennedy Expressway during rush hour. I think that was probably run by professionals," said Christy.

Clare nodded.

"Yeah, that was *The Secure Communities Task Force* that *Homeland Security* convened to gain input about these deportations. It was a five-city tour that was sabotaged by these professional troublemakers. You see, these people just want to end deportations—that's why they tied up traffic last month like they are doing today. Pat's professor buddy told him that it's part of this Sheldon Lalinsky's community organizing strategy that worked going back sixty years with the Blacks. Now the Hispanics have adopted similar methods."

Eddy shook his head.

"I didn't know any of this. So this stuff is going on all over the country?"

"Looks that way," acknowledged Clare. "And here we are and my husband is right in the middle of it. I just hope he comes home in one piece. Look, we've got a few minutes so if you like, we can take our coffees and watch the action on the other side for a few minutes."

The others were game, so they left the coffee shop and walked towards Washington and Clark. Sure enough, there was a massive crowd and police with bullhorns were working hard to keep traffic flowing and people controlled. As they drew closer, the noise grew louder but they couldn't make out what was being said through the bullhorns. They were stunned to see two, three hundred placards in Spanish and English bearing the words, NO DEPORTACION, CHICANO POWER. Horns were blaring, while tense-looking commuters and tourists tried to push their way to the edges of the mob.

"Never saw anything like this before," said Christy, barely able to believe her eyes.

Clare smiled.

"All I know is that I have one crazy husband that's going to blow this thing sky high."

"*Really?* All he's going to do is give a short speech, right?" said Jason, exchanging worried looks with Christy.

"Look, let's go—it's 9:45 a.m. I want to see this from the beginning," said Clare, avoiding the question.

Inside the County Board Room, there was standing room only in the back. The chief deputy radioed Security and gave instructions to cut off entry at 10:15 a.m. The County Clerk noted in his log that the press pen was full. Clare, Eddy, Christy and Jason entered on the City Hall side at 10:00 a.m. Clare had figured the meeting would probably start late and as she walked toward the elevators, she saw at the far end of the hall Pat, Rollie and what appeared to be Orizaga. Without saying a word, she led the group to the elevators, saying a silent prayer of gratitude that they were too distracted to notice Pat and his strange companions. What a relief to know that, so far, all was well! They got off at the Fifth Floor and then joined the long line to get through Security. Fortunately, Pat, Rollie and Orizaga were near the front of the line and entered the chambers without being noticed. Five minutes later, Clare's group finally cleared Security, and entering the Cook County Board Room, slipped into the rear of the standing room only section.

The time was 10:10 a.m. and the crowd was growing restless. Commissioner Alport scanned the audience in the hope of locating Pat. Frustrated, Commissioner Alport yelled into the microphone,

"ORDER! ORDER! PLEASE, WILL MR. MCGURN COME DOWN TO THE PODIUM. SERGEANT AT ARMS, PLEASE CLOSE THE DOOR!"

Christy, Jeff, Eddy and Clare were crunched together but Christy could make out Pat, Rollie and some blind man standing twenty feet to their right.

"Why doesn't Uncle Pat get up? Should I say something?"

Clare looked at her calmly.

"Be patient! Everything is going as planned."

Christy and Jeff stared at Clare.

"*Planned!*" exclaimed Christy. "What do you mean?"

Alport hit the podium with his gavel.

"THE MEETING WILL COME TO ORDER, THE MEETING WILL COME TO ORDER, THE MEETING WILL COME TO ORDER—

Rollie undid the nylon restraints, placed them in his pocket, took the glasses off Orizaga and left quietly.

Raising his voice above the din, Pat yelled out words he had rehearsed over and over again:

"MY NAME IS PATRICK MCGURN AND I HAVE MADE A

CITIZEN'S ARREST OF RAUL ORIZAGA, THE MAN WHO KILLED MY BROTHER. THIS BODY IS RESPONSIBLE FOR HIS RELEASE!"

Jeff, Christy and Eddy stared in bewilderment while the room exploded into a mixture of screams and cheers. A frantic Commissioner Alport pointed to the Sergeant at Arms and screamed,

"APPREHEND THOSE TWO RIGHT NOW!"

Sergeant Ross ran up the stairs grabbed Pat and Orizaga by the arm and escorted them to a room behind the stage. In the midst of the chaos, Sheriff Dypsky seemed paralyzed; he stood looking bewildered as Alport again screamed and pounded the gavel.

"PLEASE CALM DOWN. MEETING ADJOURNED. THE DEPUTIES WILL PROVIDE FOR AN ORDERLY EXIT. MEDIA WILL REMAIN IN THE BULLPEN.

The time was 10:20 a.m. Television cameras were active.

There was uproar in the chamber. Two of the deputies stood in front of the County commissioners to protect them from the surging crowd; then, as the mob pushed its way towards the exit, the deputies, escorted them to a private elevator. Upon reaching the Third Floor, they sequestered themselves in the meeting room of Finance Chairman Houma. It took Security fifteen minutes to usher the 300 attendees out of the County Board Room. Fortunately, Clare, Christy, Jeff and Eddy were among the first out. Clare noted at least ten reporters on their cell phones while TV cameras recorded everything.

Down on the Third Floor, Vic Varbanov stepped out of the conference room and put in a call to George Hallet out in Riley Plaza.

"George, I think McGurn arrested Raul Orizaga. The meeting's adjourned. It's crazy in here!"

"You're kidding! Arrested? What are you talking about?"

"McGurn had Orizaga with him and yelled real loud that he arrested him."

"That's unbelievable!" yelled Hallet. "What do we do with this crowd? You must do something, Vic."

"I don't know—the deputies got us in Riley's conference room for safety, I guess. Manny should be getting off the plane, so maybe he might figure something out."

"*Safety?* Whose safety?"

"Well, I guess they think with all the shit going down we better hide out in this room. When the deputy lets us out, I'll shoot right over."

Varbanov looked through the doorway at his fellow commissioners. Most of them were glued to their iPhones, two were sleeping and two were giggling and eating candy. Hallet called Varbanov.

"Get this, Vic. Word's out that some Indian cop busted the guys on the Picasso and the crowd is dispersing. The horse cops did a job. Scared the shit out of a bunch of our guys.

"That's no good, bro. Manny's flying in from DC and expects a crowd. He gonna call me. What should I say?"

"Think of something. I got to find out if we can get some of our hombres out of jail. Oh shit!"

"You okay, George?"

"Damn it! I just stepped in horse shit!"

•

As soon as they reached LaSalle Street, Clare promised that she would answer her family's questions over lunch; clearly, they were stunned by the events they had just witnessed and they were looking to her for answers. She suggested that they head to *Rhonda's* on Wacker Drive, and as they walked east, she called Josh Jordan.

"Hi Josh. Clare here—remember Mr. Cruice?"

"How can I forget?"

"Well, fiction became non-fiction about fifteen minutes ago—Mr. Cruice is my husband."

"I suspected as much, Clare. Does this have something to do with all that commotion by the Picasso statue in Daley Plaza?"

"You got it, Josh, but the main event was in the Cook County Chambers."

"Citizen's arrest, no doubt."

"You got it, counselor."

"Where's he at? Does he know to keep his mouth shut?"

"This time he does. Look, they took him and Orizaga behind the dais in the Cook County Board Room, so I don't know where he's at now. He should call any minute—I'll let you know where they took him. And not to worry—he won't say a word until you show."

"Well, I'm guessing they'll take him underground to the *Daley Center* because they have interrogation rooms and holding cells in the basement. Let's see—time is 10:30 a.m. My guess is that they most certainly will want to question him in some detail. My staff just told me it's getting a lot of coverage, so I'll turn on our TV. Clare, just want you to know my desk is clear for the day."

"Josh, we can't thank you enough," said Clare, beginning to choke up. She hastily put her cell phone in her purse, walking into *Rhonda's* behind her relatives. The four ordered diet cokes and chicken wraps, then sat underneath a huge photo of Waikiki Beach. Early 60's surf music played in the background. The group looked at Clare expectantly.

"Well, I'll take it from the top, but not a word to anybody because there's a chance Pat may get charged and he's got to protect the people that helped him. They could be even more at risk."

A teary eyed Christy looked at Clare.

"Uncle Pat planned all this while knowing he might be charged?"

"No, he didn't exactly plan any of it, but he had the last say or, I should say, we both did. This whole escapade was potentially dangerous, so you can imagine the words we exchanged. Well, he's safe now, so please bear with me—I'll do my best to explain. I'll start with the Sunday before Labor Day when the idea for the abduction germinated. You all know pretty much what happened the first week with the all the confusion about the release of Orizaga—you, Eddy, spoke with Eileen Murphy as well, so this is not new to you. Before I begin, I cannot mention any of the names of the men who assisted in this …"

Clare started with the Sunday afternoon three weeks before when Pat had met with an old high school chum and retired detective, Mr. X. She did her best to include as much detail she could remember and the looks on her companions' faces were indeed memorable. About half way through the narrative, Eddy interrupted.

"You just finished the 13th day—I'm counting at least 10 people recruited all over the city and state."

"Look, I know this is complicated, and I must tell you that early on I was skeptical. Try to understand that Pat was determined to return justice. Through a lot of work and luck he developed three options and the best one you saw today."

"Three?" said Jeff. "I get the ordinance and today's action. So what's the third?"

"Professor Farnsworth suggested an entity in Washington DC named *Judicial Vigilance* for legal action and, just the other day, Pat agreed to talk to them. However, he asked for a week's delay—"

"Pat's on TV—look up behind the bar," said Christy, pointing to the flat screen TV. I think TNN News is covering it!"

●

Back at *Daley Plaza*, Jake was delighted to see that at least two TV cameras had filmed the way the horse details dealt with the flag desecrators. From the sidelines, he had witnessed Officer Hokee's Lone Ranger performance. Upon seeing one of the thugs holding a burning flag, Hokee dug his spurs into Silver's sides and as the massive horse reared, eyes rolling, front hooves flailing, he had shouted, *"Hi, Ho, Silver!"* Cowering under the rearing horse, the miscreant dropped the flag, covered his head with his hands and rolled to the ground, out of harm's way. As Silver continued to rear, the crowd began to dissipate. Meanwhile, law abiding citizens on the sidelines applauded the performance. The flag burner was hauled away by a cop.

Jake watched as another clown was downed by Silver and five foot patrolmen cuffed others coming off the statue. An incoming call came from Rollie.

"Where you at?"

"I came downtown and got in the middle of all this craziness—you won't believe this. Tonto and Silver are doing their thing."

"I watched it all on TV, Jake. I'm sitting in a joint called *Katy Casey's* over on Wells, watching the action on cable. Pat's all over the news. You got time to kill, so walk two blocks west, hang a left and walk a block south— you can't miss the place."

"I'm on my way, man—I'll tell you, this may be one of the best days I've had in a long time."

Rollie laughed.

"Get your ass over here, Jake."

"On my way, marine."

On entering *Katy Casey's*, Jake was amused to see the patrons buzzing about the excitement. He spotted Rollie at the end of the bar, chatting up Rosy the bartender. She seemed intrigued that Rollie knew so much about what was happening. Slightly inebriated, Rollie introduced Jake to Rosy and the two former marines sat at the bar and ordered pints of Molanger beer and corn beef sandwiches.

"See the TV, Jake? It's all over *Wolf News* at this end of the bar and at the other end it's on Chicago's WBN. The TV anchor said a few minutes ago that they took Pat and Orizaga to rooms behind the podium."

Jake took a long pull on his Molanger.

"Look at the TV—they got the Hi Ho Silver copper clip on."

Katy Casey's patrons roared.

"This is great," said Rollie. "Now there'll be two *You Tube* clips that go viral. When I walked in there must of been twelve guys at the bar talking about it. It's a fuckin' circus—you know they got President Korshak on the air and she babbled something about maybe McGurn should be charged. And, get this, State's Attorney Hunter-Goss's press gal said Pat's in custody!"

"*She said that?*"

"Just heard it."

"I knew this town was a circus, Rol, but I'm glad we got in the ring, man. This is unbelievable. So you think McGurn's going to be all right?"

"Should be. I figure his lawyer will be there soon—they got to keep everything straight. With all the public opinion, the County would be fools to charge him. Look, you got time, so let's hang here for a while and talk old times. I gotta play one of my favorites on the Juke Box."

A few seconds later, a recent rendition of THE WILD COLONIAL BOY was blaring, with Rollie leading the whole bar in a sing-a-long.

> "*There was a wild colonial boy, Pat McGurn was his name*
> *He was his father's second son, his mother's pride and joy!*"

Two patrons at the other end of the bar also knew the lyrics and soon everyone had joined in the chorus. "*He was a wild colonial boy! That was how they captured him, the wild colonial boy.*"

Jake smiled, but his eyes were watering.

"You always loved all that Irish stuff, Rol. This is great!"

Rollie yelled to Rosy the barkeeper, "house drinks!"

The patrons roared yet again and Rollie and Jake hugged one another.

"You gave me forty-four years, man," said Jake, tears coursing down his face.

"Look, let's hang out here together for a bit—we can both take the same cab south to Midway airport, and I'll just shoot home and pay the guy," said Rollie, wiping his eyes with the back of his hand.

Motioning to Rosy that he had just the song for her, he placed some money in the box and on came THE STAR OF THE COUNTY DOWN with its famous lyrics: *"She's young Rosey McCann from the banks of the Bann. She's the star of County Down!"*

Laughing heartily, Rosey bought the next round. Meanwhile, TNN replayed Pat's proclamation and Tonto's performance again and again.

●

Spellbound, Christy, Jeff and Eddy continued to listen to Clare's narrative. Just as she was describing Jake Hawk, her phone rang. It was Pat.

"Are you all right? Where are you?"

"Basement of the *Daley Center*. I'm okay, you know, a little nervous, as they want answers, so I played the lawyer card. Call Josh, will you?"

"He can be there in maybe fifteen minutes—just don't say anything!" said Clare, trying to sound calm.

"If all goes well you should be out of there in a few hours. I'm with Christy, Jeff and Eddy."

"Give them my best—got to go."

The time was 11:00 a.m.

●

Josh Jordan had to take the long way to the *Daley Plaza* because of the demonstrators. After slogging through the crowd, he noted six TV vans parked along Clark Street and stopped to listen to an anchor from a major cable network. She had to repeat herself several times because of the loudness of bullhorns from police and demonstrators. A full-blown scuffle took place near the podium, reminding him of his days as a volunteer driver at the infamous Democratic convention in 1968. The anchor finally completed her story.

> "About an hour ago, inside the Cook County Board Room, Patrick McGurn turned over Raul Orizaga to authorities after making what appears to be a citizen's arrest. McGurn, we understand, made the arrest because county authorities had released Raul Orizaga, his brother's killer from jail three weeks earlier, instead of deporting him. He was later charged with killing McGurn's brother.
>
> Pro-immigration activists organized the crowd behind me because the County was considering an amendment to a controversial ordinance that allowed McGurn's killer to post bond.
>
> At present, we understand both Patrick McGurn and Raul Orizaga are in custody and being questioned by Cook County Sheriff's police. Earlier, authorities had their hands full here in Daley Plaza, but the horse detail led by Officer Tonto managed to maintain order."

Shaking his head in disbelief, Jordan continued on, wondering how long it would take for the segment to go national. All the talk radio shows and bloggers would sensationalize the story. He showed his lawyer credentials at the *Daley Center* and headed for the elevator. Down at the sub floor, a deputy escorted him to a rear suite of rooms. A lone detective was fiddling with an iPhone.

"Excuse me, Josh Jordan here to see Patrick McGurn."

"You are?"

"His lawyer—and your name?

"Detective Troy Toth. Mr. McGurn is in the next room. You may see him."

"Why, may I ask, is he here, Detective Toth?"

"Don't know—you know, something about needing to ask your client questions."

"I appreciate that, but I just heard a TV reporter say Mr. McGurn is in custody. Is that your understanding? Or perhaps someone from Cook County used that word incorrectly. Can you explain, Mr. Toth?"

"All I can say, Mr. Jordan, is that McGurn is here for questioning."

"Well, maybe while I interview my client you might clear that up."

Jordan asked for privacy and slipped Toth a fifty. The detective silently pocketed the note, and unlocked the door to an adjacent room. Pat was sitting on the other side of the door, looking none the worse for wear. He greeted the attorney with a grin.

"How's it going, Josh? Last time we talked it was that golf outing you invited me to. You got a sarcastic look now—is that the way for a lawyer to look at his client?"

"*Client!*" exclaimed Jordan. "I guess you are, but I'm not sure what you need. Trust me, law school didn't cover what you got yourself into, Pat McGurn. For what it's worth, my take for now is damage control and getting you out of here. Before I go on, I see we are being monitored. See that device up there?"

Craning his neck, Pat surveyed a telltale glass dome on the ceiling. He nodded.

"For now I'll do most of the talking," instructed Jordan, grabbing a wheeled office chair from behind the single desk in the room. "If I need details, whisper real soft or write on this pad."

Pat nodded.

"Pat, you made them look like fools and they don't like that. My guess is that the phones are ringing off the wall across the street in the commissioners' suites, State's Attorneys' offices and the Sheriff Dypsky's office. You must understand that you cannot tell me anything that might incriminate you or anybody else."

"You have a strategy?" whispered Pat.

Josh scooted closer in his chair, leaning towards Pat.

"Your story went national—what was it, a month ago? This will ramp it up ten times more so. With Mayor Gill and Korshak's connection to the President, you can believe all sorts of people are pissed off. And get this—on the way in I heard a reporter from one of those cable networks claiming you were in custody, along with Orizaga. If the public thinks they're treating you like a criminal, the law and order side will go viral! Let me ask, this Pat—is

Orizaga healthy? I mean, you didn't have to be aggressive to the point of perhaps causing injury?"

"No."

"Good. Now, this is important—did Orizaga know you were arresting him? I mean, did you say as much?"

"Yes."

"You used a revolver and it was licensed."

"Yes."

Okay, that's all I need for now."

Pat, looking somewhat worried, got out a pen.

"You think they want to hard ass me?" he wrote.

"Some might like Hunter-Goss and maybe Korshak," scribbled back Jordan. "I wouldn't worry about Dypsky. Sources tell me all he worries about are lawsuits and covering his ass. In the end he can't be trusted because he's two-faced. I got to tell you, there's not a lawyer in town that thinks charging you is a good idea. Now one more thing and this is important—I promise you the goofs across the street believes you did not act alone. I'm not going to ask you if you had help. They may want to go after any confederates you recruited—you understand? Again, all I want is a 'yes' or 'no. when I ask you more questions unless I say otherwise. This will protect you and whoever."

Picking up his pen again, Pat smiled reassuringly.

"No problem."

"You'll just have to sit here until they figure out a way to save face and get this out of the news. If all the media outlets pick this up, you're going to be America's hero man, modern day David kicking Goliath's ass. Look, I'll get you a sandwich and coffee. Before I go, Pat, if you have anything that belongs to Orizaga you need to turn that over."

Pat retrieved Orizaga's wallet from his jeans pocket and, with his back to the camera, handed it over to Josh.

"That's Orizaga's Mexican ID right?"

Pat nodded,

"Everything's in there, right—you got nothing else of Orizaga's?"

Pat shook his head.

"Anything else?"

Pat pulled out the Cook County warrant for Orizaga's arrest.

"Where did you get this?"

Pat whispered, "Clare."

"You keep that, Pat—no one needs to know you have that for now. Call Clare and tell her I'm here. Anything else?"

"Pastrami on the sandwich and two creams, no sugar."

"You got it. Look, here's what I'm thinking. I got a source—Chuck Cronkle at UPW who was probably there when you made the pronouncement. I think we can get him to get his New York people to run this all over the country, if not the world. Understand?"

Pat nodded.

"This ID and Orizaga's mug will do the trick. Point is to get so much coverage that the fools across the street will have no choice but to drop the whole thing."

"What about a legal strategy?" wrote Pat.

"Won't need one if they drop it. So, look—I'll get the sandwich and call my guy. Give me about twenty minutes."

Jordan walked into the next room where Toth was on a phone call.

Look, I'm going to get my guy something to eat and he's going to call his wife. Give him some privacy, will you?"

"What d'you mean?"

"You know damn well what I mean, so shut that fuckin' thing off."

Within five minutes, Jordan found a service in the downtown pedway that would copy and send e-mails with attachments. He sent the story to Cronkle before walking over to the sandwich vendor where he ordered two pastrami sandwiches and a coffee. Then he called Chuck who answered on the second ring.

"Chuck, Josh here—you covering the McGurn thing?"

"Who isn't? I was there in the press box. What's up?"

"I'm representing McGurn, so check your e-mail. I'll give you an exclusive."

"Give me a second so I can open this thing. Whoa, Josh—so that's this Orizaga?"

"Yeah, his Mexican ID and photo I figure will sell more papers."

Josh paid for the food and coffee and retrieved a diet coke from the machine.

"You should get this to your New York Office."

"My next move, Josh. Let me tell you, half an hour ago, I contacted New

York and they wanted ironclad proof Orizaga is the real deal. Now I got it with this ID. I also got a source in Hunter-Goss's office that confirms his identify."

"Do me a favor—don't tell anybody where you got the Mexican ID. I got to get back to McGurn."

Jordan returned to the interrogation room and asked Toth if he had heard anything.

"Still waiting."

"Did you tell them we want the machine turned off?"

"Don't know what you're talking about, Mr. Jordan."

"You're lying. Look, unless you got a good reason to keep Mr. McGurn, we're leaving in twenty minutes. Tell them that. Oh, and before I forget— my client gave me this wallet with Mr. Orizaga's personal effects."

Toth took the wallet and studied the ID.

"You telling me McGurn gave you this?"

"That's what I said, Detective," said Jordan, heading for the room in which Pat was being detained. Seeing the sandwich and coffee, Pat's eyes lit up. When he took off the lid, the coffee was still steaming. Slowly, he poured in the two creams and unwrapped the pastrami sandwich.

"I gave the ID to Toth—it's real obvious the 'ship of fools' over there can't think straight. Do you have a good photo of yourself on your phone?"

"Yeah," said Pat, almost choking on the sandwich.

"Let me send it to Chuck—his people will want to run your picture as well."

Deftly, Jordan slid his fingers across the keypad of his cell phone. The text read:

McGurn will agree to the following quote, **"For many reasons I did not have faith in the criminal justice system and decided to take matters in my own hands. I took this position because my brother would be alive today if the system did its job and allowed federal authorities to deport my brother's killer in 2009."** More later. I've attached a good photo of McGurn. If time permits I may patch McGurn in for a Q&A with you. If not go with the above quote.

Pat nodded approval.

•

Back at *Rhonda's,* Christy, Jeff and Eddy decided to wait with Clare until they had word that Pat had been released.

"It's hard to understand why Pat never told these professors or us for that matter," remarked Eddy.

"Detective X imposed secrecy for a lot of reasons. I don't know if I mentioned it earlier but it was Farnsworth who first suggested Orizaga might still be in the States. According to her research, many felons stay and get false ID's, so this wasn't a far-fetched theory."

"I can't believe how many people Uncle Pat recruited and how it all came together—*how on earth did he do it?*"

"He's always been resourceful, Christy—not real daring but he's always figured out ways to get things done in life. This time he had a lot of help, but he could have been killed and could still end up in jail. We had some tough discussions, but there was no stopping him."

"I'm thinking his best help came from you, Aunt Clare," said Christy.

●

Detective Troy Toth sat down across from Pat with a legal pad in hand.

"Just got my instructions—the higher ups want me to ask you some questions."

"I would prefer we wait until I consult with my client privately first, Detective," objected Jordan.

"I'm under orders, Sir, so if you don't mind, let's proceed. So, Mr. McGurn, when and where did you apprehend Mr. Orizaga?"

"Detective, like I said, we need privacy for a moment," objected Jordan.

Toth shrugged and left the room.

Turning away from the camera, Jordan whispered something to Pat, then summoned Toth from the next room.

"Detective, I see you have a list of questions. Why don't you give me a copy of the list and I will have Mr. McGurn put the answers in writing and have them to you by tomorrow noon."

"Sir, they want these questions answered today," insisted Toth.

"Detective, my conditions are clear and non-negotiable. We will wait patiently for you to check with your people. Please do what you have to do, so we can both be about our business and Mr. McGurn can go home to his family."

"Okay, but I guess this might take time," said Toth.

"We understand."

Once Toth had left the room, Jordan turned to Pat.

"Look, Pat," he whispered. "I've been dealing with these people as a defense attorney for years—trust me, they don't know what to do. You see, every time you're in the news they look foolish. If they're smart, they will keep you out of the news by dropping the whole thing."

"So I guess you're saying they may not have figured that out yet."

"Exactly. They're in a pickle. My guess is they're looking for help from the top, maybe even from Washington. I wouldn't be surprised if they're consulting Haesi's Chief of Staff, Marvin Bolevsky. Not to worry, though—they'll let us out of here shortly. They have no choice. You know, I better text Cronkle over at United and tell him there's no way we can do that interview with you before his New York deadline. He'll have enough for a story."

When the detective returned, he informed them that Hunter-Goss had agreed to the written questions on condition that they provide the answers by noon the following day and that they agree to follow up questions.

"Seems reasonable," said Jordan, amiably, "but I need a few minutes with my client, Detective."

Once more, Toth walked out, letting his displeasure be known more by his expression than by anything he said. Jordan quickly turned to Pat.

"Look, this is reasonable. I will insist the interview take place at my residence in Beverly at noon tomorrow—I'm certain they will agree. Once you're released, we go to my place to avoid the press. You call Clare, and I'll have my nephew pick us up. He and I drove down in his car today."

"So the plan is that we hang out at your place for the rest of the day, right?"

"Yeah, you're going to be bothered by the press at your house and, as your lawyer, it's best I manage the next day or so. I'll take you and Clare home late tonight."

•

At 2:30 p.m., across Clark Street in the Cook County conference room, nine commissioners, President Korshak and her counsel, Inger Nordquist, sat around the large mahogany table. Standing at the window, Korshak turned towards the group.

"It looks like most of the demonstrators have left. Does anybody know how many arrests?"

"Twenty for disorderly conduct including Zorro from ACAN and one guy named Diablo in stable condition at *Stroger Hospital*."

"Well, we should thank George and his staff because he got everybody on the busses," said Alport, staring angrily at Vic Varbanov.

"What happened to Manny?" asked Chico.

"Manny heard about McGurn when he landed at *Midway* and turned around with his group and left. He's blaming me, so I don't know," said Varbanov sullenly.

Korshak shook her head in disgust.

"Commissioner Varbanov, my staff just showed me the Picasso video—those people all look like idiots. Why didn't you stop them?"

"I couldn't," said Varbanov defensively. He was saved from having to say anything further when Korshak's phone and she saw it was State's Attorney Hunter-Goss. The call lasted two minutes.

"Well, Lisa says they'll let McGurn go in a few minutes. He's agreed to answer our questions in writing and will submit the answers at his attorney's house in Beverly tomorrow at noon."

Davida Alport frowned.

"So that sly fox Jordan runs our interrogation? He's certain to be hiding something. Tell me this, Shirley, did you get the impression Lisa wants to prosecute McGurn for unlawful restraint?"

"She seemed pissed and she hates to look bad. So I don't know. I'm going to think on this today and maybe get some advice."

"Maybe it's a good idea to go after this McGurn," said Commissioner Boller, gnawing on a candy bar.

"Damn straight!" said Rucker.

"Well, just remember that Jordan's one of the best. Tough to figure his next move, but I'm certain he wants to help McGurn avoid any legal obligations. Everyone knows McGurn didn't pull this stunt off by himself. I had my staff do a bit of research and bounty hunting is illegal in Illinois."

"Well, let's nail his ass!" exploded Commissioner Petrutis.

"Well, he wasn't seeking a bounty, so let's not get too excited here.

Believe me, he had help and he has to protect whoever was involved. That puts Jordan in a difficult spot," said Alport. "However, like I said before, Jordan's one of the best. He and I are on opposite sides politically, but he knows all the tricks."

"Commissioner Alport, you don't think these professors had a hand in this, do you?" asked Houma.

"No, they're scholars and policy types."

"I don't know about no professors," blurted out Commissioner Mayfield, "but the man makes us all look like mother fuckin' chumps."

Alport frowned and hand gestured for civility.

"Well, we may have to eat crow on this one and hope that time will let this thing fade. So Shirley, tell us what Hunter-Goss said about Orizaga."

"Well, he's acting really depressed and despondent and can't seem to remember what happened this morning."

"Well, does he say where he was?" asked Varbanov.

"He says he was taken to some sort of house late at night on the Sunday he was released and placed in the basement. His brother, Roberto, told him not to leave until he got a call."

"This sounds crazy," objected Houma. "You guys believe all this?"

They all shook their heads.

Korshak looked at Inger Nordquist.

"Anything else?"

"Sheriff's deputies were sent to look for Orizaga's brother on the North Side. One of the neighbors said they saw him and some girl drive away in a hurry."

"Looks like he ran," said Alport.

"I'd get out of here, too, man if I'm the bro," offered Rucker.

"Same prosecutor going to try Orizaga?" continued Korshak.

"Yes, she will pick up the pieces and I guess add additional charges, said Alport.

"Well, I guess that's good," concluded Korshak. "Our position has always been that we didn't want him released and that had the bond judge made it high enough, Orizaga wouldn't have run."

They all nodded except Houma.

"The right-wingers are going to blast this all over *Wolf* national and talk shows making their case," he said.

Korshak looked at Inger again.

"What do you think?"

"Well, we don't look very good."

"Ma'am, pardon my French but this is some silly ass bullshit and it makes all of us here look like fools," interrupted Mayfield. "So what they're going to do with this McGurn? A man can't just arrest some dude like that can he?"

"Yeah, man—the way I see it, you can't just grab somebody and arrest his ass. Charge the dude!" said Rucker. McAbee was next. "Damn straight!"

"Got my vote," said Chico. "Say, Davida, this don't mean we going to change our mind, does it?"

The commissioners turned to look at Alport.

"Well, there's going to be serious ramped up pressure after today. We got the right people at all branches on our side, but public opinion is going to really make my life difficult. We know Mayor Gill is ready to go with his own ordinance, but today will certainly delay action and public opinion can't be ignored."

"Any questions?" asked Korshak, rising to her feet.

There was no response.

"Let's adjourn. Oh, and one more thing—don't talk to the press!"

•

Sitting in the back seat of the car, Pat and Clare reviewed the question sheet that Jordan had passed over to them. He was seated in the front, next to his nephew, Kevin, who had graciously agreed to drive them from downtown. The questions read as follows:

1. When did Mr. McGurn first learn of the whereabouts of Raul Orizaga?
2. How did Mr. McGurn learn of the whereabouts of Raul Orizaga?
3. When did Mr. McGurn consider a citizen arrest?
4. Did Mr. McGurn have any accomplices, before, during or after the apprehension?
5. Why didn't Mr. McGurn contact the authorities to arrest Orizaga?
6. Was Mr. McGurn aware that he might have committed a felony?
7. Who else was aware of your plans?

Seeing that her husband seemed overwhelmed, Clare took out a piece of paper and wrote: Question 1=Friday; Question 3= last few days; Question 6= no. Other four questions Josh will design his own prompts or construct a statement to protect you, himself and others." Relieved, Pat smiled at Clare, as if to say, "Thank God you understand this legal stuff!"

As they exited at Halsted, Jordan turned to talk to them.

"I just got a text from my buddy at UPW—looks like you're going to be in at bunch of European papers late tomorrow and early Thursday, Pat. Cable networks around the world as well."

"Unbelievable! Didn't you say maybe thirty U.S. papers tomorrow morning as well?"

"Sure did—what gives the story traction is the Mexican ID with Orizaga's date of birth, height, weight, blood type and, of course, Orizaga's photo and yours. The public, both foreign and domestic, will eat this up."

"Jeez, that's incredible," said Pat.

"Big story, Pat. Chuck told me a few years ago that Chicago stories play well everywhere. Just think—we got an idiot ex-governor, Chicago born and bred, doing time, the Una Bomber, the *1968 Democratic Convention*, highest murder rate in the country and Al Capone still running around in people's heads!"

"You know, when we lived in Germany in 1986-87, I can't tell you how many times people wanted to know about Al Capone! Talk about being immortal!"

The car entered Beverly and took a right turn at 99th and Longwood Drive.

"Look, let's drive by your house on Roby to check on the press commotion. Then we'll head to my place."

Kevin drove slowly down 91st Street. Sure enough, there were three TV crews and any number of print reporters standing around, anxious to get some footage for the evening news or content for print deadline in a few hours. Pat saw some of them interviewing neighbors—it would be amusing if any of that footage was aired, he thought.

"If you want, I can have the 22nd District coppers chase them," offered Jordan.

"Don't bother—this is giving the neighbors something to do."

The three got out at the beautiful Heatherington house on Seeley. Built in the 1920's by a legendary local architect who had single-handedly created much of Beverly's charm, it had been completely refurbished over the years under the watchful eye of Jordan's now deceased wife. Clare looked around appreciatively.

"Just beautiful, Josh—everything just as I remembered! Your oil paintings of Bavarian scenes are gallery quality."

Jordan smiled.

"I think Maude's happiest moments while decorating the house were in art galleries. You know she acquired two of these from Wolfgang Schmidt who still has a gallery on 95th Street. Well, enough of that—let me get you something to drink. I'll order a large cheese and sausage pizza from *Fredo's*."

The three sat down in the living room and Jordan flicked on the popular *America Tonight* news hour on *Wolf News*. The consensus among the conservative analysts was that this was the wildest news out of Chicago in a long time. The lone liberal on the show stopped short of condemning Pat but suggested possible kidnapping charges. The other three scoffed at that possibility.

"Wow! Well, we know *Wolf* will have field day with this for days to come," laughed Clare.

Jordan switched to local Channel 8. Veteran reporter, Peter Wilkof, was standing outside President Korshak's office reporting live:

Reliable sources confirm that this may be one of the worst days in Cook County history. Egg is on the faces of ten commissioners who voted for the sanctuary ordinance passed last August 11th. and only one of them, Commissioner Vic Varbanov, would offer comment when asked. He believes that McGurn should be arrested. Meanwhile, the killer of Denny McGurn is in custody and proceedings to prosecute this man will be as soon as next week. Mr. McGurn was in custody at the Daley Center, which houses the Cook County Sheriff's administrative offices. We understand he left an hour ago and his whereabouts are unknown.

"Too late for the European papers to get that quote for the morning said Jordan, "But I guarantee you Chuck Conkle heard that idiot blabber from Vic Varbanov and it will be all over the United States by morning."

"And rumor has it this guy wants to run for President of the County Board in three years?" commented Clare. "So what about the commissioners stonewalling?"

"My guess is that one or more of the legal counsels, or maybe Korshak, encouraged the 'no comment' simply because they don't know what to do. Believe me, that's exactly what we want," said Jordan as he left the room to accept the pizza delivery.

It seemed the entire country was buzzing about this citizen's arrest. One cable outlet interviewed a legal scholar who argued that in medieval England these types of arrests were encouraged by local authorities. Most of the comments, however, were speculative rather than academic, and were directed more to the sheer nerve of pulling off such an act. Viewers were calling in and sharing comments on social media; it seemed that taverns everywhere were filled with patrons who were happily cheering their new American hero. Pat's cell phone rang.

"Pat, Rollie here—you okay, man?"

"Hey, we did it!" said Pat. "Can't thank you enough. Look, I'm lying low with the lawyer. So Jake's okay?"

"Oh yeah. I got hold of Jake and we watched the whole thing at *Katy Casey's*. After a few hours, I got a cab and took him to Midway. I'm home now. The news is unbelievable. Looks like you're busy, so call me when you can."

"How about Boz?"

"No problem. He dropped the van off as planned and he, Mike Dukavich, Clem and I are going to meet at *Muldoon's* at 8:30 p.m."

"Thank those guys for me, will you? I'd join you, but we're still not out of the soup."

"I hear you, Pat. Take care."

"Well here's the pizza, guys, so let's chow down," said Jordan as he returned, balancing the pizza and a stack of paper plates and napkins.

"I guess we watch TV and wait, huh?" said Pat, helping himself to a gooey slice of *Fredo's* famous pizza.

"Yeah, and we can watch that clip of you for the umpteenth time," laughed Jordan. "Every time I change channels, it seems your mug's on the screen yelling in the *Cook County Board Room* or Tonto is doing his thing on Silver."

"I should have combed my hair," said Pat.

"No, looking a little wild was good for dramatic effect," remarked Clare, leaning forward to take a bite of her pizza slice.

"I got an idea Pat," said Jordan, waving his pizza slice in mid air. "Let's get Chicago's own WBN here at the house ASAP so they can get an exclusive with you for their 9:00 p.m. news tonight."

"What's the rush?"

"Look, if we do this right I'm betting the County may just drop the questioning. I know what they are after and that is to get you in a lie, Pat. Think about it—the whole news industry and the public seem to be on your side on this. You have just torpedoed the pro immigration policies out there. You see, the County wants blood to save their pathetic faces. I know these people and, trust me, integrity is foreign to them."

Pat looked at Clare who was listening attentively.

"What do you think, Clare?"

"Go for it! You're getting good at this TV stuff. I think I get what you're trying to do, Josh."

"Me, too, but I still have to answer the questions," protested Pat.

"Well, the questions and answers we can tie in with the TV spot— let me call WBN's night producer, Warner Russell and I'll work a deal with him."

Within minutes, the interview was a done deal. Journalist Ray Fogarty would arrive within thirty minutes and had already been briefed on the questions he could ask.

"We got work to do, Pat and here's the deal," explained Jordan. "You and I are going to script Fogarty's opener—you'll get to answer most of these questions on the list the detective gave me. You follow?"

"Sure, I guess, Josh," said Pat hesitantly. Clare squeezed his hand re-assuringly.

"Now, I'll control everything on the question side," continued Jordan. "First question will be how you learned of his whereabouts. You got information—somehow you knew where Orizaga was, right?"

"Yes."

"One could call this information an anonymous tip?"

"Well, yeah."

"Was this a written or verbal tip?"

"Written—you know, typed."

"Placed in your mailbox at home?"

"Yes."

"This written tip gave you a locale?"

"Yes."

"Did you confirm the information?"

"Yes, well I—"

Jordan stopped him. "'Yes' is all I need."

Clare smiled at Pat approvingly; he was doing just fine with the interrogation drill.

"Was the arrest early this morning?" continued Jordan.

"Yes."

"Was it on the South Side?"

"Yes."

"Did the tip indicate a time frame of some sort?"

"Yes."

"Perfect! Pat, you've given an honest account of the arrest so far. The County will want more specificity but that can wait. Next, we'll script your reason for the citizen's arrest. Now you have to be careful here. I'll have Fogarty ask you why you didn't go to the police. You see, I'm trying to address some of the County's concerns while allowing you to ratchet up your reasons for the arrest to build more public support. You follow?"

"Yeah," said Pat, taking another bite out of his now cold pizza.

"Okay, tell me why you did not go to the police and how you found out about citizen's arrest?"

Pat chewed reflectively, swallowing a mouthful of coagulated cheese.

"Well, first off, I wanted the County to change the ordinance, so this would not happen to others. However, I became convinced about a week ago that this was not going to happen and that today's forum was just a farce. In fact, several commissioners and other county officials lied to me to from the beginning. When I learned of Orizaga's whereabouts, I figured the police might be more interested in protecting the politicians than arresting him. I was already distrustful of the authorities because they let Orizaga go last February after terminating probation for another felony. They never contacted Immigration. In fact, I became convinced Denny would be alive today if county officials were not so corrupt."

"So you thought taking unilateral action rather than contacting the authorities would return justice?"

Pat carefully selected his words.

"Exactly. I didn't trust the criminal justice system. Also, I came to the conclusion that by turning him in at the Cook County Board meeting would be appropriate"

"Great!" said Jordan. "So here's what I'm going to do. I'll write Fogarty's opener based on your answers. Fogarty's free to question you about anything he wants *after* your announcement this morning, but not one question on events prior. Otherwise, it's no go and my guy Russel at WBN knows the score."

"So what we are trying to do is give plenty of detail but stop short of anything specific that happened before I turned in Orizaga that could be problematic?"

"You got it! At the same time, we'll garner more public support and convince the County big shots to drop the whole thing. Hopefully, the law will get changed. My job, though, is to keep you out of trouble—can't promise anything else! Give me a few minutes to type up the script."

"I think I see the WBN News truck outside," said Clare. By the time Fogarty and his cameraman walked to the front door, Pat was already there there to greet them.

"Ray Fogarty, here," said the journalist, stretching out his hand. "My camera man, Beau Blake—you must be Mr. McGurn?"

"Yes, good of you to drive down!" Pat smiled, stepping aside so they could enter.

"I understand there are some time restraints, Ray?"

Fogarty looked at his watch.

"Yes, we need a wrap on this in about half hour or so. I'd like to get started."

Jordan walked in, script in hand.

"Hi, Ray. I'm Josh Jordan. Look, I went over this with your boss—you will read this script for your opener and after that you're free to ask any questions pertaining to the period after Mr. McGurn's pronouncement at the County Board this morning. It's in upper case and in bold type. Now time is running, so let's proceed—I got your boss on speakerphone so he can monitor."

Fogarty checked the script and clipped it to the camera so he could read it when he went live. Then, taking out a mirror, he smoothed his hair into place and sat in one of the chairs flanking the fireplace; Pat was already seated in the chair on the other side. Beau took a few minutes to get the lighting set up.

The camera rolled.

"WBN News Chicago has been granted an exclusive interview with Patrick McGurn who many are referring to as a folk hero. McGurn made a citizen's arrest this morning, on the South Side of Chicago, at approximately 5:30 a.m. He tells us that he learned that his brother's killer, Raul Orizaga, was at a certain location by an anonymous tip and that after careful planning, he made the arrest. When asked why he did not go to the authorities Mr. McGurn said—and I quote—'I do not trust the criminal justice system in Cook County because they failed my family in, 2009, 2010 and 2011 when no one contacted immigration and customs enforcement to tell them Orizaga was illegal after he was convicted of a felony in 2009.' McGurn goes on to say that authorities again failed when they released Mr. Orizaga from custody last month even though he was being prosecuted for killing his brother. Patrick McGurn remains convinced his brother would be alive today if Cook County was not corrupt.

When asked why he arrested Mr. Orizaga today, McGurn said he thought it best to surrender Orizaga before the Cook County commissioners at their meeting since it was clear they were never going to seriously address the releasing of illegal alien criminals at this sham forum earlier today.

At that point the cameraman turned the camera on Pat and Fogarty began questioning him directly.

"Sir, your arrest today has been extensively reported. Would you please tell our listeners what happened after your pronouncement today?"

Looking relaxed, Pat responded.

"Well, I was escorted behind the dais in the Cook County Board Room and placed in a room where I was left with a couple of deputies who gave me a cup of black coffee. After a half hour or so, the same deputies escorted me over to the *Daley Center* to a subterranean room that appeared to be a holding place of some kind. There, a detective gave me a glass of water and a newspaper. He said he would ask some questions in due course. I called my wife who, in turn, called our lawyer."

"What did you think they were going to do?"

"Can't say—I mean, they needed to ask questions and I understand that, but I figured a lawyer was a good idea so we waited."

"What questions did they ask, Sir?"

"Well, we said we would answer them tomorrow so that's where it stands."

"What were the questions?"

Jordan shook his head emphatically.

"I'm not at liberty to disclose that," said Pat, catching Jordan's eye.

"So did you feel that you were being held like a criminal?"

"Yeah, sort of—it's like I did their job and they then held me for close to six hours."

"Well, what do you think will happen tomorrow?"

"Who knows? What do you think, Ray?"

Fogarty ignored the question.

"So you blame them for your brother's death?"

"We had a great expression in the army in the early 70's, 'If the shoe fits … '"

Fogarty signaled Blake to shut the camera off.

"Okay, with that, guys? We've got less than an hour to get this in."

"Looks good to me," said Jordan as the TV crew packed up their gear.

"Let's see," he said, turning to Pat and Clare. "We got an hour—maybe a bit longer. We'll have some drinks, kick back, watch the news and then I'll run you home."

"That's a plan," said Pat. "I'm beat—say Josh, got any beer?"

"You bet—I got some German beer. Clare?"

"White wine, if you got it."

Jordan returned with a tray of drinks and, having handed Pat and Clare their glasses, he settled into an Easy-Boy armchair alongside the sofa where his guests were seated.

"Josh, tell me about the press going forward," said Pat.

"I was going to talk to you about that. My advice is to get lost for a week—maybe two, if you can, but first we have to get rid of any Cook County obligations. No matter what, Pat, I would just avoid the press for a while."

"What's your take, Josh? Are you banking on the County leaving Pat alone?"

"After this WBN interview, I'm hoping wiser heads like Commissioners Alport and Riley and maybe Sheriff Dypsky are going to weigh in and insist the County just drop the whole thing."

"Makes sense to me," said Pat, "but what if some of the others do something stupid?"

"Always a possibility, but unlikely. Say, I better call Warner to make sure Ray doesn't screw this up."

•

About a half mile west from Josh's house, huddled at a corner table in *Muldoon's Saloon* were Sheriff Dan Dypsky, press spokesman Guy Grodecki and attorney Paul Nikos, with a bucket of Burger beer bottles in front of them. A little distance away from them, seated at the bar, ten to twelve patrons were watching re runs of *Marshal Dolan* on WBN, a local Chicago TV station that was going to air the news after the show.

"Gotta hand it to McGurn—that took guts," remarked Dypsky. "So, Guy, you must say something for the press tomorrow—what do you suggest, Paul?"

"Well, here's my take. We looked weak at the time the ordinance passed and probably should have said we would ignore it and comply with federal law."

"No, Paul—that would have ruined me politically! I would have had Hispanic protestors up my ass and surrounding my house! You know how that *Illinois Immigration Cooperative* operates. They organized that stupid rally today. There's a congressman somewhere in DuPage County that is harassed by that bunch all the time."

"That's right—just the other day they surrounded his house because of his opposition to liberal immigration measures, said Grodecki.

"Here's what I think we should say," said Nikos. *"Sheriff Dypsky believes that the ordinance should be amended to honor detainers for certain felonies."*

"Which felonies?" asked Dypsky.

Nikos looked at Grodecki.

"The key in a good press report is being forthright but not too specific. How about you say serious felonies are under review, Dan?"

Dypsky nodded.

"So my political ass is saved."

"Hope so," said Nikos, not looking too optimistic.

"Okay, good work, boys! Let's open three more!" said Dypsky forcing a smile.

Five minutes later, Rollie and Mike Dukavich walked in together and, taking a seat at the bar, and ordered three lite beers from owner, Moon Muldoon. When Moon handed them the bottles, Rollie introduced Mike.

"Glad to meet you! Say, you guys follow the action today?"

"You bet, Moon."

"Say news is on in a few. My guys can't get enough of it," said Moon happily. "Look, I got to get Digger and his bowling team a round."

"Sure, go ahead, Moon," said Rollie, winking at Mike.

"The whole world is zeroed in on this, Mike. First time on Western Avenue?"

"Yeah."

"Welcome to the strip, Mike. Look—see those three over in the corner? That's Sheriff Dypsky and his staff. I'm thinking of having a little fun in a bit."

Just as the WBN news was coming on, in walked Clem accompanied by Boz. They walked over to Rollie's table and exchanged introductions.

"We did it!" said Rollie as they clinked bottles.

The WBN News opened with Pat's scene at the Cook County Board meeting, followed by the well-scripted interview at Jordan's house, ending with Hokee's (aka Tonto's) theatrics at the Picasso. Bottles clinked again, this time with high fives all around at the bar. Jack the mailman claimed Tonto was a good buddy. Serving up a new round of beers to their table, Moon put in his own bid for fame by association.

"You guys know this McGurn that everybody's talking about? He comes in afternoons once maybe twice a month and talks to Kevin Garrett and sometimes to Terry McFee, the retired Fire Captain."

"Moon, I tell you what—that guy's something else. I gotta meet him sometime. Say, do me a favor and send three drinks over to Dypsky and his boys for me."

"You got it, man. You know the Sheriff?"

"Yeah, sort of you might say," said Rollie, grinning broadly.

While Moon served the drinks, Rollie and his comrades turned around and hoisted their bottles in the direction of Dypsky's table. Without taking a sip, Dypsky stood up to leave.

"We're out of here!"

"There's some guys smiling at us and hoisting their bottles. They must have bought the drinks," observed Nikos. "You know them?"

"I said we're out of here! I'll handle this."

As they walked out, Dypsky stopped at Rollie's table.

"It looks like retirement suits you well, Rollie," he said, forcing a smile.

"You might say that, Sheriff," said Rollie, smiling back.

"Busy day today, I'll bet," said Dypsky, his voice bordering on the hostile.

"Not really—spent the day with an old pal from my Vietnam unit. Hey, did you see Tonto and Silver out your office window at the Riley Center?"

"Nope, I spent the day trying to figure out who was helping McGurn. You wouldn't know anything about that?"

"Can't say that I do, Sheriff, but I can tell you he did the right thing. Don't you agree? Or maybe I should ask if you're going to let the scumbag who killed his brother out again? You proud of that, Sheriff?"

Dypsky turned without answering, and headed for the door.

"How the boys in Marion doing, Mike," asked Rollie, now that there was no possibility of being overheard by Dypsky's crew.

"Talked to them last night—the headmaster thinks they can enroll in one or two college classes at *Southern Illinois University* next semester. They were in great spirits."

"Clem, did the horse detail get back okay?"

"Oh, yeah—you know the guys all felt pretty good about it. I had a TV on while they were grooming their mounts and they were proud of their work."

They stayed for a few more drinks, left a generous tip and as they walked out, Moon yelled, "HI HO SILVER!"

●

Back on Seeley Clare, Pat and Jordan had also watched the news.

"Hey, Pat—not bad! You handled it pretty good."

"I owe it all to Josh—" began Pat.

"Well, we'll know more tomorrow," cautioned Jordan. "Before I take you home, let me tell you what my clerk learned. This citizen's arrest by and large is legal, in a matter of speaking, if a crime is imminent. However, it gets murky if there is no apparent crime going. In your case, that's a problem."

"So I could be charged?"

"Well, technically I suppose, but extenuating circumstances and this media frenzy clearly will help. Let's hope I'm right. So enough of all that— let's get some sleep. Big day tomorrow."

Josh drove the McGurns home at 9:30 p.m. Fortunately, the news crews were gone. They ignored a few nosy staring neighbors standing on the corner. Once home, the McGurns were fast asleep within minutes.

●

A few hours earlier, after an exhausting day at the Cook County Building, President Korshak ordered her two man police security detail to get the limo ready to drive to her Kenwood home. The day had not gone well, and she had spent the entire afternoon on the phone explaining the situation to the Democratic State leadership. All were concerned that their support for pro immigration policies led by Cook County's ordinance was going to damage them politically; all wanted assurance that the damage would be minimal. While heading south on South Shore Drive, Korshak called Dilbert Redstone.

"Dilbert, Shirley here. I want to meet with you and Bernice tonight at 8:30 p.m. at the club."

"No problem—you okay?"

"I'll make it."

At the appointed time, Bernice, Shirley and Dilbert sat at a table in the *Philosophers' Hut* and ordered a bottle of French wine and appetizers of spinach and goat cheese tartlets.

"Now, as I recall," opened Korshak, "You two pushed for the ordinance and it came right from the top."

"Well, you also had Commissioners Varbanov, Alport and others here locally. I guess we'd better think about tomorrow, Shirley."

"Go on—I'm listening," said Korshak, toying with one of the tartlets. "You know my future is on the line."

"So are Vic's and maybe a few others," Bernice reminded her. "But if I may, Shirley, what's been decided about McGurn and this so called arrest?"

"Not sure," she said, grimacing across the table. "I suppose I can leverage this somehow, but Lisa Hunter-Goss is the chief prosecutor and, between us, I don't think she has a clue."

"Well, I spoke with my contacts a few hours ago and they're furious," said Dilbert. "We must keep this as far away from the President as possible. I guess Senator Congelosi will issue some sort of press release as damage control."

Korshak looked at Bernice.

"What do you think?"

"I'm mostly interested in how immigration issues affect juveniles, but maybe I can contact our friends up north and see if the Gay and Lesbian community would be interested in an article in their community newspaper. They owe us because we support gay marriage and convinced President Haesi to change his position.

Korshak nodded.

"That's right—the key is to keep our progressive allies engaged. The LGBTQ group have been key supporters in this struggle. Maybe you can organize a rally at one or two universities."

"Not a bad idea," said Bernice. "You know there are pro immigration groups at most of the Catholic Universities in the area. I'll e-mail my faculty contacts tomorrow and we can set up lectures and rallies. I'll call Hallet and maybe he can get his people and some La Fuentes people to help."

Korshak shook her head vehemently.

"No more street rallies downtown. I'm telling you, we all looked stupid with those fools trying to burn the flag."

"No, No, Shirley strictly campus. We have ACAN agents on every campus in the region that can stir up a protest overnight."

"That's all good and all but I really need to know what went down at the big house?"

"I did speak with his Senior Advisor, Jahnna Suhud, this afternoon," said Dilbert, clearing his throat. "She wants this to go away—I had to assure her that no connection to President Haesi will ever be mentioned. You got to keep in mind the President supported this because he figured there'd be a snowball effect in Democratic controlled jurisdictions. You know, the other day Vice President Boland went off half cocked at a press conference, babbling about how he and the President love immigrants in general and Chicago's in particular."

"The man's a fool. This isn't about love," said Bernice.

"So what else did you learn from Jahnna?"

"I was going to call you in the morning with this," said Bernice, wiping her mouth in her napkin. "Jahnna conferred with a slew of people and wants you to drop the whole thing. The sooner this dies the better—and that means first thing in the morning. She's really worried about a leak. You know, the 2012 campaign starts in a few months and we got to win a second term. This is not going to help us politically."

Korshak rolled her eyes.

"Be more specific," she said, fanning herself with the dessert menu.

"No more interrogation of McGurn and prosecute Orizaga to the hilt. Period!" said Bernice emphatically.

"*You're sure?*"

"Yep."

"Lisa's not going to like this!" said Korshak.

Haesi ordered his Chief of Staff Bolevsky to call her and she knows the score."

"The problem for the President is that public perception will get spun on *Wolf News* every night," added Dilbert. "That will tie him in with what they call the *Chicago Way* or maybe the *Cook County Way*, meaning dumb policy made by amateurs."

"Look, I didn't realize the President's future is on the line with this," said Korshak. "My first call tomorrow will be to States Attorney Hunter-Goss, followed by a call to Davida Alport."

Korshak reached for her purse. Wearily, she rose to her feet, holding onto the table for support.

"My driver is waiting, so I'm going to take off," she said.

Dilbert stood up to help her with her jacket.

"Our movement has setbacks all the time, Shirley, but each time we get stronger."

"Keep in mind that we have managed to convince our friend Haesi that he can use his executive and regulatory powers to empower feminists, gays, African-Americans and Hispanics and that must continue."

"Hope you're right," said Korshak, not sounding at all convinced. "Thanks for the wine."

"Our pleasure," said Bernice.

The Redstone siblings watched her leave.

"I'll never forget the words of Ulbricht," said Bernice. "He always told his people that the key is to look democratic, but control always must be maintained."

"Power to the people!" responded Dil.

DAY TWENTY-FIVE, WEDNESDAY, SEPTEMBER 21, 2011

Phones were ringing all over the County Building and *Daley Center* that morning. After a lengthy conference call between Alport, Korshak and Hunter-Goss, the State's Attorney issued a press release at 10:00 a.m.

> **Yesterday, on September 20, 2011, a citizen's arrest took place in Chicago. Mr. Raul Orizaga who had an outstanding warrant out for his arrest is now in custody without bond. He will be prosecuted for death and aggravated DUI. Mr. Orizaga will be assigned a public defender.**

There was no mention of Pat McGurn.
Later in the day, Guy Gorecki prepared a press release on behalf of his boss.

> **Sheriff Dypsky is well pleased that Raul Orizaga is back in custody. He supports a measure that would require the Sheriff of Cook County to cooperate with Immigration and Custom Enforcement for certain felonies.**

Back in Beverly, Clare McGurn took a call from Jennifer and Giles Gardner, old friends who were teachers at the *Heidelberg American High School* in Germany. It was 5:00 p.m. their time.

"My God—front page in the Frankfurt paper this morning!" said Giles. "My guess this will be all over the world. How did Pat pull this off?"

"Long story, Giles. The news will get some of the story. What's important is that Pat's okay. I really can't tell you anymore. If all goes as planned, Pat and I will be on a flight to Shannon airport at 5:30 p.m., our time. We think a month's stay in County Limerick, will do us both some good. If you don't mind, we could jump on that discount airline that goes into Frankfort and maybe one of the weekends we can visit."

"Any weekend, Clare, Love to have you guys!" said Jennifer.

•

The McGurns managed to get a flight to Shannon Airport later that day. Clare secured lodgings at the historic *Coffee Manor* in County Kerry. On the way to the *O'Hare International Terminal,* they stopped at a newsstand and purchased three papers with national distribution. All three gave Orizaga's arrest front-page coverage and all three carried Pat's photo, cropped from a recent birthday party when he was holding his three-year-old grandson, Matt. During the flight, Clare slept, but Pat, wide awake, wrote letters to several families that had lost loved ones to horrific crimes committed by illegal alien felons. Joan Farnsworth had encouraged him to network with them and agreed to send additional name and addresses. She indicated the numbers would be in the hundreds. The letters Pat wrote while crossing the Atlantic were addressed to the following families:

1. Joseph Rimini whose brother was murdered by an illegal alien that authorities released in Colorado in 2008.
2. James Buber whose son was killed by a Guatemalan illegal in San Francisco in 2009
3. The parents of Ryan Kerry, a Border Patrol agent who was killed by a Mexican drug cartel operative in 2010.
4. Veronica and Ford Hogan whose son Darin was brutally murdered by an illegal alien in Texas, also in 2010.
5. Fred and Wilma Guzman whose daughter was stabbed over 30 times by an undocumented alien in Colorado in 2011

6. Marie Knightly whose son, Cormac, was killed by an undocumented hit and run driver in suburban Boston also in 2011.
7. Ruth Rocco whose son, Josh, was killed by a Belize alien hit and run driver in Florida in 2011. The alien had multiple felony convictions and was never deported.

Farnsworth had given him thirty additional names with similarly tragic stories. Pat would work on the remaining letters in the next few weeks, and over the next two years, he wrote over 100 additional letters.

EPILOGUE

\# Pat McGurn continued working with pro enforcement groups and *Judiciary Committee* staffs in both houses of the United States Congress. Clare helped with correspondence and accompanied her husband on his many trips to Washington D.C. Over the next few years, three more grandchildren were born.

\# Rollie Dufner was never discovered as McGurn's key confederate. He took Frank Higgins and Schus to Fuller's Pub on Wabash for dinner.

\# Mike Dukavich continued to help troubled students at Rowan and Jefferson.

\# Boz was never discovered and meets other retired cops daily for coffee.

\# Jake Hawk was also never discovered. He was involved in an altercation the weekend following the abduction that left two men unconscious on the floor of the **Bar Fly Saloon** in the **French Quarter.**

\# Ron Ralston learned the details of the abduction several months later and is currently writing a book on immigration enforcement issues.

\# Tonto aka Hokee took an early retirement and joined **the Western Ho Circus.**

\# Mario and Jose completed training at the Chicago Police Academy and were sworn in on March 1,2012.

Dools checked into a long-term care facility underwritten by the *Illinois Department of Veterans 'Affairs*. Pat and Rollie assisted.

President of the Cook County Board Korshak, Commissioner Varbanov and State's Attorney Hunter-Goss were not reelected the following year.

Roberto Orizaga and Angela Montoya were never caught.

Raul Orizaga was sentenced to ten years.

The Democratic majority on the Cook County Board never allowed what came to be known as *The McGurn Amendment* to be voted up or down.

March, 2012 Senator Strobe Irwin from Alabama introduced a bill, "Safe America Act" that would withhold funding to any state or local jurisdiction that refuses cooperation with federal immigration enforcement. The measure also mandates notification of feds about apprehension of criminal aliens and to honor detainers. The measure failed in 2012 and passed in 2015 when Republican majorities had enough votes to override a Presidential veto.

Justice has been returned to the McGurn family.

Printed in the United States
By Bookmasters